BECAUSE I KNOW IT'S TRUE

JUNO HARVEY

mandurang
press

Mandurang Press

PO Box 2063, Bendigo DC, Victoria 3554, Australia

First published by Mandurang Press 2020

Book design by Vellum

Book cover by Mariah Sinclair

Printed and bound by Ingram

ISBN: 978-0-6484776-9-3(paperback)

ISBN: 978-0-6484776-8-6 (ebook)

A catalogue record for this book is available from the National Library of Australia

To the Masterclass of Spring 2017

PROLOGUE

1987

The SUV hurtled through its red light determined, demented.

His sedan was slow-moving into the traffic prompted by the green traffic light. Beside him, head resting on the pillar of the door, his wife dozed. Behind them, the baby slept -finally - encased in her capsule by a wide Velcro strap. It had only taken three turns of a city block. Two turns, and his wife had stopped her exhausted sobbing. One turn and he'd thought about smashing his car into a pole. Anything to stop the colicky cries: the incessant, terrible noise.

Just before impact, he looked around. The plummeting SUV driver's head was down, hands slipping on the wheel as sleep took her over. It was instinct that made him thump the brakes, his old vehicle skidding on the wet road and turning a near-perfect half circle. The blunt nose of the big car slammed brutishly into the passenger side door. He flung his arms up to cover his face. His head hit the side window anyway, giving him a moment of deep peace.

Then he was back.

The sedan was on the wrong side of the road, turned to face home. Rain was coming in through the smashed windscreen.

The air smelled of hot fuel and twisted metal and thick blood. He put out a hand to his wife and felt the river cascading from her split scalp down her arm. The locked seat belt wouldn't let him look to the baby. It was eerily quiet in the back seat of the ticking car.

Perhaps he lost consciousness again because it was only a moment later that men in dark shirts were reaching for him, lifting him out as if he weighed less than a feather. He arrived at the hospital ahead of his family but could see them from his emergency department trolley as they were wheeled in. She was pale and blood splattered. A blanket shrouded the baby.

They weren't the only accident on that treacherous night. The sleeping driver had also taken out a pedestrian, and the papers reported later that three other incidents had occurred within the same block almost simultaneously. The weather, you see. Oil spills on the road. Potholes. Drink driving. It didn't matter; the results were the same.

He remembered little except clinging to the side rail of his silent wife's bed, the tubes in and out of her criss-crossing like fencing wire. The baby was somewhere else – where? – and he didn't get to see her until they'd confirmed that his wife would never walk again and maybe not even remember who he was.

The baby, miraculously, was untouched.

ONE

2017

The packing chest was a solid summary of Grace Worthington's life. She put one hand on its sandy-coloured top, feeling how the winter sun had warmed the wood as it crouched on the small veranda of the terrace house. At the end of the narrow street, a tram dinged indignantly and the echo of voices as people crossed the road drifted towards her. She traced the small label on the chest that read *Andrew Worthington*.

'That's all he had?' said Claudia, arms crossed against the occasional chill windblast.

'This, too.' Grace held up an envelope. 'The money from the sale of his car.'

'I'm hoping that he owned a Mercedes.' Claudia pulled it from her friend's hand and took the cheque out. 'I see he owned an old bomb.'

'It's a bit of play money.'

Claudia handed the envelope back. 'Don't play too hard then.'

Grace rubbed the top of the tea chest, her palm catching soft splinters. She stopped, brushed the wood from her hands, lifted her head to stare at Claudia. 'What do I do now?'

'With this stuff?' Claudia shrugged one shoulder. 'Best to give it away if you don't want it.'

Grace shook her head. 'No, I mean, what do I do now that my father is dead, and I have no family left?'

The wind kicked up, spraying the women with grit from the worn asphalt of the narrow suburban street. Claudia shook her head, making her hair bob, and tugged her woollen coat tighter. 'You still have your best friend.'

Grace's face felt stiff. She patted the chest and turned away, staring at where, minutes before, the delivery van had parked. She'd been expecting the packing chest, but not this deep ache gripping her body. And was it anger, that darkness brooding beneath the pain? It was as if the truck driver, whistling loudly as he unloaded his gift, had delivered her father's ghost in the box. Part of Grace wanted the driver to put it back in the vehicle and go away, while the rest of her wanted to climb in among the familiar smoky-smelling clothes and drown herself in them.

'Grace?' Claudia's hand was on her arm, blood-red enamelled nails fierce against Grace's navy coat sleeve. 'You'll be okay. You're tough. Right? It's one day after the other. That's all you have to do. One day then the next.'

Grace nodded again, putting both hands up to run her fingers through her wind-strewn hair. Claudia's hand dropped away. 'One day after the other.'

'That's right.' Claudia gave the packing chest a gentle kick. 'Let's get this inside. You can decide what you want to do with it then.'

Grace pushed the envelope deep into a pocket and helped Claudia walk the chest through the front door, the fly screen catching on a metal edge. It tore before they could stop it and Grace crouched down to push the edges together.

'Leave it, Grace.'

Grace felt Claudia's hand on her back and shrugged it off.

'Okay.' She took a moment to rise, then they pushed the chest into the middle of her room. It sat like an obelisk. They stared at it.

'Cup of tea?' Claudia said into the silence. 'Something to eat?'

'Thanks.' Grace glanced at her watch. 'Is there any bread? I've got to go in half an hour, and I haven't had lunch.'

'I'll make you a sandwich.'

Grace heard Claudia's voice brisk with relief at having something to do. 'Claudia?' she said as her friend reached the hall. 'This would be so much harder without you.'

Claudia wiped at her face, smudging dark shadows under her eyes. 'You'd do the same for me.' She disappeared towards the kitchen.

If only I'd have the chance, Grace thought to the sounds of Claudia filling the kettle. She chewed the inside of her cheek. No one should have to experience what Grace had – especially not Claudia, whose biggest fault was her kindness. Besides, there was little chance she would. Claudia still had her entire family, including two pairs of grandparents. Even the infirmities of old age hadn't caught them.

Grace felt herself sliding into exhaustion. She shook her head, making the room spin, took the cheque out of her pocket and put it into her handbag to deposit on the way to the theatre. Scissors worked to lever the lid from the packing chest. Working quickly, she pulled out jeans and tops, a hairbrush and electric razor, and a pile of papers that looked like paid bills. The boarding house owner had offered to pack the box and Grace hadn't argued. She'd only visited the place twice since her father had been there. The first time was to make sure he was in his room and hadn't slunk back to the streets. The second was to collect some clean underwear for his hospital admission. When he'd died, she'd rung the boarding house. They were quick to clean his room up, but she understood. A sudden vacancy meant one less homeless man left in the cold.

By the time Claudia called her into the kitchen, the tea chest was empty, and Grace had pushed everything into a garbage bag to give away. At the last minute, she retrieved the razor. Short hairs, pavement-grey, caught in its teeth. She bit her lip and placed it in the top drawer of her bedside table.

'Here.' Claudia slid a plate towards Grace as she sat down at the laminated kitchen table shoved hard against the wall. 'Cheese and lettuce. That's all we had.'

'Thanks.' Grace took a bite, the cheese sharp in her mouth. Chewing felt a chore, and she wondered whether she could keep the sandwich down. She swallowed carefully, looking at the newspaper on the tabletop for distraction. 'What's this?'

'The local paper. You know, the one they put in the letterbox once a week.'

'I never read it.'

'Usually, I don't either but look at this.' Claudia spun the paper around for Grace to see the front page. *Thirty Year Mystery Continues.* The headline topped a photograph of two men standing outside a construction site. She pointed at the one on the left. 'It's a sad story, but he's a bit of alright.'

Grace heard the strain in Claudia's voice. *A bit of alright?* It was not Claudia's language; she was more the he-seems-very-nice sort of person. Grace felt irritation close her throat, but she forced out, 'You into redheads?'

'Of course.' Claudia flicked at Grace's hair. 'Not burning-bright red, like yours. I like it more subtle.'

Like my father's had been, Grace couldn't help thinking. 'Subtle red. What's that?'

'Bleached, the fading-sun-on-sand red.'

Grace tapped the picture. '*His* red, in other words.'

'Exactly.'

'What about the other guy?'

Claudia pulled the paper around again to study the dark-haired man standing slightly behind. 'Too heavy.' She waved a hand around her face. 'He looks like thunder.' She slid the paper back to Grace.

Grace leaned over. The second man had serious eyes. Waves of rich chocolate-coloured hair fell over his forehead. She wondered vaguely whether *thunder* would be alright. Thunder spoke of passion. 'At least he doesn't look as vulnerable as his friend.'

'He's as hard as a brick. Give me pale-faced mournfulness any day.'

'You vixen.'

Claudia smiled briefly, grasping her mug with both hands. 'Sadly, though, Mr Vulnerable is not hanging around here. He's going back to where he came from.'

'Why was he here in the first place?'

'Read it.'

Grace forced in the last of her sandwich and scanned the article. *Brother seeks missing sister thirty years on. The mysterious disappearance of baby Norah Cameron from Paxton Community Hospital remains unsolved. Alexander Cameron, a resident of Scotland, has not given up hope that his sister will one day be found. "We're not a complete family until Norah comes back to us," said the thirty-four-year-old. "I'm convinced that she's somewhere in Australia, waiting to recognise who she really is." Colin Astle, Mr Cameron's friend, declined to comment.*

'Poignant, isn't it?' Claudia poured the last of the tea into her mug. 'They're standing outside the old hospital site.'

'Poor guy,' said Grace. 'His family is incomplete.'

'Oh, Grace!' Claudia put a hand over her mouth. 'I'm sorry. I shouldn't have shown you. I didn't think.'

Grace shrugged. It was not Claudia's fault that Alexander

Cameron was on the front page of the newspaper with his sad story. It wasn't Claudia's fault that she was friends with Grace, who carried sadness around as an everyday item. Claudia was untainted. Here was this man, Alexander, desperate for his sister. There was Grace, desperate for anyone. Pain knifed her stomach. 'It doesn't matter.' She stacked her mug on her plate. 'I've got to go. Full dress rehearsal this afternoon.'

'Here, I'll take those.' Claudia took the dishes from Grace, giving her a quick one-armed hug. 'Me and my big mouth will clean up here. I'm working tonight so I'll be back very late.'

'Okay. Have fun with the drunken night club crowd.'

'Thanks.' Claudia grimaced. 'Friday night at *Stillers*. Fabulous.'

Grace put her hand up in farewell, went back to her bedroom, and settled her handbag carefully onto her shoulder. Her body felt fragile, riddled with soreness. She hoisted the garbage bag up, pushed it through the door, and lugged it to the corner of the street where she poked it down a recycling skip's mouth. As it thumped to the bottom, her stomach seized in agony. She leaned her arm on the skip, winded, one hand across her stomach, until she could move, one step after the other, towards the tram.

THE *PAXTON PEOPLE'S THEATRE* was housed in the ghost of an old movie house. Grace pushed open the back door and entered dimness. She wasn't the first one there. From the stage, a snatch of loud, off-beat music sounded followed by a shout, then silence. The music came back on as Grace made her way to the open change room. Renee was already there, practising lines in a mirror. 'Hey,' said Grace as she put her bag on the bench. 'Everything all right in here?'

Renee shrugged and pulled at the ponytail falling thickly down her back. 'Ivan thinks the sound system is stuffed. I think it might be the *sound*, not the system.'

Grace nodded. 'Usual dress-rehearsal blues.'

'Well, you sound like you've seen it all before.'

'I've seen everything.' Grace unlocked the cupboard to pull her kit out.

Renee came over and peered at the range of eye shadows filling the top layer of Grace's box. 'Right. Don't you ever want to be on stage instead of always being backstage?'

Grace watched the top of Renee's head as she hovered over the make-up. Regrowth darkened her part. 'Ah, no,' she said, pulling out brushes to lie across the bottom of a bulb-lined mirror. 'I prefer to do this.'

'You're good at it, did you know?' Renee flung back to the mirror and used a finger to dab a dust of stolen blusher to her cheeks. 'You make everyone look good even when -' she turned her head to whisper loudly at Grace '- they are butt-end ugly. You *transform* us.'

'Right,' Grace said as she unpacked cotton wool balls, but Renee was back to talking to herself in the mirror, her lines clutched behind her back.

Make-up for the cast took three hours, starting with the minor players, finishing with Renee's big look and the boldness of Charlie the lead actor. Everyone sweated under the lights. Grace was kept busy as people moved off stage and came in for a dab here, a colour fix there. Roberta worked the costumes, saying little to Grace as she pinned back shirts that were too large and unpicked a seam for Renee who swore she hadn't put on any weight since she'd tried on the costume two weeks ago. Ivan appeared occasionally, poking his bearded head around the door to see how everyone was going, then hurrying back to his viewpoint in the empty auditorium to frown at the action on the stage. Grace had a few moments to get a drink from the fridge in the kitchenette as he coached the players during interval.

Offcuts of set building crowded the kitchenette. Grace pushed paint tins from the newspaper they'd sat on to make room for her glass.

There was that article again.

Alexander Cameron stood cross-armed in front of the security fence of the old hospital. Grace sipped cold, flat soda water and studied the man's face. His hair, Claudia's bleached-red, hung down to his jawline, hooked behind both ears. He frowned towards the camera, looking beyond the lens to where Grace imagined he might see his sister walking towards him. He's *yearning*, she decided. The hollowed appearance of his face, the straight set of his mouth, and the slightly squinted eyes made him appear lost. No, *lonely*. Alexander Cameron was the loneliest man she'd ever seen. Had he been that way for thirty years?

Grace turned to the sink to rinse her glass. From the stage, Ivan was finishing his comments, leading the cast with his 'let's do it!' exclamation that Grace always thought more suited to a grand final football match than a play about unrequited love. She went back, reaching her stool in time to fix Renee's bleeding lipstick before the actor flounced back on stage without a thank you.

It was a few minutes before midnight before Grace got off the tram in High Street and started towards home. The street was bright enough, high fluorescent lamps keeping the shadows away, but Grace thrust her hand in her pocket, fingers curled around her protruding house key, ready to stab if needed. Even as she unlocked the door, she stayed wary, despite never having been approached by anyone before. Except, on that one occasion, by her father.

The door clicked open and Grace stepped inside. How

weird it was that her father would never turn up on her doorstep again. Once, more than a year ago, he'd come in behind her as she had stepped into the hall. It took a moment to recognise him, a small time period in which she felt her insides contract. Then the stranger morphed into her father, that sad man who felt he had nothing since his wife had died despite, as Grace repeatedly said to him, having a daughter.

Grace sighed. She threw her things on her bed, kicked off her shoes, and padded to the kitchen in her socks. The house was quiet without Claudia, and *quiet* was dangerous. She switched on the radio, tuning it to a happy pop station, and made herself tea. When she put the mug on the table, she had a flash of when her father had sat in the same place. Maybe he'd even used the same mug. Grace had known then that he was dying of that broken heart, the one that had started to crack decades ago on the night of the accident that had rendered his wife helpless.

Grace picked the mug up and emptied it into the sink. What she really wanted was a burning whiskey, but they didn't have any. She compromised, pouring the dregs of a Riesling into one of Claudia's best wine glasses, and sitting back at the table with a packet of chips.

If I go to bed, she thought as she picked at chip crumbs, I'll only see *him*. Then I'll see my mother sitting soundlessly in her wheelchair. Then I'll see me, first at her funeral and then at my dad's. Such happy family pictures. She took a gulp of wine, coughing as it hit the wrong spot, and spilling most of it on the newspaper left on the table.

Alexander Cameron stared past her as she blotted his face with the kitchen sponge. She stopped suddenly, the sponge damp in her hand. Alexander's head was grey with moisture. Behind him, his friend glared. Small drops of wine dripped back onto the table as Grace closed her eyes and unconsciously squeezed the sponge. A coldness clamped her limbs and the pain, tempered by her busy evening, returned to her stomach. When she opened her eyes again, Alexander Cameron was still there. Yearning. Lonely.

THE DOOR finally opened at three o'clock in the morning. Grace was at the table, a fresh bottle of wine half-empty beside her. 'Claudia,' she called to the wall.

Claudia's bag dropped heavily onto the floorboards of the hallway and then she was there in the kitchen, face flushed and eyes wide. 'What? What's happened? What are you doing?'

Grace raised her glass to her friend. 'Having a drink. Many drinks. Want one?'

Claudia drifted to the table and sank into a chair. 'Grace, I've been serving alcohol for eight hours straight. I don't want to touch another glass for at least a day.' She tipped her head. 'Are you alright?'

'No.' Grace drank deeply.

'It's been a tough few weeks for you, with your dad and everything. I'm worried about you.'

Grace put her glass down and ran her hands through her hair. 'Worried? I'm fine.'

Claudia shook her head. 'When you say that, I *really* worry.'

'There's no need for you to worry.'

'Sorry, but you said that last time when your dad got sick. You said *there's no need for you to worry* and then you quit your job.'

'I couldn't concentrate. Something had to give.'

'Now you have no money.'

Grace slumped. 'I've saved a bit. I've got that cheque from Dad's car.'

Claudia leaned forward. 'Grace, you also told me not to worry about you when your mum died and look what happened then.'

'I was in high school. We were kids.'

'You refused your university offer.'

'So? You don't have a degree and you're fine.'

Claudia reached for the chips. 'Right. I work in a bar. *You* don't even have any work.'

Grace shook her head. 'We have freedom. There's nothing holding us back. We can do anything we like.'

'I can't.' Claudia took more chips. 'I need to work. I took out a loan for my car. And if you think I'm staying in this dump forever -' she waved her hand to indicate the tiny kitchen '- you're wrong. As soon as I get enough money, I'm buying my own place. No offence, Grace, but we've been renting since we left school.'

Grace drank the last of her wine and placed her glass back on the table. 'That's very nice, Claudia. You go for it.'

Claudia sat straight. 'Something's going on in that head of yours. Are you having a melt-down? If you are, I get it -'

'I've found out something. I've discovered a new life.'

'What's wrong with your old life?'

Grace shook her head slowly. 'You're kidding, aren't you? I've got no family, one friend, and a volunteer job as a stagehand.'

Claudia frowned, dark hair falling over her face as she leaned forward. 'Grace, I don't like this. You're being weird. Did something else happen while I was gone?'

Grace turned the newspaper around so that her friend could see the crinkled photo of Alexander Cameron. 'Not while you were gone. It happened a long time ago.' She took a shaky breath in. 'Don't you see? *I'm* Norah Cameron.'

TWO

Colin Astle braced his shoulders against a sudden breeze. Despite the temperature staying in single figures, the café's outdoor tables were crowded. Everyone had coats buttoned to their necks, some wore beanies. He wished he'd brought one, but they were back in Edinburgh. Instead, he ordered more coffee. 'Come on, Alexander,' he said as the waiter left the table. 'You've got three days left in Melbourne.'

'I know.'

'Well, what touristy things do you want to do?'

Alexander put his coffee down untouched. 'Haven't we seen everything?'

Colin leaned back against the hard, wooden back of the café chair. 'No. We've seen a construction site several times, and lots of Paxton. Not really the highlights of this city.'

Alexander shrugged. 'Not feeling like being the tourist.'

'Mate.' Colin pushed his hair out of his eyes so he could stare at his friend. 'We've looked around, we've asked people lots of questions, and we haven't found any clues. How about giving it a rest for a day? Or two.'

'One.' Alexander sat straight and clasped his hands on top of his head. 'One day of being a wee tourist, then we go back and look around again.'

Colin nodded. 'One day, okay. You can start by drinking your coffee. This is proper barista coffee, not that muck you get back home.' He raised his head as Alexander put his fists on the table. 'Don't get worked up. It's the truth. Can't find a decent coffee in the whole of the Borders.'

Alexander picked up his cup and gulped. Colin frowned. It was a measure of how hard his friend was finding this trip down bad memory lane that he hadn't argued back. His coffee arrived. He sipped. It was already cooling down.

'So. Where next?' Alexander put his empty cup down.

'Somewhere warm.' Colin zipped his jacket up tighter. 'The weather is usually all four seasons in one day. Today it's stuck on the dead of winter.'

Alexander stood up, shaking his head. 'This isn't winter. It's a cool summer's day.'

Colin grinned. 'He jokes! The coffee has warmed him up.'

'Shut it, Astle. Let's go.'

In truth, Colin was finding it hard to think of somewhere that would cheer Alexander up. They were in Southbank with the Yarra sluggishly brown in front of them. Fine drizzle and hanging cloud meant it was useless going anywhere that offered a view. The art gallery was not Alexander's thing, and there weren't any sporting matches on anywhere. They'd already walked through the narrow laneways crowded with gas heaters and people and found themselves back near the dreary water. 'Come on, we'll take a tram and see if there's anything on at the Astor.'

They didn't have to wait long before a number sixty-four arrived. Alexander sat against the window, staring at people as they huddled at their stops. Colin saw him follow joggers as they ran through the Royal Botanical Gardens and down the broad footpaths and then study the occupants of a horse-drawn tourist carriage as it bounced its way around the corner. He shook his head, but not so Alexander could see. They'd been in Australia for nearly four weeks, and Alexander couldn't focus on anything but finding a sister who'd been missing for thirty years. There are millions of people in this city, he wanted to say. Millions more across the country. What makes you feel that you could find anyone here, even if you knew they were alive? Instead, he pointed at the view. 'See the Shrine?'

'Aye.' Alexander nodded, his gaze flicking across everyone walking the streets.

Colin sat back and crossed his arms. He hadn't wanted to come back, not yet. Yes, it was good to see his parents. They'd stayed with them up north when they'd arrived, and his Dad had flown to Melbourne the previous week to see the football. But Melbourne, the city he'd escaped from... it was haunted. Colin clutched his phone. She couldn't call, but still he felt tense. Three days to go, he thought, and then I can stop thinking about her. Three days, and Alexander will stop this useless, heart-wrenching quest.

'There!' Alexander leaned forward and spread his hand across the window glass.

'What is it?'

The train was jerking to a halt for its next stop. Alexander pushed past Colin and the line of people getting off and leapt down the steps.

'Alexander!' Colin went after him, muttering 'sorry' under his breath as commuters growled. He hit the ground moments after his friend and saw Alexander already across the road and sprinting back the way they'd come. Colin missed the lights and had to stop or be hit by streaming traffic. He stood, one hand on his head, as cars went by lanes deep. In the distance, he saw Alexander put a hand on a girl's shoulder and turn her towards him.

By the time Colin got to Alexander, the girl had a finger jabbing at Alexander's chest. '... idiot!' was the only thing Colin heard as she adjusted her shoulder bag and swung around to walk off. Sandy hair bobbed on her back as she went. Alexander nodded towards her. 'She could be Norah. Look at it, hair like mine, right age -'

Colin grabbed Alexander by the coat and hauled him off the path, shoving him on to a bench on the edge of the parklands. 'That's it, mate. That's enough.' He gripped the back of the seat and leaned over Alexander. 'Can't you see what it's doing to you? God almighty, you just grabbed a strange girl! You could get arrested for that. Lucky she wasn't the type to scream. Alexander.' He took his friend's shoulder and shook it. 'That's *enough.*'

Alexander still stared down the path, even though the girl had disappeared into the crowd. He glanced at Colin, then put both hands over his face. Colin let him go, swinging around to sit beside him. This was not turning out anything like he thought a quest would be. 'How long does this have to go on?'

Alexander was silent for another minute. When he lowered his hands, his face was blotchy but his eyes dry. 'Aye, alright. It wasn't her.'

Colin lowered his head. 'It's never going to be her.'

Alexander studied his fingers.

'Come on.' Colin put his elbows on his knees. 'You have to let it go. Do you know how many missing people there are in the world?'

Alexander hooked hair behind his ears. 'Aye, I know.'

'This is too hard. You're beating yourself up about something you can't change.'

Alexander nodded and said something Colin didn't catch.

'You agree?'

Another tram rumbled past. Alexander sat up, pushing both hands into his coat pockets. 'She knew how to look after herself.'

'Who?'

'That girl.'

Colin shrugged. 'Yeah. You didn't stand a chance.'

'I deserved it.'

'Yes, you did.'

'I'll stop.' Alexander turned to Colin. His eyes were grey in the winter light. 'I came, I looked, I failed.'

'Not failed. No one can finish an impossible task.'

'No, I failed.' Alexander stood up, hitching his coat to settle on his shoulders. 'I'll stop searching.'

'Good.'

'Colin, I'm never going to stop hoping.'

Colin heard the sorrow in Alexander's voice. He put one hand on his friend's back as they walked through the drizzle to the city. Sorrow, he knew. Pain, he knew. 'I hear you.'

He let Alexander go and put his head down against the rain. It was raining when...

Alicia came into his mind, her face dark, beautiful, cunning.

'You alright?' Alexander said as Colin stumbled.

Colin didn't answer.

———

BACK AT THEIR BED-AND-BREAKFAST, Colin moved into the kitchen as soon as Alexander connected his mother's call. Even through the clatter of dishes, he heard Alexander's voice break as he said, 'There's no trace, Mum. None.'

The kitchen window overlooked a derelict backyard. The house had been unlived in all winter, its owners on a trip up north where it was always sunny, and the loudest sound was the smash of surf on the sand. Good for them, Colin thought, brushing at the line of ants marching steadily along the sink before he filled it. Good for us, too, the place a cheap rental while its usual occupants were away.

Still, he felt strange being in someone else's house in his city. *His* city, that's how he thought of Melbourne. Over the back fence, he could see a row of new townhouses, their windows black and unfriendly. *His* city, although it had changed since he'd been away. The view from the plane as they'd banked over Tullamarine was unfamiliar. Since when had the city centre stretched so far out? Since when had skyscrapers edged it like that? He'd had to look left then right as the plane nosed down, unable to take in the whole view at once.

This house, with a trace of wallpaper on the lounge room walls and the floor vinyl cracked in the kitchen's corner, reminded him of his childhood home. Back then, there'd been the warm smells of his mother boiling potatoes and the comforting drone of the television on the six o'clock news.

Colin carried two beers into the lounge room and sat one next to Alexander's computer. His friend lifted a finger in thanks, his attention still on the screen.

'Hello, Colin.'

'Hi, Julie.' Colin moved so that Alexander's mother could see him over Alexander's shoulder. 'How's things over there?'

'Warm.'

'That would be nice.'

'Well, you'll be home soon.'

Home. Colin rolled the word around his head.

'Three days,' said Alexander, tipping beer into his mouth.

Colin shrugged. 'He's on the countdown.'

Julie's face pixelated momentarily as she smiled, making her mouth square and freezing her upturned eyes. She jerked back alive. 'See you then, Colin.'

Colin nodded, moving away from the computer so Alexander could finish his conversation. He sat at the tiny kitchen table and put his feet up on a chair opposite. Edinburgh was cold in the winter, but he'd forgotten how damp and miserable it could be in Australia. He rubbed his toes through his socks.

'Get them off.' Alexander walked in and pushed at Colin's legs until he could sit down.

'Your mum okay?'

'Aye. She's helping out at Uncle Euan's practice.'

Colin nodded, feeling momentarily vague about who Uncle Euan was. Then, oh yeah, *Dr* Euan Cameron. 1988 UK Medical Practitioner of the Year, or so he'd said once or five times. Tall, stern, grey-bearded. Trophy second wife. Arched eyebrows. Something of an enigma. 'Right. *Uncle* Euan.' He shook his head. 'You want to go to the pub for dinner?'

'Why not. Give me half an hour to have a shower.' Alexander drank the last of his beer, sliding the empty can towards Colin before standing up.

'Half an hour? Easy to see you haven't been on water restrictions.'

'What are water restrictions?'

Colin shook his head and waved the beer at him. 'I'm going to watch the news.'

Alexander had closed the bathroom door before Colin realised what he'd said. Watch the news? He hadn't done that since he was eighteen and still living with his mum and dad. Chuckling, he went into the lounge room and dutifully turned the television on, filling the room with a concerned news reader's voice and the sounds of screaming as something awful happened somewhere.

Colin plonked on the couch to watch, sitting on a pile of newspapers Alexander had thrown there. He pulled them out and saw his own face staring at the camera in front of the construction site that used to be the hospital. That had been a bad day. Alexander had not known they had demolished the hospital the year before. He'd stood at the fence, both hands blanching as they clenched the wire. Was he thinking that they were digging up the body of his baby sister? Or maybe that they were covering her up as she lay hidden somewhere on the grounds? Colin didn't dare ask. They'd stood for about an hour until it was clear that, with the foundations set for yet more square-faced town houses, no one had uncovered anything to do with Norah Cameron.

The shower water started, pipes rattling through the wall. Colin reached over for Alexander's computer and flicked on an internet tab. It opened to a site showing the faces and projected ages of missing people. There she was, baby Norah, current age listed as thirty.

Colin didn't have much to do with babies. They all looked the same, didn't they? This one had her fists at her shoulders, as if she was waving. Light fluffy hair decorated the top of her head and she smiled so that her cheeks pushed out. A chubby kid, he thought. I can tell that much. She had Alexander's loch-water-blue eyes. Maybe. It was hard to tell.

What would she look like now? Long and lean like her brother? Rounded and blonde like her mother? Or would she have drawn the short straw and be as large and lumbering as her father? That is, if she was alive, Colin thought as he clicked through the site. She couldn't be. Not after all this time. What-ever had happened that chaotic night at Paxton Community Hospital when Julie had gone to the cot and found her sick daughter missing, Colin was convinced the girl was dead. Just as most of these people must be. How could all these missing people, thousands and thousands of them across the country, be wandering about with no one knowing who they really were?

A thought speared him: Alicia didn't make it onto any missing person's website.

The shower turned off with a thunk of pipes. Colin slid the computer back on the table and turned his attention to the news. It was harder than ever to concentrate, and it wasn't the three beers he'd had since they'd got home. His knee jerked up and down as his foot jittered.

'Ready.' Alexander was in the doorway, rubbing his wet head with a towel.

Colin heaved himself up from the hollow in the couch and shook his legs out. 'Right. Me too.'

'You don't look it.'

'We did a lot of walking today.'

Alexander snorted. 'Wait until we bag Ben Nevis. That'll sort you out.'

'Something to look forward to.' Colin snatched his wallet and keys from the kitchen bench. 'Come on.'

The pub was only a ten-minute walk away, a loud classy place that Colin couldn't remember being in before. He'd seen plenty of interiors like it. Wooden tables with metal chairs, waiters in black aprons taking orders on electronic tablets, 70s rock posters on the walls. They sat in one corner; the rest of the crowd spread out in front of them.

It was too loud to talk. Colin was glad. Alexander sat under a light and the dark shadows under his eyes made his face even whiter. His hair was still damp and hung in strands to his shoulders. He'd got thinner. How was that possible when Colin knew they'd eaten out most nights, drinking beer to wash it down? This trip to Australia, this strange anniversary visit, had sucked something out of Alexander. He seemed less than he'd been, a sad clone of the man Colin worked with, who he knew could go all day laying stone and slate.

'You need a steak,' he said when the waiter came to take their order.

'Do I?'

'Don't argue.' Colin's tongue felt thick. 'Me too.'

'We had steak last night.'

'We're having it again.'

Colin saw Alexander raise his eyebrows at the waiter who smiled sympathetically. 'Where you from?' she asked.

'Melbourne.'

The waiter kept her gaze on Alexander.

'Edinburgh.'

'Cute,' the waiter said.

Colin found his beer empty and went to get two more, leaving Alexander talking to the girl. She left as he came back. Alexander took the drink without looking at his friend.

'Any luck?'

'She was just talking, Colin.'

'She thought you were cute.'

'Ha.' Alexander sipped the froth from his beer.

The steaks arrived by Colin's sixth drink. Alexander ate hungrily, but Colin felt uneasy looking at the brown mass before him. The pub was louder than before. It was hurting his ears. People's faces swam in and out of focus as he looked around. Maybe some of them were people missing from their families? Maybe here, in this room, was one of those from the website? He wished he hadn't read their names. It made him think that he knew them.

'Why aren't you eating?' Alexander was halfway through his steak, his face warmer with the effort. Colin picked at his dinner, eating a bit, staring at people more than he should. He thought of his mother in Queensland, wondering what she was doing. Was she at Tanya's with her grandkids? Mum and Dad often ate there, sometimes minding the kids so that Tanya could go out with her girlfriends. What if she didn't have Tanya? What if Tanya had gone missing like Norah?

'I can't eat anymore.'

'Give it to me.'

Colin watched as Alexander ate his chips, his steak, his vegetables. 'Last full day tomorrow. What do you want to do?'

'We haven't made it to the Astor. We could go there.'

'Okay.'

Alexander pushed his plate back. 'I never did say thanks.'

'I gave it to you.'

'What?'

'My dinner.'

Alexander laughed. 'Not that. Thanks for following me around Melbourne.'

'No worries.'

'I owe you.'

'Yeah, you do.' Colin pushed his chair back, feeling prickly. 'Come on, let's go.'

They paid and left, frosty night air chilling them as soon as they stepped outside. Colin felt his senses return. They walked in silence, watching as a possum balanced awkwardly on a power line.

Colin studied his friend briefly. 'It's going to be too hard to stop looking.'

Alexander shook his head at the animal. 'It's a possum, isn't it?' he said, eyes skyward.

Colin shook his head. 'Not that. You'll always be looking out for *her*.'

Alexander hunched his shoulders up and breathed into his coat to warm his face. 'Yes.'

'She's definitely not going to be in Scotland. You can stop once we get there.'

'I'll try.'

'I'm going to hold you to that.'

Alexander nodded, his face long.

Damn it, Norah Cameron, thought Colin as they reached the house. If you ever turn up, you've got a lot to answer.

THREE

Claudia sat in the kitchen, legs crossed, foot bouncing as Grace came in and switched the kettle on. Grace's head felt foggy from lack of sleep. Claudia said something she didn't catch. 'What?'

'You feeling better?'

Claudia's foot was making the table shake. Grace leaned over to rescue the sugar bowl. 'What do you mean?'

Claudia crossed her other leg over, hauling her foot up across her thigh. The table stilled. 'Feeling better. More sensible.'

Grace leaned her back on the bench and rubbed her eyes. Claudia's hair puffed all over her head. She had her sleeping T-shirt on, the one that read *I don't need beauty sleep.* Toast crumbs littered a plate in front of her. 'Sensible? I'm not sure what you mean.'

'Last night, you went to bed straight after you said something strange. You'd had a lot to drink. Maybe you don't remember?'

Grace shook her head. 'I remember what I said. I am Norah Cameron.'

Claudia pushed her chair back noisily and threw one hand

in the air. 'Come on, Grace. That's impossible. You're Grace Worthington!'

'Am I?' Grace closed her eyes for a moment, feeling slightly dizzy. 'Who have I got left to tell me that?'

'Me.'

'You. My best friend. How do you know I'm Grace Worthington?'

'Because you are. Because you always have been. It says that on your birth certificate, for god's sake! It's how you got your passport.'

Grace nodded. 'Yes. That's right.' She stared at Claudia's reddening face. 'How do you know that I'm *not* Norah Cameron?'

Claudia paced the tiny kitchen, then stopped. 'Grace.' She held out her upturned hands. 'You've had a rotten week. You just got your dad's things back. You aren't thinking straight. Just give yourself a bit of time.'

Grace shook her head. 'There's no need for time. It makes sense. Alexander Cameron comes looking for his sister, who would be the same age as me. She went missing in Paxton, where I lived thirty years ago. More specifically, she went missing from Paxton Community Hospital, and our accident - when Mum was taken to hospital - was thirty years ago.'

'That means nothing.'

'You think? How about Alexander and I looking like siblings?'

'You don't know that from one photo.'

'We've got the same colouring.'

Claudia shook her head violently. 'You mean, red hair and blue eyes? Like your *dad*?'

Grace put both her hands behind her head. 'I only remember Dad as grey. You're going on old photos.'

'Like you're only going on that one photo in the paper.

Grace. Please.' Claudia tugged at Grace's arm until it flopped to her side. 'This whole dead dad thing has made you loopy. Surely you can see that.'

Grace shrugged her friend off and turned to the kettle. The dizziness was lifting, but a nausea was taking its place. As she reached for the tea bags, her hand over the scarred grey vinyl of the bench, she felt a sudden loathing for where she stood. Behind her, the kitchen had beige walls that needed painting and a ring of damp staining two corners. Their kitchen chairs sat slightly tilted on the sloping floor, stumps no doubt eaten by termites. Outside, they had a courtyard where, when they bothered cleaning it up, they found used needles and empty stolen wallets that had been flung over the wall from the laneway. Beyond that, the city stretched winter-grey and familiar, tiredly so. *Tired, that's what I feel,* thought Grace as she poured boiling water into mugs stained with use. *Exhausted. In need of a change.*

She slid the tea across the table. 'Sit, Claudia.'

'I don't know that I can. You're making me crazy.'

'Please. *Sit.*'

Claudia slid into a chair.

Grace sat as well, her elbows on the table. 'I've been thinking about this all night.'

'Grace...'

Grace lifted her hand to silence her. 'It probably sounds crazy to you. But it doesn't to me. And I think I've got a chance to be someone other than myself.'

'You have to be joking.'

'I'm not. I'm serious. I can let the sad loser Grace Worthington go because she's not me.' She sipped her tea and put her mug down. 'I feel relieved.'

'Grace, this is not a theatre production. This is real life.'

'I know real life more than you do!'

Claudia looked down into her tea. Her fingers pressed hard against her mug, making the tips white. 'Grace,' she said without looking up, 'think about this. I know you're hurting. I know you've been through more in your life than I ever will, but you can't change that. You need to make some sort of peace with it. Maybe go to the counsellor again? Talk this over with someone other than me. Grace, stop shaking your head. You know I'm making sense.'

Grace pushed herself back in her chair. 'You're not. You're trying to stop me from starting fresh.'

'Grace, you'll be pretending to be someone you're not.'

'No, I'll be who I really am.'

'Which is Grace Worthington!'

'No, it isn't!' Grace leaned forward and slammed her palms on the table. 'I'm Norah Cameron, with a brother and...'

'And what?'

Grace stared at the wall behind Claudia. A brother, and maybe a sister, probably parents. Grandparents, aunts and uncles. 'A family.'

'Ah.' Claudia folded her hands together and put them on the table. 'I get it.'

'No, you don't.'

'I do.' Claudia spoke gently. 'I do, really.' She was quiet again. The room felt smothered by silence until she pushed her untouched drink forward so it slid noisily across the table. 'Can you promise me something?'

'What?'

'Wait a bit. Just think on it a little longer before you do anything. Please? For me?'

Grace shook her head.

Claudia reached out and gripped Grace's hands. 'Come on. Wait. Think on it.'

Grace felt the warmth in her friend's hands. She saw the

concern in her eyes. But there was also a tension in Claudia's face, the sort of guarded, frozen, ready-for-action look that you had if you were encountering an unfamiliar large dog or a deranged person weaving past you on the street. Mistrust. It stabbed at Grace jaggedly. 'No.'

'What?'

'No. I'm not waiting. There's no need.'

For a moment, Grace thought that Claudia hadn't heard her then she sat back, her mouth open and eyes startled. The dog was dangerous.

'Did you hear me?'

Claudia stood up, rocking the table and spilling her tea. 'I heard. I'm going out.' She pulled her keys from the hook near the door and ran down the corridor. The door banged shut. The entire house shivered.

Grace sat on, thinking numbly that Claudia was out in her pyjamas. She finally rose to make toast, carrying it back to her room and sitting on her bed to eat it. A long, pale streak of sunlight speared its way through her window across her father's empty packing chest.

Claudia eventually came back. Grace was still in her room, the toast abandoned on her bedside table.

'Grace?'

Claudia's voice was small. Grace barely heard it.

'Grace!'

'Yes?'

Claudia pushed the door wide open. 'What are you doing?'

Grace looked down at the pile of clothes in her arms. 'Sorting things out.'

'Okay.' Claudia stepped into the room. 'Do you need a hand?'

'I don't think so.' Grace held the clothes tight. 'I was just wondering...'

'Wondering what?'

'If Norah Cameron would wear the same things that Grace Worthington does?'

Claudia made a strange, strangled noise but said nothing. After a moment in which Grace put a shirt down on the floor to her right, Claudia said, 'Do you want to go out to dinner tonight?'

'You're going to give me therapy over food? I'm not crazy.'

'What? No. We haven't been out for ages. Anyway, there's nothing in the fridge. I'll go shopping tomorrow.'

'We never go out. We can't afford it.'

'Please.'

Grace looked at Claudia. She had coffee spilled on her sleeping T-shirt. 'Why don't you go out with whatshisname?'

'Paul? No, he's boring.'

'You didn't say that on Tuesday night.'

'I did on Wednesday when I woke up. Things have a way of becoming clear when you think about them more.'

Grace sighed. 'I see what you're doing there, Claudia.'

Claudia leaned back on the doorframe. 'Please, Grace!'

Grace put a skirt into the pile of clothes to her left. 'I will go out to dinner tonight on one condition.'

'I can't -'

'Then I'm not going.'

'Alright! Alright, we won't talk about it.'

Grace nodded. 'Where do you want to go?'

'The new place down the road. That pub they've done up.'

'I know it.' Grace placed a pair of shoes to the left.

Claudia straightened. 'Just what are you doing?'

Grace pointed to the biggest pile. 'I don't think Norah would wear the same clothes as Grace. That's Grace.' Then to the right. 'Norah.'

Claudia flinched. 'Right. I think I'll go have a shower.'

'Good idea.' Grace pointed at the coffee stain. 'Better soak that. How did it happen, anyway?'

'I was a bit... agitated.'

Grace put a T-shirt to one side. 'Claudia, there's no need to worry. I'm okay.'

'You don't seem okay.'

'Well, I am.'

Claudia backed away, hands in the air. After she'd gone, Grace studied the piles of clothes on the floor. She normally wore jeans and loose shirts, most often bought from second-hand clothes shops. Her favourite jacket was caramel-coloured leather, a find some years ago. The shoes on the left were comfortable slip-on types of things, ballet flats and elastic-sided ankle boots. It was casual dressing, styled from years of frugal living.

But to be Norah...

Grace flicked through the second pile of clothes. Three dresses, unworn, and a couple of shirts with princess sleeves. Seriously feminine. One pair of shoes had joined the stack, a wedged sandal with a crest of white daisies, worn once. Grace bent to rub her ankle. There was still a mark from the blister she'd got from going out in those.

It would be easier to lose Grace if Norah dressed nothing like her. Grace felt a tingle in her stomach. Transformation or reclamation?

An hour later, Grace was still sitting on her bed, clothes on her lap as she studied them. Claudia put her head in the room again, keeping her distance and trying not to frown. Grace saw her contortions and pushed the clothes away. 'What time are we going out?'

'Can we make it early? I'm so tired after last night.'

'Six?'

'Okay.'

'I'm going out now for a bit then.'

'Oh.' Claudia came into the room. 'Do you want company?'

'I'll be alright. I need to get some things...' She waved her hand around.

'Can you get the groceries then?'

'Sure.'

'I'll get the list.'

Grace checked the time while Claudia was away. She had three hours to get into the city and back. She snatched the shopping list off Claudia and headed out the door. It wasn't so quick that she didn't catch the concern on Claudia's face.

Half-way to the city, rocking in the tram, Grace felt the decision she'd made settle comfortably into her soul. They passed the boarding house. A man sat on the front veranda staring at the road. It was already a distant place, somewhere Grace had once known. I don't feel any *longing*, she thought. Not for Dad, not for Mum either. Instead, her heart was beating quickly in anticipation of newness.

For two hours, she walked the city. Crowds were thick, the rare sunshine tempting them outside. Grace pushed her way through the slow walkers, her body itching with restlessness. The city centre looked different, as if Norah's eyes were looking for the first time at the colours, the trams, the mix of architecture. Grace stood tall at the pedestrian lights, pulling herself straight and staring out at the people opposite. When the lights changed, the crowds crossed paths, the surge hiding the individuals. Grace reached the curb and paused, a man colliding with her stationary figure and pushing her to walk again. As she muttered an apology, the man moved past without a glimpse. *I am completely anonymous to him*, she thought.

I am completely anonymous to everyone except Claudia.

Grace had shed tears at her mother's funeral, great floods of them. Not a drop had come at her father's. She'd wondered at the time whether she'd already used her life's quantity up. It was almost a relief then to have her eyes blur and warm wetness run over her cheeks as she stepped haphazardly towards the tram stop. She wiped them away with the back of her hand but still they came, making her nose run with it, and giving her hiccuppy sobs that made the others on the tram glance at her before looking pointedly away.

By half-way home, the tears had stopped. Grace used her sleeve to dab at the ruined make-up trail she could see reflected in the tram window. She took a deep breath in and exhaled slowly, keeping her head turned away from where she knew the boarding house was and concentrating instead on a group of people standing together on the footpath, clearly impatiently waiting for others. Among them stood a wan-looking golden-headed woman, her arms clasped behind her back, a small smile lighting her face as she listened to her friend berate the absent ones with violent hand gestures. She was, thought Grace, incredibly beautiful, not only in looks but in the gracious way she bent her head to listen and the one soft, bent knee deferring to her friend. She had layered her clothing with a silvery trench coat and crushed floral cotton shirt falling over dark pants. Delicate threads patterned her heeled boots.

Grace kept watch until the tram had trundled too far away to see. Someone like that would never be anonymous. She was someone who stood out from her friends. She was someone so exquisite that no-one, including complete strangers, could resist.

'ARE YOU READY YET?' Claudia banged on the bathroom door again.

'Hang on...' Grace was having trouble with her eyeliner.

Her eyes felt bloodshot from her afternoon's grief, and the pencil scraped painfully along her eyelid.

'At last.' Claudia's bag swung as she stepped away from the opening door. 'We're late.' She leaned forward. 'What were you trying to do?'

'Nothing.'

Claudia frowned. 'Looks like you've been stabbing yourself in the eye.'

'Thanks.'

'You're welcome.' Claudia patted Grace's shoulder. 'Come on. We should be there by now or we'll lose our booking. And then we'd starve, seeing as you forgot to do the shopping.'

'I'm sorry.'

Claudia shook her head. 'It doesn't matter. Come on.'

Grace glanced in the mirror. In an attempt to change her look, all she'd done was to outline pale eyes to make them look like targets. She sighed. 'Okay, I'm with you.'

They walked under the same umbrella to the pub. Its dark interior was at least warm, and they found a table next to a wall heater. The soft air soothed Grace. She dabbed at her cheeks, trying to bring life back into them.

'I'll have the steak,' Claudia said once the waitress was there.

'Is it really big?' Grace put her thumbs and forefingers together to show an enormous piece of meat. 'I can't eat that much.'

The waitress tipped her head as she thought. 'Most people who order it manage to get through it.'

'But what sort of people order it?' Claudia put her hands out to puff up her size.

'All sorts,' said the waitress, frowning. 'Last night, a really skinny Scottish man ate one and a half.'

Claudia laughed. 'He ordered one and a half steaks?'

'He ate most of his friend's as well.' The waitress tapped the top of her tablet. 'So, what will it be?'

Grace put her menu down. 'You said that man was Scottish?'

'Sorry?'

'You said the man who ate the steaks was Scottish. What did he look like?'

'Grace...' Claudia reached out for Grace's arm.

'I'm just asking.'

The waitress shifted her weight to one foot. 'Red-headed, skinny, cute.'

'And his friend?'

'Grace!'

'His friend was darker.' The waitress shifted to the other foot.

Grace squeezed Claudia's arm. 'It was them.'

'So?' said Claudia.

The waitress asked, 'Who?'

The room swayed a little. Grace blinked and stared straight at the waiter. 'My brother.'

Claudia cringed.

'Oh. I see. Well, your brother ate a lot of steak with no worries.'

'I'll have one, too.' Grace saw Claudia lean back in her chair and sigh.

'Okay.' The waitress tapped her tablet, then turned shyly to Grace. 'He's on his way home, he said.'

'Oh?'

'You didn't know?'

Claudia fanned herself with the menu.

'He's going home to Scotland.'

The waitress frowned. 'You don't sound Scottish, not like him.'

'No.' Grace wiped a crumb from the table. 'I've been in Australia a long time.'

'You're not a stonemason, too?'

Claudia let her head drop.

'No, I'm not a stonemason.'

The waitress's face reddened. 'Sorry. I thought he said it was a family business.'

'Not for me.' Grace swallowed. 'Did he say anything else? My brother, that is.'

'No.' The waitress went even redder. 'We only had a quick chat.'

Grace leaned towards the waitress and whispered, 'Was he lonely?'

'I'll have chips with mine,' said Claudia loudly. The waitress scurried away.

'He was lonely,' said Grace.

'Grace.' The low light shadowed Claudia's face, making her eyes unreadable. 'He is not your brother.'

'His name is Alexander.'

'Alexander is *not* your brother.'

'He's missing a sister.'

'You are not his sister.' Claudia folded both hands on the table.

'You promised not to talk about this.'

'I wasn't the one to start it.'

Grace shrugged. She got up to order drinks, careful not to look at Claudia. The warm air had become abruptly unbearable, burning the top of her head and shoulders. It wasn't the fault of the air conditioning; it was the sudden anger that rose at Claudia's words. She wasn't even trying to understand. Still, she bought her friend a cocktail.

Claudia sipped at the green drink, fingers tapping the glass, and studied the room until she saw someone she knew. 'There's Purani.'

'Why don't you go and talk to her?'

'I will but let me know when the food arrives.' Claudia stood, taking her drink, and frowning down at Grace. 'I hear your family can eat more than one.'

Grace chewed her bottom lip as Claudia left. If Claudia wouldn't understand, Grace had no choice but to keep her thoughts to herself. She was only alone for a couple of minutes before the waitress arrived with two brimming plates. 'Thanks,' said Grace as she placed the meals on the table. She caught the girl's sleeve before she went. 'Can I ask you something?'

The waitress's eyes widened. 'I wasn't trying to get on to him or anything.'

'What?'

'Your brother. I was only talking to him, nothing else.'

Grace shook her head. 'I wanted to ask you whether you thought I looked like him.'

The waitress dropped her shoulders in relief. 'Oh, okay.' She wiped some hair out of her face and had a good look at Grace. 'No, not really. He was sort of... paler.'

Grace nodded, her hands tight under the table. 'Paler.'

'But, you know, you've got the same coloured eyes.'

'Really?'

'Yeah.' The waitress turned. 'Enjoy your meal.'

Grace stared at her steak. Alexander and she had the same coloured eyes?

It was enough.

FOUR

Julie Cameron paused in the middle of folding a towel. *I have adopted my mother's routine. Baking on one day, washing on another. I have become middle-aged.*

The thought made her sit up sharply. The bright kitchen was rimmed with cut flowers, the clean counter sported a jaunty range of Mackintosh-inspired mugs. The washing spread out on the table was that of two people, Julie and Donald. Julie was thrust back to a kitchen table in the 70s Melbourne suburbs, with clothes spread over the top of the *Herald* as her mother patted and folded, a cigarette in the corner of her mouth. At least I don't smoke, thought Julie, touching her lip. Her mother's lips were puckered from years of drawback, pink lipstick filling in the lines radiating out from them.

Baking on one day, washing on another, work for the rest of the week. At least that was different. Her mother didn't work, not for wages. She carried the noble title of a housewife long after her children had fled and her husband had died. It would be strange now to hear someone so proud of being one hundred percent house maker. *None of my friends would be,* Julie frowned. They saw themselves as better than that.

She picked up the towel again and finished its fold. There was a sense of order in a folded towel, something that Julie had been struggling to find lately. She stood, carried the washing to the linen press and stacked it neatly, taking care to flatten each layer so it fitted. The renovated stables had been Donald's idea, and he'd forgotten about storage. Or maybe it was just the Scottish way. Julie's mother's linen press had taken up an entire wall.

There she was again, thinking about her past life, her childhood in fact. *Why am I doing that?* Julie thought. *I've never been nostalgic before.*

It was time to check the Wallace messages. Donald would be home late, the summer evenings a good time to work with stone. Not too hot, the light enough to keep a good line. Julie had the late afternoon and early evening to herself in the big, bright, empty house. Her legs itched to be outside.

On a feverish day, when she was genuinely busy and eagerly doing multiple tasks, Julie could walk the winding track to the monument in twenty minutes. On slower days, days like this, she was deliberately more gently paced. The path wound up to the top of the hill, thick summer leaves blocking the views around each corner. There was a horse ahead today. As Julie hit the forest track, she could hear its hoof-falls on the bits of the path that were solid. Girls talked. There must be two horses and, yes, she got a glimpse of a white and a brown rump as they rounded a corner a way ahead. Julie wondered how old the riders were. Probably teenagers but, around here where everyone could ride (except Julie), the girls could be older. Maybe even the age Norah would be.

Julie stumbled over a stick. There it was, the reason she'd been reminiscing about retro kitchens and mothers who smoked. Alexander and Colin would be on the plane now, heading for Doha, leaving Melbourne behind in a trail of jet fumes. They'd spoken most nights while Alexander was away. It seemed more important to Alexander than her that he continued the never-ending search. Julie stopped, scratching at her arm. *Does that make me a bad mother? I'm not searching enough?*

'Hello, Julie. You alright there?'

Julie spun at the voice behind her. 'Oh! Louisa! You startled me.'

Louisa stood with feet apart, looking assured in sturdy walking boots. Julie was acutely aware that she had running shoes on, not because she ran, but because walking hurt her big toe these days and walking boots were far too rigid. *A middle-aged bunion?* The thought startled her more than Louisa's hearty boots.

'You're scratching at your arm something terrible. Nettle?'

Julie twisted her arm around to see where she'd been itching. Raised lumps, blanched and bulbous, decorated the underside of her forearm. She'd scratched crimson lines around them, as if she'd been trying to colour them in. 'Goodness, I can't remember doing that.'

'You shouldn't touch the nettles, Julie. I know you haven't grown up around them, but you really shouldn't touch nettles.'

Julie gritted her teeth. Louisa often wanted a walking companion, but it would not be Julie if she could avoid it. It wasn't the big woman's speed or her tendency to head straight up a hill instead of adopting a more considered zig-zag path; it was the way she thought of Julie as a newcomer. 'I've been here thirty-five years, Louisa.'

'Aye. Still the nettles get you.' Louisa threw back her head to laugh. Julie immediately thought of the horses ahead on the path. 'Are you walking to the Wallace?'

'Yes. Taking my time, though.' Julie indicated her shoes. 'Got a bit of a sore foot.'

'You won't be wanting me to hurry you then.' Louisa folded her arms and looked down. 'You should get a decent pair of boots, Julie Cameron. Those spindly little things are no good for your feet.'

Julie stretched her lips into a smile-shape. 'Thanks, Louisa. Well, I won't keep you.'

Louisa strode forward. 'Bye then.'

Julie waited until the noise of Louisa's tramping disappeared and let out a sigh. Spindly shoes today. Last week it was a paper jacket, the week before a floaty hat. Whatever she was wearing when Louisa came along, it was wrong for the climate, wrong for Dryburgh, wrong for the country.

The path was at its darkest on the long section of path before the last bend. Julie moved softly forward, Louisa and the horses long gone. The dimness was comforting. Julie felt protected by it. In these steps, she allowed herself deeper thoughts she tried to keep under wraps at home. Mostly they were images, and nearly all of Norah. Wispy hair, clenched fist in sleep, a pale pink blanket stretched over the cot. Sometimes her eyes were open, staring up at her mother. Mostly, they were closed. Pale cornflower blue when they were open, not hazel like Julie's. *How much would she have looked like me?*

The track hair-pinned and the monument came into view. William Wallace stared into the trees, his right hand on the hilt of his long sword. Julie glanced up, gave him her usual respectful nod, and headed to the tin box on the edge of the viewing area. Inside, another five notes reported visitor's origins. A couple had witty comments, one a quote from *Braveheart*, another a heartfelt *I wish I was as brave as you.* Julie slipped them into her pocket to take to the Wallace Monument Society meeting. It was her one contribution to the committee. The paper supply was getting down, and the pen had seen better days. Tomorrow's visit would fix that.

But I'm working at the surgery. She pursed her lips.

Julie decided to go the long way home, taking the road to the Abbey rather than the path through the forest. Dinner was an easy chicken casserole, something a little too heavy for Julie. Donald, on the other hand, would be starving. His work was hard, especially doing without the boys for a few weeks, his appetite enormous whether or not they were there to help. Julie tried not to imagine Dr Euan Cameron and his super-trim physique in the same thought as his brother's rounded, swollen guts. Not that she desired thin-ness in a man. No, not at all. Not again, not after... well. Donald's increasing bulk, though, was bordering on dangerous. Yet she fed him casseroles and cakes.

The Abbey was closed, but Julie went to stand at its gates to stare into the gardens. The greenness still amazed her. Summer in Australia was bleached bones and dirt. The gentleness of the heat here was, she thought, the reward for the many months of grey. She missed the dry, though: the scorched air and the need for iced ginger ale and Pimms. The air could dry a complete load of washing instantly, and tan skin in a ten-minute exposure.

Julie turned swiftly towards home. *I do not miss sunburn,* she thought savagely. *I do not miss lying awake at night perspiring into the sheets. I certainly do not miss the smell of bushfire smoke settling on the city.*

She'd pushed through the house gate before she realised that Donald was home. The van had crunched awkwardly to a stop, leaving a spurt of gravel behind it. The money they'd spent on the yard... Julie hated to think of it but hated more the way Donald parked so carelessly, as if they were back in Melrose and he had the empty field next door. Her little car stood neatly at the garage entrance as if waiting patiently to go home. She would take it in later, after she'd locked the chickens up for the night.

'Julie, where have you been, love?'

Donald appeared at the kitchen door. Even from the distance she was from him, Julie could see how his skin glowed. Donald preferred to work in singlets or, as Alexander often reported, topless, depending on who was on the building site. 'Did you put sunscreen on, Donald?'

'No, love.'

'I put it in your bag.'

'I don't like the slimy stuff.' Donald stepped back to let her pass. She smelled the heat rising from him. 'Don't waste our money on it.'

Julie shook her head. She'd trained Alexander, but not Donald, about skin cancer. Colin, of course, had arrived to do his apprenticeship fully versed. Nothing that the boys did could convince Donald that his skin needed protecting. She stared at him as he filled the kettle. Would he always be so flippant about his health? Was she doomed to look after an ailing older man full of diabetes, skin cancers and gout? Could she be bothered?

'Sucked on a lemon, love?'

Julie shook her head, rubbing her mouth as if to take a taste away. 'What are you doing home so early, anyway?'

'Can't a man be home early for once?' Donald scooped Julie from behind, his arms trapping her. He breathed into her ear.

'Of course you can.' His arms tightened. Julie felt her tummy ooze out between them. Donald is not the only one who enjoyed casseroles and cakes, she thought, trying to suck in. 'You're squashing me.'

'What about a little afternoon delight?'

'Can you have a shower first?'

He landed a kiss on her cheek and let her go. 'Give me ten minutes.'

Afternoon delights were quite regular with Alexander away. Not that he lived with them, preferring the drive back to Edinburgh to staying in the Borders. When he worked with Donald, though, they pushed each other to longer, harder days. Donald might come home with delight on his mind, but he was usually too tired to do anything. A quick morning fling was more their style. Julie wondered what she preferred. Sometimes it was the briskness of morning, particularly if she had a whole day of activity. The more languid love-making of early evening suited her when the day had been long and lacklustre. At least it filled in some time.

They lay in bed afterwards, Donald with an arm under her neck, his other hand tapping out the rhythm to a hummed song. She heard the noise deep in his chest, a contented rumble similar to a cat's purr. It stopped as he said, 'Our boy will be home tomorrow.'

'You'll give them a day off to adjust, won't you?'

Donald laughed. 'I'm not their keeper, love. They'll do what they want, which I think will mean working as soon as they can.'

'They are good workers.'

'Aye.'

They lay for a moment quietly, Julie thinking about how the rough stones had calloused Alexander's hands. Donald's were permanently thickened, but Alexander's hands, Julie noticed, had taken time to weather. They still had the spring of youth in his skin. How long would it last?

'They didn't find her then.'

Julie stiffened. In the weeks the boys had been away, Donald had never mentioned Alexander's quest. He had barely mentioned Norah in the last ten years, her name gradually fading from his lips as time went by. The desperation that had consumed him in the first five years after Norah went missing had diluted with every passing birthday. It was a shock now to remember how passionate he'd been. Julie felt as if she was recalling something taboo when she thought of his obsession with the streets of Paxton. He'd knocked on many doors, harassed the wrong people, accused the neighbourhood of nasty and terrible things. Then he'd hollowed, softened, becoming a pudding rather than a zealot. She swallowed. 'No. Did you expect them to?'

'No.' Donald sighed. 'I knew they wouldn't. He had to go through the motions to know she's not there.' He tucked Julie into his side a little more.

Julie felt her limbs tighten. It was an effort to keep from pulling herself away from her husband, from throwing back the covers and saying cheerily, 'Well, I'd better get the dinner on! Thanks for the orgasm, but I've got chicken to cook.' Instead, she practised some deep breathing before saying moderately, 'Isn't Colin a good friend to Alexander?'

'Aye. It was a lucky day for us when he chose stonemasonry.' Donald chuckled. 'I've always liked that he can take our boy in all of his moods.'

'Alexander doesn't have *moods*.'

'Of course he does. Thinks too much, that one.' Donald shifted so that he could look at Julie. 'I've caught him with a piece of sandstone, looking at it as if it was going to talk to him! I said, what are you doing, boy? And he said, Dad, it's got a story. All these stones have stories. I mean, what do you say to that?'

You say, thought Julie, *that he is right. Stones do have stories, historical or otherwise.* 'He's a thinker,' is all she said.

'And that Colin, he doesn't seem to mind. Thinks it normal.' Donald rolled onto his back. 'They remind me of brothers. Of Euan and me. Are you alright, love?'

'Just getting comfortable.' Julie shifted a little more along her pillow.

'Of Euan and me. Euan being the one that thinks, but I guess you knew that.'

Julie shuffled down the bed. 'Lift your arm a bit, Donald. You're digging into my back.'

'Sorry, love.' Donald moved his arm and folded his hands on top of his stomach. The sheet lay across his waist. Julie tugged it up to her chin. 'I used to wish that Alexander had a brother.'

'You never told me that.'

'I didn't think it until later. Too late then, love, for more bairns. And it doesn't matter now because Colin came along.' He put his hands behind his head. 'Euan and I couldn't be any more different. Are you working for him tomorrow?'

'Yes. Three days a week, like we arranged.'

'I said to him you'd be a great help. Being a nurse.'

'I was only an enrolled nurse, Donald.'

'A very good enrolled nurse. You know it all. That's what happens when you work at something a long time. If I didn't lay another stone for years, I'd still know exactly how to do it. Anyway, alright then?'

'What?'

'Working for Euan?'

Julie sat up, pulling her clothes from the end of the bed and slipping them on. 'Fine,' she said with her head in her T-shirt. 'I'd better get dinner on, Donald. You'll be hungry.'

'Always hungry, love.' He put a warm, heavy hand on her back. 'Especially for my little Aussie girl.'

There were two things wrong with that statement, thought Julie as she slid out of bed. *Little*, and *girl*. She pulled jeans on, fighting the zip until it went right up, and patted her hair down. She imagined Donald's eyes on her back as she hurried to the kitchen. What do I look like to him? The twenty-year-old he'd met in a disco in Melbourne? The twenty-two-year-old he'd married? The twenty-four-year-old who screamed her way through labour to present him with a little ginger-haired lad? She was waiting for him to recognise that she was fifty-eight now, with none of the long summer-bleached hair he'd wrapped around his fingers on the dance floor and no sign of the willowy golden-bronzed body that had caught his eye. She was sure, one day, he'd suddenly see her as she really was. It was only one step then to seeing her as she'd really been...

The chicken nearly slipped from her fingers. She trapped it against her body, feeling it splodge through her T-shirt to the skin on her stomach. She chopped it up and put it in a sizzling dish before going to change. Donald was asleep, his hands still under his head, his stomach rising and falling contentedly.

She paused to watch him. He'd been nineteen when they'd met, already on the big side, but strong-looking rather than large. He was confident on the dance floor, holding her close despite the jumpy solo moves of the others. Instant love? No, but he was exotic. A glimpse of another world, one far away from the *Herald* on the kitchen table. Was he still exotic?

Julie took a carefully folded T-shirt from its stack and threw the other one in the laundry basket, despite knowing she should at least rinse the chicken juice from it. She tried not to look at her sleeping man, his open mouth and twitching REM eyes. Exotic? No, not after the wedding. Not after she'd met Euan - her family doctor and her brother-in-law - already well on his way to being recognised as a top clinician. Euan was exotic from the tip of his smooth auburn head to the point of his Oxfords. She'd tried to stay healthy to keep away from Euan Cameron.

That hadn't worked so well.

Now Julie was back in Euan's vicinity, thanks to the faith her husband had in his wife and, stupidly, the faith he had in his brother.

FIVE

The plane trip had been horrendous. Alexander had never been so glad to step into a terminal. The family that had surrounded him through the last eight hours were still carrying on, teenage boys punching each other tiredly while their mother moved ahead with her head averted.

'At least it's warm,' Alexander said to Colin as they walked to the passport checkpoint.

'Warm*er*. Not *warm*.'

'And I can't smell farts.'

'What?'

Alexander nodded towards the teenage boys now queuing at border control. 'For the last four hours. Ever since they ate whatever it was we had.'

Colin laughed as he made his way to the non-EU passport area. 'I definitely got the right seat then.'

Alexander grunted. He'd beg for a seat away from irritable boys next time.

'You returning home?' said the man checking his passport.

'Yes.'

'Enjoy it?' The man studied Alexander's face. 'Being away?'

'No.'

'Och.' The man handed the passport back dismissively. 'Welcome home. Next!'

Alexander moved away to wait for Colin, who was stuck in a long queue. Hadn't he enjoyed it at all? His first trip to Australia since he was four years old – there must have been parts that were good. He tried to think. Yes, there was the ocean near Colin's parents and the brief visit they'd had to the hinterland. Before they went to Melbourne. From that moment on, he'd had Norah on his mind. He was tired of people-watching, of asking questions about something that no one could remember, of flicking through old newspaper articles from thirty years ago, even if it was in that magnificent State Library.

'All set?' Colin was in front of him, baggy-eyed but hoisting his backpack energetically on to his shoulder. Alexander followed him as they went to the luggage carousel. He stood a little way back, feeling nauseous from lack of sleep. The teenage boys, he noticed, were sitting against a pillar, their heads on each other, dozing. He felt like shaking them awake.

It took a long time to locate their baggage. Colin sprang forward to lift both cases up as they travelled around the belt close together. 'Customs, the bus, and we're home.'

'You called it home.'

Colin jiggled the handle on his case. 'It is for the moment.' He slapped his friend on the shoulder. 'Come on. You look like a zombie. The sooner we get there, the sooner you can remove your ugly pale face from my sight and have a sleep. We've got work tomorrow.'

'That wasn't good planning.'

'I think it might help. Nothing like flinging rocks around to fight jetlag.'

They went through customs smoothly and were almost at the bus when Alexander heard his name called. He ignored it. Norah had sometimes come to him like this, usually in the moments before he fell asleep, saying his name in a voice that sounded like his mother's. He hadn't told Colin. It would stop now, surely, because they were home. He just had to ignore it.

'Alexander!'

'Someone's after you.' Colin looked back over his shoulder. 'I'm not sure you want to say anything.'

Alexander frowned.

'Alexander!'

It was very real. He turned to find Brenda reaching out to grab his arm. He stopped and she collided with him.

'Alexander, I've been yelling at you for ages. I almost got arrested!' She flared her amber eyes at him. 'Hello Colin.'

Colin nodded. 'Brenda.'

'You just got back then? I've been away, too. Not as far as you. Visiting my Granny in Glasgow.'

'You flew to Glasgow?'

'We hired a car. Mine broke, you know, again. You been to Glasgow lately? It's a lot of fun. Amazing night life. Would do you good, Glasgow.'

'Why?' said Alexander.

'Why what?' Brenda flicked her hair away from her eyes with carefully lacquered nails.

'Why would Glasgow do me good?'

'Oh, Alex! You're so prickly! I mean, it would liven you up, Glasgow would. Put a smile on your face.'

'Alexander,' said Alexander.

'What do you mean?'

'My name. Alexander.'

Brenda's face closed down, as if water had drenched it. 'You know, you haven't changed. All doom and gloom. I don't know what I ever saw in you.'

'It was the great sex,' said Alexander, pulling his case away. 'That's what you said.'

Brenda let out a noise like a horse. Alexander was at the ticket queue for the bus by the time Colin caught up with him. 'Whoa, brother, what was that all about?'

Alexander shrugged. 'I haven't got time for people like Brenda.'

'She was your one and only! For years! Couldn't you at least be nice to her?'

'Why?' Alexander looked over Colin's shoulder, but Brenda had disappeared. 'Three years we went out together. It was like dating a white sandwich loaf. You know? Cheap and not very substantial.'

Colin's laugh made several heads in the queue turn. He was still chuckling when they climbed into the bus and stowed their luggage on the rack. 'Mate, you are *mean*.'

Alexander looked out the window, feeling sick. Yes, he was tired, but he had no right to be so awful to Brenda. She couldn't help who she was. He couldn't believe that he'd gone out with her in the first place, let alone stick with her for so long. He blamed returning from Glasgow. Brenda was right – Glasgow did liven him up. It's just that it wasn't home.

Colin folded his arms beside him, elbows sticking into Alexander. The bus pulled away from the terminal and swung its way onto the main road. With each car passed, Alexander relaxed. Gone was the strange concrete and asphalt of Melbourne. Glimpses of familiar semi-detached houses soothed him. Here was a place Norah had never been. He could leave her behind, as he'd finally left Brenda and her un-satisfactoriness.

They had a way to walk once they left the bus. Colin began to lag. Alexander reached the flat first, unlocking the foyer and dragging his case up the one flight of stairs to their door. He crashed it open, taking in the narrow corridor with their work boots still sitting at wild angles where they'd left them weeks ago.

'Let me in.' Colin pushed Alexander in the back, and staggered in, dragging his case into his room before falling flat-faced on to his bed.

'I thought you said that I was the one who needed sleep?'

'Shut up.' Colin's voice was muffled. After a moment, Alexander heard soft snores.

There was no way Alexander could sleep now. He stowed his case, made coffee, and sat on their couch to sort his backpack. Anything to do with the Norah quest went into one pile. He tried not to look at it, instead concentrating on a quick clean out. Maps, photos, plans of the old hospital – the entire history of his visit. He gathered them into a folder and pushed it onto the bookcase next to Colin's collection of Tolkien.

His phone rang just as he drained his mug.

'Alexander?'

'Mum, hello.'

'Oh, it's good to hear you're back. Long trip?'

'The worst.' He told her about the teenage boys.

She laughed. 'Sounds awful. I've had journeys like that. Makes Australia seem even further away.'

Alexander heard the wistfulness in her voice. His mother had returned to Australia every few years, but not now that her parents had died. She had one brother who lived in South Africa. Alexander had much more to do with Uncle Euan. 'Your turn to go there next.'

In the silence, Alexander wished he'd phrased that better. He hadn't meant that it was his mother's turn to look for Norah. He was pretty sure that he'd been the only one prepared to do that. But now? 'I mean, you need to go catch up with Ray and Doreen.'

'Yes, I haven't seen them for a while. They said they'd come and visit.'

'They've been saying that for years.'

'Well, Ray's retired now. It might be easier for them to get away.'

Her voice gave nothing away. Alexander was never sure how much she missed her old friends. She seemed to have plenty here. 'We'll be over tomorrow.'

'How is Colin?'

'Sound asleep.'

'Poor boy. Maybe you should have a nap as well.'

'I'll wait until tonight.'

'It's easier going this way in time than the other. I always got worse jet lag going back to Australia.' She paused. 'All right, I'll go. Leave you to unpack. See you tomorrow.'

'Bye, Mum.'

Alexander threw his phone down and stretched his hands over his head. He imagined his mother in the new kitchen, flour at the ready, maybe baking biscuits or whatever recipe she'd found this week. Later, his father would come in and swoop three off the cooling rack. There'd be yells of indignation and insincere apologies through mouthfuls of biscuit.

This was what my life could have been like. An image of Brenda came into his head, her fly-away hair pulled into a rough knot on her head, whisking a bowl full of butter and sugar. Brenda was big on cupcakes iced with pink and silver frills. She'd made a lot of them when they were together, but Alexander ate very few. They didn't seem to last long, or he was never at her place enough. Sometimes she brought a few to the flat, blinking expectantly at him as she took off the lid. Pink and silver decorations weren't his favourite. That had never worried her. Maybe, if he'd married Brenda, he would have become like his dad, eager to consume, eager to please, large and happy. Perhaps that's where he was going wrong?

Colin groaned from the next room. He staggered out, pushed Alexander's feet from the couch and sat down, rubbing his eyes. 'I fell asleep.'

'Pathetic.'

'Yeah.' Colin yawned widely. 'What are you doing?'

'Sorting stuff.'

'Yeah. I need to do that.'

'Do you think I should have stayed with Brenda?'

'What? Where the hell did *that* come from?'

'Just thinking.'

'Then don't.' Colin got up and stormed into the kitchen. He clanked around and came back with a glass of water. 'Thinking is over-rated.'

'At least she was someone to go out with.'

Colin drained his glass and sat it on the table. 'I don't like where this is heading.' He sat down heavily. 'Did you see how you were one hour ago? She rocked up to you, all sugar and spice, and you were sarcastic and foul. That's how your relationship would have been.'

'Like yours and Alicia's then?'

Colin stood up again. 'Don't.'

Alexander felt the wall vibrate as Colin shut his bedroom door. He chewed his lip. He hadn't meant to say that, had sworn never to mention Alicia. Yet she came up sometimes, usually when he was angry at Colin. Sometimes he only thought about what he'd like to say. Other times, like now, he spoke the words out loud. Alicia was the poisonous, gaping wound in Colin's side. It would take a miracle to heal him.

When Colin didn't emerge, Alexander went shopping. He came back and started on dinner. Finally, frying onions and bacon lured Colin out. He came into the kitchen, took a beer from the fridge, and leaned against its door. 'Get some music on,' said Alexander, head down over the chopping board.

Colin headed to the tiny lounge room. After a minute, *Guns 'n' Roses* played, making Alexander grind his teeth. He put meat into the frying pan, stirring roughly so that the spitting sounds covered the other noise. A wave of tiredness rolled over him. He propped his arm on the overhead cupboard and leaned his head onto it. It had been a long day. A long month.

Colin didn't talk until they'd finished dinner. He slid his plate across the coffee table and adjusted the cushion at his back. 'We need more furniture in here.'

'It won't fit.'

'I hate this couch.'

'No, you don't. You hate sharing it.'

Colin shrugged. 'True. You go to bed so I can have it all.'

Alexander pushed his friend with his foot. 'It's my couch.'

'So? I pay rent.'

'Not on the furniture.'

Finally, Colin looked at him. 'What are you going to do when I go home? The rent will kill you.'

Alexander stared at the television. Someone was shooting someone in a blaze of gunfire. 'I'll get someone else to come in.'

'That's why you were asking about Brenda!'

Alexander glanced at Colin, but he was on his feet, grinning. 'Hey,' he said, as Colin left the room, 'at least she'd know to pack her dishes up.'

A one-finger salute appeared in the doorway and just as quickly disappeared.

'WE SHOULD HAVE HAD the day off.'

Out of the corner of his eye, Alexander saw the yawn split Colin's face. 'Toughen up.'

Colin rubbed both his hands over his face vigorously. 'Where we going?'

'We're meeting Dad at his place. Mum wants to see us.'

'Lovely Julie. What's she cooked for us?'

'Nothing for you. Only for her son.'

'Yeah, right. I am her *other* son, remember?'

'You wish.' Alexander turned the car onto the slow winding road to his parents' house, pulling in carefully on the recently raked gravel. 'There they are.'

Donald was loading the truck. He half-waved at his son before turning back. Julie was at the car door before Alexander could stop. He got out to allow his mother to wrap her arms around him. 'Welcome home, darling.'

'Hi, Mum. Good to see you.'

'Hello, Julie.'

Alexander's mother swapped her hug to Colin. 'We're glad to see you.'

Julie turned her head to wipe at her face, but Alexander couldn't tell whether or not it was teary. He walked to his father and exchanged back pats. 'Good trip, lad?'

'Aye.'

Donald shook Colin's hand and indicated the truck. 'We'll take this today. Leave your car here. We're going into Selkirk.'

'I'll get going, too, boys,' Julie called, shrugging on a navy-blue jacket. 'I'm running late. We'll catch up properly another time.'

'Where's Mum going?' Alexander waved as Julie headed off in her little car.

'Working for Euan. He was short-staffed.'

'I thought she was only doing that for a few days. How long has she been working? She looks tired.'

'Weeks.' Donald paused to think. 'She started just after you left.'

'She didn't tell me that.'

'Well, she doesn't have to let you know everything she does, eh?' Donald opened the door of the truck. 'I'm sure she doesn't tell me everything.'

'That's because you don't ask.'

Only Colin heard what Alexander had said. 'Mate...'

They slid into the truck, squashing in together on the bench seat. Donald drove like he walked, so they lumbered up to the main road and made for Selkirk.

'I thought the idea was that she retired once you'd shifted.'

'Son, it's not the end of the world that your mother is working again.' Donald twisted his hands on the steering wheel. 'I didn't push her into it. She had a choice.'

'So you're going all right then? The business?'

His father didn't answer straight away. After checking both mirrors and tugging at his seat belt, Donald said, 'The house cost a bit more than I thought. It's good to have extra money.'

'So you did coerce her into working?'

'Alexander, that's the end of it. Right?'

Colin was first at the back of the truck when they reached the wall they were re-pointing. He handed Alexander a bag of tools. 'What's with the interrogation? I'm sure Julie would have said no if she didn't want to do it.'

Alexander checked the bag before closing it. 'I don't understand why she'd want to work there. Mum doesn't like Euan.'

'Doesn't sound like she had a choice. And why doesn't she like him?'

'I don't know. She's never said directly. I can tell. She avoids him like the plague.'

'He's a doctor, isn't he? He knows how to treat the plague.'

'Ha ha.'

Colin set some buckets on the ground. 'Does your dad know?'

'Know what?'

'That your mum hates his brother.'

'No. Look at him.'

Donald was stretching, his shirt riding up to expose the top of his underpants. There was a smile on his face, the one that came when he was about to start work. He rubbed his stubbly head with one hand before clapping his palms together.

'What about him?'

'He's not good with noticing things.'

Colin shrugged. 'I can't tell that by looking at him, can I?'

'I think you can.'

Colin clapped a hand on Alexander's shoulder. 'Listen. You think too much. Really. Stop thinking.' He threw him a trowel. 'Work, don't think.'

It rained on and off during the day, much to Alexander's relief. The work wasn't hard, only tedious. The sun was scorching when it was out, so the drizzle helped cool him down. His eyes shut now and then without control. Colin's were doing the same. So much for getting back into the rhythm of work straight away. They were both doing half a job.

Donald did seem to notice that. 'Okay, lads. Time to call it a day.' There was still a good working hour or two to go.

'You sure, Dad?'

'Aye.' Donald grinned at them. 'You aren't a lot of use today, the pair of you.'

Alexander slept on the drive back to Dryburgh. He woke with a start as they pulled into the house yard.

'Here already, are we?' said Colin, his head against the window.

'Mum's not here.'

'She'll be working late tonight.' Donald heaved himself out of the truck. 'You'll not be seeing her until tomorrow.'

Alexander pulled bags from the truck, handing Colin's over as his friend stumbled out. 'Did she leave anything for us?'

'Like what?' Donald fumbled for his house key.

Alexander felt ridiculous. 'Any cakes or biscuits, maybe?'

'No. I think I ate the last of the cake.'

Alexander looked at Colin. 'It's not that I expect anything.'

'It's just usually there.' Colin raised his eyebrows. 'You've been disinherited.'

'Your mother's been busy.' Donald opened the door. 'Are you coming in?'

'I think we'd better go. It's still an hour to Edinburgh.'

'You boys could live closer to your work.'

'Dad, you don't know where jobs will take you.'

Donald grunted. 'City boys, aren't you?'

'I am.' Colin ran a hand through his hair, grinning. 'See you tomorrow.'

Alexander raised his hand to his dad in farewell. He took the keys from his lethargic friend. Colin was asleep before they hit the main road. Alexander veered through Melrose, driving slowly past the surgery and seeing his mother's red car tucked away in the car park. He thought about her face as they had left this morning. It was not his imagination that made it appear strained. Were his parents in terrible debt? Was something else going on?

Colin mumbled in his sleep. His head slid down to rest on the window sill.

Alexander felt unease run through him, a rippling cold, as if a glacier had touched him. The family felt at the brink of change, but what change he couldn't say.

SIX

The last show of the run finished at ten-thirty. Grace squeezed into the changing room area to pack her kit up, pushing past the sweating, celebrating actors. Only she and Roberta wore grim faces. The rest of the cast whooped and danced as if they'd all won Oscars.

The after party was being held at a nearby pub. It wasn't long before Grace and Roberta were alone, dresses and shirts covering the floor, soiled make-up sponges in piles on the bench. 'Now for the real work,' said Roberta, flinging a jacket into her laundry bag.

'Here.' Grace reached into the cool bag at her feet and pulled out a can. She tossed it to Roberta who cracked the ring gratefully and drank.

'Nice. What is it?'

'McEwan's ale.'

'Never had it before.'

'No, it's Scottish. I had to hunt it down. I ended up at Taylor's.'

'That British produce shop? I should go there.'

'Did you know that Cadbury's chocolate has slightly

different ingredients in it compared to here? Something to do with our high temperatures.'

'Get on!' Roberta took another swing. 'Okay, I've got to get going with these or I won't be home until dawn.'

'I'll give you a hand after I pack this lot up.' Grace swept the sponges into a garbage bag.

'Don't you usually wash those?'

'Yeah. Not this time.' She followed the sponges with hairspray cans.

'What's going on, Grace? Looks like you're packing up for good.'

Grace paused with a half-empty cotton bud packet in her hand. Roberta had started in the company just after Grace. They'd both seen their share of divas and, although Grace had got used to the more temperamental of them, she knew Roberta didn't like what she was doing. She pinned costumes and sewed stretched seams muttering and frowning and was known to let pins jab to make someone stand still. 'I'm going on an extended holiday.'

'Lucky you.' Roberta squashed stockings into her bag. 'If you're not going to be here, then I'm not sure I want to be.'

Grace put the packet into her kit. 'Why *are* you here, Roberta?'

'It's one of those things you do.'

'There's plenty of other things you could do.'

'Like what?' Roberta stood straight and stretched her neck from side to side. 'I haven't had a job in five years. I do four days volunteering in an old folks' home and I come here at night. Despite this *community service*, no employer will touch me with a barge pole. I'm too old, I don't have the right skills, it's been too long. I know all the excuses.'

Grace put her head down and slid squares of foundation into their case. 'I didn't know that you were looking for a job.'

'Well, I get sick of talking about it. Do you know I apply for about twenty a week? It's become a bit of a joke. No one looks at online applications, but that's how they want you to apply.'

'Shouldn't you see the employer directly?'

'And let them see that I've pushing sixty? There's no point.' She tied the top of the garbage bag. 'Hang on to your job, Grace, that's my one bit of advice for you. You're lucky they've given you leave.'

Grace shrugged. She closed the lid of the kit and stacked the remaining bits and bobs on top. She'd been three weeks without work now. Her savings were getting skinny. It was time for action before she begged for her job back.

'So you won't be back here after your holiday?'

Grace gathered the remaining costumes and put them in another bag. 'I'm not sure what I'll do afterwards.'

Roberta gave her a hip bump as she staggered out the doorway with three bags in her arms. 'I hope it works out for you.'

Grace carried her things out to her car. The night was bitter. The windscreen ran with condensation, blocking her view as she slid into the driver's seat. She turned the car on and let it warm up. A dying fluorescent light starter made the theatre's lights flicker. Grace pulled the car out onto the road, watching the twinkling in the rear-view mirror until it other buildings hid it and the lights were gone.

CLAUDIA HAD MADE spaghetti bolognaise and left a bowl neatly wrapped in the fridge for Grace. The curly pale pasta with its covering of weak red sauce made Grace feel sick. She made a pot of tea instead, swapping it at the last moment for the red wine they reserved for cooking. She spread the make-up from her kit across the table, carefully choosing the bits she'd take with her. Norah needed to be magnetic, the best make-over Grace had ever done. She had imagined thick brown lashes framing Norah's eyes. Grace had ordered extra pairs of good quality falsies for the play. They were untouched in their box.

Grace sat back and took a gulp of wine. Roberta had been so busy picking up used costumes she hadn't noticed Grace in the storeroom gathering some items for herself. 'Borrowed,' Grace said firmly to herself. She would return them when...

And there was the sticking point. *Return.* Norah Cameron would not return to the narrow house Claudia and Grace were renting, not once the family welcomed Norah back. Grace felt her life shift sideways. What would Claudia do without her? Would Claudia come and visit?

Grace packed the excess make-up away in her kit and carried it to her bedroom. As familiar as it was, the small room was looking worn, as if it could be folded up and discarded. She put the kit into the empty tea chest that had not been moved, not one centimetre, from where she'd pushed it after getting her father's things out. Beside it, hidden from the doorway, was the case in which to pack her new life. The items from the theatre storeroom rolled tightly into one corner of it.

The sound of the key in the front door made Grace jump. Claudia paused on the way to her room, smiling tiredly at Grace. 'Hey,' she said.

'Hey yourself.' Grace followed her down the hall. 'Want a drink or something?'

'What have you got?'

'Tea. Hot chocolate. Vinegary wine.'

'Fantastic choices. Hot chocolate.'

While the milk heated in the microwave, Grace bundled the good make-up into a bag and took it away. She got back to

Claudia slumped at the table, holding out a concealer brush with one hand while the other supported her head.

'Thanks,' said Grace, putting the brush in her jeans pocket. She stirred chocolate powder into the milk and put the drink next to Claudia's elbow.

'I made you dinner.'

'I saw it.'

'You haven't eaten it yet?'

'No. Don't feel hungry.'

Claudia straightened slowly and pushed her wavy fringe off her forehead with both hands. 'What's going on, Grace?'

'Why?'

'You haven't eaten in days.'

'I have.'

Claudia shook her head, letting her hands down to wrap around her mug. 'Not like the Grace I know.'

Grace perched on the kitchen bench and drank more wine. It was awful, burning her throat. The sting was good. 'I've been doing some research.'

'On what?'

'Norah Cameron.'

'Grace...'

Grace slid off the bench. 'She was at the Paxton Community Hospital because she had croup.'

'Grace...'

'Shoosh. Listen. The family were visiting Australia. The mother was Australian. Norah had croup, but she was almost better. They'd put her in the nursery with some other babies. When the nurse came to check her, she was gone.'

'Someone took her?'

'They searched.' Grace walked around the table. 'The hospital was old. They had added on to it. Lots of corridors leading to other buildings. Lots of different exits. A basement with a laundry and rubbish bins. Balconies. Back stairs. The place was a security nightmare.' She sat opposite Claudia. 'They looked for her and didn't find a trace.'

'Who would take a little baby?'

'Someone who couldn't have their own? A jealous relative? A mad person? The police interviewed every nurse, doctor, visitor, parent. Even the other kids on the ward.'

'They interviewed the other babies?'

'It was a children's ward, Claudia. Some of them were teenagers. No one saw anything unusual.'

Claudia swilled her milk around in its mug. 'Your point?'

'There's never been a trace of Norah since. She totally disappeared.'

'I still don't see your point.'

'She totally *disappeared*, Claudia. The family stayed to help the search, but eventually they went back to Scotland. There was no reason for them to be here.'

'They all live in Scotland?'

'I've tracked them down.'

'How?'

'The family are stonemasons, remember? It was easy enough to find out where the business is.'

Claudia pushed her mug away. 'And what's all this got to do with you?'

'Because I'm their missing baby!'

Claudia knocked her forehead on the table. 'No, Grace, this doesn't make sense. How could you be the baby that went missing? Do you mean your father stole you from the Camerons?'

'Maybe.'

'*What?*'

'I don't know, Claudia! Something happened, that's all. Probably something bad or sad or both. What does it matter? I can find them, Claudia, I can find the Camerons and give them back their baby.'

Claudia was silent. She frowned, eyes so hidden under her fringe that Grace could only see darkness. 'This is wrong, Grace. Morally and *legally* wrong.'

'Why is it illegal?'

'Because you will be an imposter. Oh, come on! You aren't so stupid that you don't know what you're doing!'

'I'm not trying to trick anyone.'

'Grace!' Claudia stood up. The table tilted, chocolate milk ran like a river over its top. 'You can't do it. It's cruel. What if the family believes you?'

'I expect them to believe me.'

'But why?'

'Because I know it's true.'

Claudia reached for her mug and picked it up with her other hand, catching drops of spilt milk. She carried it to the sink and brought the kitchen cloth back to the table. 'Grace,' she said, wiping the table, 'it's not true. They won't believe you and then you'll be branded a criminal.'

Grace felt something harden in her gut. 'I'm not trying to get their wealth or their house or their stonemasonry business. I want them to have their *girl* back.'

'That's not really what you want.'

Grace propped herself on the cupboard, one hand holding her stomach. 'It is.'

Claudia rinsed the cloth and wiped her hands on a tea towel. 'Do you remember the story about Frederic Bourdin?'

'Who?'

'He was a man who took on the identity of a teenager who'd gone missing. He went to the family saying he was their son, and they believed him. He didn't even look like their boy. His eyes and hair were different colours. They believed he was theirs.'

'So?'

'You know why they believed him? Because they really *wanted* him to be their son.' Claudia put a hand on Grace's shoulder. 'They wanted so much to have their son back that Frederic got away with it.'

'But he wasn't their son.'

'No. He got found out and he went to gaol.'

Grace stepped away from Claudia. 'What happened to the family?'

'I don't know.'

'Maybe they were grateful.'

'What?'

'Frederic Bourdin gave them time with their son they thought they'd never have.'

'How can you say that?' Claudia threw her hands up and turned her back on Grace. 'This is crazy.' She swung around. 'If you so desperately want a family, you can have mine. I'll get Mum to adopt you. We're practically sisters, anyway.'

'You can't be adopted if you're an adult.'

'You know what I mean. Mum likes you a lot. She's always asking about you. Dad's the same. They call you-' Claudia stopped. She put her head down.

'What do they call me?' Grace put her hands on her thighs. 'Go on, say it.'

Claudia took a deep breath in. 'They call you the lost girl.'

A car went past the house, its headlights flaring for a moment on the house wall outside the window. Light ricocheted into the kitchen. 'Claudia,' said Grace softly, 'I'm not someone's pity package.'

'You aren't. They know your life's been hard.'

'The trouble with people I know is that they've heard my

story. They feel sorry for me.' Grace shook her head. 'I don't want people to feel that way about me. I want to leave it behind.'

'You can do that without being someone else.'

'But I am someone else. I'm Norah Cameron.'

'Grace! Stop it!' Claudia closed her eyes briefly. 'Okay. We can sort this. Have you talked to a psychologist?'

'Hundreds of times! When school found out I was looking after Mum because Dad was useless, they set me up with a counsellor. She said that I would become a stronger person because of what I was doing! You know the saying, what doesn't kill you makes you stronger? Well, it didn't kill me. So I must be strong.'

'You are one of the strongest people I know.'

'Only because I had to be. Can you imagine what it's like to look after your brain-damaged mother when you'd rather be watching cartoons on the television?'

The kitchen echoed with shouts. Grace saw Claudia cringe and lowered her voice.

'Sorry, Claudia, but I've seen so many psychologists. Before Mum died. After Mum died. When Dad was homeless.'

'Not since your dad died.'

'I'm not seeing any more. I'm nearly thirty-one years old. I can look after myself. Especially now I've found out who I really am.' She sat abruptly, rubbing her eyes. They felt scratchy, as if she'd been in a dust storm. Behind her, Claudia had the kettle on. She opened a packet of biscuits and slid them on a plate, pushing it in front of Grace. Once she'd put two mugs of tea on the table, she nodded at the biscuits. 'Eat.'

Grace took one and ate. The sweetness made her nausea increase momentarily and then die away completely. She took a mouthful of boiling tea, loving that the heat of it took away some numbness that was creeping into her body. 'Thanks, Claudia.'

'You're welcome.' Claudia took two biscuits, dipping one into her tea. 'I'm trying to work out how to help you.'

'I don't need your help.' Grace put her hand up. 'I don't mean that in a nasty way.'

Claudia ate her second biscuit. 'I've got an idea. Why don't you take that money of your dad's and spend it on an adventure holiday? Go bungy jumping in New Zealand or climb Mount Everest. Be the first woman to ride a camel across Australia. Maybe trek the Pacific Crest Trail.'

'I have a feeling that those things have been done before.'

'Does it matter? The result was the same. People *found* themselves.'

'You are so New Age.'

'It makes sense, though. You said your dad's money was to play with. So, go play. Come back when you're ready, when you've found yourself. I won't even rent your room out.'

Grace spun a biscuit on its plate. 'I don't have that money anymore.'

'*What?* Where did it go?' Claudia looked around as if the money might be hiding in a kitchen drawer.

'I've spent it.'

'On what?'

Grace put her shoulders back and stared at her friend. 'A plane ticket to Edinburgh and a month's accommodation.'

Claudia's mouth quivered. 'You're going to The Edinburgh Festival?'

'No. Well, maybe. It hasn't started yet.'

'There's something else on?'

'Claudia. Please.'

Claudia stood up. Her chair fell backwards. 'So I've been talking for nothing? You've already made up your mind what you're going to do! Even though you know it's sick and cruel and illegal, you are going to upend another family's life for your own benefit?'

Claudia's face was blotchy. A scarlet blush stained her neck. Grace saw her hands shake as she pushed at the hair falling madly across her face. 'I don't see it that way, Claudia.'

'No.' Claudia picked up the chair and banged it under the table. 'Obviously.' She stormed to the doorway, turning back at the last minute. 'If you go ahead with this insane plan of yours, don't expect any support from me. Don't you dare ring me for help. You got that? If you do this, then you are no longer my friend.'

Grace stared straight ahead.

Claudia slammed a flat hand against the wall, making the plastic clock fall off its nail and smash to the floor. She kicked it across the room, ran down the hall to her bedroom and crashed the door shut.

Grace bit her bottom lip, hard. When she let it go, it wasn't trembling at all. That's when she knew she was right and Claudia, well, Claudia was gone.

SEVEN

Julie parked her car well out of the way of anyone else's. *Patients come first* was the central rule she'd instigated at the practice. It was met by immense surprise to those working in administration where lack of change was evident in the fax machine at the front desk and two archaic typewriters still in place in the back room. Discontent followed the surprise, as Julie made people shift their cars to the back of the carpark to leave room for patients at the front. The discontent grew. When she held a short professional development session on how to communicate effectively on the phone, there was almost a riot. Did Dr Euan Cameron support her in any way? Julie snorted at the thought.

Donald had made it clear that Euan would highly value her skills as a practice manager. Or that was the way Julie had interpreted the way Donald had said, 'Julie, the place runs like a girl-guiding group high on red jellybeans. Euan is going out of his mind. See what you can do, love.' Mind you, Euan had not objected to Julie accepting his brief emailed request for short-term work, so perhaps it was his idea and not Donald's. *I don't want to know*, thought Julie.

She approached the practice through the back, hoping to check on the flow of work without disturbing it. Meredith was on the phone. 'That's how it is, Mrs Drake. I cannot do any more for you.' Cynthia stood next to Meredith, rolling her eyes and nodding encouragingly. She had the grace to blush heavily when she spotted Julie and scuttled away to the end of the desk.

'What's the problem with Mrs Drake?' Julie said quietly as Meredith hung the phone up with a clank.

The older woman jerked back, her elbow knocking a pen container, sending gel tips everywhere. Julie caught a couple rolling towards her but kept her eye on Meredith.

'Oh, she's ringing again demanding to speak to Dr Cameron, but I told her... I *explained*... that Dr Cameron was very busy this morning and didn't speak to patients directly, although if she could come in she could see him later.' Meredith licked her bottom lip.

'That doesn't answer my question, Meredith. What's Mrs Drake's problem?'

'Her problem is that she couldn't talk to Dr Cameron.'

Julie's arms drooped. Her handbag slid off one shoulder, the tote bag containing her lunch from the other. So much for the effectiveness of the communication session on effectiveness. She almost turned back to her car. A nice little run out to Scott's View would be so much better than standing next to oafish Meredith McKinley, trying to explain the nuances of listening. 'What was she wanting to talk to Dr Cameron about?'

'Oh.' Meredith frowned. 'I don't think that's my business now, is it?'

'Meredith, you are *triaging*. When you answer the phone, you are trying to work out how to prioritise a patient's concern. You ask just enough to work that out without delving in to personal details.'

'That's it, then. That's the issue. I can't ask Mrs Drake or anyone about their problems because it's too personal. My mother always said that it's not anyone else's business what people want.' She folded her arms.

'Did your mother work as a doctor's receptionist?'

'My mother was a good mother. She stayed home -'

'I'm not accusing your mother of any fault. I'm trying to point out that your job, as a doctor's receptionist, is to triage patients and to treat the information they give you confidentially.' Julie resisted the urge to shake Meredith out of the bovine-like stupor she was in. 'Ring her back.'

'Eh?'

'Ring Mrs Drake back and ask her what she wanted to speak to Dr Cameron about.'

'Someone wants to speak to me?'

Both women turned at this voice, Meredith eagerly. 'Dr Cameron, I was just explaining to Julie here that I can't go asking personal details of a patient, it's not the done thing.'

Euan lifted his glasses and pushed them gently back up his nose. 'Then how do you know what she wanted to talk to me about?'

Julie bent to retrieve her bag, hoping that the action would hide her face. He had been noticing what she was doing with his staff. The back of her neck tingled. Had he been listening in on her sessions or, worse, watching her through the opaque glass of the tearoom? She collected her other bag and walked to the tiny office that was the hub of the business. Euan gathered his next patient and disappeared into his room. As Julie sat down, she caught Meredith mouth at Cynthia, 'Australian dragon.'

I don't want to be. Julie switched on the computer. I don't want to be the dragon lady in this tiny practice in this small town. It was bad enough still being considered the Australian, even though she'd lived in the Borders for thirty-five years. Country towns were the same all over the world. No one was considered a local unless they were born there, and perhaps not even unless your parents had been born there as well. She smiled to herself. That counted Alexander out then. And Norah, if...

Emails were demanding things. Always present, never-ending. Another fourteen had come in overnight, adding to the fifty-six she hadn't got to the day before because Mr Holland had collapsed in the waiting room, needing first aid. Then there'd been the boy from the bakery burning his hand on his oven. A vicious game of soccer meant three badly sprained ankles. It was, as Julie's mother used to say, one of those days. She leaned over to add to her to-do list: *first aid training for Meredith and Cynthia.* She sighed. Probably a waste of money.

She stayed in her office until lunchtime. The surgery closed for an hour. Cynthia stayed in to manage the phone so the others could head out if they wanted. Julie stepped into the sunshine to buy a Selkirk bannock for Donald, and to check – without prying, of course – on the bakery boy's burned hand. She walked back on the other side of the road, sitting for a moment on a bench to catch the sun.

'Mind if I sit as well?'

Euan held up a book, as a shield or a peace-offering, she wasn't sure. 'I was about to go.' She stood up and nodded towards the seat. 'It's all yours.'

'I have a few minutes to read.' He didn't sit. Standing there, tall and wiry, he looked nothing like his brother. Gestures were familiar though. Julie flinched a little at how he waved his hand toward her before he spoke. 'I don't think I've properly said how thankful I am that you could step in after Heather left.'

'Donald was keen that I help out.'

'He knew how good you would be.' Euan spoke without a hint of flattery.

'I've had a lot of experience in practice management.'

'Yes. But not in such a small town.'

Julie tucked the bun under her arm and turned towards work. 'I worked in Galashiels. It isn't very big. Nowhere around here is.'

'Do you miss city life?'

Julie stroked hair away from her eye. 'No. Melbourne was too long ago.'

'I hear that Alexander was there.'

Had the sun gone under cloud? Julie shivered, tugging her cardigan across her chest. Euan watched her, head tilted down to see through the top of his glasses. New frames since last time she'd studied his face. Cobalt trim, highlighting his eyes. 'He's back now.'

'He was on holiday?'

'Of course. Why else would he go?'

'I thought there might be another reason.'

She had to go or be swept into the tornado that always surrounded Euan Cameron. She felt it tug at her as she walked, so she went faster until it wisped away. What had she been thinking when she took this job? That she'd never have to encounter him? That she could communicate through the other doctor? That she'd never see him outside the marked confines of the practice walls? That she would always have Donald there to act as a barrier between them? Yes, all of those things.

She'd taken the job for Donald's sake, to get them a little ahead on what they'd had to borrow to finish the renovations. Julie had written out strategies in her diary. 1. *Only talk about professional matters. 2. Seek out others if there is a chance of being alone with him. 3. Don't look in his eyes.* Meeting him in the street had stripped her of these safeguards.

The back door opened as Julie reached it. Cynthia nodded once and tripped out to her car. That was another thing Julie had to correct - Cynthia's skirt length and skinny heels. For the patients' sake, she didn't care about anyone else. Julie didn't want anyone to have to avert their eyes in case they saw more skin than they should. She went to the front door and unlocked it, ready for patients to enter.

It was an unexpectedly busy afternoon, with the two doctors fully booked and requests for more appointments. Meredith had contacted Mrs Drake. She'd been having strange pains in her left side. Julie felt vindicated by the poor woman's troubles, feeling so guilty about the minor victory that she met Mrs Drake at the door and showed her straight in to Euan. Meredith's face was stony when she returned.

After Meredith left for the day, Julie dithered at the front counter. Dr Jayasekera had three patients left, but Euan had four. Strategy number 4: *Never be the only other person left in the surgery if Euan finishes late.* This was by far the most difficult. Cynthia worked until early afternoon, Meredith to five o'clock. Someone had to remain if the session continued late. Heather had taken that role when she was in charge. Julie jotted down *rostering* on her to-do list.

It wasn't a problem in the end. Euan's patients were managed quickly while Ravi's were complicated. Euan left with a nod of his head, which Julie was able to ignore with a timely ring of the phone. When everyone had gone, she got into her car and sat for a moment, head resting back. Exhaustion dragged her down. Her arms felt leaden. It was not the hours; it was the adrenaline that coursed through her, keeping her body alert and wary, so wired was she to avoid him. She wondered how long, seriously, she was going to be able to work for Dr Euan Cameron.

THE BOYS WERE LONG GONE by the time she reached home. Donald was asleep in front of the television, still in his work clothes, a beer on the table beside him. She let him sleep. Unlike her, he'd been on his feet all day. Perhaps he'd been lifting rocks all day too. He had two young men working with him and still he lifted. Most nights, he took painkillers to ease the aches in his back and neck. That was another reason for Julie to work. Donald was not going to be able to be a stone-mason forever.

What if she'd married someone who had a less physical job?

Julie crashed the kettle on to the stove. Donald had fixed the stonework of the very building they now lived in. Other builders envied the craftsmanship. He was a genius. Well, not a genius but a careful craftsman who had learned from his father and was now teaching his own son.

Alexander might have to take over sooner than he thought.

Julie sat on the kitchen stool to drink her tea, watching Donald. It was late, she hadn't started dinner, but the gentle breathing of her husband was memorising. Idly, she pulled the computer tablet they shared along the bench and entered the password. Perhaps she'd check her emails before starting work or do some online clothes shopping. Without going to Edinburgh, shopping was limited, and, now she was working, a few more shirts...

The tablet had opened to the last website Donald had been looking at. For a second, it pulled Julie back through time to a bright hospital ward and the little baby who lay sleeping in its plastic crib. There she was, Norah Cameron, fluffy hair and all, in the grim square photo on the missing persons' website.

Julie rushed to the toilet, gripping the bowl and dry retching into it. Her hair fell out of its clasp and flooded her face. She retched again, eyes closed. The finer details of Norah's face were lost in the photograph, but not in Julie's mind. People say they forget how loved ones looked, but not Julie. Norah's eyes were the colour of the horizon in an Australian autumn, the blue that rimmed the sky just after the night finished and as the sun was rising. The left eye had a gold fleck, just one, radiating out towards her ear like a shooting star. Her hair was fluffy, intending to be thick and full. It glowed golden in the artificial light of the ward, although Julie knew it was more coppery in the real world. She had no teeth but perfect pearly nails on her soft fingers and toes.

She sat back, reaching for a towel before wiping her mouth. It was clammy in the bathroom, making her sweat. Julie rubbed the towel over her face, make-up smearing its white surface. Strange how much fingers could shake and still be functional. When the trembling had calmed a little, she pulled herself up, shed her clothes and stepped into the shower.

Donald was still asleep when she emerged. Without both-ering to wake him, she chopped a salad into a bowl, then fried some fish fillets. Nothing tempted her to eat. She left the fish to cool, took a glass of whiskey to the bedroom to fetch a cardigan, and stepped outside. The tiny porch at the back of their room had been an afterthought. Julie used it while she could. The winter depths would leave it abandoned.

The shaking and sweating stopped. Distressing though it was, Julie always marvelled at how those attacks landed on her and, just as quickly, stopped. She imagined them like tigers, flicking their tails from side to side while hiding in the shadows until her defences dropped and they could leap, digging their claws in and biting at her head. She'd once asked how long they would go on for. The psychologist had smiled sadly. 'Until you no longer care.' Forever, then. The tigers would attack her until she died.

'Julie, love? Are you there?'

Donald's silhouette appeared in the doorway. Without her

noticing, twilight had spread. Julie downed her drink, stood to pull her cardigan around her, and opened the door to let herself back in. Donald hadn't noticed her in the dark and had wandered off to the bathroom. She didn't chase him. 'In the kitchen,' she called when she arrived there.

'Right then.'

'I've got your dinner.' She stuck the fish in the microwave.

Donald's phone rang as he appeared. They both went for it automatically. Julie saw the caller's name – Carl – before Donald reached and turned it off.

'You could have answered it.'

'It's all right, love. A client. I'll call back.' Donald reached for his plate, walked away, thought about it more, and turned to peck her cheek. 'Thanks. I fell asleep, didn't I?'

She didn't bother to answer but took her own meagrely piled plate and went with him to the lounge. The late news came on, so they ate in silence. At the weather report, Donald sighed and put his plate on the coffee table.

'Donald?'

'Mmmm?'

'Do you ever think we might do something different with our lives?'

'What like?'

'Go on holidays, for one. We never go away.'

'We went to Skye last year.'

'No, away. Plane-flight away.'

'We could fly down to Bristol. Maybe look around Devon.'

'Further than that.'

Donald turned his head. His eyes were unblinking. 'Where exactly are you thinking?'

'I'm not sure.'

'Love.' Donald heaved himself up a bit in his chair. 'Do you want to go back to Australia?'

'No! No.' Julie waved her hands. 'No.'

'So where?'

'I don't know.' Julie stood, bent to pick his plate up, and carried them to the kitchen. 'Don't worry. I've been watching too many travel shows.'

She didn't miss the slight shake of his head as he reached for the remote and turned the telly up. As she scraped the plates, the trembles returned. They stayed until she'd wiped the bench vigorously and polished the front of the dishwasher.

Australia. Should I? Could I?

Donald's phone rang again. He punched it silent, instead typing a lumpy-fingered text message. He glanced up at her. 'You have the television now, love. I'll get ready for bed.'

'Early start?'

'Got to finish up the job in Selkirk. Might have to travel north for a big one soon.'

'Lucky you've got the boys.'

'Aye, but not tomorrow. If I don't finish, I might leave them to do it later.'

'That means they're improving.'

'Aye, they're good.' He yawned.

'You go. I'll finish up here.'

He nodded.

There was nothing to finish up but Julie didn't feel like going to bed yet. She turned the noise down and sat in Donald's chair, feeling the hard lump of his phone on the seat. When she pulled it out, there was a text message from Carl. *What day?* A job, most likely. She opened the phone using Donald's birthday as the code, and it went to messages. The one from Carl was the only one under his name. There was no indication that Donald had texted before.

'Carl texted,' she said, as Donald came out in his shorts. 'I was trying to check a day for you -'

Donald snatched the phone from her outstretched hand. 'Don't do that.'

Julie twisted in the seat to look at him. 'Do what?'

'I mean, I can arrange my days, love.' Donald tucked the phone away. 'You've got your own work now. No need to worry about me.' He kissed the top of her head before leaving.

A mild tremor wriggled through Julie and stopped. She never worried about Donald doing things without her knowledge. Should she?

Could she?

Not with other things on her mind.

EIGHT

Colin woke in a knot of sheets. She was there, wind-swept brown hair hanging to her hips, mouth open to tell him what had happened – then she was gone. He sat up, throwing the bedclothes away from his body. The day had begun in how it did in high summer; the light infusing his room until it stole the shadows.

Alexander's door was shut. Colin took the shower first, switching the electric heater on and waiting until the water warmed. The water ran over his head, skimmed his face and chest, and cascaded to the floor. With it, he hoped, went Alicia, drawn out of his head as if she was dirt in his hair to be sucked into the bathroom pipes.

The apartment was still quiet. Colin let the steam out of the tiny room and padded to the kitchen. Five thirty. Alexander better be stirring. He made tea and toast before flicking on the radio. *A grand Saturday morning to all!* He stopped mid-crunch. They weren't working today.

Instead of relief, there was anger. A particular anger, the red-rimmed one with spikes that came with thoughts of Alicia. Alexander should not have mentioned her. Speaking Alicia's name was like uttering a curse. She rose in Colin's mind at any mention, ethereal and dangerous, sticking like a parasite in his head until time went by and she could sink, defeated only in battle and not war, into the depths of bad memory. She had woken him, taken him away from real time, and he was ready to go to nowhere in particular too early on a Saturday morning.

Colin looked around the tiny kitchen. Its walls, usually comfortable, pressed in. He grabbed his wallet and left for the Old Town, where surely he could find a decent coffee somewhere in its recesses. He would welcome the walk. Alicia hated him walking. It was harder for her to caress his thoughts when blood pumped through his legs.

The streets were quiet but not empty. Edinburgh lived high and fast through the summer months. Colin saw a couple of teenagers walking tiredly home, arms around each other for support. Another couple waited at the corner as a taxi pulled up, their carefully kept distance saying more about their relationship that the band on her finger. He crossed Princes Street to the Balmoral and walked up North Bridge.

Coming to Scotland had been good in many ways. To get to work with Donald was amazing. Donald knew things about stone and the way it worked that Colin had never thought of, despite intense reading into the subject. The man read stone like it had a language only he knew. 'How do you do that?' asked Colin one day.

'Do what?'

Colin couldn't explain. He waved his hand at the wall that was settling into shape in front of them.

'I don't know what you're talking about.' Colin had watched as Donald did it again, choosing the exact stone in shape, colour and tenacity for the wall.

The other good thing was that he was thirty thousand kilometres away from Alicia. Or, he thought as he moved into

Cowgate, thirty thousand kilometres away from where Alicia's ghost was.

The best coffee was near the university. There were several cafes around, but not that many open in the early morning of holidays. Colin passed two of his usual haunts until he found *Spoon* open on Nicholson Street. He climbed the broad stairs and headed for a two-seater table against the window. A cool breeze came into the cranked open bottom window. Colin put his head closer to catch it through his hair.

While his coffee came, he pulled out his phone and ran through his messages. The family app showed the usual array of pictures. Tanya and her kids at the snow, his mum and dad tending bromeliads in their Queensland back yard. Later in the year, his parents were planning to visit. Colin found it hard imagining his sun-loving, leathery father in the bitter UK winter.

A new message came through. Alexander, demanding he bring back milk. He sent him back *Spoon*. Alexander texted *twenty minutes*.

It was more like thirty. Alexander meandered through the tables and sat down, yawning. 'What are you doing?'

'See Tanya?' Colin held his phone up.

'She looks tired.'

Colin studied his sister. She did, too, but that was how she always looked. Three kids on your own would make you that way.

'You didn't answer my question.' Alexander rubbed at his head and hooked hair behind his left ear. 'What are you doing? Here? So early?'

'Forgot it was Saturday.'

'For feck-'

The waiter came with Colin's coffee, but Alexander pulled it in his direction. Colin shrugged and ordered another.

'And a bacon sandwich. Please.'

'Sorry, sir, we don't have a bacon sandwich, but I can do you bacon on sourdough bread. Eggs?'

'Two then.'

'Spinach? Mushrooms? Tomatoes? Avocado?'

Alexander waved her away. 'There are closer places to ours that serve proper food. Not so...' he tapped the menu '... bohemian.'

Colin laughed. 'You go all over the world and come back exactly the same. Bacon sandwich? Come on.'

Alexander grunted and took a sip. 'Good coffee at least.'

The waiter brought Colin another. 'That's why I'm here,' he said, accepting his cup with a smile.

They sat in contemplation of their drinks as the café filled up around them. It was raining in the street, a ponderous shower that took most by surprise. Umbrellas appeared like unfurled flowers. The breeze that came through the window was laden with moisture.

'Well, what have we got here?' A tall, solid man appeared at their table, his latte tipping dangerously as he leaned over to shake Colin's hand. 'Good to see y'all.'

'Neil. What's up?'

Neil held his hand out to Alexander, who shook it briefly. The waiter pushed in to deliver his breakfast. Colin saw the shadow of relief pass across his friend's face.

'Taking a break while I can.' Neil reached behind for a spare chair and dragged it across so he could sit. 'You heard this one? An Australian, an American and a Scotsman go into a bar. Correction. *Café.*'

Colin laughed. 'You working today?'

'Working every day until it starts and every day of the festival. It's not so bad when it gets going, but there's always something to fix.' He lifted his hand towards the buildings across the street. 'I'm doing the uni. Supervising.' He peered at Alexander's plate. 'Got any maple syrup for that?'

'I like plain salt, not sugar.' Alexander's hair had come away from where he'd hooked it. It hung over the side of his face, concealing it from Neil. He had his eyes on his food.

'So,' said Colin, punching Neil's thick arm lightly, 'any news? We've been away.'

'I heard. Back to the colonies?' Neil grinned. 'Don't have time for news this time of year. Festival starts in two weeks.' He leaned forward, both elbows on the table. 'Although, I heard that this comedian...'

Neil's story was full of misplaced sex and heavy drug use. To spice it up, Colin thought, there was a touch of gambling and massive debt. Also, some innuendo about the comedian's manager, who surely could not have slept with so many people in one night. Colin ordered more coffee. Neil spoke breathlessly until he'd eked all he could from the comedian's wretched life. He took a drink. 'Why was it you went away again?'

'Holidays.' Colin thanked the waiter as she came back with her tray. 'You know, those things that you deserve when you work hard. That's right, maybe you don't know.'

Neil shook his head. 'That wasn't the whole reason. I heard something.' He looked across at Alexander, who sawed determinedly at his egg-soaked crusts. 'You went for family reasons? Something about an anniversary?'

Colin shrugged. 'Nope.'

'No, I think it was you, Scotty.'

Alexander put his knife and fork down. 'We were on holidays.'

'Huh.' Neil looked back and forth between the two. Colin shrugged, Alexander finished his coffee. 'Curious, that's all.'

'No, mate, a holiday. For me, it was catching up with my

Mum and Dad. And my sister. Maybe that's where you got mixed up. It was my little niece's birthday. No anniversary.'

'Maybe.' Neil put his empty cup down, twirling it on its base. 'Right, better get back. You be good.'

'No need to tell us, mate.'

Colin leaned over to the window to watch Neil cross the road. The rain had stopped; the streets glistened. Colin glanced at Alexander. His face was warmer, less strained. Hard to tell whether it was Neil going or breakfast eaten. 'How did he know?'

'About what?'

'The anniversary.'

Alexander shrugged. 'Someone must have said something. Jacqui. Belinda. We had that party, right? One of us must have said something to someone.'

'Not me.'

'Must have been me.'

Colin tapped his finger on the table. 'Why would you do that?'

'What? I probably had too much to drink.'

'You let people know what you were doing?'

'Only Jacqui. Maybe Belinda.'

'You wanted them to know?'

'No.' Alexander scrubbed at the back of his neck. 'Maybe. I don't know. Let it go, right.'

Colin stood up. 'I'll pay.'

Alexander nodded.

They walked out together. 'I'm going this way,' Colin said, heading left. 'Thought I might check out what's being set up around the uni.'

'I'm going back so I'll see you later then.' Alexander put his hands in his pockets as he went the other way.

A loud shout made Colin turn. A man in a blue coat pushed

at a woman who tipped like a domino and was caught and dragged away from the skidding sedan that hit the kerb and leapt up as if trying to swallow them. A split-second pause. The car nosed down, and the man dived away, crashing into a pram that tipped into a girl who screamed. Her terror caused a chill to race through Colin even as he jumped back as a second, then a third car struck the first with windscreen-shattering violence. The rain started again, straight and fast and dense, blocking the zig zag of crushed cars until Colin blinked. The traffic was still.

People moved as two groups, one stepping hurriedly back as the other tore forward and gathered around the windows of the broken cars. Colin looked for Alexander, but there were too many lookalike drenched people. The girl under the pram screeched. A young woman crouched, then stood, clinging to a baby. Someone else put the pram right, and the girl emerged to clutch at the young woman's leg, howling into her dress. As Colin moved toward the wreckage, he saw the woman kiss the baby and crouch again to the little girl. The screeching stopped as they hugged, a family trio.

People backed away from the third car's driver door. A bearded man appeared, wobbled a moment, and was led to the footpath where a restaurant owner set down a chair under cover of a veranda. Blood dripped from his nose. He collected it in his hand as he sat, staring at it like he'd never seen anything so bright. The rain eased as the second driver stepped out, her elbows held by two other women, steering her inside a shop. Colin kept his distance, walking around the right-hand sides of the cars. More people crowded the first car. A tall man spoke into his phone, his eyes flicking back to the car, his voice urgent. Others called out. A towel passed from hand to hand until it disappeared inside the car.

'What happened?' said someone behind Colin.

'Don't know. Too fast on wet roads?'

'Rental car.'

'Aye.'

Colin couldn't see what they were looking at. A woman pushed into the group around the car and it parted at her authority.

'Doctor?'

'Hope so.'

The crowd closed back around the car.

The distant sound of sirens tipped a few others into action. Two large men, heads shorn like bodyguards, put their arms out and shepherded people off the road. Colin stepped back with the others. He'd seen one accident like this before, on the Monash Freeway in Melbourne. People took roles until the police arrived. Some people could do that, instant command, instant decision-making. You saw it in emergency situations. Floods, fires, terrorist attacks. It was the same all over the world. Some people gawked. Others were more useful.

I'm one of the useless ones. Colin turned to leave. He had first aid training, but so did thousands of others. It wasn't enough. You had to have a certain gumption that no one could teach. And it helped if you hadn't had a bad experience before. He gulped.

'Are they all right?' Alexander was in Colin's face, his eyes level, his own wet hair swinging.

'Two are. Can't see this one.' Colin twisted to look again at the first car. He hadn't noticed before how its front had connected with the concrete pillar of the building. Was the driver trapped behind a motor pushed into their lap?

'Do you know how many people are in the car?'

'From the way people are moving, I'd say it's just the driver.'

The self-appointed guard walked to the front of the onlookers. 'Move back. Ambulance on its way.'

'I'm going.' Colin pushed his hair back from his forehead as the rain started an infuriating drizzle. 'It's going to get crazy here.'

'Aye.' Alexander didn't move. The drizzle misted his hair. It crowned his eyelashes in drops as he glanced at Colin. 'Do you ever wonder what happens afterwards?'

'After what?'

'After accidents.'

'People get taken to hospitals. Cars are towed. It's pretty obvious.'

'Not that.' Alexander's head shake sprayed water down his top. 'After all that. What the person goes through, how it changes them. What their family does.' He looked around. 'How these people are affected.'

'Yes. And it's terrible.'

'See, I don't think it is all terrible. Perhaps it makes people realise what's important. Maybe that man -' Alexander tipped his head towards the driver sitting on the outdoor chair, a blanket tucked around him '- will stop cheating on his wife.'

'He's cheating on his wife?'

'It's an example. Or maybe he'll leave his wife and take off with his new girl.'

Colin shook his head. 'You have the weirdest imagination, mate.'

'It doesn't take much.' The rain stopped. The sun lasered through a cloud gap. Alexander used both his hands to wipe his face. 'Maybe the person in the last car won't remember their old life. They'll have to start again with a new one.'

Despite the sun, Colin shivered. 'I know where you're heading.'

Alexander took a deep breath in. Colin closed his eyes briefly and waited for his friend to launch into another Norah possibility. Oh, she'd been raised by a different family or a religious cult or wolves and had discovered who she was but on the way to the airport to find her true family she'd been in a car accident and didn't remember what she was doing and the wolves or whoever they were had collected her and she would never remember the truth again.

'Well,' said Alexander, the frantic look falling from his face, 'it's a possibility. You can't say it isn't.'

The sirens arrived. The crowd lurched back as the guard did another stern round. Colin and Alexander were pushed together, trapped at the front, and had a gold cinema seat view of the people around the car stepping backwards to reveal the silhouette of a fast-breathing person skewered in their seat. The view closed over again as the uniforms moved in. Colin tried to get away, but people surged forward. He found himself blocking their movement, arms outstretched like the guard's. Alexander glanced at him and did the same.

One moment voyeurs, the next moment barricades. Colin caught the guard's eye, who nodded at him, man to man. Shame flooded Colin at even being there at all.

Their now unimpeded front row view let them witness the driver's whimper as someone assessed her. There were calm but quick movements that passed medical equipment down to the main officer. Colin saw gloved hands, tubes, white dressings. The rain came and went as if someone was playing with a sky tap. People worked on without fuss. Colin's arms were aching.

Finally, it was time to get the driver out of the car and the real police took over, directing people back and back and back until the woman disappeared from their sight. Much of the crowd moved away then. Colin and Alexander were free to go. They heard grinding as they cut the car up and saw the stretcher brightly white against the grey of the day as they wheeled it to the car.

'She's out,' said Colin as a body shifted, held stiffly by six people, onto the bed.

'Can you see who it is?'

'No. Can't see her face.'

Alexander turned to look, still walking away driven by bands of ordinary people diverted from the accident scene and busy with their day. 'What about her hair? What colour is her hair?'

It was too far. The day was too shadowed. The crowd behind them too dense. 'I don't know.'

'I thought it was brown. Maybe sandy.'

'Can't tell.'

They got stuck then, the street narrowing and too many people walking. The accident disappeared completely. Alexander frowned, not at the people jammed on the path. Colin saw his friend's eyes downcast, working through the millions of scenarios he'd created for himself about his absent sister.

'No, it was dark.'

'What?'

Alexander shrugged, his shoulders relaxing. 'Aye. Her hair was definitely dark. I know it.' He tapped at his head.

'Okay.'

The crowd filtered through the stopgap and resumed its steady walking. Colin inhaled sharply. Her hair was dark? Alicia? Of course it wasn't. He scowled at Alexander, who didn't notice. The trouble with having a traumatised friend was that their imagination was horrifyingly catching.

NINE

At Julie's insistence, it was an Australian-style barbeque. She used to have lots when she'd first come to Scotland. The long summer evenings were perfect for cooking and eating outside. She stood at the kitchen bench staring out into the gravelled yard and thought back to the last family gathering involving slow-burned sausages. Last summer? It certainly hadn't been this summer, not with Alexander away and her new job.

Donald smiled at her through the glass, raising his ale in acknowledgement. She blinked and hastily gave a little wave back. He was meant to be at the hotplate, but Colin had taken over. She didn't blame him. Donald wasn't used to turning meat, drinking and talking at the same time. He did one or the other, rendering the sausages into useless logs of charcoal. Colin was good at all three. He had Elizabeth in thrall while flipping some hamburgers. She leaned forward to hear him over the sizzling champagne flute held between dainty fingers. Julie searched for Euan. He stood in the corner flicking aphids from the leaves of the roses. Or that's what it looked like he was doing.

'All good, Mum?' Alexander touched her arm.

'Yes.' She smiled at him, a moment too late perhaps. 'See?

All the salads are done. Go and check on Colin, darling. The meat should nearly be ready.'

Alexander nodded and ducked outside. She watched him go, her lanky son. The last few years of working had hardened his muscles but not bulked him out as they'd done to Donald. Wiry, her dad would have said. Alexander was a wiry bloke.

Julie ducked her head at the thought of her dad. These days, his image didn't come very easily to her. He'd been gone a long time now, decades. Her memories of him zoned in on when he used to take her in the car to horse riding lessons, the driver's side window down as he blew smoke out. She could still smell it. It made her feel sick. Somehow, her child-self knew that smoking was something he couldn't control. Breathing the smoky toxins out of the window, and not leaving the car closed up like some dads did, was in concession for her young self. She loved him for it.

'Need a hand to carry them out, love?' Donald stood with his hands poised over the first bowl.

Why did everyone keep sneaking up on her tonight? 'Yes, thank you.'

'Could you remind me, love, what they are? In case someone asks me.'

Julie glanced at Donald to see how much he was joking. Not at all, it seemed. His face was open and completely honest. 'Potato salad. Greek salad. Coleslaw. Coriander and couscous.'

'Aye, got it now.' He took the potato salad. 'This one I know.'

Colin was piling the meat up onto a plate when she came out. He put it in the middle of the outdoor table and smiled at her. 'At least we don't have to worry about the blowies.'

He was such a nice kid. She grinned back, feeling unreasonably pleased to have someone here who understood. With a flourish, she held out a bottle of tomato sauce.

'Home made?' Colin's eyes widened. 'Did you make it?'

'My grandmother's recipe.'

Colin rubbed his hands together.

'We had it last time, you know.' Alexander shook his head at Colin as he slid into his place.

'But that was...'

'Must have been last summer since we've had a barbeque.' Donald had trouble saying the word, or that's how it sounded to Julie. She nodded at him, however. 'That's what I thought, too.'

They tucked in. Thankfully, thought Julie, Euan was sitting on her side of the table at the end and she couldn't see him. Opposite her, Elizabeth cut carefully into her hamburger, shaking her head at Colin's offer of sauce. Alexander sat opposite his uncle. Donald nudged her. 'Lovely, love.' He waved his meat-laden fork in a circle. 'All of it.'

'You need to thank Colin for his cooking.'

'Thank you for taking over, Colin. I was failing bad.'

'That's all right. When I'm home, it's my job, too. I took over from Dad when I was about eighteen. He used to burn things all the time -' Julie saw Colin bite his sentence back before he could say 'too.'

'Tell me, Colin,' said Elizabeth in her cool voice, 'how are your parents? You visited them in Brisbane?'

'They actually live in Coolangatta. We stayed with them for...' Colin frowned at Alexander, remembering '... just over a week? Then we went to my sister's in Brisbane. That was before we went to Melbourne.'

'Was it pleasant weather?'

'Queensland wasn't bad. I mean, it's winter, but they don't really do a proper winter. It gets cool, but not icy. That's why my parents moved up there. That, and because Tanya went there. She struggled a bit after her divorce. Mum helps out with the kids.'

'And when you go back, will you be in Queensland, as well?'

'I'm not sure yet. I'll have to work out where the jobs are.'

'You don't have anyone tying you down then.'

Colin's knife squeaked as he cut his sausage. 'No. I'm free and easy.'

'A good place to be.' Donald chuckled. 'Make the most of it, lad, because the time will come when you won't be.'

Alexander glanced at his mother. She gave him a tiny shake of her head and a brief smile. Donald was still laughing to himself, his arm rubbing her shoulder. She inched away.

'What did you do in Melbourne?' Elizabeth's focus was on Colin. He was her favourite tonight, as Alexander had been the time before. Julie wondered how she chose. Was it the first one she laid eyes on? You would think that it would always be Colin, as the most outlandish member of their little family, but sometimes Julie saw a little sneer on her lips at the way Colin said things. *Mate. Eh. Tomorra.* Colin was not the most ocker Julie had ever heard, but he hadn't had to adapt his language, not the way she had to when she first came. Sometimes when Julie spoke, she didn't recognise herself, it was such a strange linguistic mix.

'We did lots of things. Melbourne has a lot to see and do.' Colin chewed a bit. Alexander was quiet. 'Actually, we did a lot of walking around. It was really weird how things had changed in the two years I've been away. Did you know that Melbourne was voted the world's most liveable city for the sixth year in a row last year?'

'No, I didn't.' Elizabeth put her elbows on the table and clasped her hands under her chin. 'Why was that?'

Colin laughed. 'I have no idea! I guess I just figured that its congested traffic must be better than anywhere else.'

'Stability.' Euan's voice came like a schoolmaster's from the end of the table. 'It was in *The Economist*. Their global live-ability index rated Melbourne very highly on education, health-care and infrastructure.'

'Right,' said Colin. 'I didn't know that.'

'Something I read.'

Julie cut through her lettuce fiercely, her knife slipping a little on the plate. The masterly voice reminded her of Euan's past political campaigns, his attempt at knowing everything about everything in case someone bothered to ask him. Even twenty-plus years on, he magpie-d information, presenting it like a gift for others to unwrap. Even if, she thought, people would rather return it and get the money instead.

'Where did you stay in Melbourne?' Elizabeth's interroga-tion continued way past her finished meal.

'In Paxton. We had free accommodation there.'

'Paxton?'

Colin coughed. 'An outer suburb.'

'You went all the way to Melbourne to stay in the *suburbs*?'

'I grew up in the suburbs,' said Colin lightly.

'I can't imagine it was very exciting. Was it?'

Had everyone finished their meals at exactly the same time? Julie set her knife and fork on her plate, aware of the lack of noise. Donald chewed quietly on a bread roll, looking out over the heads of his guests at the clouds like a meteorologist. Euan had pushed his plate forward. Julie saw his arms crossed on the table, the ring he wore on his right hand glinting in the lowering light. Elizabeth had not registered *Paxton*. To her, it was a strange place in a strange land where she had no intention of going. Elizabeth had forgotten, or maybe she never knew, the significance of *Paxton*.

'The suburbs are where I grew up.' Colin's voice was deeper than it had been. 'You know, a milk bar on the corner and dogs that bark at you through the fence because you're walking past.'

'Hmmm.' Elizabeth took a sip of champagne. 'Melbourne is where you came from, Julie?'

Julie sat up. 'Yes. Not far from where Colin is talking about.'

'Do you have fond memories of it, too?'

'Doesn't everyone have good memories of where they grew up?'

'I suppose, if you can remember it at all.' Elizabeth trilled as she laughed. A rosella, thought Julie. One of the not-so-colourful ones.

'I have strong memories of the playground at the corner of the street with a metal slide that burned you when you slid down on hot days.' Julie wasn't sure why she felt the need to explain anything to Elizabeth. 'There was a donkey in a vacant block, a brown one with ears the length of its head.'

'A donkey in the middle of Melbourne?'

'Back then, where I grew up was outer Melbourne. There were market gardens behind us.'

The table was quiet. Julie's memories were swarming in her head. The row of gum trees across from her house. A brown snake squashed on the road. Riding a dilapidated billy cart down a bumpy footpath. She glanced at Elizabeth and then at Donald next to her. They both had dreamy eyes, perhaps thinking of their own billy cart races. Although, Julie thought, Elizabeth may think more of fox hunts and first blooding.

'Memory is a strange thing.' Euan spoke into the setting sun, holding his glass up to the light. 'It is selective, of course. The strongest memories are sometimes the worst ones we had.'

'Aye, Euan,' said Donald, 'then I wonder if you remember pushing me into the nettles when I was a wee boy of five. I was covered head to toe in welts!'

'Donald, that would be something you would remember, but not me.'

Donald roared, spilling his drink onto his plate as his body jerked back and forth in mirth. Julie frowned. Whatever was behind that story, she could only see the obvious. Euan couldn't remember it at all.

'What do you remember, Alexander?' Julie half-turned from her husband, willing him to wipe his mouth and shut up. 'Tell us about your childhood.'

Alexander stared at her. At the same moment she realised what she'd asked, Donald let forth with, 'Aye, boy. Tell us something that we don't already know about you.'

Julie swallowed, trying to tell Alexander with her eyes he didn't need to say anything, that she was sorry, that this was all getting really stupid. Alexander flicked his hair off his face and drank the last of his beer. 'This is an old person's game, Mum. You shouldn't even be playing it yet.'

'Come on, Alexander.' Elizabeth held her glass up. 'Tell us something.'

Alexander dabbed at a crumb on his plate. 'I remember my first day of school. I thought Mrs O'Connell looked like Frankenstein.'

Even Julie laughed at that. Gorgeous Mrs O'Connell, with her imposing chin and unfortunate flat haircut. 'How did you even know what Frankenstein looked like when you started school?'

Alexander looked up, faint colour in his cheeks. 'Dad's book of monsters. It was on the top shelf.'

Donald grunted. 'I didn't know we still had it. My Dad gave that to me when I was a boy.'

'But you didn't read it when you were just starting school.' Julie felt slightly sick.

'It's okay, Mum. I recovered fully.' Alexander smiled at her.

Julie let her mouth copy his. There it was again, that ridiculous guilty-mother feeling, raising its ugly head even though her son was nearly thirty-five. So he fully recovered. Had he fully recovered from the intenseness of parenting that came from unexpectedly being an only child? How terrible had she made his life?

Colin leaned forward. 'It's okay, Julie. I can vouch that he's mostly okay.'

Julie broadened her smile, trying to settle her thoughts. She felt Colin's gaze on her. He was that sort of boy, one who could see deep into people. She often wondered what had happened to him to make him that way. She also felt pity. His empathy was dangerous for him.

'You spent some time in Australia, Donald.' Elizabeth leaned back in her chair and shook her head so that her shoulder-length hair bounced around her shoulders.

'I've only been twice. I stayed eighteen months the first time.' Donald put his arm around Julie, settling his open hand on her shoulder. 'I went for a holiday and found this beautiful thing.'

'Donald...' Julie shifted under the weight of his arm.

'And then we came back.' Donald moved suddenly, his hand pressing down on Julie. She winced. He pulled his arm back, putting both hands on the table and leaning on them to help him stand. 'I'll help you with desserts, love.'

Julie gathered plates and led him into the kitchen. Outside, Colin was leading the conversation into music. As she bent to stack the dishwasher, she heard his scratchy baritone start on *Farewell to old England forever.*

'Sings like a cracked record.' Donald held a plate out for her, head cocked towards their visitors. She stood, and he took her hand. His skin felt thick, worn, dry. 'Are you alright, love?'

She squeezed his fingers. 'Of course. Thanks for asking.'

'Things were going sideways out there.'

She let his hand go, patting it once as she did. 'Let's get the pav.'

Donald carried the sweet out for her. She watched him move carefully through the glass doors, high-stepping over the ledge. She waited for him to return and gave him the fruit salad.

'Coming out, love?'

'In a moment.'

Julie wiped the bench. Outside, dishes clattered. Alexander laughed, a sweet sound to her ears. Colin was trying another song, but his mouthful of pavlova made him un-intelligible. Elizabeth joined him, humming along earnestly until she put her spoon down and giggled. Julie's stomach roiled.

What was Elizabeth's game? She was the second wife, that of privileged status, she who got the lot doing none of the hard yakka of wifedom. Julie frowned at herself, but she had liked Rachel, Euan's childhood partner, even though she was far too mousey. She had had good chats with Rachel, as one young woman to the other, but Rachel couldn't seem to continue the flow of conversation with Euan close by. It was as if she expected him to be listening. Euan didn't listen, even if he was standing in front of you, if he thought it not worth his while. Rachel gradually faded into everyone's background. One day, it seemed, she just vanished from their family. Julie made a half-hearted attempt to contact her that failed, as Julie had really wanted it to. Some years later, there was Elizabeth. Smiling, charming, empty Elizabeth.

Was she another of Euan's patients? Euan had been doing a year of locums. He'd travelled as far as Inverloch and down to Newcastle, two weeks here, six weeks there. He'd arrived back in Melrose with a Londoner. Julie had never thought Elizabeth would stay, especially without children to keep her grounded. Elizabeth went back to the city most weeks to keep in touch with her wholesalers and workers, but otherwise managed a very successful flower delivery service from right where she was in Euan's vast manor house.

Outside, Elizabeth laughed again. A lot of champagne had passed through her flute. Champagne and barbeques clashed in Julie's mind. She served it as a concession to family at gatherings that weren't entirely hers. When she was a young woman, and her parents celebrated their birthdays using the portable gas barbeque set up in their overgrown backyard, she'd drunk the ubiquitous shandy or two, a fact she had told no one who hadn't been there at the time. Tonight, she was drinking mineral water. She'd tipped her wine down the sink. Tonight, it tasted sour.

Julie picked up her glass and went outside. Donald had served her a piece of pavlova with extra strawberries, as she liked it. She thanked him with a hand on his shoulder and used the excuse of eating to not join in on the conversation.

Colin had stopped singing. He sat back, rubbing his stomach, and pushed his beer away. 'Beer and cream really don't mix.'

'You want something else, lad?' Donald twisted around to look back in the house as if he expected a bar tender to appear. 'I've got some whiskey.'

'No, thank you. That'll do me. We're bagging a Munro tomorrow.'

'Which one?'

Colin grinned. 'The smallest one we can find. We aren't that adventurous.'

Donald raised his glass. 'To the mountain climbers.'

'Not me.' Alexander put both his hands up.

'I'm going with the A.L.I.E. group. *Australians living in Edinburgh.*' Colin shrugged. 'We're trying to assimilate.'

'By climbing hills?' Elizabeth flicked her hair again. 'That's a lovely idea.'

'Not just a hill,' Colin said. 'I had to buy walking boots.'

'You big softie.'

Colin pushed at Alexander so he nearly fell off his chair.

'Did you go hiking when you went back to Australia, Colin?' Elizabeth leaned over to tip the bottle into her glass, but it was empty.

'No. We weren't near any decent mountains.'

'So what did you do again? In Melbourne, the most liveable city in the world?'

'He's already answered that, Elizabeth.' Euan was on his feet, pushing back his chair while glancing at his phone. 'Thank you for the lovely evening. I'm sorry, but I do have some work to do when I get home.'

'Perhaps you'd like some help packing up?' Elizabeth said hopefully as Euan helped her out of her chair.

'No, we've got help.' Donald pointed at Colin and Alexander.

Julie walked her guests to their car, standing back on the gravel as Euan swung his car around. Elizabeth leaned out the window, her hair tangled artfully around her face. 'Goodbye! Bye!'

Julie waved once. As she turned back, the dying light silhouetted the three men left at the table. It occurred to her that Elizabeth couldn't know anything about Norah or she surely should have twigged to the lack of conversation. That meant that Euan hadn't told her about the baby girl. Or anything else, hopefully.

Julie thought of Rachel, her sad, wide-eyed face. Hopefully, she had known nothing either.

'Right, love?' called Donald.

Julie walked back to her husband, wishing that he wasn't waiting for her while she had those thoughts in her head. She gave him a smile as she went to pick up some plates. 'I'm fine, Donald. Of course I am.'

TEN

Airlines demand customers at airports three or so hours before an international flight. Grace had reckoned on six. Six hours beforehand landed squarely in the middle of Claudia's shift at *Stillers*. Grace would be gone before Claudia had rinsed her last glass.

With half an hour to go before the taxi came to take her away, Grace finished the packing chest off with her quilt and pillow. The room was empty except for the barest of furniture, the things of her life crammed into the rectangular reminder of her father. She put the flimsy lid on and tacked it shut using Claudia's hammer. With a bit of heaving, the chest slid back under the window. Claudia could rent the room out if she liked, but Grace had left enough money for a month's rent in an envelope under her friend's pillow.

If Claudia had known Grace was going that day, would she have stopped her? Grace dragged her suitcase to the hall and went to get a last cup of tea. They had spoken little since that night Claudia had called Grace cruel. *Cruel.* Such a sharp word. Grace still didn't know what to do with it. They'd lived side by side for years, eating dinner at the wonky kitchen table if Claudia had a night off, going into the city to shop. Had Claudia noticed that Grace had been sorting, packing, preparing? Grace couldn't tell. She used to be able to read her friend. She was a closed book now.

As the kettle boiled, Grace checked her handbag again. Phone. Passport, a bit of UK currency, her travel itinerary. Debit card linked to the last of her father's money. Copy of the email confirming her accommodation. Her driver's license. The bag felt slim compared to the usual amount of junk it held. No old receipts, no jelly beans, no parking tickets. The keys to her car sat on the table next to the letter she'd left for Claudia.

The cabin bag she'd decided on was more telling. A book. Her tiny laptop. Phone charger and computer charger. A complete change of clothes folded neatly at its bottom. Shoes, too. Just in case her luggage didn't make it to Edinburgh, and she had to start her new life as an old self.

One final piece of paper tucked into the outside zipped pocket. *Cameron Stonemasonry* was easy to find on the internet. The website had a mobile phone number and email address and photos. The photos showed the type of work done: lime pointing, dry stone walling, restoration. In a couple of photos, a young man bent over his work, beach-sand hair hanging over his face. Alexander Cameron, just as pale as he had appeared in the Paxton paper.

From there, Grace searched online until it was clear from photos and comments that Alexander lived in Edinburgh. It was only a city of 500,000 people, nothing like Melbourne's four million plus. She had one month of accommodation booked, and six months of money to use if she was frugal. That's enough to sort things out, thought Grace as she culled the last of her tea and rinsed the mug for the last time. Six months sounded like a lifetime.

The taxi was fifteen minutes late. Despite the chilly wind, Grace felt sweat swell on her back. What if Claudia finished early? What if she felt sick or got a headache or sprained her ankle and was on her way home right now? Grace wheeled her bag right out the front. She stood shivering for another five minutes before the taxi came, its driver unapologetic, and took her away.

Grace had tried to prepare herself for the moment when the city receded behind her and the airport loomed. Planning it felt so final, but Grace was strangely unmoved. She didn't want to look around to see the Eureka building or glimpse the frame of the Star. Her hands were relaxed in her lap. The hum of the taxi, its cosy warmth, was secure. Even as it pulled up at the drop-off point, and the driver lifted her bag out of the boot without smiling, Grace continued on her journey without pausing. It wasn't until she was in the airport, too early to check-in, that she decided how she was feeling. 'This is one hundred percent right,' she said to herself, making a fellow traveller walking past smile.

With hours to spare, Grace wheeled her bag to a coffee bay and treated herself to an early dinner of toasted banana bread and a hot chocolate. As she ate, other tasks she'd been unsure of were suddenly clear. A new travel sim card went in and she tucked away her old one. She systematically went through every link to social media she had and de-activated her pages. They were still there but hidden, a secret treasure chest of memories. Apart from Claudia, who would want to contact her? Grace just hoped that Claudia still liked her enough to wait out the month.

It was tempting to slip into the airport bathroom and change. Grace held back. No, the new life started in another country. She needed the break clean. This was not a game. She finished her drink, shut down the laptop, and went to plane-watch by the window until she could get rid of her luggage.

Nearly the entire day had passed before she could board. Even with a person wedged either side, Grace settled comfortably in, scrolling through the list of flight entertainment as if she'd flown a million times before. She hadn't, though. She ground her teeth for a moment to let the moment pass. It was the first time, not on a plane, but certainly on one as immense as the A380. She looked across the chest of the man next to her to the expanse of people to her left. Many looked flustered, a couple were asleep already. It was after ten o'clock. Grace felt for the sleepy ones. It had been one of the longest days in her life.

It was a longer night. It stretched forever. The break in Dubai was humid. Grace peeled off two outer layers and still sat sweating at the gate. Her book finished, she bought another but couldn't get into its tale of loss and love. There wasn't an idea in the book that felt real, that she could even remotely relate to. What did she know about love, for starters? It was an abstract concept, somewhere between lust and disgust. Sitting in a remote airport terminal, looking into a pale unfamiliar landscape, was dreamlike as well but the hard plastic chair and the queue for the Western toilet was factual enough. In the bathroom, Grace wiped her face free of make-up, staring at her plainness in the mirror. Her eyes felt grit-filled and sore.

Hours later, the ping of the aeroplane brought Grace back to the present. They wheeled heavily through the sky, strange mountains and bridges and buildings flashing in and out of Grace's view from her middle seat, and settled for the runway. A whump, and they were down. She closed her eyes and let her head fill with the sound of reconnecting to the earth.

PASSPORT CHECKS. Baggage retrieval. Bus stop locating. She sank into the seat and had to wait while the coach filled. It took off at last, veering sharply, and carried her into her new city.

Phone in hand, Grace angled her suitcase from the bus and started the trek to the Old Town where she was staying. It was not the heat of Dubai, but it was warm. Her shoulder ached immediately on pulling the case across along the ascending road. People weaved around her. They walked on the right of the footpath, confusing her. The huge Balmoral Hotel squatted below. She could only glance at it before needing to swap her grip. Festival posters clung to the fence on her right. Some faces she knew. Australian faces, ones commonly on the television. It was like seeing friends.

She'd thought it early when she'd landed, but it was nearly eleven o'clock by the time she made it to the apartment door in St Giles Street. The crowds stuck to the Royal Mile, allowing her to collect the key from the gift shop owner without having to fight her way in. The door opened into a concrete stairwell. Grace let it slam behind her and began the climb to her fourth storey room. It was a lucky find in the festival town. Or was it? She left her suitcase at the second landing and carried the rest of her things to the top, turning the three locks to let herself in, tossing her bags into the hall, and running back down to get her suitcase. She leaned on the door as it closed on her temporary home, panting and holding back a wave of nausea.

It didn't matter that she spent the next hour lying on the skinny single bed in the one roomed flat, or the next half an hour after that in the bathroom, first being sick in the sink and then in the shower, or that the complimentary biscuits in the cupboard were stale because, being dry and hard, they were perfect for a stomach sore from homogenous aeroplane food. Outside, the air was light, and the clouds had stayed away. Grace pushed the window up high even though that meant she could, if she wanted, plunge headfirst out the window to the paved street below. She breathed in, swallowing the last crumbs in her mouth, and felt on the edge of something.

The internet connection was surprisingly good or maybe this was how the rest of the world had it while Australia wallowed in low speed? Grace felt her luck increase. She studied maps of Edinburgh and real estate guides to work out where the average person might live, and was soon lost in a myriad of useless information about public transport and local shops. Lady Luck hadn't stayed long. She studied the photos she could find of Alexander Cameron, but there was no trend to follow. He wasn't a huge social media user. It didn't help that he liked football teams Grace had never heard of and went to matches in places she didn't know existed.

Still. He was somewhere, and he would be the first Cameron to approach. A brother in search of a sister seemed less obstructive to parents who'd given up on a daughter. She'd ask around. She'd rely on the six degrees of separation, the three degrees of influence, or cosmic vibrations. Time was on her side. He would be working hard after spending so much time away from home. He was trapped somewhere. She could feel it.

Grace's mouth was dry. She made more tea, waiting for the kettle with her head out of the window. For all she knew, he was there, on the street walking past eating fried haggis and chips. Should she be ready for him before she started looking in earnest? What if, by some extraordinary chance, she bumped right into him as she stepped out of the door and she didn't know it was him? Worse, he didn't know her. She shivered. It was what she feared the most, the lack of recognition.

Ignoring the boiled kettle, Grace consulted her map again and located the nearest supermarket. She dressed as ordinarily as she could, pulling on worn jeans and a dark, plain T-shirt. A floppy sun hat covered her jaw-length hair, especially with it angled back over her ears. She left make-up off, rendering her eyes ever paler without their border of mascara. Instead of her handbag, she tucked her debit card into her phone cover and pushed the phone into her jeans pocket. Her hands trembled as she undid the locks on her door, and the wide, hard steps jarred her feet in their thin trainers. By the time she opened the door to the pavement, she was panting.

The streets had that excitable before-party feel about them. Grace pulled her phone out and went to maps. Her destination was obvious, but as soon as she stepped in the throng, the chatter of passers-by and the blasts of music at points along the road made her slow down. A lone bagpiper, a boy barely adolescent, played solemnly in a doorway. A woman with a pink Mohawk and dressed in a kilt spun wool in St Giles Square, a clear note on a stand behind her. *Photos $1*. A fire-eater called a crowd around him, balancing high up on rocking barrels.

Most people moved in small groups, families or tours. They cruised up and down the streets, nibbling fudge and clutching souvenirs. Grace stopped with them to watch some bird handlers with owls call for people wanting photographs with the beautiful creatures. A homeless man parked against a shop pillar had to wriggle across to prevent being stepped on. Most people staring at the owls didn't even know he was there. Grace gave him five pounds. He took it, confusion stamping his face, and had to dodge as someone's plastic bag full of tartan-boxed shortbread nearly knocked him in the head. She felt sorry for the man, but the way people ignored him was almost encouraging. Human nature was that people were transfixed by the attractive.

People were moving into restaurants and cafes by the time Grace had bought what she needed from Sainsbury and was back at the door to her apartment. She climbed the stairs slowly, pausing at each landing to look out the window and study the streets below. Yellow barriers marred the Old Town look, no doubt ready in case the Festival was targeted by terrorists. As she unlocked her door, she imagined those among the crowd with large and horrible secrets. She shut herself in, three locks and a chain across, making her secure.

She unpacked the newspaper cutting of Alexander Cameron and his friend standing outside the old hospital zone, and pulled up the website photo of him to compare. In each, Alexander's hair was the colour of blonde sandstone, a light ginger in sunlight. Grace studied her image in the bathroom mirror. She was too auburn, too richly red. She didn't want him to be put off.

Jetlag washed through her as she worked, waxing and waning like a heavy sea. In the dull moments, she paused, gloved hands resting on the sink. As it lifted, she rubbed at her head, carefully pulling each strand through. It was not the first time she'd changed colour, but Claudia had always helped. Perhaps not physically, but by sitting on the edge of the toilet pointing out where Grace had missed. Grace tried to imagine her there. *You missed a bit. No, there. Better. The other side now.* In the dreamy downward rush of fatigue, she could almost hear her friend's voice. In the moments of clarity, she knew she was alone.

It was midnight by the time she'd finished and her hair was dry enough to go to bed. The outside noises of tourists and cars had gone. Grace fell asleep with the light on, waking abruptly an hour later to turn it off, sleeping heavily again. Waking again. Sleeping. A roller coaster of a night until the sun forced her up with early morning brilliance. By any holiday standard it was early, but merry voices floated up through her still open kitchen window. She gave herself a long time for a breakfast of tea, yoghurt and fruit, then pushed her bowl aside. It was time.

First, a shower to be rid of excess dye. Grace had been care-ful, the line on her skin around the edge of her hair barely visi-ble. She upended her head and dried most of it before forcing a part down the left-hand side instead of the middle. Hair protested, falling as she wanted in an uneven wave across her face. She plucked her eyebrows into a slight 1930's arch, thin-ning them to a few finishing hairs. Already, her face had changed.

Grace leaned on the rim of the basin, taking a few steady breaths in and out. Faint cracks in the enamel surrounded the plughole, radiating out like sunbursts. She kept her gaze on them, noting their almost symmetrical beauty, until the rush of heat had gone, and she felt alright to continue.

It was easier after that, as if the weak moment had flushed away a blockage. She applied a lighter foundation, accentuating her cheek hollows by clever strokes of a thick make-up brush. Her eyes took longest. The false lashes went on last, curled and heavy brown.

Grace pulled her clothes from her suitcase. She hung most in the tiny built-in robe of her room and layered the rest in two drawers. She glanced out the window to the speedy cloud-ridden sky and decided on a floral maxi and sandals. The fabric settled softly on her shoulders as she pulled the dress on.

The full-sized mirror on the door of the wardrobe was in shadow even with the bedroom light on. It was all Grace had. She stood in front of it for a long time, slowly pulling herself upright until a taller, paler, wide-eyed version of herself stared back. The newspaper photograph of Alexander Cameron was rippled, but she held it up next to her head. There they were, brother and sister. She was an exquisite female version of the tall man in the picture.

The tip of Grace's tongue came out to touch her dark lips, and she pulled it back in. The newspaper settled on the bed when she threw it down. She packed her new lichen-green leather tote with cat-eye sunglasses and the earth-brown lipstick, and swung it confidently onto her shoulder before unlocking the door.

Grace Worthington had entered the building. Norah Cameron exited.

ELEVEN

Did the myriads of people in the Royal Mile notice the new girl? Grace felt shiny and obvious in her long floral dress and roman sandals. She walked downhill, her long skirt swishing the sides of her legs. People parted around her. Some glanced up, others adjusted their holiday stride but didn't stop talking to their neighbours or staring at the sights. It was a short distance to St Giles Cathedral. Grace paused at the mohawk'd spinner, the wind gathering her dress and making it embrace her briefly.

'Would you like a photo, lassie?' A man moved forward from where he'd slumped against the church. 'One pound for a lasting memory.'

Grace smiled. The *first* memory, she thought. 'Yes, thanks.' She moved to stand next to the woman at the spinning wheel who nodded sternly at her.

'Your phone, lass.'

Grace got the phone ready and passed it to the man, realising at the last minute that this could all be a scam, that he might take that phone and run. He wouldn't get far, she realised. A fence of people had formed around the picture-taking scene, and the man had to shoo them back a little in order to get the shot. He took several, waited for Grace to fumble for the unfamiliar coin, and handed the phone back.

'Thanks,' said Grace to the woman at the wheel.

'You are welcome, my gorgeous.' As the woman nodded, her pink Mohawk cut through the air stiffly.

'Anyone else?' The man swept his hand towards Grace.

A couple stepped forward.

Grace moved out of the way. She stepped into the shade around the corner, stopping close to a floating Yoda, and opened the photo. This is insane, she thought, grinning. A woman in a kilt seated at a spinning wheel with a pale, fair-haired stranger next to her. Grace was no one she recognised. Had she ever stood that way before, with her hands demurely in front of her, one on the other's wrist? The long dress, cinched at the waist with a thin belt, gave her the appearance of someone beyond her usual average-girl height. The make-up she'd so carefully applied that morning lifted her eyes. Her lips were fuller, dark with colour. It was a little like being photo-shopped, but in real life. Grace Worthington really looked nothing like Grace Worthington.

I am free, thought Grace.

The thought made her walk purposely down the street. The ingrained bleakness rose from her. She imagined that it ascended like a cloud and veered off into the skyline. Something had clung to her after her father's death, which the terrible delivery of his life in a box only made more tenacious. Now? There was no reason to cling to his memory or to wonder how she might have helped him more. Grace closed her eyes and tipped her chin up, feeling for the sun. It caressed her cheeks.

'Are you alright, dear?' An older couple had stopped, bags of fudge in their hands. Grace opened her eyes to find that she was statue-like in the middle of the path.

'I'm so sorry,' she said. 'Yes, I'm fine.'

The woman nodded. 'It is lovely, isn't it?'

'Yes, it is.'

'From New Zealand, are you?' The man was peering at her closely, as if she was stamped with a silver fern.

'New Zealand? No, Australia.'

'Ah,' he said doubtfully.

Grace smiled. Even her country was anonymous. 'Can I ask where you got that?'

The man held the fudge up. 'Over there. They have samples, you know.'

'Thank you.'

As Grace turned, she heard the woman say, 'Such a lovely girl. I hope the heat hasn't got to her.' Grace was still smiling as she stepped into the fudge shop.

Strange how the expression on a random person's face was catching. The serving girl grinned back broadly and pointed Grace to the samples on the counter. Grace tried a humble morsel of each one, letting it sit on her tongue until it melted and showered her mouth with flavour. She pointed to three different types, ordering enough in each batch for her and Claudia, and carried the bags outside.

Within a stone's throw from Holyrood, she halted. The group of chattering Germans behind her swerved. She lifted a hand in apology, a fudge bag hanging from her fingers. Claudia hadn't fled her thoughts like she'd thought she would. Was Claudia looking for her or was she doing as Grace had instructed, leaving her alone? Grace had promised contact within the month. Maybe she should ring Claudia today?

An oncoming crowd started down the hill, so Grace took a few faltering steps forward before walking onwards again, the sweeties crammed into her tote except for the bag of salted caramel. This one she ate through steadily. Claudia didn't really like salted caramel, she said it was fundamentally wrong to have those taste sensations assaulting her mouth at once. She was a straight sweet girl. Grace had bought chocolate toffee for that reason.

Holyrood Palace was shut for the day. Grace leaned her forehead on the iron gate, staring in at the buildings. Mary Queen of Scots had lived there, had witnessed the death of David Rizzio in the closet next to her bedchamber. Grace had seen the movie or read the book; she couldn't remember. She read so much but could hardly recall anything about any book. Was it worth reading at all? she often wondered. Claudia read nothing but the magazines at hairdresser's and doctor's places.

Grace shook her head, standing away from the gate and tightening the slim belt so it pressed firmly against her waist. She combed her hair with her fingers, careful to keep it over to one side. Her sleeve rode up, falling past her elbow then sliding down to cover her wrists as she put her arm back down. She read lots of books. Fantasies, adventures, thrillers. It was why she took the risk to find her family. Stories fuelled her.

Grace let Claudia's fudge drop into a bin as she walked around the outside of the palace. There were plenty of walkers on Arthur's Seat. Maybe she would go there tomorrow; it would help to get the lay of the land. She would definitely start her search for the Camerons. She crossed the road and started up the street again, moving alongside Parliament House. Her feet weren't used to her sandals, and the arches ached. She also had soft winter skin. The strap around the back of her left ankle rubbed. She swapped her tote to the other shoulder and dawdled. Cloud which cooled the air had bleached the sun. The smell of fish and chips at a shop near her apartment enticed her in to buy dinner. As she waited for them to cook, Grace flicked idly through an old newspaper.

Inside the little apartment, she locked the door and then, just in case, put a kitchen chair against the door handle. She hesitated before taking off the dress but, surely, she could relax while no one was watching? She flicked her laptop on and pulled up the Cameron Stonemasonry site. It had been such a rush to get here, to change, to adapt to the new season that she realised that she didn't have a solid plan of how to introduce herself to the Camerons. She could just ring, but what if they thought she was a hoax? A Frederic Bourdin, but one that wasn't welcome?

It wasn't until she'd finished eating and looked at the photos on the site again, walked to the bathroom and back, that she had an idea. The view from the window – not the one that overlooked the street but the window at the back – was over rooves, right down to the bay. Most of the buildings she could see were blonde sandstone, grey and brown with time. Not that she'd seen them, but surely the residential buildings were similar? Any one place in front of her could need the gifts of a stonemason. What if she asked for a quote and summoned her family to her in that most unassuming of ways?

Somewhat unsteadily, she pulled up Google maps and studied a likely street. It didn't matter where it was, as long as it was vaguely local and therefore thoroughly authentic. Of course it would need repair of some sort. She didn't even have to know exactly what. She was arranging a meeting, not a real job.

Grace flicked the tab back to the contact number of Cameron's Stonemasonry. She got her phone out, stared a little longer, then put the phone down to change back into Norah's dress. She even slipped the nasty roman sandals on. Only then did she feel she could ring the number.

It rang for a long time. Grace braced herself to leave a message. Should she mention Alexander's name? It wasn't on the website. No, not if she was pretending to be a customer. Best to make him think that she was ringing cold, having discovered their wonderful website and making a considered call.

'Hello.'

The voice was thicker than she'd imagined, older.

'Hello. Is this Cameron's Stonemasonry?'

'Aye.'

'Is this... Mr Cameron?'

'Aye. I'm Donald.'

Donald? Of course. The father. *Norah's* father. She swallowed. Grace's father had not sounded so robust, not ever. But then he wasn't her father, was he. Grace felt momentarily dizzy.

'Hello? You still there.'

'Yes. I'm here.'

'Can I help you?' The voice was even brusquer.

Grace took an unsettled breath in. 'I'd like to arrange a quote.'

'Aye, what for in particular?'

'My husband and I have bought a house in Macdonald Street and it has one wall that needs repair.'

'Macdonald Street. Melrose? Galashiels? Selkirk?'

'Pardon?'

'Where is the house, what place?'

'Oh.' Should she have chosen Melrose or Selkirk? Where were they anyway? 'No. Edinburgh.'

'Aye.' Grace heard shuffling and scribbling. 'Can you be more specific with what needs to be done?'

'No. Sorry.'

More shuffling. 'You're not from here then?'

Where was *here*? 'Pardon?'

'Your voice. Not from around here.'

'Oh. I'm Australian.'

'Are you now?' Donald sounded pleased. 'So is my wife.'

Julie. The wife's name was Julie. Grace had read that, too. Julie, not Jeanette. Grace put her hand on her forehead before saying, 'Is she really? Does she go back much?'

'No.'

It was said so firmly that Grace paused with 'why not?' stuck on the edge of her tongue. 'I read on your website you have workers in Edinburgh who could come to quote?'

'On the website? Is it now? I leave that internet stuff to my son. Now he's in Edinburgh. I'm in Dryburgh. I'll get him to quote your job. Wait.' The phone clunked on metal and Grace heard paper pages turning. Donald took so long, Grace's mouth dried out. 'We're working a job at the moment in the Borders, but he could come and look after work, I suppose. Tomorrow do you?'

'That would be great. Thank you.'

'What number?'

'Pardon?'

'Your house, lass. What number?'

How did house numbers work in Scotland? Grace took a punt. '7.'

'Right. It'll be Alexander. He might have Colin with him.'

'How will I know it's him?'

'What do you mean?'

'My husband won't be with me. I'd like to know who to look out for.'

Donald paused as if he had to think about it. 'Alexander's got ginger hair that's too long. Colin's the opposite. He's dark, got a proper haircut now.'

'Are they tall?'

'They'll have the van. It's got the name on it. He'll call you. I've got your phone number on mine. Now, what's your name so I can let him know?'

Grace hesitated. 'My name is Norah.' Your Norah. She held her breath.

'Right. Spell that for me.'

'What?'

'Spell your name for me, love. N-o-r-a?'

'N-o-r-a-h.'

He paused. She listened to him breathe in and out, in and out. When he spoke again, it was brisk. 'All right, Alexander will see you tomorrow. I'll let you get on now.' He hung up before Grace could say anything more.

She put the phone down, palms sweating. The whole of her was sweating, she realised. The dress clung damply to her chest and thighs. She wrenched it off, sitting back down in her under-wear on the clammy kitchen chair. She'd spoken to Donald, and he hadn't even known how to spell her name. There was hardly a tremor at his lost daughter's title. Grace trembled. What was he like, this Donald?

What about Julie? Grace felt oddly empty. Mothers were, she thought, more complicated than fathers. Jeanette Worthington had been a shadow of a mother, someone whose face lit up when Grace came into view but closed almost imme-diately as the memory slipped away. Grace was sure that she loved her. There was unexpected stroking of her hair while Grace knelt at Jeanette's feet to tie her shoes. Sometimes, Jeanette reached for her hand at the kitchen table and clung to it, forcing Grace to eat with just a fork. Once, she said 'Gracie' softly, a whisper that Grace caught and still held in her heart. Once only had her mother said her name.

Andrew tended to Jeanette, handling her like a treasure that needed the lightest of treatments and would be best left alone. He lifted her from the wheelchair, carrying her with his face slightly averted, a *devoted husband*, one that couldn't shake the blame for the accident. When he'd put her in bed for the long evening and night, he took up his position in his chair and drank until he fell asleep with one hand wrapped around a bottle. It was Grace who spent the night alert for Jeanette's whimper, sleeping in spasms, afraid she might miss something.

Claudia's mother was large and noisy, a counterpoint to Jeanette's frailty. She had wild, curly grey hair that refused control. When she talked, she outshouted everyone, even if it meant joining in on someone else's intimate discussion with a third party. She hovered over Grace if she went to visit Claudia, but not in a motherly way. More, *'Your father still drinking too much, Grace Worthington?'* as if it was Grace's fault Andrew had slid into despair. Claudia thought it all quite normal and became angry if Grace even hinted that her mother was overbearing. Claudia could, Grace thought, be very similar.

As for other mothers, well, there weren't many more examples in Grace's life. Her grandparents, aunts, relatives were non-existent. As Andrew often said in his moody times, which were often, *we are loners. The last of the Worthingtons. We are very alone.*

Not, thought Grace as she pulled on her own shorts and T-shirt, as alone as I am now.

Pain grabbed her stomach, so violent that she bent over, grabbing the doorframe to steady herself. It went, just like that, a one-off stab to remind her that she was still functioning, breathing, living, even if she'd thought she couldn't keep going. She'd never really thought she couldn't, it was just that she wondered how alone she could get. This was it, the pain told her. This was as alone as she could get. Even if the total population of the world died of a pandemic, it was difficult to think she could get much lonelier.

Grace picked up her phone. Her contacts were there, she could ring Claudia anytime. She could ring to hear her speak. There was no need to hold a conversation. Maybe in Claudia's voice there would be a tone that would tell Grace if she was missing her friend or if she remained angry. It was a powerful reason not to ring her because what if Claudia, after years of being Grace's only confidant, didn't care anymore? Grace put the phone down, pulling her hand back as if it was hot.

Outside, finally, the sunlight was weakening into evening. Grace took the floral dress and washed it in the bathroom sink, the room dimming around her. She hung it to dry in the shower. She needed it for tomorrow, for first impressions. What did she want Alexander to do when he saw her? Come running in to give her a hug? Slap her on the back and say, 'Hey, sis, where have you been?'

Yes. All that and more.

Grace leaned on the wall, exhausted. She'd set it all up, a cog in motion. She'd even talked to Donald. The one thing she hadn't factored into her plan was if Alexander reacted in the same unconcerned way as his father.

TWELVE

The night had been long. Alexander got up before his alarm just to get out of bed and stretch. In the bedroom next door, Colin muttered and thumped as he did now and then, night ghosts calling to him. Alexander didn't ask what infiltrated Colin's dreams like that. He didn't want to know what made his strong and forthright friend so rattled.

Maybe night ghosts melted through walls to infect others? Alexander shook his head, scratching early morning hair out of his eyes as he waited for the sun to strengthen and the kettle to boil. He didn't have dreams. His nights were usually blank, but something had stirred last night. The remnants of it throbbed behind his eyes. He closed them to concentrate but could only see a black mass twisting and twirling. Nothing solid at all. He sighed, shook himself, made strong tea. It was luckily a workday with a job to finish and one to quote. Busy and long, hopefully utterly exhausting.

Stonemasonry was the family business but, Donald had said a decade previously, there was no pressure to continue it. Now Alexander realised his dad had said that with the conviction of someone who knew that his son, his only child, would pick up the rock hammer and nod with a broad grin to indicate *Don't worry, Dad, of course I'll follow in your skilled footsteps just like you'd followed your dad's and he'd followed his dad's...* It wasn't what happened, either in the past or now. Only Donald's father had been a stonemason, with Donald as his apprentice. Their forebears had been shepherds.

Alexander broke eggs into a pan and watched them turn. With his affinity for early mornings, maybe he should have been a shepherd? Instead, he'd declined his father's generous offer and gone to Glasgow to study architecture. The image of his father's broad face as he'd driven away aged eighteen and gleeful emerged at times. Lips curled into a faux smile, eyes squinting in dismay. His mother waved with genuine happiness for him, but his father was completely lost.

Well, Dad, Alexander thought as he hustled eggs onto his plate, *it was full circle.* Architecture led to an interest in restoration which, as inevitably as the snow, led to stonemasonry. Donald only had to be patient and wait for his prodigal son to return.

The eggs were good, a present from a client who had Buff Orpingtons in his backyard. Alexander ate them standing at the window, looking out across the street. Some cars were out, the couple across the road were walking their dog, a jogger leaned forward as he ran at the hill. An ordinary day had begun.

There was another image of his father's face that reared more often. Most days, in fact. The first time was when Alexander had come home for the weekend – the old home, the one in Selkirk where he had buried a toy truck in the back garden to see if it would turn into a skeleton – to ask about becoming his father's apprentice. The smile on Donald's face widened, his mouth had opened to show stubby mustardy teeth. His hand shot out like a lever and at once gripped Alexander's so hard he winced. The question was what his father had been waiting for since that day Alexander had driven happily off to university. It was like most days Donald still couldn't believe his luck. That grin showed itself regularly when Alexander turned up for work.

It wasn't what Alexander had thought. He had been twenty-five after all, a man used to setting his own agenda, even with the menial type of tasks flung his way at the commercial architects. Menial tasks didn't take long. There was plenty of time to take part in the office goings-on that were more interesting, but not his responsibility. He got to shadow project leaders, take minutes for seriously interesting meetings with town planners, and browse through the online library they kept of past projects. Once he calculated that he spent forty percent of his day doing his job and sixty percent priming himself for another.

He hadn't realised that, in Donald's industry, everyone did menial tasks, and one hundred percent of the job was *his* job. Donald set the pace, decades ahead of his son in technique and work-fitness. Alexander felt like a shapeshifter, albeit one that took months to morph. His skinniness became toughness, long limbs hardened rock-like. Donald had an agility that didn't match his bulkiness, and Alexander developed it as well. After the first year, they could both lean into a pile of raw stones and take the best one for the job, resetting the heap so it didn't tumble by a subtle shoulder or knee movement.

The jogger ran back down the hill, arms flaying to keep control. *You may be fit*, thought Alexander, *but I bet you couldn't lift rocks all day.*

'Talking to yourself again.' Colin lifted a hand as he passed the kitchen and disappeared to the bathroom.

Alexander ran his finger around his plate and licked the egg off it. Colin helped with the stonemasonry. He'd become more Alexander's apprentice than his father's. Out of Donald's eye, Alexander had things to teach. Sometimes, thanks to the only useful skill gained from university (research ability), he had things to teach that weren't from his father. *They worked well together, Colin and Alexander.* Donald said that a lot. *You boys work well together.* Alexander knew that he hoped Colin would stay on, becoming an ex-pat like his mum.

And what was with his mum? She could hardly eat for jitters at the barbeque.

Colin came in and leaned on the bench as he waited for his toast.

'Did you notice anything about Mum the other night?'

'Huh?' Colin yawned. 'What about her?'

Alexander shrugged. 'She seemed...I don't know.'

'She had your uncle there. She doesn't like your uncle. You've told me hundreds of times.'

'She's working for Uncle Euan.'

'That probably makes her hate him more.' Colin popped the toast and bit it.

'Jam in the cupboard.'

'I know.' He reached into the cupboard and smeared the slice before taking another bite. 'Better. Why's she working there again?'

'Uncle Euan's manager's left. Dad asked Mum to help him out.'

'Family guilt, then. She's stuck there until another manager comes along.'

'I don't think it was that worrying her the other night. Something else.'

'What?'

'I don't know.' Alexander slid into a kitchen chair. 'I think they're hiding something.'

'Who?'

'Mum and Dad.'

'Good!' Colin shook his shoulders in mock-horror. 'You don't want to know everything about your parents.'

Alexander shrugged irritably. Colin's parents were see-what-you-get types, Victorian retirees to the Gold Coast, happy and tanned. They wove around each other smoothly. Alexander was in awe of their easy way, their lack of emotion, and their late-night cocktails. It was as if they'd been working towards it all their lives. 'I'd like to know it, whatever *it* is.'

Colin pushed his plate onto the table and sat backwards on a chair. 'Why?'

'I think it has something to do with Norah.'

'Mate.' Alexander heard the carefulness of Colin's tone. 'You think everything has to do with Norah.'

'Why wouldn't it be?'

'Because other things happen. Problems occur. People argue and fight over stupid things.'

'You think they're fighting over what television station to watch?'

'I don't know if they're fighting at all. You're the one who said something was wrong.'

'Aye.' Alexander put his hands behind his head and stretched backwards, eyes on the ceiling. 'Sorry. Didn't sleep well.'

'Come on, princess.' Colin stood up. 'We've got to drive to Innerleithen today.'

'Right. And be back for that quote.'

'What time?'

Alexander reached for his phone. '5.30.'

'What's it for?'

'Don't know.'

'Who's it for?'

'Dad didn't say.'

'You have got the address, haven't you?'

'Got the address.'

Colin opened the fridge door and rummaged around for lunch. 'If I could get your dad to listen long enough, I want to tell him about a different booking system.'

'Good luck with that. You'll have to wait.'

'Until you take over?'

'I think so.'

'When will that be?'

Alexander was sorting his bag. 'When either Dad decides he's got enough money to retire or when his shoulders give out.'

Colin grunted. 'I'm going with the first one because I don't think he'll stop even if the second one happens.'

By the time they hit the highway south, the sun was glaring. Colin drove, his elbow on the windowsill with his fingers loose on the steering wheel, tapping to the radio. Alexander had the workbook on his lap. His father's handwriting was large and scrolled. He wrote as if he was being marked for neatness. It made him slow, but it was easy to read. It was an old-fashioned way of record keeping. They had one book between them, Donald writing notes in a spiral-bound miniature notebook that he later transferred. Whoever had the new jobs kept it in their van. Bookings on one page, quotes on the other side, the sort of system that kept their minds on the present while planning for the future. They started a new book every financial year. Alexander smoothed the paper in front of him, feeling the dents and scratches of pen marks. That he liked it so much, this feel of paper and pen, made him wonder if he was the one stopping Colin's technological ideas and not his father.

They arrived at the new job in time to get the full brunt of a summer shower. They stood in the doorway's shelter, the smell of fresh wood behind them as carpenters worked inside. Another new café. The Borders were full of them. Fix the outside, totally refurbish the inside, then invite the customers in with a menu rich in simplicity. Toasted sandwiches, soups, Empire biscuits to finish. Alexander glanced in and noticed a stack of old chairs in the corner, fresh from someone's grandmother. Everything that was old is new again.

'Right, it's stopped enough.' Colin was already at the truck, pulling a work shirt on over his flimsy T-shirt.

'Bit warm for that. Raining, too.'

Colin raised his eyebrows. 'Skin cancer, mate. Will you ever learn?'

Alexander grinned, grabbing another long-sleeved shirt and putting it on. *Cameron's* was embroidered across the pocket. It still felt like he was putting on a school uniform, but it was getting second nature now. Another Colin influence, but heavily backed by Julie. She'd even hugged Colin when he suggested it and got Donald's approval to get them all sun shirts.

The rain fled as they worked, the clouds with it. By lunchtime, the sun was directly on their backs. Sweat ran down Alexander's shoulders. He was working the other end of the wall while Colin had the ladder. He knew by Colin's silence that he too had realised it was a one-day job if they could go hard enough. Lunch was only time enough to eat thickly cut bread and cheese. Alexander wished he hadn't eaten anything. His mouth was dry, and his stomach felt tight. It was a relief to call it a day. He bought drinks while Colin packed the truck back up.

The routine was that Colin drove to a job, Alexander drove back. Mainly it was because Alexander knew the roads, the sneaky shortcuts, to get them home quicker. The other reason was more subtle. The truck was a heavy drive, difficult to get into gear most times. Colin had said nothing to either Alexander or Donald, but they both knew that Colin had had knee surgery back when he used to play Australian Rules Football. They'd both caught him rubbing his knee at the end of the day. He was doing it now. Alexander watched him put the cold bottle against the side of his leg.

'Are we going to make it in time?'

Alexander put his gaze back on the road. 'There's a road I know.'

'There's always a road you know.'

'You'll never be a local, Astle.'

'Don't want to be, Cameron.'

The roads were dry again. Alexander drove the van a little faster, keeping it to the line, making it rev higher. They were running later than he liked. Having time to survey a job properly, without the pressure of a client breathing down his neck or tapping at their phone every two seconds as if their time was the most precious of anyone's, was essential to a good quote. Too high, they lost the job. Too low, they lost the job for the workers. Alexander hadn't got it right for his first year or so. Donald had trouble teaching him the intricacies, having done it on his own for a long time. One thing he had taught his son was to allow plenty of time.

The gods are looking out for me, thought Alexander as they pulled into Macdonald Street at five twenty-five.

'What number?' said Colin, peering out his window.

'Seven.'

'You sure.'

'That's what he texted.'

'He's got it wrong.'

'I'll pull over and check again.'

Number seven was right. It was wrong, though. Number seven was a vacant block, building rubble piled in its middle decorated by weeds.

Colin laughed. 'Better give them a quote a bit more on the higher side.'

'He's got it wrong.'

'Text him again.'

Colin opened his door and stretched his leg out while Alexander texted his father. 'Seven. That's what the client said.'

'Maybe we have it wrong.' Colin stepped out of the van.

Alexander got out as well, slamming the heavy door. He looked up and down the street. Semi-detached all the way down one side. Random ones down the other. 'This is the street he said. Maybe it's a build?'

'Must be.' Colin walked over to the pile of rubbish and began poking through it, pulling out an occasional stone. 'Not with this lot,' he called back. 'Must be coming in from elsewhere.'

'We didn't need a site visit then.' Alexander rubbed his head. 'We need to speak to the architect.'

'They might come as well?'

'I don't know.' Alexander checked his phone again. 'Dad just said it's a quote on a renovation.'

'He might have clients mixed up.'

Alexander shook his head. Donald was slow but methodical, his book-keeping precise. He might have given them the information by text, but it was written somewhere, word for client word, in his navy-blue notebook. All of his dad's notebooks were navy blue. Only Donald could instantly tell them apart. He separated every client contact with a neat black line from a gel pen, dating it meticulously. Over the top detail, Alexander thought, when an email trail or a text conversation was already in place.

'Well, is anyone coming then?'

Alexander looked up the street again. A few people were wandering up and down, intent on their own business. Mostly getting home, he thought. Lucky them. 'Not yet,' he yelled back.

Colin walked over to join him. 'How long do we wait?'

'Fifteen minutes.'

'Right. I'm sitting in the van.'

Alexander leaned on the old truck's bonnet as Colin swung himself back on his seat. His head went down, emailing or messaging or using some sort of app. Alexander admired Colin's many contacts. Colin could spend hours a day keeping up to date with the world. Was it that he had a huge number of friends? You wouldn't think so, thought Alexander. The trip back to Australia mainly involved family. Whenever Alexander had said he'd go away for a few days so that Colin didn't have to keep baby-sitting him, Colin refused. 'I'm fine,' he'd said. 'I've caught up with everyone I need to.'

Now that they had finished for the day, Alexander let tiredness seep into his limbs. The truck was warm and pressed into his back where there was a little niggle of pain from all that driving. He pushed into it, idly scanning the street again. Only a girl this time, walking down the street on the other side. No, *floating*. Her long dress grazed the tops of her feet as she went, splitting open to reveal her shin as each leg thrust forward. The sun lit her hair golden, but as she touched any shadow, it darkened to ginger. Sunglasses hid most of her face, red cat-eyes that matched the straps of her tote bag.

Alexander stood away from the truck.

'What is it?' he heard Colin say.

The girl was crossing the road now, still a distance away but keeping the same pace. The street led to a major road into the city centre, but Alexander had the feeling that wasn't where this girl was heading. She shifted her tote to the other shoulder, flicking it around in a fluid motion that made her ear-length hair swing over one eye.

'Alexander? Are you alright?'

Now she was on the footpath, walking straight down its middle. He saw that the dress was patterned with large blue flowers, daisies perhaps – he wasn't good with flowers. The strap of her sandals flashed as her feet pushed forward. Beads?

'Do you think that's her?'

Ten metres away, the girl came to a sudden stop as if someone had blocked her way. Alexander saw her chest rising and falling as she took a deep breath in. She brushed hair away from her sunglasses, then lifted them up to balance on top of her head. Then she was walking again.

Colin was next to Alexander now. He felt his friend nudge his shoulder, but he couldn't turn away. The girl walked right up to them, stopping a metre away, her eyes on Alexander. Her eyes! He was looking into a mirror, one that had his late-spring bluebell-coloured eyes looking back. A flick of breeze spilled her hair over one of them and she pushed it back.

'Are you looking for a quote from Cameron's Stonemasonry?'

Alexander was vaguely puzzled why Colin sounded so aggressive. Was he speaking to the girl? He glanced at his friend. Yes. Colin had his arms crossed, frowning, but was definitely staring at the girl.

When Alexander looked back, the girl hadn't taken her gaze from him. She smiled happily, relieved, even joyful. 'Not really,' she said in a voice that mimicked Colin's Australian one. 'Hello, Alexander. I'm Norah.'

THIRTEEN

Julie heard the phone as she stepped through the glass doors. It was Alexander ringing his father, the tone something to do with Star Wars. Even she could recognise that. Donald had left his work bag strewn on the kitchen bench. His jacket muffled the phone noise.

'Donald, it's Alexander!'

He didn't answer. Deep in the house, she heard the shower and someone singing Tom Jones woefully. Julie went for the phone, but it stopped. She swept the bag onto a kitchen stool.

The day had not been great as a day off. Donald's term, that one. *Day off*, as if she froze on that day, contributing nothing to the world. When it was a *day on*, he spoke to her differently. *How was your day?* meaning *How did your wage-earning go today?*

Stop it. Julie put her handbag on the other stool. You make him sound like a wicked man.

She had started the day with a walk to William Wallace, collecting a week's worth of notes, and coming back down the hill through the forest again. She'd met Louisa, a group of lost Welsh tourists, and three large women on enormous horses who'd forced her into the undergrowth to avoid being stomped on. Louisa had been in the mood for a long chat, having completed her ten-kilometre daily work and was *winding down*. Julie knew she should invite her to tea. Instead, she felt for her phone, read out a non-existent text from Donald demanding her presence, and scuttled down the path to the sanctuary of home. She half-expected Louisa to steal one of the giant horses and come after her.

Home didn't have the feel of sanctuary. Even after two months of living in its modern glory, Julie entered gingerly. It was someone else's place, despite the transported furniture and the framed family photos. Their old house was grey and gloomy, Axminster maroon floors and a suffocating staircase. She hadn't realised she loved it so much until it was replaced by this gleaming, vacuous interior so carefully designed to be new and invigorating. There was no memory in the house. Could there ever be when so much was left in the other?

Julie baked biscuits for the men's lunches. That's what you did on your day off. It didn't matter that, these days, she couldn't eat a sweet crumb without it settling around her hips. Really, Donald couldn't either. She fed him the same way as she had since they were married, a labouring man's dinner with extra potatoes. I am complicit, she thought, in his growth. The smell of baking didn't linger in this house. Extraction fans, gigantic windows, great spaces – they took it away as if they forbid it. The old house held smells for days.

Was there a time during the day that she'd stolen for herself? An hour of reading? More like twenty minutes over lunch and then out she went into the garden to kill weeds and squash snails. Then over to the Wallace Monument Society's meeting to deliver the month's notes. Dorothy Waller, president. Georgie Magee, nee Waller, secretary. A mother and daughter show with a few cake-nibbling lackeys around the edge.

'Thank you, Julie dear.' Dorothy had large hands for a woman of her size. She seized things rather than take them. The notes looked diminutive on her palm as she flicked through them. 'Got any of those funny ones?'

'Sorry?' said Julie, trying to smile at the lackeys who kept their eyes on Big Dot.

'Aye, the funny ones. Here. Look. *Bravery is acceptance of things we cannot change.*' She snorted. 'You cannot say that about William Wallace.'

Julie glanced at Georgie, but she, too, was staring at her mother. 'I don't think the notes are all about William.'

Big Dot's eyebrows shot into her straight fringe. 'Then what are people putting them in for?'

Julie opened her mouth to explain. She chose a shrug instead. 'Ladies,' she said as she retreated into the fresh air. Oh, Dorothy would love to have her on the committee. She'd said it a hundred times. *Can't have too many lackeys.* Supporters. Dorothy had said *supporters*. Julie drove home the long way, ending up back in the unfriendly kitchen.

The phone rang again from a galaxy far far away. Julia swooped on it. 'Hello, Alexander, it's your mum.'

A beat of silence. 'Mum. Hello. Is Dad there?'

Julie tightened her grip. 'What's the matter? Are you alright?'

'Yes. I'm fine. I'm with a client. Is Dad there?'

'Hang on.' Julie half-ran to the bathroom. Tom Jones had been put to bed, and it was only Donald leaning over the sink, checking where he'd missed his whiskers. 'Donald! Alexander. Quick.'

Donald's eyes widened. He took the phone, his other hand

tucking the towel in more firmly at the waist. 'Alexander, have you a problem?'

Julie leaned on the architrave, her head in the steamy bathroom. Donald frowned.

'I'm not sure what you're talking about. Did I know what?'

Julie heard Alexander's voice, but not the words. He sounded calmer now, as if he'd sorted it out.

'I can look at my notes. I'm sure I told you her name. Okay, I won't bother. Listen, if you think the job is more trouble than it's worth, drop it, right? We've got plenty of work.'

Again, the tone of the phone voice was regular, nonchalant even.

'Okay, then. Anything else? No? See you here in the morning. We'll take the one van.' Donald checked the phone and handed it back to Julie.

'Was he alright? He sounded, I don't know, *shocked.*'

'Oh, aye. They're fine.' Donald chuckled. 'You get the odd one when you do quotes, although she sounded very nice when she rang. My bet is that she's gone ahead without thinking and the cost is going to be out of her reach.'

'And Alexander?'

'He'll over-quote if he doesn't think we can work it. Don't worry, love.' Donald leaned over to tweak Julie's cheek. 'I'll finish up here. Is dinner ready?'

'Donald, I've just got in.' Julie rubbed her face.

'So, we could fill our time doing something else?'

If he hadn't just treated her like she was three years old, she might have nodded. Instead, she felt a flicker of irritation pass through her. 'Not tonight, Donald.'

He turned back to the mirror, but she saw the disappointed look on his face. They'd had more sex in this house in the last two months than for twelve months in the old house. The walls of their previous house were thin, and their bedroom faced the street. Not that they had many neighbours, but they were more exposed than the solitary position of the renovated stables. Julie didn't know whether or not this was a good thing. Donald flounced about in his birthday suit. She still covered up, even at their most intimate.

'I'll get dinner on. You must be hungry.'

'Aye, always hungry.'

She took the phone back out to the kitchen, leaving it on the bench in case Alexander rang again.

ALEXANDER CLUTCHED the phone in one hand.

'What did he say?' said the girl in front of him, brushing flyaway hair from her eyes.

Alexander turned to Colin. 'He didn't realise.'

Colin pulled his friend aside. 'Listen, I don't know what's going on in that head of yours, but this is not what it looks like. She is not *your* Norah.'

Alexander looked back. The girl stood, one hand now gripping the other's forearm, shifting her weight from one side to the next. The sunglasses were down again. Her eyes may have been hidden, but Alexander knew – he *knew* – that she was his Norah. He edged back from Colin. 'Hello, Norah.'

They were the first words he'd said to her. She smiled, not broadly, not ecstatically. It had a tinge of *Finally!* Alexander grinned sheepishly back. Yes, finally. He'd been looking for her for so long, when she finally turns up his first response is to ring his father to confirm that she isn't a fabrication.

'I'm sorry to startle you.' Norah spoke quietly. He leaned forward to listen. 'I didn't know how to go about...' she shrugged one shoulder '... this.'

'Alexander,' said Colin, staring at Norah. 'Don't get sucked in.'

Alexander stepped closer to her. 'How did you find me? I mean, we went to Australia...'

'Well, it's quite a big place!' Her laughter was harsher than he thought it might be. As if she'd noticed the quick frown on his face, she stopped. 'I know you were in Australia. It's how I knew you were looking for me. You, and your friend, were in the newspaper.'

'You saw that? You saw that wee article?'

Norah shook her head. 'My friend did. And you went to a pub in Paxton.'

Alexander frowned, tipped his head towards Colin. 'Did we?'

'We did a lot of things.' Colin crossed his arms. 'Look, I don't know what you're doing but stop it. Got that? Leave him alone.'

'Shut up, Colin.' Alexander's hand closed into a fist, but he didn't raise it.

The girl watched them both, her face impassive. Her hand still held her arm casually. 'I read about you.'

'But...' Alexander went closer. She wore a thin silver band on her left wrist. It had slid right up her hand. She let her arms go and shook her hand, so the bracelet went back to her forearm. He watched it move. Her skin, he thought, is freckly like mine. 'But where have you been? How did you know?' He hooked his hair behind one ear. 'I've got so many questions.'

'Yeah, so have I.' Colin kept his distance. His face had darkened.

'It might be enough to know for now that I tracked you down because of your website.' Norah pointed to the pile of rubble in the centre of the vacant block. 'I made up a street number, but there could be a bit of work to do here, don't you think?'

Again, the laughter, this time lighter. Alexander grinned again. She was a joker, not like him, more like Colin. Was it an Australian thing, then? Making jokes when the situation could not get any more serious. 'We'll pass on this job, thank you.'

A couple of teenagers walked along the footpath. Alexander stepped back to let them on their way. Colin went forward, ending up next to Norah. In the few seconds he was alone with her, Alexander saw him lean towards her and say something. Norah frowned. Her face stayed turned towards Alexander.

'What did you say?' Alexander walked over to Colin, who put his hands up and shook his head.

'Absolutely nothing.'

'I've shocked you both,' Norah said, 'for different reasons, obviously.'

The wind swept an old paper bag along the path. Alexander watched as it hurtled by, tumbling over and skidding wildly onto the road. The thoughts in his head were doing much the same, hurtling and tumbling and especially skidding. They'd been working all day, but that didn't account for the weakness in his legs that was threatening to move right through his body. He wiped trembling hands on his pants. A headache throbbed behind his right eye. The longer he stood, contemplating Norah, the more ill he felt. He bent over, hands on knees.

'Are you alright, mate?'

Alexander nodded, nausea rising. He needed to keep perfectly still, breathing carefully in and out, in and out, until he was normal again. It didn't help. He closed his eyes.

'Alexander?'

Suddenly, a hand was on his back, a soft light hand. The scent of strawberries reached him. He opened his eyes to Norah's face level with his, her sunglasses pushed back on her head again. Her eyes were wide, and her eyebrows twisted towards each other. If he'd felt steadier, he would have reached out and smoothed her forehead. Instead, he gave her a small smile. 'I'm okay.'

'Shock. Told you.'

'Not content with lying to him, now you're trying to kill him.'

'Don't be stupid.' Her voice was hard. 'What's your name? Colin. Don't be stupid, Colin.'

Alexander shifted his head, so he was looking across at Norah. 'Aye, don't be stupid, *Colin*. I'm not dying.' He straightened slowly, Norah with him. 'I'm fine. Sorry.'

'This is a strange place to talk.' Norah waved a hand at the vacant block. 'Do you think we could go somewhere else?'

'You're not coming to our place.' Colin had his arms crossed again.

'You live together?' Norah glanced swiftly at Colin. 'Cute. But we don't have to go to your place. Just somewhere better than this.' She put a hand lightly on Alexander's arm. 'Somewhere for a drink?'

'Aye, I think we could.'

'I don't think so.' Colin spoke over Alexander who shook his head.

'Drink, Colin. Come on.' He pointed behind him. 'In the van.'

Alexander slid into the driver's side of the bench seat. His hands were clammy as he gripped the steering wheel. Beside him, Norah shuffled into the cabin, bringing with her that summer-fruit scent and a softness of skin as her arm accidentally touched his. She arranged her dress across her knees as Colin heaved himself in to sit beside her. 'Where will we go?'

'I'll have to park this somewhere and then we'll walk.'

She nodded, eyes to the road. Alexander glanced at her as

he started the truck. Her nose was straight, more like his mother's than his father's. He chuckled at that. Donald's statement nose on a slim thing like Norah? Inconceivable.

They drove without speaking, Colin's arms crossed again, and his feet shoved hard up against the front wall of his foot space. The town centre was busy. Alexander found a park further away than he'd wanted. Did it matter? The walk to the bar was downhill and breezy. I've got my *sister* beside me, he thought, the faint remnants of nausea disappearing.

When they got to the Cambridge, it was full of workers relieved to have finished the day. The courtyard had one table left. They squeezed three chairs around it. Colin reluctantly went to get drinks, narrowing his eyes at Alexander as if he thought someone would steal him before he got back.

'First things first,' said Norah, as Colin disappeared from view. 'Could I have your phone number? Because, this is nice -' she raised her eyebrows as she took in the buzzing yard of people '- but it would be great if we could get together sometime. Privately.' She stared meaningfully in Colin's direction.

'Aye. Here.' Alexander read out his number as she typed it into her phone. Long fingers, he thought, like mine.

'Here's your lemon.' Colin was back, sliding two glasses of beer onto the table and thrusting another glass in Norah's direction.

'Thanks.' She shrugged. 'I must be the only Australian in the world who doesn't drink.'

Colin sat down, arms folding immediately into each other.

Norah turned her gaze to him. 'You trying to show me your guns?'

'What?'

She nodded at his arms. 'Your muscles. When you sit like that, it pushes them forward.' She tipped her head to Alexander. 'Surely you guys know that trick?'

'No!' Alexander laughed again, his head back. 'Colin, did you know that?'

'It's a teenage trick.' Colin let his arms go and took his beer up instead. 'That's not what I was doing.'

'Right.' Norah took a sip of her drink.

Alexander leaned on the table with both elbows. She was forming right in front of his eyes. A sister who was funny and smart, able to take Colin down a notch or two, and beautiful. Oh, yes, she was beautiful. *Can I say that about my sister?* Alexander wondered. There was no other word for her. The way her hair sat over one eye now she had her glasses in her bag, and her long pale arms decorated lightly with that bracelet and a small band on her left index finger – beautiful. Colin didn't seem to think so. His scowl was so heavy his eyebrows almost buried his face.

'I think you'd better tell us,' said Alexander quietly.

Norah shifted in her seat and didn't look at him. 'Tell you what exactly.'

'Why now? Why, after all these years, do you show up?' *And present yourself to me,* he thought, *gift-wrapped and complete.*

'I told you that.' She swirled her glass, making the wedge of lemon in it ricochet. 'I saw the newspaper article. I heard people speak of you. I found your website.' She shrugged. 'It was easy.'

'No.' Alexander finished his drink and set his glass carefully back on the table. 'There's something else. Why now? It's only weeks since we were in Australia. It took months of planning to get us there. Why did you suddenly come over, with your flimsy bits of information guiding you? As my grandmother used to say, *It's a folly.'*

Norah pushed her glass away and sat back, her hands in her lap once more, her head up. She studied the cheerful crowd for several minutes. Alexander shifted uneasily. She turned to him at last, eyes watering. 'The person I called my mother died fifteen years ago after living a brain-injured life since I was a few months old. My so-called father died of a broken heart, but it took him forever to do it. I buried him last month. I don't have anyone else in this world, no aunts or uncles, no one. Until I found you in that newspaper. My brother.' She slapped the table. 'My *brother*.' She reached over and grabbed Alexander's arm. 'You came thirty thousand kilometres to find me. Why wouldn't I do the same for you?'

Alexander felt her grip strengthen and then let go. Norah stood up, her tote bag on her shoulder. A single tear ran down her left cheek. Her hand shook as she wiped it away.

'I've got to go. I'll see you soon.'

As she swung away in the crowd, Alexander rose to follow, but Colin pulled him back down into his seat. 'Let her go.'

Alexander sat. He didn't need to look at his friend to know that he was shaking his head in disbelief. Alexander had heard the pain in Norah's voice. She was telling the truth; he could feel it.

FOURTEEN

Grace made it back to her tiny apartment before the real tears came. She flung the dress off and lay down on her bed, holding the pillow under her chest and letting her grief soak into the quilt. She sobbed silently, as she knew she did when she was anguished. That's how she described it to herself. *Anguish*. She'd felt it two times in her life already, on both her parent's deaths. It was a singular emotion, one confined to a real catastrophe. It happened when the ordinary emotions wouldn't do, when sorrow was not deep enough, when sadness was too shallow. She hugged the pillow tighter.

It wasn't meant to be this hard. She'd told Alexander her life's truth and it hurt. Leaving Australia was leaving Grace behind and starting again with Norah. Leaving the anguish. Yet it had followed her. How unfair was that? One question from the man sitting with his long, pale fingers wrapped tightly around his beer, and she felt freshly wounded.

And what if her pain repulsed Alexander?

She'd found him, she couldn't lose him. He needed a sister, was ripe for one. She could see it in every pore. He wanted Norah. She *was* Norah. What if he had a moment of doubt and thought how improbable the situation was? It would destroy him. It would destroy her.

Her body gradually calmed. Sweat dried, making her shiver. She sat up, pulling on a T-shirt and shorts. More time had gone by than she'd realised. Her stomach hollowed as she breathed. She had a shower to wash Norah's make-up away then made a dinner of sorts out of bread, cheese and an over-ripe tomato. She'd have to do proper groceries before long. She sat the sandwich in front of her and stared at it. Alexander. She couldn't eat until she'd contacted him.

Her text was answered straight away.

Eleven o'clock. Can you find Spoon? Good café. He'd sent a map link.

See you then.

Grace put her phone on the kitchen bench. It dinged. She didn't look at it, couldn't look at it. All this time thinking how wonderful their reunion would be and she'd ruined it. Why couldn't she now just let herself be taken in by Alexander's joyous, heartfelt emoticon? Her skin was tingling. Goose over her grave? Allergic reaction to the tomato? She shook her hands to loosen them up and walked a few paces around the tiny kitchen. The apartment's walls were high and narrow. They squeezed in on her. She shut her eyes and practiced a slow, deep breathing until the tingles faded and her face relaxed. When she opened her eyes, outside had turned a soft navy, and streetlights kept the road below warm. She sat on the windowsill, leaning her forehead against the closed glass. People strolled by, oblivious to their spy. Grace let the apartment darken around her until her leg went numb from being curled up on the sill.

She was meeting Alexander alone tomorrow. This would be the real test. The shock would have gone. Colin was probably talking to him right now, telling him the truth as he saw it. Would Alexander come along with a steely look in his eye?

Perhaps he wouldn't turn up at all? She had to be prepared for whatever happened. She was Norah, and Norah would not leave that café table until she was sure Alexander had no doubts. If that man Colin was watching with his raven eyes to see if she shed Norah on the way back to her accommodation, he would see nothing.

Fatigue hit her, as solid as sandstone. She staggered to bed, slipped her clothes off, and fell into the sheets. She slept without dreaming.

TEN O'CLOCK and Grace's phone pinged. She woke, sat up. Why was it light? It was too early, too wintery, to have that powerful sense of summer in her room. She blinked and remembered where she was. The unfamiliar shape of the room's closet morphed into Scotland.

I can be earlier? read the text.

Grace pushed the hair away from her face. *I can't. See you at eleven.*

She bounded out of bed, dithered on the spot until she could think clearly. Shower first. Something to drink. Her mouth was as parched as if she'd been walking in the summer suburbs without carrying a drink bottle. She ate a banana, hoping to settle the shaking in her hands.

Ten-thirty. She'd hung her clothes in order of brightness. A gathered skirt caught her eye. She matched it with a white top that dangled tassels across her stomach. Her make-up took the longest, but she was quicker with the eyelashes. Finally, she parted her hair cruelly on the side. It kept wanting to go back into the middle, springing joyfully until she sprayed it under control. The cat-eye sunglasses, the leather tote, and the softening roman sandals. Ten-fifty.

It was humid in the street, a thin grey haze keeping the heat in. Norah slowed her pace and swung her bag from her hand to stop patches of sweat forming on her back. She was fifteen minutes late climbing the stairs to *Spoon*. Alexander sat in a corner, his eyes on the street below. She breezed up to him. 'Hello.'

The worry in his eyes made Norah reach a hand towards him.

'I'm so sorry I was late. I slept in.' She sat down, shaking her head. 'I never sleep in.'

'Jet lag?'

'I guess so. I wouldn't know.'

Alexander rubbed his face with one hand, as if trying to remove his concern. 'You've never been here before?'

'I've never been anywhere before.' Norah coughed as her voice caught. 'I've barely been out of Victoria.'

'This must be strange to you then.' Alexander nodded towards the outside.

'Not as strange as I thought it would be. I watch a lot of BBC.'

Alexander smiled briefly and was quiet.

Norah looked around the café, twitching her shoulders at his silence. The interior was like what she saw in her own city, scattered round tables with austere floral decorations, menus on blackboards, a bar stretched at the back. Even the same sorts of people were there. Men in neat shirts and jeans, women in floaty scarves. No children, as if they didn't exist. A group of university staff members, their lanyards prominent, at the largest table in the centre, nodding their heads earnestly as a balding man spoke with his hands.

'It's my favourite café.' Alexander passed her a menu.

'Did you go to uni around here?'

He shook his head. 'Glasgow. What about you? Did you go to university?'

Norah took a deep breath in. 'No, I didn't.'

The waiter interrupted them. Norah ordered the first thing on the menu, her head suddenly skittish.

'It didn't help me much,' said Alexander, leaning forward a little to put his forearms on the table. 'From architecture to stone masonry.'

'You don't want to be a stonemason?'

'Don't worry, I do. I came at it the long way around.'

'I think that's okay. We all go around in circles for a while.'

'What is it that you do?' Alexander's face blotched. 'You don't have to tell me. If I'm asking something that's none of my business.'

'Alexander.' Norah slid her hand along the table, her bracelet scratching quietly on the wood. 'This is why we're here, isn't it? To find out about each other.'

He looked at her, those smoky eyes in sharp focus. 'Colin said I was to drill you.'

'He doesn't believe me, does he?'

'No.' Alexander shrugged. 'I do.'

Norah's stomach lurched. She put one hand on it. 'Thank you, Alexander. That means a lot.' She gave him a small smile. 'What do I do? I'm a secretary for a legal firm. *Was* a secretary for a legal firm. I quit after Dad died.'

Alexander moved back to let the waiter in with coffees. He watched her walk away before saying, 'Your dad died. What about your mum? How did they...' He stopped, stirred two sugars in his drink.

'You want to know about my mum and dad?'

'That's the biggest part of the mystery, isn't it? Did your mum and dad ever say you were adopted? Or... anything else?'

Alexander pushed his hair behind his ears, still staring into his cup. 'It's odd.'

'Alexander, I don't know everything. Really, I don't.' Tears threatened to destroy her make-up. Norah patted them away. She took a deep breath in, letting it out slowly before she spoke. 'They didn't tell me anything. I saw your picture in the paper. I worked out that I was in the hospital thirty years ago, too. And... well, I just knew.'

He nodded, eyes unblinking. 'They stole you from the hospital, do you mean? What sort of people were your parents?'

A man at the next table paused in his conversation at Alexander's raised voice.

'Not that sort! I don't think so, anyway. I don't know anything anymore.' Norah grabbed his arm. 'Listen. Two weeks ago, I was the only one left in my family. Then I got to know about you. Understand? I have come over here because I knew you were looking for me.' She held her breath, closing her eyes for a long moment before looking at him.

Alexander stared, first over her shoulder, then back at her. She kept his gaze until his eyes softened. Only a little, but she knew he was listening.

'You don't have any other siblings?'

She shook her head. 'You?'

'No.' He rubbed his face again.

'There was a car accident. My father had a broken arm, but my mother was seriously injured. See? I always imagined that my father had a family and then overnight it was gone. He had me, a baby. He had his wife, brain damaged. That's how I see him. Broken. Going off the rails.' Norah took a gulp of coffee. 'Maybe he did do something, but we'll never know now he's dead.'

The silence was hers this time. She traced the rim of her cup until Alexander put his hand lightly on hers. 'What was it like, growing up with that?'

She put her hand down, making his move, and shook her head. 'It sounds bad, but it wasn't. Mum was easy to look after. She was in a wheelchair for most of my teenage years, but she never complained. She couldn't talk much after the accident, but she could use her hands to tell us what she wanted. She moved around by herself, at least for the first few years.'

'Norah.' Alexander had her hand again. 'I'm so sorry.'

'Oh, don't be sorry. It was okay, really. It could have been worse. I spent a lot of time looking after her, but it's a privilege, right? She would have cared for me if she could have. So I cared for her.' She drank more coffee. 'Mum died when I was fifteen. Her injuries, you see. They made her vulnerable to ordinary things. The doctor said it was pneumonia.' She drained the cup.

Alexander nodded. A picture was forming in his mind, she could see. Maybe he saw her in a parallel version of his own life. Did he imagine a pretty house in a green garden? A smiling father, a benign mother? A little girl in a floral dress, dancing around the kitchen to make her parents happy? Norah could see it herself. The little girl had long, pale-red hair tied back in a ribbon that her father had lovingly but crudely formed into a bow. The mother couldn't laugh but there was a relaxed look on her face and the one arm that still worked tapped a joyful rhythm on her thigh. Norah kept the image in her head as she smiled at Alexander.

'That must have been very sad.' His voice was low.

'Yes, it was. But I had a good friend...' Her tongue felt thick. 'Tell me, though. What about... your parents?'

He grinned then, upright and happy. 'Our parents, Norah! We need to tell them.' His posture dropped. 'It will be a huge shock.'

'What, more than yours?' Norah tapped him on the arm.

'Aye.'

A trickle of cold ran down Norah's side. She turned to see that it wasn't spilt water. Nothing. Just a triggered nerve. 'Why?'

'Your shadow.' Alexander shrugged.

'What do you mean?'

'Your shadow is everywhere, always. There's a photo of you in every room, mostly the same one. You in your cot, waving your arms at the camera.' Alexander moved his shoulders in imitation. 'Even in the new house. I thought Mum would pack them away when they shifted.'

'She kept them out...'

He nodded. 'They aren't as noticeable in the new house. It's much bigger, in a way. Or brighter. Something about it. The old house, now everything was dim in there. I'm not sure why your wee photo stood out more.' He looked at her. 'Probably because you'd been living in that house. I didn't think Mum would ever shift.'

Norah shrugged. 'Maybe she's over me.'

Alexander shook his head once, sharply. 'You don't get over that.'

Norah frowned. She almost said, *don't tell me about grief, Alexander Cameron. I have lived with it every day. Your mother doesn't have the monopoly on it.* Instead, she said, 'I'm so sorry.'

'Not your fault, is it? Someone's fault, but not yours.'

'No.'

The food arrived. Norah studied her plate and was glad to see she'd ordered something she liked. She pushed it away for the moment.

'Listen, Alexander.' He didn't look up from his plate. 'We have a choice to make here. Right now, right at this point in time, we can honestly say we have no idea why -' she stopped, coughed '- why I went missing that day. All we know is that somehow I ended up with my parents and they are now dead. I've come home to you, Alexander. Isn't that enough for now?'

Bacon steam invaded her nostrils, making her stomach gurgle. Alexander hadn't moved. His head was down slightly, his hair had escaped their hooks and hung over his face. The skin was pale again, cream with faint freckles that Norah suddenly wanted to touch. Her bacon cooled. Alexander tipped his head up, decided. 'Aye. It is.'

Norah nearly sank off the chair in relief. She gave him a wide smile and started on her late breakfast, feeling oddly like they'd scored a massive win together. Over what, she wasn't sure. Fate? The little girl whirling around the family kitchen lodged in her head as she ate, keeping the happiness on her face. Alexander seemed to pick it up. He tucked into his eggs. They didn't speak until they'd finished their ferocious munching and had ordered more coffees.

'So,' Alexander said.

Norah waited, but he said no more.

'So,' she said, 'I don't want to talk any more about me. Tell me more about you.'

'Should we walk?'

'If you like.'

They paid and made their way outside. The haze was almost gone. Sunshine patched the footpath as they walked. 'I went to university in Glasgow,' said Alexander.

'What's it like? Glasgow?'

'Red instead of blonde.'

'What do you mean?'

'The sandstone. The buildings are red.'

They went up and around the streets as he talked. Norah didn't catch all that he said. Sometimes the traffic was too noisy, other times it was the constant flow of pedestrians. She guessed most were tourists. They had a stunned look about them as they tried to take in the sights and leave nothing unnoticed. Even when there were quieter moments, Norah listened to Alexander's cadence rather than his words. His sentences rolled, reminding her of hills. At times, he used words she didn't know at all. She smiled at them. He smiled back and kept talking, getting faster and using his hands in places so he sometimes gently knocked a passer-by.

Even though she couldn't take it all in, Norah got the drift. Alexander had lived in Selkirk with his parents until he left for Glasgow. His father, Donald, had continued the job of his father before him. His mother, Julie, a nurse's aide, worked in medical practices as a secretary and later as a manager. Alexander had scores of friends through school and uni, many who'd left Scotland. Girlfriends? Here, his voice dropped, and he talked instead of moving to Edinburgh where he moved easily into social circles. Colin came to work with Donald through a sponsored apprenticeship, and then he'd had an Australian friend. It was a nice life, one full of movement and hard work.

Alexander stopped. People moved past him, frowning. Norah was a little ahead before she realised his voice had gone. She turned back to him. 'What is it?'

'All that I've said.' He pushed his hands into his jeans pockets. 'It sounds like you were never on our minds.'

'It was a long time ago.'

'I want you to know that we never stopped thinking about you.'

Norah felt that prickle of cold run its icy finger down her back again. 'Thanks, Alexander. I get it. I'd forgive you if you had, right? It's a long time to be sad.' She tipped her head. 'Is that why you left your home to go to Glasgow?'

He looked at her for a moment, then grinned. 'No. They have better pubs.'

They started moving again, Alexander taking up his story.

There was an uncle, Euan, and his much younger wife. No grandparents alive, not on either side. Julie had a brother in South Africa. There were cousins he'd never seen.

'That's a shame.'

Alexander shrugged. 'It's what happens when you have relatives in far-off lands.'

Norah felt the icy stroke and shrugged it away. The sun was warm on her back. They were close to Holyrood. Alexander pointed to the towering hill to their right. 'We could climb that?'

Norah held a foot out. 'I haven't got the right shoes on.'

Alexander shrugged. 'Next time.' He grinned. Next time. She smiled back.

They continued around the park, Alexander still going but faltering. He'd had a dog when he was young - had she? He used to go horse riding - could she ride? He learned guitar for ten years - did she play an instrument?'

Perhaps it was the shaking of her head that finally silenced him. They were walking back up the Mile now, the street even busier than before. Buskers drowned out any other sound. Alexander took her elbow to steer her down a side street, into the sanctuary of a pub. It was still noisy but not bagpipe-loud. He ordered drinks, remembering what she'd had the evening before.

'What do we do now?' he said after his first sip.

Norah clutched her hands together under the table. What had she imagined would happen next? She'd presented herself at the door, but she hadn't stepped inside yet. Alexander swirled his beer. 'I don't know,' she said finally, truthfully.

He gave a slow nod. 'You'll have to meet Mum and Dad. They need to know.'

'Not yet, Alexander. Please. I need a bit of time.'

He dipped his head again. 'For what, exactly?'

'I'm not sure.' She looked around. 'I've just got here. It's a long way from anything I know. I feel like I need to...'

'It's alright, Norah. Don't explain.' Alexander drank deeply and put his glass down with a thunk. 'There's time. Only, the more time that passes, the more I have to fake it. Aye? I work with my father. I see my mother most days. I'm not sure I can keep you a secret for long.'

Dizziness threatened Norah. 'A week? Can you give me until next week?'

'Next week.'

'Thanks.' She left her breath out. 'That will give me time. Give *us* time.'

'What will we do this week?' He smiled. 'I could stop work for the week.'

'No. Don't.'

'No?'

'I need time, Alexander. And space. You know? I need to be alone for a few days, sort out things.' She indicated her head. It felt stuffed full of images she couldn't untangle, Alexander's words and his presence and his family. Her *new* family. Did this mean she had to forget her old family? She stood. 'Would you mind if I went now?'

He looked pained.

'I'll see you again soon. Next Wednesday, after work. Yeah?'

After spending hours talking, Alexander seemed to have run out of words. His face was blotching again. She leaned down and kissed his cheek, little stabs of stubble on her lips.

'Goodbye,' she whispered.

He smiled then, his eyes bright. She left before the urge to hold him was too great to resist.

FIFTEEN

'Is he sick?'

Colin took his time climbing out of the van. Donald's hands were on his hips, making him wider than ever. 'Not really. Just needing a day off.'

Donald frowned. 'Needing a day off? He's either sick or on holidays. A day off?'

Colin folded his arms, then let them fall to his side. He tilted his head as if contemplating the garden bed beyond Donald. Alexander had been sitting as usual in the kitchen when Colin had risen. His first morning words were, 'I'm seeing Norah at eleven o'clock. Tell Dad I'm not coming in.'

Colin threw his hands up, feeling early morning fuzz in his head. 'Tell him yourself.'

'Colin, please. Tell him for me.'

The drive to Dryburgh hadn't been long enough to make Colin's fumes abate. He wondered whether Donald could see the anger that was cooking his skin. 'In Australia,' Colin said, careful to keep his voice neutral, 'we call it a mental health day.'

'A mental-' Donald shook his head, turning to face his wife

who stood at the sliding doors looking puzzled. 'What the... Julie, a mental health day?'

Julie shrugged. 'They weren't around when I was working back home.'

Colin felt the word *home*. Julie had been here for decades. She still felt the pull? Home. Was it needling at him? 'We've only got the Patterson's job today. We'll manage with the two of us?' Colin only just remembered to put the question mark in. It was Donald's business, as much as Alexander and Colin knew they could manage it, well, differently.

'No choice. We'd better get on.'

Donald gathered his things from his truck and threw them into the van. Usually, if two of them and not three were on a job, they took the smaller one, Donald driving, lumbering along the road as if deadlines were a myth. That Colin was to drive... he saw Donald's heavy face and stiffened back as he parked himself on the bench seat with an elbow out the window and a gaze fixed on the landscape. Colin lifted a finger to Julie, who waved back briefly. Donald was a stony sculpture as they drove away.

The Pattersons were on a lonely stretch of road past Traquair. Donald didn't speak until the news came on the radio. 'Is he alright, then?'

The news had been about George Pell. Colin frowned. 'Cardinal Pell?'

'Alexander. Is he, you know, alright?'

Colin pictured Alexander frying eggs, his eyes bright. 'Yes. He's fine.' He clamped his lips closed as if they might betray him.

'I wondered. The trip to Australia. All that. Looking for Norah. I thought it would disappear, that he would be alright when you didn't find anything.' Donald sighed, long and hard. 'He was obsessed.'

Colin nodded. A good, right word.

'What was he like, in Australia?'

Colin hesitated. Frail, he wanted to say as another good, right word. Disturbed, even. Desperate, always. 'He really wanted to find out what happened,' he said finally, eyes on the quiet road.

'Wouldn't we all.' Donald rubbed his hand over his face, just as Alexander did when he was thinking. 'I don't know why it's getting to him now.' He sat up. 'Does he know something? Has something turned up on the internet?'

Colin gripped the steering wheel. 'There was nothing new when we went to Melbourne.'

'He had the same information that we did?'

'Yes.'

Donald slumped. 'I tried to not think about how it affected him.' Colin could hardly hear him over the van's engine. 'It was so hard.'

Colin's shoulders tensed. They'd been working closely together for nearly two years, and he'd heard nothing from Donald about Norah. He glimpsed something now, a deep pain that edged Donald's voice, something sharp that still cut, like having a knife sewn into your guts. If you moved even slightly the wrong way, it sliced your soul, glistening beads of new red on its steel. And yet Donald was always so *here*, so *in-the-moment*.

A deep shame rocked Colin. He knew that nothing went forgotten. Why would he even think it possible? He had his own agony. Why wouldn't others have the same? This *Norah* person, turning up as she had, presenting herself as the solution to Alexander's burden, was evil. Despite the likeness to Alexander (those eyes, pale but intense), it couldn't be her. No one turns up in your backyard after thirty years, not in such a spectacularly beautiful way. You could almost hear the muzak when she walked towards them, thought Colin. Mancini's *Mr Lucky*, Andre Rieu's violins, possibly a bit of Whitney Houston in there somewhere. Yes, she was a vision. A *calculated* vision.

Alicia had taught him well. Fake it 'til you make it. It had taken him years but, in the end, he could see her disguise. It was in the way she glanced at him to see if he was looking at her, the tiny movements of her body as she straightened her posture, the biting of her lips to keep them ruby. There was not a gram of Alicia that was her true self. Not until the end, heralded by the minute mistakes in her make-up. It was a harsh lesson he learned about not believing what you see.

'Watch the road, lad.'

Colin moved the van back into the centre of the lane. 'Sorry.'

'Maybe you need a mental health day.' The smile was back in Donald's voice.

Colin relaxed. 'I'm perfectly fine. If you're offering me a day off…?'

'Day off? Not likely. I've never had a day off myself. Can't afford to…'

Colin let Donald drift into his monologue on the hard life of a self-made man. He'd heard it before, not only from his boss. His father had been the same, drumming into his children that the road to success was paved with sweat. He'd heard it from his uncle as well. It wasn't unexpected that his cousins all went for cushy public service jobs, and that his sister had made sure she married a man who'd inherited his father's money. Colin had felt the same about avoiding the life his forbears had had until he discovered the adverse pleasure of hard work and the satisfaction of a clean, straight wall. He smiled to himself. Donald went quiet as he strained to see down the road.

'Turn here.'

Donald was all business, his seat belt already off, hands

flexing in anticipation. Colin parked the van and set his mind to the tasks ahead.

THEY HAD A LATE LUNCH, the job almost finished. Donald lay on the grass, stretching his back out before they tackled the last bit. It was the silent signal for Colin to take over, let the younger man have a go, watch the apprentice hone independent skills. Colin didn't mind. He stood up, sliding his lunch bag back into the van. His phone was in his hand, empty of messages. He was on the verge of calling Alexander to see how he was, but he was also on the verge of letting it all play out. There had been no doubt in Alexander's mind that morning that he was off to see his sister. Maybe there was now?

An hour later he knocked the last stone in place, checked for stability, and packed up their tools. Donald was asleep now, bathed in sun that was slowly roasting his face. Colin crouched and shook him gently. Donald raised one hand from his belly. 'I'm awake,' he said, clearly only just. 'Give me a moment.'

Colin went back to the van and leaned against the warm bonnet. His muscles were pumped, as they were after a day's work. It would take him hours to relax, for the weariness to sink into them. He felt his best at the end of the working day, adrenaline-sharp. He snatched his phone up with unintended force as it rang.

'Colin.' Alexander's voice blurred into the noise in the background.

'What's up, mate?'

'Come for a drink.'

'I'm still at work.'

'Come for a drink.' It wasn't the noise making Alexander's voice blur. 'Come on.'

'I can in about two hours. Where are you?'

There was a rustle, as if Alexander was holding the phone against his chest. 'Castle bar. I think. Pictures of castle here.'

Could be anywhere in Edinburgh, thought Colin. 'Should you go home? Sounds like you've been there too long.'

'Don't want to go home.'

'Is she with you?' Colin glanced back at Donald, who was on his feet now, doing some limbering exercises.

'Norah?'

'Yes. Is she there?'

'No. Norah not here. Gone.'

Colin felt a thrill of triumph. 'Gone for good?'

'No, gone for now.' A glass clinked against the phone.

'Alexander, why are you drinking by yourself?'

'I'm not! I found friends.' Sound roared through the microphone as men cheered.

'Do you actually know them?'

'Aye. Now I do.'

'Mate, you haven't told them about Norah, have you?'

'Norah!' Colin imagined Alexander lifting his glass. 'No, should I? Aye-'

'No, Alexander, don't say anything. Hear me? Nothing about Norah.'

'Norah!' Another cheer, but only Alexander's voice.

'Listen. Go home. Catch a cab if you have to. I'll get us some take-away.'

'Take-away!'

'Are you listening?'

'Aye, Colin. Going home now.' The phone deadened.

Colin turned to find Donald staring at him from the back of the truck. 'Everything all right?'

'Oh, yeah.' Colin lifted his phone as if Donald wanted to see its good condition. 'The ex-pats wanting me to join them. Some of them have had the day off.' He rolled his eyes, hoping Donald would see the joke.

'A day off? Maybe your friends are a bad influence on my son.' Donald grinned and went around to slide into his seat.

Colin switched his phone onto silent in case Alexander rang again and Donald answered to ask him about the infamous mental health day.

It took an hour to get back to Dryburgh and sort the van, another hour to drive back to Edinburgh. Colin let himself into the apartment to find Alexander prostrate on the couch, arm over his head and the television on some sort of English game show. The place smelled of mustiness, alcohol and eggs. He opened up the window in the living room, sucked in a few gulps of fresh air.

'Did you bring any food?' Alexander's voice was flat.

'Not yet. What do you want?'

'Anything that has fat and salt in it.' Alexander shifted so that his head was up on the arm of the couch. 'How's Dad?'

'Wondering where you were.' Colin shrugged. 'Easy job though. All done.'

Alexander nodded. 'Patterson's, right? Knew you two could handle it.'

Colin sat on the arm of the couch near Alexander's feet. His friend's eyes were rheumy. 'You going to tell me what happened?'

'Can you get food first? I'm empty.'

'Have you been drinking all day?'

'No. I had second breakfast with Norah.'

Colin waited, but Alexander's attention drifted to the game show. He pushed himself upright. 'So I'll go out and get something.'

'Thanks.'

Colin stumped down the stairs again, went to the nearest

take-away, and came back with fish and chips. Alexander sat up as if he'd brought lobster, tearing the paper away and burning his fingers on a chip. Colin sat on the floor, stretching his legs out under the coffee table and pouring vinegar on his fish. 'Okay, tell me now.'

'Nothing much to say, really. She told me about her parents. They're both dead.'

'How convenient.'

'She knows you don't believe her.'

'She's got some sense then.'

Alexander took the last chip. 'I told her about growing up. Mum and Dad. Stuff like that.'

'What did she say?'

'Not much. She listened.'

'What did she look like?'

'Like she did yesterday. Different clothes.'

Colin shook his head. 'No, what did she look like when she was talking to you? Did she, I don't know, look around to see if anyone was staring at you or touch her ear as she talked?'

'Why would it matter if she touched her ear?'

'It's a sign of lying.'

'You want to know if she was lying? If I could tell?'

'Yes. Could you?'

'Cross my heart, Colin. She was genuine.'

Colin wiped his hands free of salt on his work trousers. *Genuine.* She'd burned herself into Alexander's soul, that was clear. 'You don't think this is all too coincidental? I mean, we've just got back here after looking for Norah and, hey presto, Norah's followed us back.'

'It was because we went back that she found me. That's not a coincidence. That's how it should be.' Alexander scrunched the paper up.

'Why did you go drinking then?'

'I met Neil. He was with Ross. We went back to the pub.' Alexander stared at the television again.

Colin frowned. 'What happened after you talked? Or did she go to the pub with you?'

'No, she left after we ate. She said she needed some alone time.'

'Ah.'

Alexander leaned forwards, elbows on knees. 'What is *ah*, Astle? This has been pretty big for her, too.'

'I bet.'

'Come on, what do you mean?'

'I'm reading her code language, Alexander. *Alone time* translates to her planning what to do next. How she's going to act next time she sees you. There will be a next time?'

'Wednesday after work.'

'Right.'

'You can come.'

'I will.'

'Colin...'

'What? I'm only looking out for you. Someone has to.'

'No, they don't.'

'Take it from me. Yes, they do.'

Alexander dropped his head, then lifted it up to the television again. 'Would it have made a difference? With Alicia. If someone had been looking out for you?'

Colin stood, snatching at the paper ball. 'Who knows? It didn't happen, so I'll never be sure.' He lobbed the paper out of the doorway into the kitchen where it hit the top of the bin.

'Coffee, thanks.'

'You ingrate.' But Colin went into the kitchen, putting the kettle on and picking the paper up to fire into the bin again. As he spooned coffee into mugs, the grains spilled from his unsteady spoon. He brushed them on to the floor in one swift, hard action. No, it wouldn't have made any difference to him if someone had been watching him when Alicia struck him down. He was hooked, lined and sinkered. Just like Alexander.

He turned, a coffee in each hand, and Alexander stood in the doorway. He had that post-drinking pallor, a dehydrated weariness. 'Where do you want this?' Colin held a mug up, dripping coffee on to the floor.

'I've got to tell Mum and Dad.'

Colin chilled, tried for a joke. 'It's okay, I'll clean it up.'

'But she said to wait a week.'

Colin set the mugs down, scrubbed the floor clean with a cloth and threw it into the sink. 'Good idea.'

'What if they find out before I tell them?'

'How are they going to do that? Unless you take the whole week off. That'll drive your dad spare. He'd be up here in a flash.'

Alexander came right into the room, picking up his drink and holding it with both hands. 'I should wait a week?'

Colin nodded. A week would be enough to bring out the truth from Norah. 'Definitely. Come on, mate. What if it turns out to be a hoax?'

'It's not.'

'Okay, you keep saying that, but what if it is? Do you want to put your mum through that?'

Alexander shook his head.

'Or your dad, for that matter.'

'He wouldn't care. It's past history to him.'

Colin thought of Donald looking out the car window. 'I wouldn't be so sure about that.'

'He didn't ask a single question about her when I got back!'

'He didn't have to, did he? Your mum did all the asking.'

Alexander slurped his coffee. His face was sickly, a wan yellow highlighted by the bright orange cup in his hands.

'I'm going to suggest something.' Colin leaned his backside on the bench. 'You aren't going to like it.'

'What is it then?'

'If we're going to meet with Norah again, then we – you – need to be prepared. We need to see whether she's prepared to go the whole way to prove that she's who she says she is.'

Alexander put the mug back on the table. 'How do we do that?'

'We get her comfortable, let her tell you more about herself. Maybe we go out for dinner, make her feel like she's at home. Then we hit her with the big questions. Where's her birth certificate? She must have one. And when would she like to have genetic testing?' He'd got louder as he spoke, and it took a moment for his voice to fade from the little room.

Alexander traced his finger around a stain on the table. 'You think she won't answer.'

'I expect her to have some sort of answer. I want to see her reaction. It might be the last we ever see of her.'

Alexander's head moved, as if he was flicking hair out of his eyes. Colin studied him. No, there was something else. As Alexander's fingers started a staccato drumming on the laminated surface, Colin realised what it was. His friend didn't want to know the truth if it was not what he wanted to hear.

'It has to happen, Alexander. For your mum's sake.'

It took a while, but finally there was a clear nod. 'Genetic testing?'

'The only way to make sure. Sibling testing first so your parents aren't involved.'

'How do you know all this?'

'It's called the internet. It's not hard to find out.'

Alexander stood up, pushed his chair back, thrust his hands into his pockets and left the room. Colin heard his bedroom door slam. It would not be an easy week.

SIXTEEN

Julie was ready for work well before Donald. She'd risen early, chased out by Donald's volcanic snores. She sat outside near the barbeque, watching swallows shooting across the sky, trying not to think of the day ahead.

Donald came looking for her. 'You right, love?'

'Yes. Just finishing my tea.' She leaned back to look past him. 'Your lunch is on the bench.'

'Thanks.'

She raised her cup in acknowledgement. He turned away to the kitchen, and she heard burnt toast being scraped into the sink. She wriggled her shoulders. Not enough sleep. Her neck and her skin prickled irritably at the noise behind her. Donald set a plate on the bench, knocking it so it wobbled loudly. He was so clumsy in the house, so large and ungainly. Before she could stop herself, she was thinking of Euan.

'No.'

'What was that, love?'

'Nothing, Donald.'

She wished it was nothing. It was one month since she'd

started working for Euan. One month of keeping her head down to the computer screen or concentrating on reception or casting her eye over the patients in the waiting room in case one of them was in urgent need. He'd appear, disappear. Her peripheral vision caught him, let him go. She felt like a hunter, acutely aware of his every move. Or was she the hunted?

'Going now, love.' Donald had inhaled his breakfast. He stepped through the door and came to give her a kiss. She could smell toothpasty mint, sandy dust from yesterday's clothing, and the sharpness of coffee spilt down the side of his thermos. 'I'll be seeing you.'

'Is Alexander going to work?'

Donald shrugged. 'I haven't heard. The boys are up north today. I'm by myself in Kelso.' He turned to go, his bag ready in his hand.

'Do you mind? Working alone.' Julie shrugged. 'It wasn't meant to be that way. Alexander was your assistant.'

Donald put a dismissive hand up as he walked to the truck. 'Nothing goes according to plan, not really.' He clambered in, waving heartily, and drove carefully across the stones and away.

Julie stared at the tea leaves marooned in her cup. Did Donald really mind working alone? Probably not. His overall cheeriness with the world should have been a comfort, but Julie often found it wasn't. Not today, anyway. She stood up and put her cup in the kitchen before making a last trip to the bathroom. Donald came home from work with the same smile on his face as he'd left with. His ideal night in was a chair-sit in the living room with the television on car-chase movies. Most nights, he fell asleep watching the action. She liked that he didn't follow her around, demanding attention, but sometimes... oh, a deeper conversation about their son or a ratty one on climate change or even some sort of considered opinion on Theresa May would be enough for Julie. Something to fill the empty evenings on long summer days.

The drive to Melrose was quicker than normal. Julie realised that she was earlier than she'd meant to be, despite the prolonged think at the outside table. The practice was warm and dark. She went around flicking lights on and opening the waiting room windows. One stuck, peeling paint jamming the runner. She stepped in as close as she could to put her weight behind it.

'Here, let me.'

Euan's arm brushed hers as he reached to help. She couldn't move, chairs blocking her escape. In the few seconds it took for him to steer the pane up, she smelled heady aftershave, laundry powder, and fresh print from the newspaper he'd placed on the sill.

'There,' he said, head tilted down to her and a swift smile on his lips. He took his paper and moved into the back of the surgery.

It was a long time since Dr Euan Cameron had been on a political trail, but it easily took Julie back to it. Earnest speeches on television, firm handshakes with his constituents, lists of promises if only he was elected. The youthful version of Euan was confident, shrewdly handsome, powerful, especially after his prestigious award. The older version had flashes of the same, tempered by what had happened and his failure to gain a seat.

Julie shook her head, rubbed her hands where the window-pane had dug into them, and unlocked the front door. She stood at reception and fired up the computers, aware of Euan in his room, her empty office to the side and the general lack of people anywhere near the building. She answered emails still standing at the desk until Meredith came in the door and slung her sad bag under the desk.

'Good morning,' Julie said, shaping her voice to be just that right amount of managerial efficiency.

'Not so good when you haven't slept all night. Neighbour's cat howling his love across the fence. Love? I threw my slipper at him. Yowling don't get you love, I said to him. Just ask me on a bad day.'

Julie nodded, unwilling to ask more. Meredith was full of bad-luck stories. One day, Julie's guard would be down, and she'd tell Meredith the worst of all stories just to witness the shocked realisation that really terrible events had never happened to the dull receptionist.

The real day started with Mr Turner having a heart attack in the waiting room. From her office, Julie saw his body slink out of sight and Meredith leaping from her chair to assist. Julie checked that first aid management was underway – secretly pleased that her insistence on updating the team's competence was turning out to be of use – before knocking firmly on Euan's door. They had a signal for catastrophe, two firm knocks followed by two quick ones. As she went back up the corridor, Euan came out behind her, long-striding until he was level.

'Mr Turner,' she said, not slowing. 'Collapsed but conscious.'

Euan nodded as he steamed past. One hand stroked her arm. She flinched, but he was already kneeling on the carpet. The gesture was consoling, she told herself. A pat turned into a caress by his momentum. She tried to concentrate on Mr Turner's painful pallor and was glad to leave for the phone when Euan requested an ambulance.

Events like Mr Turner's weren't unusual, not in a country practice where people sometimes staggered half-dead into the surgery, preferring to see their own doctor than call out for unknown care. Mrs Barton, for example, had waited until nine o'clock opening time before almost crawling in with her temper-

ature at thirty-nine degrees and barely able to breathe for the
pneumonia-induced constriction of her lungs. Miss Campbell
hadn't actually made it. The butcher found her on the footpath,
her hand clenched around an appointment card. Mr Turner was
at least alive and improving according to his hospital report.

No, things happened in doctors' consulting rooms, but Julie
couldn't settle. The rest of the bookings were for quietly ordinary complaints, as if the rest of Euan's patients didn't want to
cause further trouble. He was the lone doctor, Ravi taking a day
to travel to London to see his mother. Julie prowled behind
Meredith, who frowned at the attention. Cynthia came in later
and Meredith told her about Mr Turner in such an understated
way that Julie was suspicious that Cynthia had already been
told. She couldn't fault either of them, though, and was careful
to say to Meredith as she left for the day, 'Well done on your
response to Mr Turner. Very professional.'

It was rare to see Meredith give an un-scornful smile. It
made Julie smile back, an action she must not have done that
day as it pulled at a patch of dry skin on her cheek.

The waiting room emptied. Cynthia gave a last tidy and
left. Julie felt the air thicken as she turned off excess lights and
went back to finish up. Euan was in his room, his door open, the
click click of his keyboard a soft sound in the empty building.
Julie answered one last email and powered off. Her in-tray was
empty, her desk clean. She slung her bag over her shoulder.

After hours, the phone went to Euan's mobile. She heard it
go and paused. There was a chance she could leave, no reason
not to, but then Euan came out of his room with the phone stuck
to his ear. 'Aye, yes. I see. Alright. Ten minutes?'

'Everything okay?' Julie said as he put the phone down.

'Mrs Laurie. She's on the floor, may have been there for a
while. Trudy saw her through the window.'

'Shouldn't you call the ambulance?'

'She's diabetic. I'll do an assessment first.' He paused, looked at her through the top of his blue-rimmed spectacles. 'Could you come with me? Sorry to ask but there could be some social issues as well.'

Julie nodded automatically. She went with the doctors on house calls if she could, usually to see to the domestic side of things if the patient had to be taken away. Occasionally, she actually had to help in a quasi-medical way. Staunching blood. Stroking foreheads. Supporting necks. What the practice really needed was a permanent practice nurse, someone who was still registered, as well as a manager, but they'd battled on without one forever. It would not change now, especially after upskilling the staff.

'We'll go in my car.'

Julie waited until he had his travelling doctor's bag and followed him to the sleek SUV. For a split second she thought about getting into the back seat but, of course, slid into the front. She tugged her skirt down to her knees, patting it firmly. Euan glanced at her hand as he started the car. Heat rose in Julie's face.

Mrs Laurie lived alone in a house under the enigmatic looming of the Eildons. Trudy stood at the front door, twisting her hands. Of all the people to see someone in need, Julie thought, Trudy was the worst. No, she hadn't tried the back door. No, not the windows either. It wasn't right, was it, rattling the locks of a house that wasn't hers, not even if its occupant was lying panting on the floor and beckoning with an arthritic finger for help. No, she didn't wish to intrude, but she had to ring Dr Cameron because he'd know what to do, what with his vast experience and calm manner.

'Thanks, Trudy.' Julie steered the woman away down the path. 'Thanks for the call. Dr Cameron has it now.'

'Trying to help, trying hard.'

'Yes. Thank you.' Julie even shut the gate on her before Trudy got the idea and left.

Euan had gone around the back where the door was open. He unlocked the front for Julie. She pushed hard to open it. Not a regular entrance, she thought as three cats, startled by the light, rushed back to the kitchen. Mrs Laurie now had her fingers curled around Euan's arm in a thanksgiving grip. 'Julie?' he said, nodding slightly at the clamped hand.

'Mrs Laurie,' Julie said, kneeling on the floor next to the old lady. 'What's happened?' She gently put her hand on top of Mrs Laurie's and wriggled her fingers into place to be the one in Mrs Laurie's grip. Euan moved his arm away. Julie felt the warm pressure of it leave.

Mrs Laurie, it seemed, had tripped over one of her cats, twisting her ankle on the way down to the lush mat she now lay on. That had been breakfast time. Her thin hand was cold despite the warm day. Euan examined her attentively. When he was satisfied she could move, Julie helped him heave the trembling Mrs Laurie into a chair. Julie made her tea and sandwiches while they waited for the ambulance.

When the cats were fed, and the house locked up for the duration, Euan and Julie watched the ambulance as it disappeared towards the hospital.

'What happened, Doc?' said a neighbour, one of many standing in a respectful crowd along the footpath.

'We aren't sure.' Euan said, unlocking his car.

'Will she be alright? I mean, she hasn't been alright since Bertie died, but will she be alright after this?' The neighbour's eyes were too bright for the solemn occasion. 'Perhaps she'll need to go into care?'

Property-hungry galoof. Julie scowled at the woman who had the decency to blush.

'We'll have to see what happens.' Euan shrugged non-committedly. 'If you'll excuse us...?'

'Of course, Doc.' The woman stepped backwards with, Julie thought, a slight bow. Euan's presence had that effect. It was why he'd nearly made it to parliament. Nipped at the post, she thought the expression was, by some conservative local with a petulance for Highland cattle.

'Julie?'

She moved forward at his voice, sliding into the passenger seat and clicking on her seat belt before he'd said his last good-byes to the crowd. 'If only,' she said as Euan got in, 'they'd been more interested in why Mrs Laurie hadn't come out of her house all day.'

'They're not to know everything.' Euan started the car.

'Oh, but some of them would. It must be nosey Parker's day off.'

Euan gave a low chuckle. 'Which one is nosey Parker?'

'Rosie Doyle.'

'She's visiting her sister in Glasgow.'

Julie turned. 'How do you know that?'

'I'm one of those who knows everything.' He glanced at her with a smile before pulling away from the kerb.

Julie studied his profile for a moment before looking back to the road. Over the decades they'd known each other, he had changed very little. Sure, there was some slight sag of his skin around the jaw, but he had kept the sharpness of his cheekbones. He'd always worn glasses. This pair gave focus to eyes that were a deeper ocean blue than Donald's or Alexander's. It could also be that his dark hair, despite its silver layering, contrasted fiercely. Donald always said that Euan took after their Irish father while he collected his mother's freckled skin and sandy hair.

Donald had been more like Euan in his youth. Not in

colouring, but they were both tall although even in their twen-
ties it was obvious that Donald would not keep lean. His work
muscled him up, and soon his body matched the broadness of
his shoulders and hands. Hard work made him hungry and
thirsty. There was no time for delicate wine drinking or
counting of calories in Donald's world. Euan, on the other hand,
kept his fine suit figure as he travelled around the countryside,
first working then campaigning and then back to medicine. Julie
supposed that a fat doctor wouldn't be quite right, although
she'd seen plenty. That image wouldn't suit Euan.

They pulled up at the surgery before Euan spoke. He'd
turned the car off, released his belt, but did not try to get out.
'So,' he said as if their conversation had only been interrupted,
'Alexander found nothing when he went to Australia?'

Julie shifted uncomfortably, the seat belt suddenly pressing
heavily on her chest. She pushed the button, so it sprung away.
'What do you mean?'

'I do know why he went back,' Euan said softly. 'I heard him
talk about it before he went away.'

'Thirty years, Euan.'

'Yes. Did he find anything?'

Julie shook her head 'Nothing at all.'

Euan nodded. His face was expressionless. She hadn't
wanted hysterics but, surely, he could have given her a hint of
melancholy?

'Thirty years.'

'I keep track, Julie. I know how much time has gone by.'
Was that irritation in his voice?

'How much do you wonder, Euan? How many hours of
every day do you think of her?'

He gazed at her then, a doctor's analysing stare. 'I don't,
Julie. You know me to be blunt.' He opened the car door and
went to get out. 'I don't think of her at all.'

Julie struggled out of her side, her chest still tight despite the lack of a seat belt. She flicked her hair so it settled on her shoulders and tugged at her shirt. Euan's presence made her feel like she needed to make more effort, over what she wasn't sure. She held her handbag under one arm as he walked around to the surgery door.

'I need to update Mrs Laurie's record,' he said, unlocking. 'Are you coming in?'

She lifted her chin. 'Why is it,' she said clearly, 'that you don't think of our daughter at all?'

Euan pushed at the heavy wood panelling until the door swung wide, revealing the inside of the waiting room as a homely, comfortable place of refuge for the sick. 'Because,' he said, head turned towards his surgery, 'she was here in a time and place long ago. Other events happen, each decade swamps the next.' He looked over his shoulder at Julie. 'I locked her in to that time and now she isn't present. She doesn't, for the here and now, exist.'

Julie felt her body try to slump to the ground. She tensed, determined to stay upright. The arm clamping her bag to her side was sweating. She used one finger to move some hair out of her eyes. Her mouth had gone so dry she didn't want to speak in case her voice betrayed her.

'I'm sorry, Julie.' Euan was half behind the door. 'I know that's not what you wanted to hear. Maybe I'm a cynical medical man, but sometimes you have to keep things in the past.'

Julie nodded stiffly. 'I'll see you tomorrow.'

'Thank you for your help tonight.' He tipped his head.

She turned before he had shut the door, feeling for her car keys, trying to focus back on Mrs Laurie's accident to see that they'd covered everything. Had she got someone to feed the cats? She could check on them tomorrow on her way in. Best to be sure about these things.

She was halfway home when two tears ran slowly down her cheeks. She wiped them away, biting the inside of her cheek, and blinked sternly until her eyes were clear. *Oh, no you don't, Euan Cameron*, she thought. *I'm not wasting any more sorrow over you.*

SEVENTEEN

Grace hadn't left her apartment for three days. She sat now on the dangerous windowsill, her back against the side edge, one leg tucked up under herself. Today's skirt was paisley, its swirls mauve and green. The frilled edge of her top sitting on her hips was lifting slightly in the occasional breeze, exposing a line of pale flesh. Grace smoothed it down, feeling how hollow her stomach was. She'd eaten very little since her lunch with Alexander.

It had taken days, but she was feeling better. Good, even. Wearing these clothes helped. They made her feel taller, svelte, impartial. She kept her hair parted to the side and developed a habit of casually rolling her head to move her hair out of her eye. She'd caught herself in the bathroom mirror, rolling and flicking. It wasn't bad. Nothing too effectual. She noticed that she'd developed a few different gestures since coming to Scotland. Holding her forearm with her other hand so that her arms were loosely arranged in front of her. Standing with her feet together but pointed slightly out, plie. Grace had never done ballet, but she could have. Norah felt that type of elegant.

The alarm on her phone went, a soft song that lilted and

lifted until Grace hit the stop button. For a blurry moment, she wondered why she'd set it. Of course. Getting ready to be Norah.

It took less time than originally, although Grace was still experimenting. She curled the ends of her hair under using a rolled brush and the dryer so they tucked into her neck. The same cream foundation on her face, but a smoky-blue application of shadow around her eyes. Brown eyelashes this time, just as long as before but slightly thicker. The finished effect was Norah, ever so slightly different. Can't have Alexander getting used to one look, thought Grace, as she slipped into a second pair of sandals. Wedged, they drew her up, so that Grace had to duck to check the mirror. She wondered: is this really me?

She dabbed at her mahogany lips before going back to the kitchen and dialling Alexander.

The first ring went to his message bank. Grace frowned. She put the phone down, walked around the tiny flat. That's quite normal, she reasoned. He's working. The phone's in the truck. His hands are covered in mortar. He has his music on. He's not yet thinking about meeting Norah for drinks.

She made tea, not drinking it yet, and tried again. The phone gave three rings before 'Hello.'

It was ridiculous how relieved she was. 'Alexander! It's Norah. Where do you think we should meet - '

'This is Colin.'

Now Grace heard the lower timbre-ed voice. She swallowed, tapped a nail on the bench. 'Colin. Can I speak to Alexander?'

'He's talking to a client. So, no, you can't.'

'Could you please ask him to ring me back?'

'What about, *Norah*?' The disdain was heavy in his voice. 'So you can check that he's still hanging on every one of your words?'

'No, we're having drinks and -'

'Why did you give him your number if you weren't going to text him back?'

Grace thought of the messages she'd left unanswered. *What are you doing now?* then *Are you finding your way around okay?* Only after the second one had she put Norah's clothes on and waited for the third that didn't come. 'I couldn't. I was...' *trying to let go,* thought Grace '... busy,' Norah said.

'Listen, whoever you are. Stop. Whatever it is that you're trying to do, just stop. You're going to break him.'

'I'm not going to break him.' Grace felt the flare of anger she needed heat her face. 'I'm giving him back his sister, moron. Can't you see that's what he wants?'

'It doesn't matter if that's what he wants! If it's not true, then he can't have it.'

'What makes you think it isn't true?'

Her calm voice seemed to make him pause. Grace flicked her hair back, keeping the phone carefully to her ear.

'Because it can't be. That's not what happens.'

'It can happen, Colin. It has happened.'

'Not if I've got anything to do with it.' She heard him take a breath. 'Drinks are off. We're too busy, and we need to get the van back to Dryburgh for Donald. Goodbye, Norah No-one.'

Grace listened to the finality of the beeps with her mouth slightly open. She put the phone down slowly, letting it slip from her fingers. Her hand brushed her skirt. All dressed up and nowhere to go.

Nowhere in Edinburgh, that was.

She glanced at the time as she turned on her laptop. *Cameron's Stonemasonry* featured on the map of Dryburgh, an easy find. Dryburgh was an hour away, even from the airport. The airport was about 30 minutes from the centre of Edinburgh. Within two or three hours, she could be in the heart of her new family. She glanced at the clock. In time for dinner.

The spasm caught her by surprise. She bent over, groaning, clutching her stomach. If she went to Dryburgh, she would meet Donald and Julie, and there would be no turning back. And yet it had to happen. She couldn't keep meeting Alexander in cafes for the rest of their lives, even without Colin's interference. Grace wiped her mouth and pushed herself up. Once it happened, once she met Alexander's parents, Norah would take over and Grace would be gone. Was she ready for that?

Grace glanced down at her clothes. She plucked her skirt from where it clung to her legs and gave it a shake. She went to the bathroom, drank from the tap, and brushed her teeth. Two coats of lipstick, a top layer of sealer. More deodorant, a spray of perfume. She tucked the corners of her hair back under with the rolled brush.

Before she left, she squashed her old clothes into a shopping bag and pushed it into the back of the wardrobe along with her backpack and walking shoes. She hadn't brought much, so Grace was easy to dispose of. Norah packed her tote and locked the window. Pulling her shoulders back a little, she left the apartment, turning the three keys, and made her way to the airport.

'WHO RANG?' Alexander combed his hair from his hot face. The sun had burned into them that day, punishing on their backs.

'Just a query about a job. They sounded like they didn't know what they were talking about.'

'Do we have to do a quote?'

Colin shook his head. 'No. I think that one's finished.'

'Good. I couldn't stand the thought of more work tonight.' He held out his hand. 'Phone.'

Colin handed it over and watched as his friend scrolled for messages. Nothing, as Colin well knew. No history of the previous call either, but Alexander wasn't looking for that. 'What's up?'

'She hasn't texted or called.' Alexander checked again. 'I don't know where she's staying.'

'Mate, she's gone.' Colin tried his gentle voice. Alexander shook his head. 'Mate. Listen. She was a fraudster. You're better off with her gone.'

Alexander walked away, still fiddling with his phone. Colin watched him warily. When the phone went to Alexander's ear, he called out, 'Don't do it.'

Alexander lifted his other hand but didn't turn around. Colin heard him talking, but in the explanatory way of a voice message. Alexander tucked the phone into his pocket and crossed his arms.

They were near a wood about forty-five minutes from Dryburgh. The old home they'd been fixing sat skeletonised in the yard. One wall was half-repaired, the others gaped. Colin liked these sorts of jobs, ones that created something. They'd be spending weeks on it, not all at once, as the owner could only afford bits done at a time. A shame, really. There was something about the thick stand of trees that reminded Colin of Queensland. The likeness was only in the shadows, for none of that vegetation could prosper in northern Australia. Colin had sat in the shadows to eat lunch, watching the patterns on his skin as leaves waved back and forth, thinking of the damp darkness of the rainforest near his parent's home.

Alexander turned, worrying at the top button on his shirt until it gave. His face shone with sweat even though they'd finished working nearly half an hour ago. The owner of the ruins had come to visit, picking his way around the wall, asking detailed questions of Alexander who patiently answered everything.

'I packed the van while you were mucking around with Mr Renovation Man.'

'Patrick.'

'What?'

'Patrick is the owner.'

'Great. So has Patrick got any more money?'

'Only enough for us to keep on this wall.'

'He'll be 103 by the time he finishes it.'

Usually Alexander would roll his eyes at statements like that. There were so many clients who had jobs that couldn't be finished. Colin and Alexander often joked about the waste of money. Today Alexander frowned, pulling his phone out again and sighing.

Colin wiped his hands on his pants. This was worse than Alexander in a relationship. *Lovelorn* was how he described Alexander's reaction to girls in general, except when Alexander realised what they were really like. Take Brenda, for example. Whatever was going on between Norah and Alexander was not love or lust, but it was still pathetic. Queensland flashed again in Colin's head. The great escape. He rubbed his head. He must be tired. 'Come on, let's go.'

Alexander climbed into the cabin, and they trundled towards home. The back roads were stovepipe-narrow. They had to reverse several times for tractors, once for a raging BMW that bulldozed its way through. Even on the main road, the traffic slowed for roadworks. The sun dropped to an uncomfortable angle. Colin tried the air-conditioner, but it hadn't been turned on since 1972. 'Cameron, you need a new van. One with a few mod-cons.'

'Tell that to Dad.'

'I wouldn't waste my breath.'

'When we take over, we'll trade this one in.'

Colin turned sharply. 'When we take over?'

'Aye.' Alexander kept his eyes on the road. 'When the business is ours.'

Colin was quiet.

'Is it a possibility?'

Colin shrugged. 'Mate, I hadn't thought that far ahead.'

'Dad won't be able to keep going forever. I'll need a partner.'

'I'd have to move here.'

Alexander laughed. 'You are here! You've been here for nearly two years.'

'That doesn't mean...'

'What? That you aren't going to stay?' Alexander passed a car in front. 'What else were you going to do with your life?'

Yeah, thought Colin. What am I going to do with my life? He had the skills now to return to Australia and set up as a stonemason. There would be work, although he'd have to travel to find it. It was coming to decision-time, at least on paper. His family was in Australia. That hadn't stopped him fleeing when he could, running from the ghost.

'I don't know, Alexander.'

'Well, it's not happening yet. You've got time to think. Dad's not moving on until Mum forces him to stop.'

'She won't do that. Your mum's too nice.'

'Aye. Eventually, though.'

'Eventually is a long time.'

Alexander nodded.

Colin looked out the window, forcing himself to imagine this country his home. Undulating green hills, even in summer. Rain like waterfalls, even in summer. Sheep with black faces, horses in the middle of towns, Selkirk bannock for breakfast. Would he miss the vast flatness of outback New South Wales, the glitter of Sydney Harbour, the affectedness of Melbourne's inner-city lanes? If he returned, could he cope with daily reminders of Alicia in every molecule of Australian air? He shivered.

'Visitors.'

Colin turned to the front as Alexander wheeled the van onto the white gravel of the yard. Dr Cameron and his botoxed-wife. Elizabeth was handing a bunch of flowers to Julie who stood, still in her work clothes, at the kitchen door. Donald was in a pair of shorts – nothing else – and offering a glass to his brother. Julie accepted the flowers, raised her hand to her son, and stepped backwards into the house, Elizabeth following her daintily. By the time they'd parked, retrieved their bags, and locked the van down, Julie was outside again with a tray of drinks. She slid it onto the outdoor table and beckoned.

'Our homecoming present,' said Colin.

Alexander checked his phone again. 'I'll ring one more time.'

Colin waited until his friend had left another voice message, this one a little less eager, a little more defeated. They walked together to where Julie was emerging from the house again, a selection of cheese and biscuits on another tray. 'Just in time for pre-dinner drinks.' Her voice was slightly higher than usual.

'Thanks, Mum.' Alexander gave his mother a peck on the cheek.

'I'll be back in a moment. I need to change.' Julie patted Colin's arm as she went by. He raised his eyebrows at Alexander, who shrugged.

'Mum got flowers?'

'She helped Euan out last night. Above and beyond the line of duty!' Elizabeth laughed, a tinkling sound that couldn't be real.

'Oh?' Donald sat heavily on a chair. 'Did she now?'

'An after-hours call. Didn't she tell you?' Euan sipped and wiped froth from his moustache.

'You make her work all hours, Euan.'

'Well, this time,' Elizabeth said, putting a light hand on her husband's arm, 'Euan wanted her to be thanked properly. Flowers have a way of doing that, don't you think?'

Colin took a glass from the table, keeping his eyes down to not look at Alexander, who surely would be staring blankly at his aunt.

'She's a worker,' Donald said, smiling.

'You make her sound like a horse, Dad.'

'No. No, I don't, boy. I mean, she's a good worker, one that puts in-'

'Only joking.' Alexander raised his glass to his father.

'Joking about what?' Julie sat in the chair next to her son. She'd changed into a summer dress, fresh pink lipstick glossing her mouth.

'I'm teasing Dad. You look nice, Mum.'

'Thank you, Alexander.' She smiled, tossing a shirt in Donald's direction before reaching over to take a glass from the tray.

They sat in silence as Donald slipped the shirt over the broad expanse of his stomach. Now that he was sitting still, Colin felt his muscles give. He stretched his legs out and rolled his shoulders. He noticed Alexander doing something similar. Donald was pulling at his sleeves, wincing slightly at the movement.

'Shoulders hurting?' Euan's voice was mild, as if Donald's shoulders were hardly worth mentioning.

'Only the left one, thanks, *doc*.' Donald sat up a bit. 'I don't need you assessing me every time you lay eyes on me.'

Euan shrugged slightly. 'I can't help it. You'd be doing the same if we were facing a stone fence.'

Donald grunted.

'I had a wonderful day today.' Elizabeth moved her glass around as she spoke, as if trying to capture the whole table. Her husband turned to her, frowning. Donald's mouth opened. Colin grinned at Alexander, who shook his head.

'Tell us about it, Liz,' said Julie kindly, glaring at her son.

'Well, I went to help with the show...'

Colin felt his body relax to fit the contours of the chair. Elizabeth's voice, despite its occasional shrillness, had an unrelenting rhythm, a soprano-ed lullaby. He put his glass down and let his hands fall to his lap. He had an aunt similar to Elizabeth, one of those who had to have attention, one who others let have the attention for the sake of peace. That aunt was rarely invited to ordinary family events which made her worse in the times they were all together. At least Elizabeth was entertaining to watch with her blonde waves falling to her shoulders, and the flashing of many diamonds on her gesticulating hand. But even that couldn't stop Colin from closing his eyes for a moment.

'Who's this?'

Colin sat up, blinking at Julie's voice. Elizabeth stopped her story mid-flow, tossing her hair and frowning as Donald pushed his chair back. 'I'll go,' he said. 'Could be a client.'

'It might be Louisa.' Julie was on her feet as well.

'Doesn't she drive something smaller?'

The car had crept into the yard and parked at an awkward angle behind the van. Whoever was in it kept it running as Donald made his way down the steps. He stopped as the car turned off, looking back to his wife and shrugging as the car door remained closed.

Colin's neck prickled.

The car's windows were tinted, but there was a slim silhouette of a person inside. Someone tall and slender. A woman, by the way she tipped her head, allowing the fall of her hair to blunt her shadow.

Alexander stood up, his chair toppling over backwards.

The door opened. A pale leg emerged, the folds of a paisley skirt draping over it as the woman stepped out. Colin looked at Alexander, whose face was mottled.

'Are you alright?' Julie said at Alexander. He didn't answer but tipped his head in the strange woman's direction.

Donald took a step forward. 'Can I help you?'

She pushed the car door closed with a gentle click and moved towards the house, stopping after a couple of steps to stroke the hair from her face.

'No,' said Colin, starting forward.

'Leave it.' Alexander reached for his mother's hand. Julie took it, staring out into the yard.

'Hello,' said the woman, taking her cat-eye sunglasses off and smiling at Donald. In the sunlight, her hair was gold. 'I'm sorry to take you by surprise.'

'She's Australian,' Julie said softly to no-one in particular.

The girl put her hand on her chest, the slim bracelet sliding down her arm. 'Hello,' she said again. 'I'm Norah.'

The mild summer breeze took her voice and spilled it over her family, who stood still and were drenched.

EIGHTEEN

'Norah...' Donald's arms hung at his side.

'Yes. That's right. I've talked to you on the phone.'

Julie heard the familiar lilt of the girl's voice. She shook her head, trying to get a grasp of what was happening. Alexander's hand was tight in hers. She tugged at it, but he wouldn't let go.

'Did I?' Donald said.

'Yes. I'm sorry about that. I wanted to get in touch with Alexander. With all of you. With Alexander first.'

'And did you?'

'Yes.' The girl pushed her sunglasses up onto her head. 'Yes. I did.'

Donald turned, slowly, stiffly. Julie felt Alexander squeeze her hand and finally let her free. 'Alexander?'

Alexander stepped forward, lifting his hand as if to calm his father. 'I met with Norah before. I was meant to meet her tonight. Not like this.' He glanced at his mother. *Stricken*, was how she would have described him if asked. 'We were going to talk more about...' He waved his hand again.

'This is quite ridiculous.'

Donald shifted his open-mouthed gaze to his brother. 'Euan...'

'It's all right, Donald.' Euan came forward to stand at the top of the steps. His arms were crossed, his head down so he looked through the top of his glasses. 'Are you saying, Miss, that you are Norah Cameron?'

'Yes.' Norah's voice was firm, but Julie noticed a tremble of her hand as she stroked at her hair. 'I am.'

'Can you prove it?'

'She doesn't have to prove it,' said Alexander loudly. 'Look at her. This is Norah. My sister.'

Julie frowned. The scene was happening around her. It was like watching television, a particularly unlikely soap opera when people who had been killed off in a previous episode were now back on with the excuse of amnesia or mistaken identity or plastic surgery that made them look different from how they used to be. Except, she thought, this girl looks exactly how I imagined my Norah would be at thirty. Hair and eyes like Alexander. A slender Cameron form, similar to Donald's mother. And some of Julie, there, in the tip of her head and the pursing of her lips. I do that, she thought. I do that very same thing.

'Alexander, I appreciate your feelings about this-'

'I'm sorry, Uncle Euan, but you don't. It's not exactly your business, is it? I don't like to be rude, but this is one for our family, not yours.'

'Euan's trying to protect you, darling.' Elizabeth was at her husband's side, looping her arm through his. Euan didn't move. 'Aren't you, Euan. Euan?'

Euan shook his head once and Elizabeth fell quiet.

Julie's legs were suddenly wobbly. She reached out a hand and Colin was first to it. He gripped her around the waist, and she couldn't help but lean into him. It was so strange, the feeling that her legs had disappeared. 'Someone get a chair,' Colin said above her. They manoeuvred her into a seat, but it didn't help. Dizziness gripped her. Euan's firm hand was on her back, pushing her head forwards. She took deep breaths in and waited for the world to settle.

'Alexander, tell her to stop. Look at your mother!'

Colin's whisper was not meant for Julie, but she heard it all the same. 'No, wait.' Julie made herself sit up and wiped drops of sweat from her forehead. 'Let her come forward.' She stood, relieved to find her legs active again. 'Norah, please.'

The girl stepped forward, the long skirt clinging to her legs. She paused next to Donald, but he only stared, one hand on his head. A few more steps and she was in front of Julie. A floral perfume, a hint of cloves, came with her. Julie breathed it in. Was this the grown-up version of how her baby would smell? No longer Johnson's baby soap and newborn skin, but something with depth, with an enigma. She smiled at the girl, more broadly as Norah mirrored her.

'Hello. Hello, my darling girl.'

'You see,' Alexander was hissing at Colin. 'You see, Mum knows.'

Julie held out both her hands, and the girl slipped hers into them. There were tears flooding Norah's eyes, darkening the blue. She blinked, and they spilled over. Julie let one hand go and wiped them from Norah's cheek. 'Where have you been all these years?'

Norah gave a little sob. 'I'll tell you everything. All that I know, that is. I don't know everything.'

'How did you find us?'

Norah looked over Julie's shoulder. 'Alexander came to look for me, but I guess I found him first.'

Julie turned, one hand still in Norah's, to see her son standing wilted on the bottom step. He was scarily white, the patches of red gone from his face, leaving it drained. 'How long have you known?'

'Less than a week.'

'You've known for almost a week?'

Alexander shook his head. 'No. Well, aye. We've only met twice.'

'You met twice?' Julie pushed her shoulders back, tightening her grip on Norah's hand. 'You met twice, and you didn't tell me?'

'Mum, I had to make sure.'

'And when were you sure?'

Alexander hesitated. He looked at Colin, but his friend had his hands in his pockets and his face averted. 'I was sure from the first minute.'

'Oh, this is quite absurd.'

'Euan, dear, hush.'

'Shut up, Elizabeth.' Euan came down a few steps so that he was towering above Julie and Norah. 'Julie, really, this can't be right.'

'Uncle Euan, don't.'

'You've been taken in, boy. How could it be Norah after all these years? Don't you think that, if she was alive, we would know it? What about her birth certificate? How about when she went for her driver's license? There are one hundred situations when you need to prove your identity. What, she didn't know?'

'She can't help it if no one told her the truth!'

'The truth?'

'There is no one that knows anymore.' Alexander went to Norah's side. 'Her parents are dead.'

'How convenient.'

'You leave my parents out of this!' Norah's sharp voice cut through the argument.

Euan threw his hands up and turned away. Julie shook her

head at him, but he had his back turned. Fear grabbed her stomach. Was he going to say something? She glanced at Donald. Her husband stood staring at Norah, his arms hanging loosely now. He looked side-swiped.

'Norah.' Alexander was holding the girl's other hand now. 'It's alright. There will be plenty of time to go through everything. Right now, it's important that we just get used to each other. We'll go gently.'

Norah nodded, more tears on her cheeks that Alexander swept away before Julie could. Behind her, Julie heard Colin's harsh breathing, as if he'd come back from a run. Poor fellow, she thought. He probably doesn't believe Norah. How could he? He can't tell, like Alexander and I. Julie reached out to stroke Norah's hand. It was so obvious that she was theirs. Every molecule in her body told her. Surely Euan could see it, too?

But what about Donald?

Julie's hand dropped away. She stepped back to look at Donald. He stood, forgotten, mouth closed now, eyes narrowed. 'Donald?' she said. 'Come and see Norah.'

When he did nothing, panic seized her throat. He knew! How did he know? He couldn't! He hadn't known when Norah was born and still hadn't known when she went missing. There was nothing he could have found out since, not if Julie hadn't told him. Euan certainly wouldn't. So what was wrong with him?

'Donald,' she said again, keeping her voice steady, 'come and see your daughter.'

Donald blinked and shook himself as if he'd only just woken. He came towards Julie, eyes on the girl. Norah smiled at him. She was so lovely, thought Julie. Beautiful. I knew she would be -

'Get off my property.'

Julie sucked her breath in. 'What did you say?'

'You.' Now Donald was pointing to Norah with a finger cracked and grime-filled. 'You. Get off my property!'

'Donald!'

'Dad!' Alexander held his hand up. 'Dad, it's Norah.'

'Go! Get off! You're not welcome!' Donald's roar made Norah pull back from Julie and Alexander. She stumbled to the edge of the garden. 'Go! Now! Go!'

'Donald!'

'Dad, no!'

Donald kept yelling over the top of them. The noise filled Julie. She heard herself shrieking, shrill and pleadingly. 'Donald! Donald!' Alexander's rapid voice layered over hers. 'No, Dad, no. No, Dad, no.'

Norah freed herself from the garden edge and backed towards her car. Both her hands were up in defence, but Donald only swivelled on the spot, roaring increasingly loudly. His face, red before, purple now, was screwed up. Spit flew. Norah reached the car as Alexander ran towards her. She slammed the door closed on herself. Alexander tugged at the handle, but she'd locked it. The car started, moved backwards violently. Alexander lost his grip and lunged for the windscreen, but the car was out on the road. He fell as it turned. It swerved around him and sped up the hill.

Alexander ran back. Blood dripped from his elbow where he'd hit the road. The van was locked, and he fumbled with his keys before opening the door.

'Alexander, wait!' Colin ran now, but it was too late. The van left deep trenches in the gravel as Alexander hauled it around. He fishtailed out onto the road. They left Julie with its receding sound.

Silence settled. Colin stood in the yard, frantically dialling his phone and getting no pick up. Donald turned slowly to face his wife, eyes squinted, breathing fast. Three strides, and she was near enough to hit him hard across the face, the heel of her hand blunting his nose and making him yell.

'You bastard,' she said, swinging at him again and missing. 'You big bastard!'

'Julie,' he said, holding his face, 'it wasn't her. It can't be her! She's gone now, Julie, gone!'

'She isn't! She isn't gone. She's back! Can't you see? Couldn't you tell?'

Snot and tears covered her face as she scrubbed at it, the pain inside her head screaming no, no, no! She felt Donald's hand on her arm. She jerked back.

'Julie...'

'Get away from me. Leave me alone!' She turned to leave but swung back. 'If she is gone and we never see her again, it's your fault. Do you hear me? Your fault!'

He winced as she made a fist. She turned before she killed him, pushing her way past Euan and Elizabeth on the steps, and made for her bed before the burning in her heart felled her completely.

THE OLD VAN WAS STRAINING. Norah's car had surged ahead and now Alexander couldn't be sure that he'd kept it in his sights or it was another white car in front. His hands twisted on the steering wheel. What the hell was wrong with his father? How could he do something so cruel, so unexpected? The change in him... Dr Jekyll and Mr Hyde. Never had Alexander seen him so raw and uncontained. Thinking about it made Alexander shudder. The wheel was slippery with his sweat and he wiped his hands on the seat before driving the van faster on a straight stretch of road.

The phone in his pocket, ringing and vibrating ever since

he'd left, made him increasingly angry. Trying to keep the rickety van steady on the road, he wrenched it out, flinging it across the seat, catching the caller's name as he did. Of course Colin would be ringing. He'd be wanting to say, 'told you so. I told you' and Alexander couldn't stand it. *Did you see the look on Mum's face?* he said to Colin in his head. *She was so happy. You saw it, surely? Norah was back in our family and the wound scored into us could finally begin to heal.*

A wound, he thought, that was now likely to fester uncontrollably unless he found Norah again.

He accelerated. The corner was a little sharper than he expected, and the van rocked. He gritted his teeth and held it on the road. There, what was that? A white car one hundred metres in front, the shape of its driver unclear until it had to come to a stop for an intersection. He was almost on it, but it pulled away, rewarding him with a glimpse of a girl profiled in the evening light. Norah.

It was easier to keep her in view once they closed in on Edinburgh. The road widened into the highway and even the van could keep up its speed. Alexander lost her again as they wound into town but saw her in the distance as she rounded a corner, and then another. He was close enough to see all the car's movements, far enough away so that when he pulled up behind the car, its engine still ticked hotly. He looked around. Norah was running. He bounded after her.

She was fast. Driven by the force of his father's anger, Alexander was not surprised that Norah could bolt as she had. The tiredness of his day had gone. He ran like the sprinter he'd been at school, dodging the crowds, covering so much ground he caught her as she paused at the door of an apartment building, the keys rattling too much in her hand to work.

'Norah.'

Maybe she didn't hear him? Anyway, she still fumbled blindly with the keys.

'Norah!'

This time she jumped, the keys cascading from her hands and landing on the street's cobbles. He swept them up, pressing them into her hand and keeping hold as she wept.

'Norah, I'm so sorry. I had no idea he would do that. It's crazy. It's not like him. I've never seen-'

'Don't. Please. Don't apologise. I should never...' The tears choked her words.

He couldn't help but hold her close, pulling her head to his shoulder and rubbing her back. Through the thin material of her shirt, he felt the bones of her spine. It hurt him, her frailty. She was his sister, and yet he couldn't stop her feeling this pain. First, her parents had died and left her. Second, her family – her actual family – hadn't been as open-armed as they should be. As they had to be. Anger made Alexander screw his eyes up. What was wrong with his father? It was madness!

'Norah,' he said into her ear, 'I want you to know that I will always be here for you. Now that we've found each other, we are to never let each other go. I swear this. Do you?'

She mumbled something, pushed her face deeper into his shirt.

'Norah?' He shifted his hands until he had her shoulders and could pull her back. Her head was down. Traces of make-up smudged one cheek. 'Norah? Swear. Whatever happens, we have each other.'

She nodded, small at first, then deeper, more urgent. He pulled her close again, but she'd finished crying. One of her hands went around his waist, the softest of pressure on his back. He held her until he felt her stiffen. When she straightened, her face was dry.

'I must look a mess.' She smiled wryly, a hand on her cheek.

'A bit.' He shrugged.

'I need to clean up.' She took the key from his hand and placed it, expertly this time, in the lock. 'Do you want to come in?'

He followed her saying nothing, and climbed the worn, concrete steps behind her. The outside door closed on any noise but their footsteps, hers light in her sandals, his heavy with work boots. She took a while to turn the three locks, and he pushed the door open for her when eventually it was free. She locked it behind them, pointing down the hall. 'I need to clean up. Help yourself to anything in the kitchen.'

Alexander had not had a sister but sensed that Norah would be like the three or four girls he'd known well. He nodded as she locked the bathroom door and set about making coffee. The adrenaline of his flight was gone. He was bone-weary. In the little refrigerator, he found cheese and tomato, and made up a plate with oat crackers. The coffee revived him, but his body shook for a beer. The water still ran in the bathroom as he ate all the crackers and made up more. Another coffee, and she was there, rosy-cheeked and wearing a fresh pink dress. She slid into a chair opposite him and took a biscuit.

'So,' he said, offering a drink.

She took it, sipped, grimaced. 'You call this coffee?'

'Colin says that, too.'

'Well, that's one thing he got right.'

Alexander chuckled. 'So,' he said, again.

'Look, Alexander.' Norah broke her biscuit into bits. 'I'm not sure I can do this.'

'What's to do?' he said. 'If this is all it is-' he indicated the room, them in it '- then that's fine.'

'It isn't, you know. Without your mum and dad, this isn't going to work.'

'*Our* mum and dad. And, aye, it would work without them.'

Norah sighed. 'I'm tired. Never been so tired. Can we make a pact?'

'A pact?'

'Let's talk about other things than our stupid families. Politics. Pop groups. Castles. Anything but bloodlines.' She widened her eyes. 'Okay?'

He shrugged. 'That's the best idea I've heard today.'

She smiled.

A little burn of hope warmed his chest. Norah. My sister.

NINETEEN

After Julie went inside, Elizabeth said, 'Well,' and gathered glasses as if she was the waiter at a wake. The three men watched her. She slid the door across with one elbow and went to the kitchen. Colin moved first, sliding the door shut to stop the flies getting into the house. An Australian habit, he thought. Flies around here weren't the angrily buzzing, maggot-laying variety. Instead, they zoomed lazily and slowly, easy targets.

'Donald, are you okay?' Euan scrutinised his brother from where he stood. It was Colin who went to Donald and steered him onto a patio chair. Elizabeth had left a jug of water and a few glasses. Colin poured one for Donald, placed it in his hand, and saw that he drank it. And another. Donald's face had the sheen of someone just out of a swimming pool. The front of his shirt clung wetly to his chest and stomach.

Euan came over and crouched beside him, taking a wrist in his hand to feel Donald's pulse. Colin went to stand at the edge of the outdoor decking, and rang Alexander again, grunting as it went to message bank once more.

'You'll be alright.' Euan's voice, calm and clinical, did

nothing to show to Colin that Donald would be alright. Donald's heart might be pumping along the way it should be, but his eyes were glazed. He kept wiping at his head with his forearm to remove the sweat running down it, but his arm was equally soaked. Colin came over and poured another glass of water, but Donald shook his head.

'That girl.' Euan stood, taking out a hanky to polish his spectacles. 'You know her.'

His question was to the table, so it seemed, and Colin didn't answer until the doctor slid his glasses back on, his gaze now directly at Colin.

'I was there when she turned up. Since then, I've spoken to her once on the phone. Alexander has met up with her.'

'Where did she come from? How did she concoct this imaginary tale of hers?'

Colin put his hands up. 'It was nothing to do with Alexander or me.'

'She got it from somewhere.'

Colin felt his hackles rise. Was Euan looking to blame Alexander? 'Look, Alexander's caught up in the romance of it all, but he didn't start it.'

'He did.'

Colin and Euan turned to Donald. His voice was husky and breathy with effort. 'What do you mean, Donald?' Euan said briskly.

'Alexander, he got this...' Donald held a clawed hand out '... *thing* in his head about not knowing what happened to wee Norah. The entire trip to Australia, that was what he did.'

'We did other things as well.'

'Don't defend him, Colin.' Donald leaned his arms on the table. 'You know as well as I do he had one reason for that trip. Mind, I was glad you went with him. I was worried he might not come back.'

Colin shrugged. 'He was always coming back.'

Donald shook his head.

'I should involve the police. She's attempting fraud,' Euan said.

Donald shook his head again. 'Leave it, Euan. It will blow over.'

Euan raised his eyebrows. 'If she shows up again in the next twenty-four hours, contact me. I'm in touch with the local police.'

Colin tried Alexander's number again. Nothing. Alexander was a good driver, steady, used to the roads. Even at speed, even full of emotion, he should be able to handle a screaming trip to Edinburgh. Norah, in that sleek sedan, would surely speed away and not be found, leaving Alexander to search the city uselessly. Colin stretched his neck a little to ease its tightness. 'Look, I should be getting back. Alexander will end up at our place. I want to check he's okay. Donald, can I take the other van?'

'I'll drive you.' Euan was already searching his pockets for his keys.

'The lad can take the van.' Donald sounded exhausted.

'No, you might need it. I'll take him. Elizabeth can wait here until I get back.' Euan glanced in at his wife standing at the sink. 'Julie might need company.'

She might need it, thought Colin, but not want it with the fluffy Elizabeth. 'It'll be okay. I'll take the van.'

'Get in the car.'

Euan was already striding towards it so his voice, thrown over his shoulder, was like an afterthought. Colin looked at Donald, but the big man could only stare back at him and shrug uselessly. Colin went to Euan's car, slid into the leather seat. 'Thanks,' he said, curtly.

Euan nodded. He turned the car carefully across the gravel

and onto the road. No one spoke until they got to more open roads. The car glided almost noiselessly.

'You knew this was going to happen.'

Colin bristled. 'I had no idea.'

'You knew this girl was around.'

Euan's tone was light. Colin glanced at him and saw the way he sat slightly forward so that his back skimmed the seat. One hand was on the wheel, the other fiddled with air-conditioning controls, radio volume, speed settings. In close profile, Euan's face betrayed more of his age with a spread of deep grooves on the side of his face. It didn't help that he was frowning. Whether that was at the traffic on the road or at the situation, Colin couldn't tell.

'I knew she was around, but I didn't know she'd turn up.'

Euan shrugged a shoulder. Maybe his arm was uncomfortable because he did it again. 'How dare she disturb our family.'

It seemed an overly intimate reflection. Colin knew Euan had no children, but he didn't seem close to Alexander. Yes, he and Elizabeth spent regular time at Donald's but Colin thought that reflected generosity on Julie's behalf. It was not as if Euan had helped Alexander through university or acted in any other way like a benevolent uncle. Alexander had once said to Colin that he suspected Euan wasn't Donald's real brother but a changeling.

The thought made Colin smile. He turned so that Euan wouldn't notice. Ahead of them somewhere, Alexander was racing into the city in pursuit of a girl he clearly thought was a foundling. True, Julie had reacted the same way. Colin kept his eyes on the road as he said, 'Could it be true?'

'I beg your pardon?'

'Could that girl actually be Norah?'

'It's hardly likely.'

There was a warning in Euan's voice. Colin pushed on. After all, he thought, you're not my uncle.

'Why not? She went missing as a baby. There was never a body found. There's a slim possibility that she might have been adopted out. Perhaps by mistake.' He shrugged, waiting. A logical man like Euan would have a realm of statistics about missing people. The likelihood of the girl being Norah was, of course, ridiculous.

They drove for miles before Euan cleared his throat. 'We searched. The authorities searched. There was no trace of her after the third day of admission.'

Colin pulled himself up in his seat. 'You were in Australia as well.'

Euan gave that one-shouldered shrug again. 'It was a holiday of sorts. We were all there. Alexander was a toddler. My first wife, Rachel. She was there too.'

'I hadn't realised that.'

'We were holidaying with Julie's parents, showing them the baby. Norah.'

Colin nodded slowly. He'd never asked about the details of Norah's disappearance. He saw them now, the holidaying family, perhaps getting a phone call from the hospital that said, 'We can't find your daughter.' Or, worse, arriving to find her cot empty and asking, innocently, 'Where is our Norah?' and seeing a frightened look flit across a nurse's face as she realised something was wrong. The chaos that would have reigned from that. The scandal. Colin knew that Paxton Community Hospital had been closed for ten years, demolished not so long ago. How much had Norah Cameron's disappearance contributed to its demise? What would happen now if she reappeared?

'How long did everyone stay in Australia?'

'We left almost immediately. Donald brought Alexander back first. Julie stayed much longer.'

'That is awful.'

Euan nodded. 'Very sad. But in the past, do you see?'

Colin frowned. 'What do you mean?'

'Over the years, we've all gone through a lot of grieving. We'd finished. When this girl turns up, it brings it back to the present. For some.'

'You mean Julie.'

Euan's fingers twisted on the wheel. 'Mainly Julie.'

'Donald, too, by what happened just before.'

'Donald is a different matter.' Euan leaned forward to adjust the air-conditioner vent. The air directed onto his face lifted the hair swept across his head.

Colin shifted again in his seat. The car smelled new, a slightly sickly odour of plastic and cleaning liquids. Even from where he sat, he could sense the richness of Euan's aftershave. The radio hummed classics. Euan drove into the city to the flat where there was no sign of Alexander or the van.

'Thanks,' Colin said as he climbed out of the cool car. He thought about inviting the doctor in, but instead gave a farewell wave. Euan pulled the car around effortlessly and drove back the way he'd come.

The air was city-scented and warm. Colin shook his head clear of the confines of being close to Euan and rang Alexander once more.

TO HIS CREDIT, Donald didn't disturb her at all, padding down the hall to sleep in the spare room after Elizabeth left. Julie emerged after midnight, the house now dark and empty. Moonlight brightened the outdoor area where a jug still sat on the table. She made tea, her trembling hand shivering the kettle, and sat on the living room couch facing the window.

Alexander hadn't answered her calls. Colin had texted very late to say that Alexander had made it home. That was one child safe. What about the other?

One last tear slid down. She patted it away. The hours, days, months she had spent crying in her lifetime... really, it was a miracle that her tear ducts hadn't seized altogether. She felt that, given half a chance, they would start all over again. Tears of worry, tears of guilt, tears of regret. Norah was here, but what sort of life had she had? If Julie had stayed looking for her longer, would she have got her back sooner? Would Norah hate her now that she had trekked out to find her family, only to discover that she wasn't welcomed by everyone?

Donald did not, could not, know he was not Norah's father, so why had his reaction been so arrogant? He'd sent away her *daughter*. Julie put the cup down so the angry shaking consuming her body wouldn't spill tea everywhere. If Donald disappeared overnight, she wouldn't look for him. *I hate him*, she thought. She put her hand to her mouth. *Hate*. Such a strong word, full of spitting fire. Exactly how she felt.

She finished her tea and rose to make herself a sandwich. She would drive to Edinburgh before dawn and make sure she was at Alexander's flat before he even thought about leaving it. He would take her to Norah. They would reunite. Donald would be nowhere near them and neither would Euan. Norah would see that she was wanted, needed, loved. Julie smiled. It was a coherent plan with a definite end. A family, at last! She ate, still smiling, standing at the bench.

But the dawn was a long way off and the thought of sitting in the dark in the car on the streets of new Edinburgh seemed anti-climactic. Julie drummed her fingers on the bench. Her skin felt itchy, her legs jittered. A quick walk up the hill in the moonlight to William Wallace would calm her restlessness. The urge to see the monument, Wallace glaring through the trees, was almost overwhelming. Julie put her shoes on, struggling with the laces in the room's dimness, and slid the door open. Outside was bright, the pale blue light making friendly shadows of her garden.

It was darker on the path through the forest. Julie used the light on her phone for the first little while, but it was too fierce. She turned it off and let her feet pick the familiar path. At least, she thought wryly, there shouldn't be any horses or Louisas bounding past her. Things scurried through the undergrowth, but Julie wasn't worried. They weren't the Australian snakes she'd had to be always on the lookout for growing up. What did it matter if a fox or a mole crossed her path?

Where had Norah grown up? Was she a city girl, as she looked, or a country girl dislocated? Had she been happy? Julie hadn't seen any signs of stress etched into her skin. A happy life then, with loving parents nurturing her as their own. A mistaken adoption perhaps, paperwork fumbles at the busy hospital, the parents never knowing what had happened but so very glad to have their own little girl.

The path hooked around, overhung by rocks. It was immediately dark. Julie looked down at the ground, little steps now, feeling tiny stones roll under her feet. But what if those very parents had been the ones to take Norah in the first place? Plucking the recovering Norah from her cot as Julie ate tea at a local hotel before going back to see her daughter? Disguising the infant in a pram already made up with pink blankets and teddy bears? Turning their backs on the pain they'd created in their selfishness? Even if they were the most loving parents, they still had the stench of evil ready to trickle through their actions. What else had they done to Norah?

The path turned again. She was almost to the top. The moonlight was stronger now, clear of clouds for the first time. It sat behind William Wallace as Julie climbed the last bit. He cast a long shadow down the hill, his face hidden in it. Still. There he was. Comfortingly steady, feet apart, right hand on the hilt of his sword. 'Hello, William,' said Julie, voice husky and lonely. 'Thanks for being there.'

She was being ridiculous again. Of course he was there, he was a *statue*. Honestly, the world was wobbling. She made her way to the note box, opening it to reveal a whole busload of good wishes and thankyous. The wad was thick in her hand as she retrieved them. She paused at the top of the track. The darkness of the upper section was waiting for her. The road was the better option. She almost ran back down to the house, the creaking in her knees stopping a faster flight. Home, and it was time to go. She left Donald a different type of note and started on the drive to Edinburgh.

The road ran out in front of her smoothly. It was hard not to gather speed.

Officer, I'm going to meet my daughter after thirty years!

I'll give you an escort, Ma'am.

That was what should be happening. Instead, she rang the surgery phone to leave a message about her absence.

'Dr Cameron.'

The car swerved as Julie jerked at the phone. The Bluetooth controls confused her. Where was the off button?

'It's Dr Cameron. Can I help you?'

'Euan.' Julie focused back on the road. How ironic would it be if she was killed going to see Norah? 'I won't be in today.'

'What are you doing, Julie? It's very early.'

'I could say the same about you. Did you get called out?'

'No. Catching up on paperwork.'

Rubbish, thought Julie. She knew the status of the paperwork. 'You're trying to find out more about her, aren't you?'

'What are you talking about?'

'Norah. You're hoping it isn't her.'

'Julie, it's not Norah.' Euan frowned. 'And I'm not doing anything I wouldn't ordinarily do on a normal working morning.'

The first glimmer of morning was lighting the sky. Julie angled the rear vision mirror slightly, glimpsing her face. Flushed, red-eyed. She'd forgotten to put any make-up on. No, she'd forgotten to take off yesterday's. The lines around her eyes were collecting mascara. She wiped a finger under her eyelashes, patted and poked at her hair. She felt slightly wild. 'Euan, please. Tell me honestly. Is there any chance that this girl could be Norah?'

The question seemed to surprise him, or perhaps he was taking his time to think of a delicate answer. 'Julie, the baby disappeared thirty years ago without a trace. No one in that time has found anything of her. Could she still be alive? Julie.' His voice dropped. 'It doesn't seem likely.'

Julie nodded dutifully, catching herself again in the mirror as her hair bobbed. 'Not likely,' she said. There's a chance then, she thought. 'Euan, if it is Norah – no, say she *is* Norah – what should we do?'

'Why would we do anything different? There's nothing to gain by Donald finding out the truth now. Julie, don't do anything... hasty. This will all blow over.'

'I'm not about to tell him, Euan. I didn't then. I won't now.'

'Good. It's best not to stir up trouble.'

Trouble, was she? Julie gritted her teeth. Did Euan mean her or the baby? 'I need to go now. Concentrate on the road.'

'Be careful.'

Somehow, she knew he didn't mean her driving. 'Goodbye.'

Without the radio, the car noise was restricted to a continuous road hum. The little car was nearly new but without the solidness of her old sedan, the one that had seen her through most of Alexander's childhood. She missed it. Things feel flimsier the older you get, she thought. You need more to hang on to.

Norah. She had to hang on to her.

TWENTY

Grace woke, tightness around her throat. She sat up, pulling at her sleeping shirt. It was already day, with strong sunlight through the window. *How could I sleep so heavily after yesterday?* she thought. Her body felt post-marathon heavy. She suspected it would have felt worse if she hadn't spent the evening talking to Alexander.

Halfway through discussions about the ludicrous state of Australian politics, Grace decided that Alexander was a nice guy. It came to her, an epiphany unrelated to the talk, *Alexander is really nice*. He was serious when thinking, but his eyes brightened easily. He listened, he nodded in the right places; he laughed when she bought take-away haggis and chips. It felt so easy to be with him.

Three quarters of the way through the night, she wondered whether she was falling in love with him. It made her falter. You can't fall in love with your brother! She made more coffee, feigning a salty-chip-dry throat. After that, she watched him more carefully. No, it wasn't the rosy feel of love or lust. There was no spark. She'd had that before, sometimes with disastrous consequences. This feeling was of *companionship*.

'What's the matter?' he'd said once she'd smiled inappropri-ately and inanely at him.

'I'm so glad you're my brother,' she'd said simply.

She was, too. If Norah had discovered that her family was awful, she'd have faded back into oblivion. Alexander, Julie too, kept her here.

But what about Donald?

Grace shuffled her legs out of bed and went to get a drink. Outside, on the Royal Mile, early crowds were wandering up and down the street. Most of them were in raincoats. The road cobbles glinted wetly in the sunshine. She hadn't heard the rain at all.

Donald's face had no trace of niceness. In her head, it was round and furious, slashed in red. What, didn't he want his daughter to come home? Was he the one who'd got rid of her in the first place? Why would a father do that? Grace wriggled off the window ledge she'd perched on and made herself tea. Donald was unnerving. He made her feel sick.

The sound of her phone was faint, but she heard it. One person had that number. She rushed into her bedroom and rummaged among the sheets until she found it. 'Alexander?'

'Norah.'

Was that a question? 'Are you okay?'

There was a slight pause. 'Mum's here. She wants to see you.'

'Oh.' Mum. Julie. Of course. 'I've just got up.'

'Lazy.' There was a hint of a smile in Alexander's voice.

'Too many chips make you sleep in.'

'I'll eat them all next time.'

'You can try.'

There was a beat of silence.

'So, where can we meet you?'

Grace glanced down at her sleeping shirt. 'I'll need an hour.'

'Can you remember where we met the first time?'

'Macdonald Street?'

'No, the café.'

'*Spoon*, yeah?'

'Aye. We'll be there at ten o'clock.'

'Ten o'clock, then.'

'I'll let you get on. Bye, Norah.'

'See you later.'

One hour before she was face to face with Julie, without the element of surprise, Grace flicked through Norah's clothes and found a pea-green raglan sleeve dress. She made up her eyes to match, smoky grey with a teal shimmer to her eyeshadow. She dried her hair so it fell over one side of her face and swapped her cat-eye sunglasses for a round, amber pair. The dress fell from her shoulders straight to the floor. She buckled on white plat-form shoes and finished Norah with a cluster of simple gold bracelets. That was it, she'd run out of different clothes. Next time, she would be recycling. One step closer to being more familiar.

The dress was a little heavy for the weather. She swept the hem up as she walked through weeping rain, making on-comers smile at the loop of skirt over her arm. The way was not as straight-forward as she had thought. She was a block over and had to check her phone map before trudging back past the museum. It made her later than the planned ten minutes. She stayed for a moment at the bottom of the steps, shaking her dress out and rearranging her hair. The glasses were a poor accessory. They'd been too dark to see through the grey streets. She put them in her bag before climbing to the restaurant.

Grace hadn't even seen them before Julie was in front of her, first smiling, next holding her tightly. Grace's heart pounded to the beat of the other woman's – she could feel it through their chests. 'Norah,' said Julie into her ear. 'Norah.'

'Mum...' Alexander came into view over Julie's shoulder. He raised his eyes at Grace, who tried to grin back. Although she was a head taller than Julie, she was anchored. 'Mum, let her go.' Alexander reached out and gently pulled Julie back.

'I am so sorry.' Julie put her hands on her cheeks, then tugged her shirt down. 'I couldn't help it. I've been wanting to do that from the moment you stepped from the car.'

'That's alright.' Grace could still feel the imprint of the hug on her skin. She wriggled, plucking at the dress's damp material.

'Over here.' Alexander led them to a window table, pulling the middle chair out for his mother and then sitting next to her. Grace let her bag drop to the ground as she slid in. Julie's knees knocked hers.

'So,' said Julie, 'here we are.'

Grace smiled, taking the glass of water offered from Alexander for something to do. Yesterday, driving to Dryburgh, she'd felt strong and purposeful. Today, drinking water, Julie's gaze on her face, she felt slightly ridiculous. She nodded at the empty chair next to her. 'Is Donald coming?'

Alexander looked at his mother, who shook her head. 'That seat's for Colin. He's coming for coffee in between jobs.'

'I see.'

'Colin's a good friend to Alexander,' Julie said.

Grace remembered Colin's sharp looks. It made her also think of his dark, wild hair and stonemason muscles. 'I've got no doubt about that.'

Alexander picked up the menu while Julie rubbed a finger along her watch. Grace kept her hands in her lap and willed her shoulders to drop. 'I'm sorry about just turning up out of the blue,' she said, keeping her voice low.

'That's alright.' Julie sighed. 'It was a bit of a shock, I've got to say.' She smiled, her head slightly on one side. 'Actually, you literally nearly gave me a heart attack.'

'Oh, I didn't mean-'

Julie waved her quiet. 'It's not your fault. It's *his*.'

'My fault?' Alexander put the menu down. 'Hardly.'

'You should have said something.' Bitterness tinged Julie's voice, but she patted her son's hand.

'I was going to.'

'We were working on a plan,' cut in Grace. 'Something a bit gentler than what I did. I was impulsive. I am very sorry.'

'Well, it doesn't matter now.' Julie wiped under her eye. Grace swallowed at the traces of tears on her finger. 'Alexander's told me what you've said about your... other life. I want to hear some for myself.'

Grace swirled her water. 'Okay.'

'What did they call you, Norah?'

Julie's voice was almost too soft to hear. Grace leaned towards her instinctively. 'My name?'

'Yes. What did they name you?'

'Oh. Not Norah.'

'No.'

Grace put her glass down. 'Claudia. My name is Claudia Purton.' She kept her eyes down, but her head was suddenly pounding. Why did I say that?

'Claudia.' Julie said it under her breath a few more times before glancing up at Grace. 'Can I ask you other things?'

'What like?'

'Who was your best friend when you were little?'

Grace jumped. It was hard to know what was more frightening: the eagerness in Julie's eyes, or the question itself. Best friend? Only friend. There was a string of childhood friends, but none that stayed with her when Grace was constantly needing to be at home. She'd changed primary schools three times as they'd moved houses, her father chasing work that allowed him to care for his wife as well. Strangely, they'd ended up almost back where they'd started, their last house together as a little family a block away from their beginning.

'Norah? Norah, I'm sorry. Was that the wrong thing to ask?'

Julie's voice filtered in until Grace blinked and re-focused. 'No, of course not. Sorry.'

'What was her name? Your best friend.'

There was only one person Grace could ever name as a friend, best or otherwise, but she'd already blown it. She chewed her lip a moment. 'Grace.'

'What a beautiful name. Do you still keep in touch?'

'I haven't seen her for a while.'

'That's sad. What about school? What were your favourite subjects?'

'Mum.' Alexander put a hand on Julie's forearm. 'You're interrogating her.'

'No, I'm not. Am I?' Julie put a hand on her forehead. 'I'm sorry, Norah.'

Grace reached out and took the older woman's hand as it dropped to the table. It was small and soft, the fingers very unlike her long, bony ones. The edges of the nails were sharp. Grace traced them, bringing her other hand up to lie over the top. 'It doesn't matter. You can ask me anything you want.'

'It's just... thirty years, Norah. It's an entire lifetime. How will I ever be able to know you, having missed all that?'

Grace dropped her head, trying to keep her breathing steady. When she lifted her gaze, Alexander was looking at her. The same question was in his eyes. 'I think it might be impossible,' she finally said. 'Too much time has gone.'

Julie shook her head. 'No, no, it'll be fine.'

'No, don't get me wrong. I'm not going anywhere. What I think will be impossible is me trying to catch you up with my life as it was.' She smiled at Alexander, who sat nodding. 'But we could start again. From now. We could get to know each other as we are, in this café. You know, like people meeting again after they've nearly forgotten each other. We could stick to the future instead of thinking about the past.'

Alexander sighed. He leaned back in his chair, looking up to the ceiling. Relief relaxed him, and he spun the fork on the placemat, a small smile on his lips.

Julie's hand tightened on Grace's. She shook her head, ever so slightly.

'Hi.' The deep voice made Norah twitch.

'Colin, about time.' Alexander indicated the empty seat. 'Hope you're working hard.'

'Working for two at the moment.' Colin glanced at Grace. She'd been waiting for hatred in his eyes but saw something less vicious. Hardness, yes, but also curiosity. 'Hello, Norah.'

'Hello, Colin.' Grace couldn't help but hold his look. He reached for a glass of water. Grace blinked and turned back to Julie, who hadn't stopped staring at her. It was a little unnerving. She flicked hair out of one eye. 'So, tell me something about you. I've heard all about Alexander's life. Could it be your turn?'

Julie's face had high spots of colour. Grace leaned forward, but Julie let her hand go and pushed her chair back. 'Excuse me for a moment. Alexander, where's the ladies?'

Alexander stood to show his mother the sign to the bathroom, and Colin reached over to take an empty glass. 'Still going with this charade?' he said quietly to Grace.

She pulled back in her chair. Colin sipped at his water slowly. She skidded the chair forward abruptly, knocking his arm and making water slop on to his shirt. 'It's not a charade,' she whispered. 'Look at us. We're obviously family.'

'Because you're all red-headed? Give it a break, Norah.'

'No, really, Colin. Can't you see it?'

He hesitated, brushing absently at his shirt with one hand. 'Norah. Listen. You can't do this to Alexander.'

'What do you mean?'

'Look at him.' Colin nodded towards Alexander who stood at the bar now talking to a smiling man behind it. 'He's....' He shrugged.

'I like it that you care.' Grace dabbed at drops of water on the table.

Colin put his glass down heavily. 'There's one way to make sure. If you're game.'

'What are you talking about?'

'Genetic testing.' Colin looked up, but Alexander was still talking. 'Would you do it?'

'Of course, I would. But only if he asked me.'

'Alexander?' Colin shook his head. 'He's already convinced that you're his sister. It won't be him asking you. *You* need to ask *him*.'

'What do you mean?'

Colin leaned forward. Grace could smell the distant shadow of aftershave, a rich fragrance hovering among the slight sting of a working man's sweat. 'I will only be convinced that you are not out to harm this family if you're willing to go all the way to proving that you are who you say you are.'

'And if I am who I say I am – what then?'

He looked down at the table and folded his hands together over the menu. 'Well,' he said, looking at her suddenly, 'I might even like you.'

Warmth invaded her cheeks.

'Are you guys alright?' Alexander frowned as he came back and sat down. 'Don't fight, okay? This is hard enough on Mum without you two carrying on.'

Colin held up his hands. 'Hey, I'm cool. Coolest person at this table. Isn't that right, Norah?'

'People who think they're cool are usually the most uncool.'

Alexander laughed as the waiter came to take their order. 'She's got you there, my friend.'

Julie came back, smiled at Grace, and sat. Her face was normal, no smudges or spots or any sign of distress. Grace relaxed, tucking into her eggs hungrily, as did Alexander. Colin swallowed his coffee and stood to go, taking Julie's proffered hand for a moment, nodding at Alexander and giving Grace a complicated stare. She watched him go. 'Sullen sort of bloke, eh.'

'Oh, you sounded just like my aunt then!' Julie's laugh lit her eyes. 'Eh? Eh? A true Queenslander. But you aren't from Queensland?'

'No, but... Grace's cousin used to live there. The 'eh' thing went on for quite a while before she dropped it.'

'So you've stayed friends with Grace for a long time.'

Grace nodded, uneasy. She had disappeared on Claudia eleven days ago. For all Claudia knew, she was a missing person now. The note Grace had left asked Claudia to leave her alone for one month and not to worry, although Claudia had made it clear that she would not worry if Grace had done what she'd said she would. Julia was right. Grace had known Claudia for a very long time. She wasn't callous, no matter how hot-headed she might act. For the first time, Grace wondered how worried Claudia might really be.

Julie was still looking at her.

'Grace and I shared a house.'

Julie nodded. 'Share houses. I remember those. We had seven people in a four-bedroom house in Fitzroy when I was at uni.'

'You've never told me that, Mum.'

'You never asked. Five girls and two boys. Sam in the

lounge, Andrew in the hallway and Jenny taking it in turns to sleep in one of our rooms. Made the rent very cheap.'

'Is that how you met Donald? At uni?'

Alexander nearly spilled his coffee. 'Dad? At uni?'

'Donald was a stonemason when I met him.' Julie scowled at her son. 'I was travelling around. He was in the pub.'

'Captured by his Scottish charm.'

'Actually, it was his accent. He sounded like Sean Connery.' Julie shrugged. 'We got married without telling any of our parents. You'd think we'd have murdered someone, the way they carried on.' Julie traced a bubble of paint on the table. 'We didn't see much of either set of parents after that. We took Alexander to see my Mum and Dad when he was one. We took you both later.' She looked up at Norah. 'It was on that trip that you went missing.'

They fell quiet again. The table next to them lit up with deep laughter as a group of men celebrated something. When they quietened, Grace said, 'What happened?'

Alexander put his elbows on the table and dropped his head as his mother spoke. 'You had croup. We took you to the hospital, poor wee thing you were. That awful barking nose, your little face red with effort. You were only three months old. There were quite a few babies in with all sorts of things. I thought you might have caught something worse if I left you there.' Julie shrugged. 'Ironic how things go.'

'How long had I been there when...?'

'They kept you there for two days. We came in on the third and the ward was in chaos. They were short-staffed. There'd been an influx of admissions. Some children lay on trolleys in the corridor. To top it off, there'd been an outbreak of gastro and there were lots of children on drips. And there was a little injured baby, I'm not sure why. Euan and Rachel were going to wait for us in the foyer, but Euan had already gone in. He said one of his old colleagues was working there.'

Julie stopped.

'Mum? Are you alright?'

Alexander leaned towards her. She gave him a reassuring smile, a mother's smile wanting to soothe. 'Yes. Just remembering.'

'You don't have to talk if...'

Julie shook her head at Grace. 'I'm fine.' She coughed. 'We went up to the ward, Donald and Rachel. Alexander and myself.' Julie sat up, reached for her cup with a steady hand, and took a deliberate sip.

Grace looked at Alexander, but his head was still down. 'Where was I?'

Julie used her serviette to pat her mouth dry. 'No one knew. At first, we thought they'd shifted you to keep you away from the other sick children. The father of the injured baby was banging his fist on the nurses' desk and they were busy with him. It took a while before we could get anyone's attention. We waited for ages. Euan turned up. The doctor came eventually, and I knew something was really wrong. He was holding his stethoscope in his hands. So strange. They're usually around people's necks or in their pockets, you know? He said that you couldn't be found. You'd been quite well, ready to go home. Your cot was empty. You were gone.'

Grace frowned. 'But how could that happen? There's security in hospitals. Cameras. Everything!'

'Not then. It was 1987. They had built the Paxton Community Hospital just after the war. It was a maze of rooms and corridors. The children's ward was part of the old nursing home area. The nurses couldn't see what was going on all at once. The police said that area had four different exits, including a fire door to stairs going all the way to the fourth floor and right down to the basement where the boiler and the incinerator was. The shutter door was open because the gardener had the mower out. There wasn't any security because, up to then, it had been a quiet, suburban hospital surrounded by quiet, suburban houses.' Julie took one of Grace's hands and squeezed it. 'You were gone.'

Grace could imagine the panic. A crying Julie, a pale Donald. Police, nurses, the gardener out looking. Journalists and photographers. News vans, oversized 1980s microphones. How long had Norah's disappearance been front page news? A day, a week, a month? Other scandals would have eventually taken over. But not for Julie.

Grace watched the woman take another sip of surely-by-now cold tea. Norah's mother. How had she lived with the pain of that all along? Her hand was still in Grace's. 'I'm so sorry,' Grace said.

Julie turned to her. 'You said we should let all that time go and start again.' She reached over and cupped Grace's cheek. 'I can do that. Now that you're back.'

Out of the corner of her eye, Grace saw Alexander sit up and sigh. 'Well then,' she said briskly, 'let's do it. Let's start again.'

This was what I wanted in the first place, Grace thought as Julie hugged her. *So why do I feel that I'm holding something thin-shelled in my hand?*

TWENTY-ONE

It was strange how quickly something became normal. Colin rose early, leaving the apartment to drive alone to Dryburgh as Alexander kept sleeping. It was the second day in a row. For one who'd never missed a day of work in two years, Alexander was remarkably nonchalant.

'So I'll go work with your father then?' Colin had said last night.

Alexander had shrugged. 'You're the apprentice.'

Donald was expecting him at the crack of dawn which, in the long hours of summer, was crazy-early. Colin pulled up slowly on the gravel, aware that Julie would be as asleep as her son, but Donald slid the house door closed with a bang and called greetings heartily to Colin, despite Colin getting out of the van and hurrying towards him. 'We'll take your van, lad. You've been working on this one.'

Colin had been at the McAlister's house for quite a few days, on and off. It was another of those 'come-back-when-we-have-more-money' jobs, this time on a long, low wall that surrounded historic sheds. It was a beautiful property that sloped up a forgiving hill, with bald-faced sheep in droves plucking at lush grass. Colin couldn't help but think of photographs of Merinos back home dragging their feet through the dust on the way to a water hole.

Donald settled into the passenger's seat, slipping sunglasses on as they turned onto the road. Colin glanced at him. What he could see of Donald's face was expressionless. That in itself was weird. Donald was nearly always smiling or whistling or looking bright-eyed. This Donald was morose. He sat with one hand on the side of the seat, the other hanging from the bar above the window, wordless. Colin turned on the radio to fill the silence.

Old Mr McAlister was waiting for them when they pulled up. He was talking to their shepherd, a young girl with a sour face who tapped her stick repeatedly on the ground. Old Mac waved her off and approached the van. 'You're here,' he said, peering in through the window to Donald. 'I thought you had some family business to attend.'

Donald's hand on the seat curled. 'We're here. We've got a job to do.'

'Aye.' Old Mac stooped lower to see Colin. 'Not got your boy with you.'

'You know Colin. He's Australian. He can't help that.'

Colin nodded at Old Mac. The man was grooved so much it looked as if his face was carved. No one laughed at Donald's joke, although it usually got a smile at least. Delivery is everything, Colin thought of Donald's glum tone.

They worked at either ends of a section, filling the gaps with other stone, reconstructing the dry wall's integrity. Donald was on the phone a lot, always walking a way into the paddock before ducking his head to talk. Colin tried not to listen, but words drifted his way. One call might have been Julie. He heard 'can't do it, love' several times. The other calls were probably business. Donald glanced towards Colin now and then. There was a lot of head shaking.

At lunch, they sat against the wall with the sun on their faces. Colin let his eyes close after eating, the warmth oozing into his skin. At home, he'd be rushing for the shade or to slather another handful of sunscreen on his nose. This sun was gentle. He'd miss it when it came time to leave. Australian sun felt dangerous, even in winter. It could burn, even when clouds covered it.

Alicia had been too long in the sun when they found her.

Colin sat up. He had drifted off, surely. Alicia only came to him at night. She slunk into his dreams, turning them black. He blinked, wiped his face, looked around for Donald. A sheep had wandered over to the van and was nudging a wheel hopefully. Colin could see Donald's legs underneath, past the animal. He was walking back and forth, an urgent tone to the snatches of conversation Colin could hear.

Colin drank the rest of his tea and packed up his lunch things. The cure to Alicia was exhausting work. He carried his bag to the van, ready to spend the afternoon working as hard as he could. Donald's words stopped him.

'It can't be her. You've already found Norah...'

Colin let his bag drop to the end of his fingers.

'Carl, you said you didn't need more...

He brought the bag up to the cradle of his arms.

'I need proof right now...'

Colin moved carefully forward, letting his bag down in the grass next to the van. The sheep sniffed at it curiously. He shooed it away.

'Wait on, I've got to go...'

The sheep skittered away. Colin picked up his bag, opened the back of the van, and flung it in noisily. He feigned surprise as Donald stepped around. 'Sorry, I think I fell asleep.'

Donald grunted, waved the phone, and said, 'It's okay, lad. I do it too when I get a bit of sun. You right to go on?'

'Yeah, I'll keep working along the same line.'

'Good, good. Listen, I'm going to make some calls. Work out a few things.'

Colin shrugged. 'You're the boss.'

Donald had already turned away to sit in the passenger's seat, the door closing on his leg resting on the sill. Colin went over to the wall, working so that the sun, and Donald, was at his back. A faint headache was taking hold. Maybe the sun had got to him after all?

The grey stone held its history. The areas of wall that needed repair had not met with natural disaster but man-made accidents. A truck collecting sheep for market backing too far. The tractor, slasher up, turning too tightly. Feed tumbling accidentally from the tray of a truck. Simple mistakes over decades of farming. Colin smoothed each rock free of grass and dirt, turned it over and eyed its position in the wall. If the pattern held and the rock was right, it solved the puzzle.

'You knew then?'

Colin heard Donald before he saw the shadow.

'What?' He turned, still gripping a rock.

'About this lass who turned up the other night. She'd found Alexander.'

Colin lowered the stone. 'Yes, she found him.'

'It's not her, you know.' Donald's mouth stayed open, his face was red. He was leaning forward slightly, as if ready to pounce.

'How could it be?'

'Eh?'

'How could it be Norah, after all this time?'

'Oh, she's alive.'

'*What?* Donald?'

Donald rubbed both his hands over his head. 'I've had this

investigator looking for her ever since you went to Melbourne. He's found her. Norah.' He grimaced.

Colin shook his head. 'Where? I mean, we looked everywhere, read the papers, talked to Julie about what had been done before. There was no trace.'

'Well, there must be. Carl's found her.'

'When?'

'The same day as that girl turned up to Dryburgh. Funny, isn't it?'

'Not really.' Colin tossed the rock gently into the tufty grass. 'Bit of a coincidence, isn't it, this girl turning up as your fellow found another?'

Donald shrugged. 'He said he was close. He was just waiting on confirmation. I rang him the night that girl came along. He'd got it, the confirmation.'

'What was it?'

'What was what?'

'The confirmation.'

'Oh, he didn't say exactly. Only that it was confirmed.' Donald let one hand rub the length of his face. 'Carl found Norah, and he's bringing her here.'

'Here?'

'Scotland. He's bringing her from Cornwell to Scotland. She's been living in Penzance.'

'In the UK? All this time?'

'Well, she didn't know, did she? Carl said she was very shocked to find out who she really was. It took a bit of time to convince her. Carl worked hard on that, he said. Spent a few weeks talking to her.'

Colin shook his head. 'Look, I'm not really involved in all this. You should tell Alexander.'

'He's not going to believe it now, is he?'

'He's pretty sure that this girl is Norah.'

'What do you think?'

Colin crossed his arms and leaned back onto the wall. Lichen flaked off and fell on his arm. 'When people go missing, they don't usually come back. Not after all this time.' He hesitated. 'Not alive.'

'So you don't think that girl with Alexander right now is Norah?'

'There's no proof she is.'

'Well, Carl has the proof that he's found the real one.' Donald sighed and looked up at the sky. 'It's been hard.'

Never once in the time Colin had spent with Donald, either at work or at his home, had there been a mention of the need to look for Norah. Not in the time Alexander had spent planning the trip to Australia, not when Julie and Alexander huddled together over old pictures, and especially not when Colin and Alexander had come home with nothing. 'Why now, Donald? Why would you do this after all this time?'

Donald closed his eyes and lowered his head. He breathed out noisily and then stared at Colin. 'It's for Julie. She will never get over losing that baby. I did it for her.' He spoke more softly. 'I'd do anything for her.'

Colin nodded slowly. Donald's face was deep red now. His eyes were a little glazed, as if either the sun or the talking had been too much.

'I'm thirsty.' Colin indicated the van. 'Want a drink?'

Donald followed Colin back to the truck where he took a cold drink without appearing to notice Colin not drinking anything. Colin sat on the edge of the open back. After a moment, Donald sat with him, the van dipping noisily. They sat quietly, long enough for the sheep to come back with a couple of friends. They nosed around the men's feet.

'What do they want?' Colin said.

'They think we're going to feed them.'

'Ah.'

Donald finished his drink and screwed the lid back on the empty bottle. He sighed again.

'What happens next, Donald?'

'Carl's going to be here on Sunday.'

'With the new Norah?'

Donald folded his arms. 'With the *old* Norah. With our Norah.' He lifted his shoulders and let them drop. 'So it doesn't matter now.'

'What doesn't?'

'What that other girl is doing. The one who found Alexander. She'll be proven a fake.'

'Are you going to tell Alexander?'

'No. Not Julie either.' Donald stood, the van rocking in protest. 'Don't you either, hear? I want them to see Norah then that will stop this thing that's happening. Years of it.' He rubbed his face again, his head. 'It's got to stop. It will.'

'And this Norah that Carl has found?' Colin put both his hands on his knees and stared at the sheep. 'What if she doesn't want to know about it?'

'Och, she'll want to know us.' Donald looked at Colin with a benevolent smile. 'People always want to know about their real family. People who've been gone for so long, they want to come back home.' He turned, as if just remembering the wall, and went back to work.

Colin sat for a moment longer, hands gripping his thighs painfully. 'No, they don't,' he said quietly at Donald. The big man didn't hear, and Colin didn't repeat it.

IT WAS Julie's idea to travel back to The Borders the long way. Grace sat in the front of the car; the window cracked open so the rushing air played with her hair. Alexander sat, knees tucked up, in the back of the little car. Grace looked over her shoulder at him. He smiled, rolled his eyes, and used his hands to imitate his mother's gabbling.

'You were born in Edinburgh, only because I had placenta praevia – I had it with Alexander, too – and they thought you were too at risk to be in the local hospital. I was in for four days, I think, before I had you. Alexander stayed with Donald and they had a great time, or that's what Donald said when I finally got home with you. A little baby and the house like a disaster zone. Rachel was fantastic, she cleaned up for me and looked after Alexander so I had some time with you in peace. Not that you were anything out of the ordinary, Alexander, but two little kids were harder work than I'd ever thought possible, especially with none of our parents being very useful. It was why we had to go to Australia to show you off, Norah, because my parents would not travel on a plane as far as Scotland. They would hardly travel from Brisbane to Melbourne. Frankly, I'm glad they didn't fly out.' Julie stopped abruptly.

Grace had been listening more to the flow than Julie's actual words. The silence took a moment to register. Alexander, she noted, hadn't registered it at all. He looked out the window, fingers tapping on the window edge as he listened to some sort of music on his phone.

'Why do you say that?' Grace thought she'd better say something.

'Well.' Julie brushed hair away from her eyes and slid her sunglasses from the top of her head to her nose. 'I was going to say that I liked going back home. Visiting Mum and Dad gave me an excuse to return.' She turned towards Grace, then brought her head back without looking at her. 'One thing you notice, Norah, is that people here don't think about Australia. Not at all. Australia could be on another planet. To them, it's so far away it's unthinkable that anyone would want to visit. I mean, Europe's only hours away. Spain, Greece, Italy. America's half a day away. Australia? Days of flying, especially if you have a stopover. It's totally off the radar.'

Grace opened her mouth to say something, anything, to console Julie's bitterness, but Julie reached a hand out to stop her.

'No, it's all right. You get used to it. I had an excuse to go back. After you... disappeared, I didn't want to go back. Not if they couldn't help me find you.'

'So you haven't.'

'Only when my parents died.' Julie smiled. 'But I can now, can't I? I've got to go back to see where you grew up! See where you work! And your house. Where you live.' She turned all the way, her smile broadening.

'Mum! The road!' Alexander pulled his ear buds out and sat up.

'Right, sorry! All good now. Look, here's Selkirk.'

Grace stared out the window at the town. Julie continued to talk. Fatigue settled in, crushing Grace's shoulders. Selkirk, then Melrose. The tourist route. The houses set along the street, edged in flowery reds and pinks, were blurring. Another bakery, more churches. Grace tried to differentiate them. Hadn't they just been past that shop? Even the people going about their business looked the same, striding up footpaths, across roads. Grace closed her eyes, rubbed them carefully with one finger. Her eyelashes caught. She peered at the side mirror, trying to see whether they were coming unstuck. She felt slightly ill, the fug of the car and Julie's endless, relentless chatter making her stomach churn. She put the window down a fraction more.

'Mum.' Alexander had a hand on the driver's seat to pull himself forward. 'I think Norah's had enough for the moment. How about you drive us to your place? I could do with a drink.'

Julie shook her head, making her hair fly about her shoulders, then nodded. 'Yes, I'm sorry.' She fell silent.

Grace closed her eyes again and rested her forehead on one palm. When the car slowed to turn into the house yard again, she took a deep breath in and let it out slowly, opening her eyes to the sight of the elegantly restored stables. She licked her lips and turned to Julie. 'I didn't notice on my last visit how gorgeous this place is.'

Julie parked the car before acknowledging the remark. 'It's a very easy house to live in.' She smiled, her hand this time connecting with Grace's as it reached out. 'It helps that you like it.'

Grace followed Alexander as he walked with his mother up the sandstone steps and into the house. It was pleasantly warm inside. Grace lifted her hair from her neck and let it fall back to settle off her skin. Alexander was at the fridge. He held a beer up to Grace, who shook her head. Her stomach was better, but still roiled. She perched on the edge of the couch while Julie fussed with the kettle.

Only when Alexander had plonked himself opposite her did she notice the line of photographs on the wall. Three photos, the centre one of a baby by itself, the other two family portraits with a toddler peeking over the shoulder of its parents as a small baby lay asleep in Julie's arms.

'We were so cute.'

She looked at Alexander, who raised the bottle to the photos.

'That's us?'

'Who else would it be?'

Who else indeed? Grace didn't remember any photos on the wall of her home, only a scrappy photo album with photos in envelopes stuffed at the front. Not one had been put in. Her mother couldn't have done it, her father wouldn't have. Grace hadn't thought of it in years. Where had it gone?

Alexander sipped his beer. 'Why do I feel that some of this is new to you?' he said, quietly, so Julie couldn't hear.

'It's all new to me.'

'No, not us.' Alexander pointed his head at his mother, who was clattering crockery. '*This.*' He waved at the photos, the room, the entire house.

Grace blinked at him. How could he know? She stood up, gathered her skirt so it brushed against her legs. 'I'm going to help your mother.'

She heard him as she walked away but didn't turn. 'Our mother,' he'd said. Three strides it took to take it in. Her shoulders relaxed.

'Feeling better?' Julie looked up anxiously.

Grace studied the woman's face in front of her. It was soft-looking, gentle. Loving. 'Yes,' she said. 'I am.'

TWENTY-TWO

I'm not known for cowardly behaviour, thought Julie as she drove Alexander and Norah back to Edinburgh, *but that's how I'm acting.*

She hated the nervousness, the slight fear in letting her children stay until Donald got home. The end of the afternoon had promised a good future. The three of them in the living area, sprawled on couches, telling stories. Mostly Julie telling stories, but the others listened. It felt good. Donald might have huffed in and splintered it.

'Speed, Mum,' said Alexander lazily from the back seat.

Julie dropped the car back a little. It wasn't as if she was in a hurry to get rid of them; it was more that the road felt dry and smooth, the air luxuriantly warm, and she had both her son and her daughter with her. Julie was filled with incredulousness, as if she'd been waiting all her life and, here, a present had arrived.

She glanced at Norah. The girl's head was leaning on an arm propped up on the windowsill. Eyes closed, her long lashes sat against her cheek. That careful make-up around her eyes, clever really. Julie nodded to herself. Norah knew how to emphasise the dusky blue of her eyes, the alignment of those cheekbones. Her lip colour was slightly exaggerated, Julie noted, drawn just outside the natural line. A talent for style, certainly.

They came into the city. Norah woke, sitting up abruptly. She dabbed at the area of her face she'd squashed against her arm and checked the mirror in the passenger's visor.

'It's fine,' said Julie, eyes on the road.

Norah glanced wide-eyed at her. 'Pardon?'

Julie tapped her own face with the pads of her fingers. 'Nothing out of place.'

Norah nodded, checked once more in the mirror, and flipped the visor up. Her hands went to her lap, clenched stiffly.

I should have asked her about the mother, Julie thought. She pushed the guilt away. She'd asked about the father, learning about his retail jobs, the fact that he'd tried to look after the broken family. She'd asked about grandparents (dead), other relatives (dead or unknown), and pets (never had any). The mother? Julie sensed that Alexander knew more. He had lounged on the couch, eating biscuits, watching. Occasionally he added to his mother's stories, making Norah laugh. That sound! The pureness of it! She'd imagined Norah having a tinkling laugh, but that was the girl-Norah. Here was the woman-Norah. She laughed like she was singing, a staccato, descending alto. Just like, Julie remembered, her mother used to.

'You can drop me anywhere.' Norah pointed along the main street.

'I can take you right to your door.'

Norah shook her head. 'No, it's in the tourist area. You can't drive through.'

'Oh.' Julie slowed for a traffic light. 'We could go back to Alexander's?'

'If it's okay with you,' Norah said softly, gazing out of the window, 'I'll go on. I'm quite tired.'

'It's alright, Mum.' Alexander's voice was weary. 'You can come up for a cuppa with me before you drive back.'

Julie glanced at the car's clock. 'No. Look at the time. I should get back straight away. Your dad...'

In the rear-view mirror, Alexander shrugged. They hadn't spoken, father and son, since the evening Norah had turned up. Part of her didn't want the son to hate the father, but Julie couldn't say anything. Now, with Norah in the front seat and Alexander stuffed into the back, she was vivid with anger at Donald. Come to think of it, had she talked to him since that night?

'Here.' Norah indicated a parking space to their left as a car pulled out of it. Julie turned the sedan into it automatically, pulling to a crooked stop.

'We'll see you again?'

Norah smiled. Her teeth were squarer than Julie's, she noted. Bright, straight, Australian teeth. 'Yes. Alexander has my phone number.'

'Could I?' Julie ran her tongue across her teeth. 'Would it be alright if I had it as well?'

'Of course.' Norah took Julie's phone and entered the number. Her nails were the same milky green as her dress. 'Here you are.'

'Tomorrow?'

'I really should go to work tomorrow,' said Alexander, yawning.

'I've taken the week off.'

'I thought you were helping Uncle Euan?'

Julie tried not to think of Euan. 'He'll be okay.'

'I'll let you know.' Norah opened the car door, bent to the window and waved through it. Julie watched her go, the long dress whirling as she went.

'What do you think, Mum?' Alexander put his head through the seats to speak into his mother's ears.

'I can't think at all.'

Alexander laughed, pecked her cheek, and slid across to the kerbside door. 'I'll walk from here. Save you a bit of time.'

Julie nodded. He gave her a brief wave and headed towards a side street.

Traffic whizzed past. Norah had disappeared across the road and into the park. Alexander was on his way to his flat. *Here I am*, she thought, *sitting in the heart of this city, as alone as I've ever been*. She wanted to scramble out of the car and run after Norah, catching her arm and never letting her go. Instead, she steered the car out of its parking spot, and drove back to Dryburgh.

A long, slow drive. A hedge trimmer trapped her for ages. The afternoon traffic congested on the narrow roads. Even so, it felt too soon to be pulling into home. The vans were there, Donald and Colin leaning over the outdoor table, the job book stretched out flat. Donald looked up as Julie got out. There he was, her husband. Tall, broad, red-faced. Grinning at her as if she was a prize. Even heading down the steps and folding her in his dusty, solid arms. Had he realised his mistake? She sighed, letting herself relax.

'I'll be going then.' Colin had the book under his arm as he walked to the van.

Julie pulled back. 'Stay for a bit, Colin. Have a bite to eat before you go back.'

Colin lifted one hand without looking at her. 'Thanks, Julie, but I should go.'

'You sure?'

He nodded, pulling the creaking van door open and getting in. One arm went out the window as he drove past, a goodbye salute.

Julie frowned. 'Is he alright?'

'Aye, he's good. Works hard, that lad. Going to miss him when he goes back.'

'Did he say when?'

'No. Have to be soon, though.' Donald put his arm around her as they walked to the house. 'So, we're alone again.'

Julie slipped out from under his hold as she went through the door. Alone with Donald? She realised that it didn't really matter to her whether or not he was there. If he was, there was more food to cook, clothes to wash. If he wasn't, she ate by herself, read a magazine. Either way, they filled the evening with activities that suited themselves.

He grabbed her again as she put her bag on the end of the kitchen bench. 'How about some afternoon delight?'

Delight was certainly in his eyes. Julie tried a smile. 'I'm so glad, Donald, that you've come to your senses.'

'Senses?'

'About Norah. You aren't angry anymore.'

'Norah?' Donald spoke the name as if it was brand new. 'Oh, *Norah*. Aye, I have good news about that.'

Julie stepped back. 'What good news?'

'Oh, you'll see.'

'What do you mean? Donald, I spent the day with her. It was wonderful. What good news do you have?'

'You were with...' Donald rubbed his face with a large, cracked hand. 'That's where you were today.'

'Yes. Alexander and I were with Norah.'

He trembled. It was over in a split second. 'Listen, love. Don't get caught up with that one. Don't see her again.'

'But you said you have good news!'

'Aye, I do, but I'm not telling you yet. Just you listen to me and stay away from that girl.'

'Stay away from Norah?' Julie shook her head and pushed at

the edge of her hair. 'Why on earth would I do that?'

'Because.' Donald turned away, one hand on his head smoothing the stubble on its top. 'Because, Julie.'

'*Because* is not a reason.'

He spun awkwardly back to her. 'Can't you trust me just this once?'

'What do you mean, just this once? I trust you over many things. But you aren't listening to me.' Julie stepped closer and put one finger on her husband's chest. 'I am not staying away from my daughter when I've found her again.'

'That girl is not Norah!'

If not for the twist of anxiety in Donald's words, Julie would have exploded. She felt her rage simmering lava-deep in her belly. 'How would you know that? You've spent less than a minute in her company and most of that you were yelling at her.'

Donald looked down at her, pleading about something. Julie shook her head. Whatever game he was playing, it was no use to her. 'What is it, Donald?'

'The real Norah is living in Cornwell.'

'What?' Julie's laugh made Donald grimace. He swallowed.

'It's the truth, love. I've had someone investigating her. She lives in Cornwell and she's coming to see us on Sunday.'

Nausea rocked Julie. She put one hand over her mouth. What stupid thing had Donald done now? He stood in front of her, one hand still on his head. He was waiting, she knew, for gratitude. 'Oh, Donald...'

'It's the good news I was telling you about. I was trying to make it a surprise, but you seem to be all caught up with that other girl-'

'You don't see it, do you?'

'See what?'

'Her. Norah. How she belongs to this family.'

'Julie, love, you've been taken in by some red-headed beauty-'

'*I've* been taken in! You, on the other hand, are being rational, are you? Can't you see-' There she stopped. He couldn't see. Why would he? There was no connection between Donald and Norah, and he wasn't – what was the phrase to use? – *emotionally intelligent* enough to see the instant bond between herself, Alexander and Norah. 'Donald, I'm so sorry.'

His eyes brightened. 'I told you you'd see the truth eventually, love. I'm sorry, too. About that girl. How she just turned up. Wait – where are you going?'

'I need a walk, Donald. By myself.' Julie was already stepping through the door.

'Yes, of course. It's a shock. I'll make us a drink when you get back.'

She didn't bother nodding. It would take more than a gin and tonic to resolve whatever was going on in Donald's head.

The familiar path was unexpectedly empty for a fine summer evening. Maybe others sensed she needed the spongy path with its flickering canopy to be entirely hers. Powered by the now erupting volcano, Julie moved up the path with her head down. The steep bits made her pant. She went faster. Her face warmed, sweat prickled her armpits and her brow. Once she stumbled, one knee connecting to the earthy floor, but she was up again, heading onwards despite the ache of the impact. She reached William in the shadows and stood directly underneath.

William Wallace had fought single-mindedly for his cause. People thought him mad, but Julie knew how he'd done it. He had one focus, and nothing veered him from it. It was easy, she decided, because there was no choice.

WELL AFTER GIN and tonic time, she came back down the hill. The house lights were on. Donald watched her through the glass. 'Where have you been?' he said, a hint of heaviness tainting his concern.

Julie held a wad of notes up. 'I've been doing a job for the society.'

'Still collecting those things?'

Euan. On the couch in the same position as Norah had been earlier that day. A chill ran through Julie, making her shiver.

'They tell stories.'

'About what?' Euan sat up.

Julie put the notes on the bench and squared their edges. 'About people's lives. I've got thirty years' worth of notes I'm documenting for the Wallace Monument Society. There are threads in there. The same handwriting on notes for months on end. Stories stop and others start.'

'I see.'

She scowled. 'I've had one story going ever since I started collecting. Someone writes a new line to it nearly every week. Types, I should say, on a real typewriter with a faded ribbon. A small piece of paper every time. That's the oldest story.'

'And what is the story about?'

Julie looked at her brother-in-law. One long leg was flung over the other. An arm stretched down the back of the couch. His eyes were slightly magnified by his glasses, their strong blue like winter Australian sky at dusk. He looked like a politician, an aura of confidence arming his features. He looked how he was. Successful. She picked the notes up. 'Loss.'

'Ah,' he said.

'I'll put them away now.'

Julie took the neat pile of notes to her study. She could hear the murmur of voices from the living area, a low rumble of question and answer. Had Donald called Euan to tell him about the second Norah? She started back to the lounge, then stopped. Even if Euan could see Norah in the same way that she could, he couldn't argue against Donald. Even pathetic Donald, with his misplaced faith in his brother, would see something suspicious in a defence of Norah. The real Norah.

She sat at her desk and idly rifled through the notes. A bus must have been through. There was a lot of 'Sheree' from Arizonas and 'Marvolene' from South Dakotas, as if leaving a calling card like that was the response to being impressed by the Earl of Buchan's gift to the people. Why do some people even bother touring the world, she thought, if they can't stop themselves from planting a flag everywhere they went?

From the living room, Donald laughed. It was relaxed, hearty. He had told Euan, she was sure, and Euan was doing his best to reassure Donald that, of course, he was right. Anything to distract him from the truth. She flung the notes down and went down to the where they sat.

Donald looked up at her, the laughter still across his face.

'What's so funny?'

The smile slipped from his face at her tone. 'Funny? Not really funny, just something Euan said.'

Euan had his arm still flung across the back of the couch, the crossed leg displaying a smart, tan Derby. He raised his eyebrows at Julie. She frowned. 'An old family story,' he said.

She shrugged, her eyes on Donald. 'You told him what you've done?'

'Yes.' Donald wriggled. 'He's very happy for us.'

'I'm sure he is.'

Donald shifted again. 'Julie.'

'Why are you here, Euan?'

Euan uncrossed his legs and stretched them out under the coffee table. 'You haven't been at work. I was checking everything was okay.'

'Ever heard of a phone?'

'Julie...' Donald spread his hands out across his broad thighs.

'It's alright, Donald. I think I've come at a bad time.' Euan's arm stayed across the leather couch top.

'I've been with Norah. Alexander and I have been catching up with her.'

'That girl,' Donald said to Euan.

'*Norah.*' Julie heard her voice echo in the spacious, white room.

Euan stood, buttoning his jacket as he went. 'Now that I know you're okay, I'll go. Although, Julie, if you aren't coming in to work, I hoped that I could leave some bookwork here for you?'

'I won't be back in the surgery for a while.'

'All the more reason, if you wouldn't mind.' Euan nodded at Donald. 'I have some things in the car.'

Julie let Euan go out the door before she followed him. Bookwork? She had no time for that. She caught him at his car. 'Euan? I'm not-'

His grip spun her around until she met the solid side of the car. 'What's going on, Julie?'

'Let me go.' She wrenched her arm away, but he blocked any retreat to the house.

'What are you playing at? Meeting with that girl?'

'Why wouldn't I, Euan? She's Norah!'

'And what's Donald up to? An investigator? Why did you let him do that?'

'I had no idea he was!' She dodged to the side. He stepped across. 'Euan. Stop it.'

'Let it go, Julie.'

'What is wrong with you, Euan? Why would I let it go?'

He leaned closer, lowering his head so she could see through his spectacles to blazing blue eyes. 'We don't want to dig up the past.'

He was too close. Julie put a hand on his chest and pushed. He moved back a little, not enough. 'It's not digging. She is our daughter!'

He went forward again. 'This is ridiculous, Julie.'

Julie was panting. She pushed again at his chest, both hands flat against him. He didn't move. 'What's it to you? No one needs to know about us, about her. They didn't before. Why would they now?'

He shook his head. 'I don't need this, Julie.'

'Don't need it?' She slid out from behind the car. 'What does that mean?'

He smoothed his hand over his hair then stretched it out to her, letting it drop before he could touch her. 'Julie, Norah was never in my life.'

'You didn't want her back then. You could have her now.'

He closed his eyes, opening them suddenly to regard her sternly. 'No, I couldn't.' He tipped his head slightly. 'I don't want to live in the past and neither do you. '

'Euan, I-'

'You have never told Donald the truth.'

Julie flicked her fringe away. 'No.'

'Are you going to tell him now? Could you be so *unkind*?'

From behind Julie, back in the house, she could hear Donald whistling. The tune was unrecognisable, interspersed with some song words that made no sense. 'I might. Maybe he deserves to know.'

His grip on her arm was sudden and pinched. She was too shocked to pull back. There'll be a bruise, she thought even as she stared at him open-mouthed.

'If you know what's good for you, leave it.'

He let her go, got into his car, and went, gravel hitting her shins as it spun out from under his wheels. She could only watch, her arm aching, as the sleek car disappeared.

TWENTY-THREE

Alexander woke to his alarm with the full intention of going to work. He pulled on work clothes and went to find his boots. The flat was quiet, Colin still sleeping. It was light outside, and a jogger went past, his shoes pounding on the downhill, the noise rising through the open kitchen window. Alexander leaned over the windowsill and sought the familiar landscape of New Town. Somewhere over the impression of Nor Loch was Grace. No, he couldn't go to work, not with her in the city.

He texted his father.

'What's going on?' Colin stood in the doorway, rubbing sleep-strewn hair.

'Telling Dad I'm not going in today.'

Colin stopped yawning. 'Neither am I.'

'Why not?'

'Because I have an uneasy feeling about what you're doing.'

Alexander shrugged. 'That's not a reason to not go to work.'

'It is.' Colin folded his arms.

'What about Dad?'

'If you're that concerned about him, you go to work.'

'Why are you being so calm about this?'

Colin shrugged.

'I mean,' Alexander put the phone down on the table, 'you're really angry about Norah. Why aren't you screaming at me?'

Colin shrugged again.

'Do you know something I don't?'

'I'm going to have a shower, okay?' Colin moved into the bathroom before Alexander could say anything more.

Donald didn't answer the text. Alexander twirled the phone on the table. It was too early to contact Norah. He wasn't really sure he wanted to. Every time they'd met so far, it had been planned. Staged. What was she like, he wondered, when she wasn't expecting her brother or her mother? Left to her own, would she visit a museum or go hiking or maybe spend the day in a pub? She'd told him a lot about her childhood, but something was missing about the time period since her father had died. Did she have a boyfriend at home, one that was pining for her? There was no sense of who Norah was when she was not with him. When she was *Claudia*.

Alexander changed his clothes and had his keys in his hand as Colin came out of the bathroom.

'Hey, wait! I'm coming with you.'

'You don't know where I'm going.'

'I know what you're doing. Give me one minute.'

Alexander tossed his house keys in the air, caught them, tossed, caught. One minute was enough time to go without his friend, but he didn't. Colin came out, combing wet dark hair roughly with his fingers, and nodded. They left the apartment as the morning work traffic started rolling and followed some workers travelling on foot to the city centre.

They walked for ten minutes in silence.

'What are we doing?' Colin asked, pausing before he crossed a road to let a car pass.

'We're looking for Norah.'

'So, not going to *see* her but *looking* for her.'

'Aye.'

Colin glanced at Alexander. 'You sounded just like your father then.'

Alexander shrugged, heading across the road. 'You've been spending too much time with him.'

'Not a lot of choice when we're one worker down.'

'Shut it, Astle.'

They got to Princes Street and waited for the lights. There were more people now, heads down and pounding the street. Early tourists in sensible, all-weather clothes stared around delightedly. Workers dodged them. When the lights changed, a large group crossed with Colin and Alexander, and veered off towards the information centre.

'Do you know where she is?'

Alexander nodded. 'I was at her apartment the other day. But I want to see her without...'

'Without her knowing it?' Colin laughed. 'Turning into a stalker? Didn't think you had it in you.'

'I'm not stalking her. I just want to see her...'

'In the wild.'

'What?'

'I get it, Cameron. You want to see what she's really like.' Colin put a solid hand on his friend's back. 'Good idea.'

Colin followed Alexander, one step behind, as they wound up the hill. Festival posters plastered the fence. Faces glared, grinned or grimaced out at them, depending on whether they related to the book, theatre or comedy programmes. Alexander glanced back to Colin and caught him looking grimly at a poster that should have made him laugh. Alexander frowned. There was something going on, something Colin knew. Be damned if he was going to beg to find out.

At least in the main tourist drag of the Royal Mile, there was breakfast. Colin stopped next to an open café. Alexander was a few metres ahead before he realised. He came back, scowling, but Colin had sat at the outside table. 'Come on,' he said, 'I'm starving.'

Alexander looked around before he pulled out a chair and slumped into it. 'She's staying over there.' He pointed towards St Giles Street.

'You can watch the crowd from here.' Colin threw a menu at him.

'I'm not trying to catch her out. I want to know more of what she's like.'

Colin's eyebrows went up.

Alexander slapped the menu on the table. 'I still believe who she says she is.'

Colin leaned forward. 'But you've got a doubt about something.' He ran his finger down the food list but stopped halfway. 'Alexander,' he started.

Someone caught Alexander's eye. Someone lithe and graceful. 'It's her.'

'What?'

Norah was across the road, walking smartly down the hill, long skirt brushing her legs. She had the same sunglasses on that she'd had that first day, and the same bag. Alexander remembered how casually she'd hung onto its strap as she stood next to the vacant block. He'd been startled by her confidence then. He saw it now in the way she made her way straight through the straggles of people milling on the footpath. Her back was straight, her head high. 'She looks like Norah.'

'You already said that, even though you only knew her as a baby.'

'No, I don't mean that.' Alexander twisted in his chair so he could follow her. 'She looks the same as whenever we've seen her. She looks like the Norah she says she was.'

Colin was quiet for a moment. 'Where's she going?'

'To meet Mum.'

'How do you know?'

Alexander pointed. There was Julie, the morning light picking up the gold strands of her highlighted hair. She was leaning forward on her toes, her mouth open in a slight smile. Norah hadn't seen her yet. She continued on her way past Julie, who reached out a hand and touched her arm. Norah spun, a slash of anger across her features, before she stopped, smiled, let her shoulders drop. They stared at each other for a second before Julie opened her arms for a hug. Norah kept one hand on the strap of her bag, so it was a lop-sided embrace.

'We should call them over,' said Colin.

Alexander shook his head.

Without moving from their awkward position in the middle of the footpath, Alexander saw Norah bend slightly to Julie's height and ask something. Julie put a hand to her hair, patting it into shape, before clutching at Norah's arm again and talking earnestly. Norah pulled back slightly, but Julie kept talking. He stood but didn't go to them.

Julie finished talking. She was stroking Norah's arm now, soothing her as if she was a flighty horse about to bolt. Alexander frowned.

Colin stood as well. 'Alexander, I've got to tell you something.'

'Later.'

'No, now.'

Alexander walked off towards his mother, hearing his friend's urgent call but letting it go. Julie turned as he approached, a startle that turned to relief. Norah gave him a quick, narrow stare before Julie pulled them both into a hug.

Alexander's head knocked Norah's. She pulled back quickly. He felt his face warm. 'Come and have breakfast with us.'

Norah looked across the street. 'Colin's here.'

'Aye. Neither of us are working today.'

Julie made a huffing sound but moved off before her son could say anything. Colin pulled two more chairs to the table.

'Hello, Colin.' Julie patted his arm as Colin nodded. Norah lifted a finger in a brief greeting. Colin looked at her, a quick frown creasing his forehead.

'What are you two doing?' Alexander sat down heavily. 'Meeting up without me.'

'Julie had some news for Norah.' Colin's voice was harsh, and Julie gave him a wide-eyed look. He shrugged at Alexander. 'Something I tried to tell you.'

'What is it?' Alexander watched his mother. 'Have I missed something?'

Julie hesitated. Alexander leaned his elbows on the table. What could she possibly have to say that was going to disrupt the picture in front of him? His best friend, his mum, his sister. He felt light, as if a blackness had lifted from him since Norah had appeared. That crushing despair he'd felt from the failed Australian trip had gone. If only Norah was smiling. Why wasn't she smiling?

Before Julie could speak, Colin put his hand up. 'Your dad told me that he's found the real Norah.'

Alexander shook his head at the strange look on his friend's face. 'Well, aye, she's here.'

'Not...' Norah twisted to Colin, who glared back and continued on. 'Alexander, your dad has been working with a private investigator who found Norah in Cornwell. She'll be here on Sunday.'

Alexander felt a coldness touch his neck. 'I don't know what you mean.'

Colin leaned forward. 'A different Norah. Donald's found someone else who says she's Norah.'

'He's wrong.' Alexander's face felt stiff as he talked. 'That's stupid. Norah is here.' He put a hand on Norah's shoulder that still had the bag hanging from it. 'Right here.'

A breeze wafted a brief smell of summer dust over the table. Colin shrugged at Norah, who sat stone-faced in the lightweight aluminium café chair.

'I don't understand. There are two Norahs?' Alexander looked at his mother.

Julie swallowed. 'There's only one. We've found her. Your father thinks he's found another.'

'Crazy.' Alexander turned to Norah. 'What does it mean?'

Colin traced the pattern on the glass tabletop. 'It means that someone needs to provide proof that they are the real Norah.'

The table was quiet while the noise of the morning built up around them. Alexander kept his gaze on Norah. He saw her bottom lip quiver, her shoulders drop so that her bag slid off. She looked pale and shocked. He started towards her. She held up her hand. 'I can do that.'

Her words were almost lost among a burst of voices from a pack of tourists following a guide along the road. Alexander caught them. 'How?'

Norah put a light hand on her forehead, then let it drop. 'You wanted genetic testing done.'

'No, we didn't!' Alexander leaned towards Norah. 'We know it's you. Don't we, Mum?'

Julie folded her hands in front of her. 'I've never felt surer about anything.'

Norah bit her bottom lip. This morning's lipstick, Alexander noticed, was a rose pink. 'Still. It's what has to be done. Now or eventually. I have to.'

'No, you don't.' Alexander sat straight in his chair. 'Really, you don't.'

'Alexander's right, Norah. There's no need.'

Norah held up both her hands. Her mouth opened slightly, but she didn't speak. Instead, she shook her head once. Was it possible that she'd gone even paler?

Alexander scraped the hair off his face, then leaned his forehead into his hands. This was his father's fault. If only Donald had taken the chance to talk to Norah, to really see her. It was so obvious that she belonged to them. Now they would be waiting for the results of science to tell them what they already felt, doubt like poison creeping into their relationship. He lifted his head, catching Colin shaking his head at him. What would he know? He opened his mouth to tell him to shut it and caught sight of his mother.

She sat, a familiar olive-green cardigan draping her shoulders, looking smaller than usual. Her face, so often animated, was heavy. He glimpsed a deep sorrow in the roundness of her shoulders and the tightness of her clasped hands. It was easy to see physical marks of pain, but what must the scar be like inside? A lost baby, a found woman. Even though Norah was back, how could it possibly heal thirty years of emptiness?

Julie saw him looking at her. She smiled, autopilot. Alexander felt a strong urge to take one of those clenched hands and rub his fingers over the hard knuckles. Instead, he watched while Colin reached over and touched his mother's arm. She looked down at his hand, her hair swinging across her face, but not before Alexander saw the weariness in her eyes.

Colin looked up at Norah. Alexander saw the look he gave her. *He thinks she's like Alicia.* It was a disquieting realisation, one that made sense of Colin's distrust, his downright contempt for Norah. Alicia had fooled him for so long, had him convinced that she'd loved him – of course Colin would hate Norah. She'd seem just like that manipulative girlfriend, the one that had taken his heart for a ride before smashing it alongside her body on those cold dark rocks.

Alexander closed his eyes. Sometimes, the pain around him was too great.

THEY ATE, then moved as a group around Edinburgh. The walking was aimless, listless. Alexander stuck to Norah's side, glancing occasionally at the slim arm beside him, its freckled skin a shade of the same tawny tan as his own. If she turned to speak to him, her eyes reminded him of himself, although today his felt veiled by a disappointment he couldn't quite articulate.

By the end of the morning, when they had exhausted small talk about the pulsing city around them, he could say, if anyone had asked him, that the world had let him down. Here was Norah, so obviously a Cameron. There was the world – Colin, Donald, even Norah herself – questioning her place in his family.

Strangely, they had ended up in Greyfriars's Kirkyard. They wandered silently past Bobby's tribute and separated to scan the headstones and obituaries. Alexander had never been in there. He'd felt no previous compulsion to check out the long-dead. Others found it fascinating. He saw evidence of that as he followed the wall downhill. Older people in sensible sunhats clumped together trying to read the old inscriptions that were disappearing with time and weather.

Norah walked alone. She was following the other wall, also heading downhill. She moved slower than him, taking a few moments to read each monument. Or was it she was taking time, full stop? He'd felt her quietness as a distance that hadn't been there before. He followed the path around until he was next to her again.

'Look,' she said, as he approached. 'This one was only twenty. Then his brother died a few weeks later.'

He nodded, struggling to stop himself from shrugging. Who really cared about people so long gone? She glanced at him, sunglasses on top of her head, one finger up to wipe her eye carefully. Okay, *she* cared. He gave her a late smile, but she'd moved on to the next stone. 'Norah,' he said softly, 'you don't have to prove anything. Not with me.'

Maybe she hadn't heard him? She wasn't stopping now but stepping sideways down the path, concentrating on the engravings, frowning.

'Norah...'

'But I do have to prove it. Eventually.' The next step was almost on his toe. He moved back. 'It's just what has to happen.'

'No, it doesn't.'

She leaned across to read something, still moving. He went uphill to get out of the way. She said something he didn't catch.

'Say that again?'

'I said that you're a very sweet person.'

He frowned. She didn't sound like being a sweet person was something to be proud of. A warm flush grew on his face. 'I only meant-'

Finally, she stopped. 'Alexander, it's alright. I know what I have to do.' She looked at him. The muscles in her cheek were hard.

'Please...' But he wasn't sure why he was pleading.

She reached for his forearm, wrapped cool fingers around it. Her fingernails dug in for a moment. 'I've got this.' She let him go, head down again to the graves.

Alexander put his hands in his pockets, following her but not closely. A Harry Potter tour went past, their leader in an academic gown. He waited while they giggled away and by then she was at the bottom of the yard, one hand on her hip, the other gripping the handles of her tote bag. He looked around for his mother and saw Colin sitting on a seat, elbows on knees, flicking his sunglasses around in his hand. He went back and sat with him.

'You alright?' Colin said, sitting up and sliding his glasses back on.

'Of course.'

Colin grunted. 'Here they are.'

Julie came through the door in the wall at the same time as Norah walked up the path. Both walked briskly, grave-digging accomplished. 'That was interesting,' said Julie, in a practiced tone.

'I'm going to head off now.' Norah spoke before Julie had finished. 'It's been a lovely morning.'

Julie shook her head. 'But won't you have some lunch with us?'

Alexander thought that Norah was going to change her mind. Her shoulders relaxed momentarily, her fingers lengthened in their grip on her bag, then everything stiffened. Norah leaned forward to kiss Julie's cheek, a lingering touch that left a soft lip-shape. 'No, I need to go.'

'After lunch, surely?'

Alexander hated the desperation in his mother's voice but loved it, too. It was what he wanted to say. *Stay, Norah, don't leave our sides.* An ache started in his stomach that gripped tightly as Norah stepped across to him, paused, then wrapped her arms around his neck. His nose buried into her hair. He smelt rose and cinnamon. His hands felt the warmth of her skin through her shirt, the outline of her ribs. She squeezed him strongly, then let him go.

'You aren't leaving us?' he said.

'I need time, Alexander.' She lifted the sunglasses from her head and pushed them onto her face. 'I've always needed time.' She held her hand up as he stepped forward, so he stopped.

As she turned to go, Alexander saw her stare at Colin. He nodded slightly, his face behind his aviators expressionless. They watched her walk away, her skirt flapping around long legs, her hair catching the sun.

'Come on.' Colin's loud voice made Alexander blink. 'I'm starving. We've been walking around for hours.' He glanced around as if to take his bearings. 'There'll be a pub somewhere. That okay, Julie?'

'You know it is, Colin.' She glanced at him, Norah's lipstick mark the only softness left on her face. 'I've been in more pubs than you've had breakfasts. Come on. I need a drink.'

It was a good try, Alexander thought as he and Colin followed Julie out of the churchyard. Alexander saw the little stumble on the path as his mother ploughed forward with her head high. He heard the gasp and watched how she recovered. His mother's hand was trembling as she patted her hair in place and re-positioned the handbag on her shoulder.

We are both, he decided, *afraid of what's going to happen next.*

TWENTY-FOUR

Colin hadn't seen Julie really drink before. She started with a beer, grimacing at the taste before downing it quickly as if she'd been working hard lifting rocks. She'd had a gin and tonic then, and that was before her smoked salmon arrived. There was something else he didn't recognise during the meal and then another gin afterwards. He glanced at Alexander, but he was pushing his food around his plate, not looking at his mother.

There had been little conversation to start with, but there was total silence after they took away their plates. Colin ordered sticky toffee pudding but gave it to Alexander, who swapped his food-playing to that bowl until the pudding was mush. Julie got another drink. Alexander leaned back in his chair, crossed his arms over his chest and stared out the window.

'Hey,' said Colin, 'I'm going off to do some things. You want to stay and look after your mother?'

Alexander nodded and let his shoulders drop forward. 'I have to look after Mum?'

'Can't you see what she's doing?' Colin nodded toward Julie at the bar. 'When she finishes that one, get some coffee into her. Okay?'

'Right.'

'And don't let her drive anywhere. Take her home if you have to.'

'Right.'

'You listening, Cameron?'

'Aye. Stop going on. I've got it.'

Colin stood up. 'Just watch her.'

'Where are you going?'

'To do stuff.'

'Right.'

Colin lifted his hand in farewell as Julie came back to the table. She nodded distractedly, taking a sip before sitting back down. He pushed the door open and stepped into the street. The fresh air and boisterous crowds were like a tonic.

He started walking back into the heart of Old Town. The lamb roast he'd eaten sat thickly in his gut and he rubbed at his stomach. His whole body felt irritated, borne perhaps of too long a lunch with sadness but nurtured now by a swelling rage. When he got back to the café they'd sat next to at the start of the day, he dialled the stolen number. He redialled twice before she answered.

'Don't hang up,' he said, before she could say anything. He pushed the phone hard against his ear. 'Norah.'

She took a moment to answer. 'Who is this?'

'Colin.'

'Colin.' Her voice was stiff, but she didn't hang up.

'I need to see you.'

'Why?'

'Because I know what you're going to do.'

'Really.'

'Yes.'

'It's no business of yours what I do.'

She sounded stronger, the Australian twang welcome. His

stomach churned its heavy meal around. 'Maybe. But Alexander is my business.'

'What, are you in love with him?'

'I'm not in love with him.'

'So why do you so desperately want to protect him?'

He shook his head; the phone scraping his ear. 'I'm not desperate.'

'No?'

'I just would like him not to be hurt.'

Phone quiet again, ruined by the bleating of a bagpipe starting up on the steps of the cathedral. She said something.

'What?'

'My apartment. Come up.' The address she gave him was only metres away.

He hung up, head aching with the sudden music. Off the main street, it was immediately calmer. He put his back against the wooden door of the entrance and watched people idly until he heard the scrape of the lock opening. The shadow of the door hid her features until she stepped aside to let him in.

Saying nothing, she headed up the concrete stairway. He followed, hand sliding easily on the worn bannister. It took a moment to realise what was different about her. The long dress had gone, worn jeans replacing its glamour. The T-shirt she had on slipped from one shoulder, exposing a pale bra strap against milky skin. Colin glanced at the stairs, noticing how they dipped in the middle from years of pounding feet. He was panting by the time they reached the top.

'You can see why it was cheap accommodation,' she said, panting as well and taking time to open the three locks. The door creaked as they stepped into the tiny flat and then slammed shut behind them.

Colin stopped in the hallway, suddenly unsure. The door was three metres high and solid. They were on the fourth floor of a sandstone building. Was Norah worried about his abrupt phone call? She'd disappeared into what seemed a small kitchenette. There was the hiss of a kettle boiling. He walked on, silent steps on a worn rug, and stood in the kitchen's doorway. She was on the window ledge, its pane pushed up and the street hard below.

'What is it you really want, Colin?'

She spoke out the open window, the tiredness in her voice echoed in the slump of shoulders.

'You don't know him like I do. He's... vulnerable.'

'You were going to say weak.'

'No, I wasn't.'

She slipped from the sill and went to the kettle, organising plunger coffee. He watched her hands, slight and long-fingered. Her hair was pulled back, showing a small ring in the piercing on her upper ear. It was delicate, with a tiny blue star threaded through. He swallowed. He'd come here to... what? Stop her hurting Alexander, as if she was an evil narcissist? As if she was *Alicia*?

'Are you alright?' She'd turned at his grunt, spoon in hand.

He pulled out a chair, scraping it roughly along the wooden floor. 'Coffee would be good.' He coughed, trying to ease the thickening in his throat.

'That's what you're getting.' She put two mugs and the plunger down on the table but didn't sit.

'Norah-'

'Listen, Colin. I'm not out to get your friend.'

'I-'

'Shut up and listen.' She swung back to the window, changed her mind, and sat. 'I came here because I knew I was his sister. You saw us.' She leaned forward and tapped the table. 'You saw us! We are...' She put her hands in the air. 'It's so...'

Colin pushed the plunger, poured coffee, took a hot gulp. 'But you can't be, eh. It's not possible.'

'It is.'

'Not *probable,* then. It's the longest shot you've ever taken in your life.'

She put a hand on her cheek, then to her mouth. 'You know nothing about my life.'

'I know enough. You've had it tough; I get that. That doesn't give you the right-'

'Don't.' Norah stood up, the chair scraping noisily behind her. 'I'm not doing this because I have a choice. I have nothing. My life is *nothing.* If I was happy, do you think I'd be here?'

Her loud voice took a moment to fade. Outside, the world seemed to have stilled. Then normality recommenced, the bagpiper being brave in St Gile's square, the chattering crowd sounds still full of excitement. The stone walls would keep their secrets; he of all people knew that.

'Forget Alexander, what about Julie?'

Norah put both hands to her face, backing right up until she hit the window ledge. Colin stood, but she leaned away from him. The window frame banged as her head hit it.

'Careful there.'

'Julie...' Norah's eyes screwed up.

Colin stepped around the table. She opened her eyes and flinched. 'Norah, careful. You're right against the window.'

'I didn't think about Julie.'

He sighed. 'I don't think you did much thinking at all.'

A tear dripped from under her hands. 'That's what -' She wiped at her face and let her hands drop. 'I had nothing to lose, so I came here as soon as I could organise it.'

Colin let a minute pass. A breeze had kicked up, making Norah's hair flick. It brought in dust, noise, a musty smell. He stepped closer, but still she leaned away from him. He stopped.

'What happened to you, Colin?'

He was concentrating on the width of the gap, the height of the woman in front of him. He had to let the words form again. 'What happened to me?'

'Yes. It's not just friendship that makes you want to save Alexander. It's something else.'

She'd pinned him. He felt his stomach lurch. 'I don't know what you mean.'

'I can see it.' She smiled, small and rueful. 'I know pain and I can see it. Something happened to you and you don't want Alexander to go through the same thing.'

'You're being ridiculous.'

'I'm not.' She wriggled herself on to the sill. The glass rattled. 'I know.'

The wind played with her hair again. Her make-up had smeared, putting shadows under her staring eyes. Blue eyes, but nothing arctic-cold like Alicia's. A smaller face, higher cheekbones. Spots of colour now, mottled. Alicia was always so smoothly perfect, dangerously flawless. Not doll-like, more shop window mannequin posing in strained, enticing shapes. Norah slumped softly, gently, watching him with a weary earthiness.

'I had a girlfriend called Alicia.' His body froze at his words, but they were out now, whirling in the warmth of the Scottish air. 'We had an unhealthy relationship, that's what my counsellor called it. She...'

'She... what?' Norah said when too much time had passed.

'She ruled me. I lived for her.' He moved to the wall next to the window, leaning an arm on its coolness, the old plaster undulating under his outstretched fingers. 'Then she left.'

'She left?'

'Yes. Left. Gone. I went to work one morning, and she'd packed the house and gone. She took everything. Everything she wanted, that is. She left a note. *I've never loved you.*'

Norah nodded, as if she had one of those notes. 'What happened then?'

Colin studied the woman in front of him. She was gripping the window ledge, but her body was still, listening. He shrugged. 'She wouldn't take my calls, wouldn't see me. I went to her workplace and the security guards wouldn't let me in. I sat in the car outside her new flat, but she seemed to know I was there and didn't come out. The police threatened an intervention order. So I stopped and waited for her to come back.'

'And did she? Did she come back?'

Colin shook his head and turned so his back was against the wall. 'She might have. But one day she was reported missing, and the police thought I'd hurt her.'

'You... hadn't?'

He caught the touch of fear. 'No! It had never crossed my mind! I was...'

'You loved her.'

'I thought it was love.' He ran a hand through his hair. 'I went looking for her. I knew where she liked to go. I was the one who found her. She'd slipped and fallen into the sea.'

Norah's words caught. 'She was dead?'

He nodded and closed his eyes, trying to block the memory out, but it was there like an uninvited guest.

Alicia's hair was over her face, decorated with sand and a long strand of watery-brown seaweed. She was colder than the water that lapped at her feet. When he tugged the black strands of hair away, she stared at him with her one open dull eye, and a little crab, intent on escape, ran out of her blue lips, scuttled across her cheek and away.

Panicked, he opened his eyes. Norah was standing right in front of him, her face twisted anxiously. He stepped back.

'I'm so sorry, Colin.' Her voice caught. She swallowed.

'It's okay. It was a long time ago.'

She shook her head. 'Don't lie. It doesn't matter how long ago it was.'

They stared at each other. A shame filled him. He had come here too late to stop anything, and now he had made his own anguish a target. He ran a hand through his hair. 'Time helps.'

'That's what they want us to believe.'

He blinked, but she was still staring. 'Distance helps.'

'She's why you came to Scotland?'

He nodded. 'Partly. Mostly.'

She leaned forward and put one hand flat on his chest. 'And did it really help? Distance?'

I should step back, he told himself. Instead, he took her hand in one of his. 'I don't know what helps anymore. Has it helped you?'

She pulled back a little, but he kept her hand. 'I don't know what helps either.' She smiled crookedly. 'We're a fine pair. We've brought our problems to the other side of the world.'

He let her hand go, but she put it back on his chest. 'Don't,' he said softly.

'Why not? What have we got to lose? We both know what's going to happen tomorrow.'

'It's not right.'

'Stop it.' She put both hands on his shoulders. Her eyes were almost level with his. 'Maybe it will help?'

Her lips were soft on his at first, but then so hard they slipped and caught his teeth. Her hands wrapped around his neck so he stumbled, putting one arm out to the table while the other snaked around her slim back. When he straightened, she lifted off the floor and gripped his waist with her legs. He went forward to the windowsill and perched her carefully on it, his hands now under her T-shirt, feeling her smooth, warm skin. She smelled sweet, floral, nothing like the spice of Alicia. As she pulled his shirt off and moved her lips across his bare chest,

Alicia faded to smoke. There was nothing but Norah, her hair blonde in the afternoon light and her hands now tugging his jeans down.

Festive noise carried from the street below into the room, but all he could hear were their quick sobs as they moved together. His hands held her safely against the sill, but she wove hers into his hair and stayed looking into his eyes until that moment when she gasped and flung her head back. He shuddered into her warmth and they clung together until their breathing slowed.

AS THE DAY LENGTHENED, they coiled on her bed until Norah shivered and they had to move to find the sheet to cover them. Colin put his head back on the pillow next to her. She smiled, her face soft. 'Sorry,' she said.

'No, don't say that.'

'It changes things.'

'Yes.'

'But not everything.'

Colin stayed as still as he could. Move, and it was gone, whatever *it* was. He could feel the tentativeness of the moment. He saw it, too, in the way her wardrobe door was open, and the suitcase was half-out. There was a sense of movement in the room, of time not staying still.

Norah stirred first. She straightened her body, stretched, and propped herself up on one elbow. He reached out to smooth the unruly hair along her side part. She turned and kissed his fingers as they reached the ends of her cut, and rose out of bed, pulling on her jeans and T-shirt again. She padded to the bathroom. He pushed himself up, dressing slowly, but ready long before she finally emerged with hair brushed and make-up renewed.

They stared at each other.

'What are you going to do?' he finally said.

She looked down at her jeans, shook her head as if surprised she was wearing them. 'I don't know.' She lifted her head, ran her fingers through her hair and let it fall back. 'I don't want to be me.' She was quiet for a moment. 'But there's another Norah coming. The real one.'

He nodded.

'I don't know what to do. What do you think?'

'I don't know what you should do either.'

They stood for another few moments. Her gaze shifted downwards again, as if he'd been forgotten. He turned, went to the door. At the last minute he looked back.

She brought one hand up, a farewell wave. Or, he thought later after he'd gone back to the flat where Alexander was asleep on the couch while the television blared, it was a signal for him to stop and he hadn't.

TWENTY-FIVE

Julie called Norah again. Each time, the phone went straight to the generic message bank. She left another message, the same as before. *Please call me. Or text. Norah, please. Call.*

She was going back to work, Cynthia having dropped in the previous night with some questions. Cynthia dropping in? The managerial side of Julie saw the red flag the minute the other woman's dusty-red sedan pulled into the yard. Cynthia could hardly look her in the face, and the questions she'd asked were plainly ludicrous cover for something else done badly. Julie had stopped her mid-sentence. 'I'll be in tomorrow.' Cynthia's nodding face was full of relief and resentment. To have stooped so low! it read. To be in this mess because my manager had extra days off when she should have been considering the practice! Julie felt inclined to shove Cynthia down the steps but, really, it wasn't her fault she was completely incompetent.

Julie called Norah again before she went inside the surgery, shaking her head at the voice message. She sat for a moment longer. I'll call Alexander, she decided. Maybe she's talking to him. She lifted the phone. The rap on the car window made her drop it into the footwell.

Euan opened the door to help. Julie moved her feet aside as he knelt to feel around the floor. She stared at the top of his head, the lines of silver through his black hair, its careful cut staying neat even when he stood with the phone rescued in his hand. 'Thank you,' she said, as he handed it to her. There seemed no choice, then, but to get out and start the day.

'Everything alright?' Euan asked as they walked to the front door of the practice. Julie had her handbag in her hand, letting it swing heavily between them.

'Yes, quite fine.' She had the key in the lock before he could. He reached across and opened it for her, waving her in.

She headed for her office. In the empty building, though, it was hard to ignore the echoes of his questions. 'Have you seen the girl again?'

'Norah. Yes. I've spent some time with her.'

'And?'

He was leaning over the front desk now like a belligerent patient. She switched on the computers, scowling. 'She's a very nice girl.'

'Julie.'

She looked up. 'What is it, Euan?'

'How convinced are you that she is Norah?'

She shivered. It was cool in the surgery, and the ice-hard look he was giving her didn't help. 'In every way possible, Euan, I hope she is.'

He gave one slow nod. 'Hope is all you have.'

'Well, I can't know for sure.' I do, she thought. It *is* her.

He drummed his fingers on the counter.

What are you waiting for? she thought, mucking around with the booking system. A full day, that was good, and already the light was on the answering machine. Euan would be busy, she would be busy fixing Cynthia's mess, and the girls at the front would be busy keeping their heads down in shame. 'I'd better get on, Euan.' Julie picked up the phone to play the messages back.

His eyes, intense lasers, stared unblinking at her until she put her head down to note the content of the messages. She heard him walk away, footsteps long and muffled on the carpet. She dealt with the bookings, called the pathology lab and one nursing home, and was still standing at the counter when Cynthia came in a guilty fifteen minutes early.

In her office, the waiting room now filling fast, she dialled Norah's number again. This time it went straight to a disconnection tone. A quick sweat burned her forehead. Julie shut her office door and rang Alexander. 'There's no service on her phone,' she said, as soon as it connected.

'I just sent her a text.'

'She replied?'

'No.'

Behind Alexander's voice, she heard traffic and crowd hums. 'What are you doing?'

'I'm looking for her. I've tried her apartment. I can't get in.'

'Try again.'

She knew her voice was hard when he said, 'I am trying, Mum.'

'Sorry.'

Julie glanced through the pane of glass in the office door. Cynthia was shaking her head at an older woman who was trying to hand her a piece of paper. Julie could guess what was happening: the woman wanted to show the doctor something – a list of symptoms, the information from her medication box, a letter from her daughter (it didn't matter what it was) – and Cynthia didn't realise the importance of it. Just take it, she willed the imprudent receptionist.

'Mum, I'll ring you back when I find her.'

'Where's Colin?'

'He's gone with Dad.'

Donald. Her chest felt tight at the thought. She couldn't bear to look at him, so she kept him as a blur in the house, serving dinner to the large man at the table, keeping to the edge of the bed until he fell asleep and then heading for the spare one, getting up early and walking to William Wallace until Donald left for the day. She had chest tightness and a headachy rage that now and then formed into solid black words: *how dare he?*

Colin would work with him, keep him honest. She felt a surge of thankfulness towards Alexander's dark-haired friend.

'Ring me immediately.'

'I will, Mum.'

She sat for a moment longer before going to rescue the old woman from Cynthia's stupidity.

THE SUMMER HAD GONE for the day. Rain fell in brief, malevolent torrents. Alexander was soaked before he reached Cockburn Street and spent a minute squeezing his hair out under the shelter of an eave. The tourists weren't bothered. Umbrellas crashed as people made their way up and out the main streets, in and out of colourful shops. He looked for Norah. There was no slim, sandy-haired girl he recognised among the people in the Royal Mile.

He returned to the café they'd been at yesterday and stood with his back to it. What if she shifted her accommodation? Rental apartments were common here, most of them two, three or four stories above the street. So many. He rang Norah's number again, getting nothing. He rang it once more, listening to see if there was a corresponding jingle from a mobile phone nearby. Nothing. The painstaking choice was to go from shop to shop and ask if anyone had seen her.

'You've got to be joking, eh, man?'

'Seen a redhead around here? No, not a one.'

'Dressed in a floral skirt? I wish.'

Alexander wished for more rain to cool the heat from his face. He stood in the street, taking deep breaths, before ploughing back into shop fronts and asking all over again. Some people didn't bother to answer his insane, repetitive question, and who was he to blame them? How do you find a missing person among the many who'd escaped here for a holiday? There were more and more people in the streets as the Festival grew nearer. It was like a nightmare, one in which, by searching, Norah became more lost.

At twelve o'clock, Colin rang. 'Anything?'

'No. Nothing.'

'Alexander, if she doesn't want to be found, there's nothing you can do about it.' Colin's voice was scratchy.

'Yes, there is.'

'Give it a rest.'

'No.'

Colin sighed, his voice a long gust of wind through the phone. 'Your dad's happy.'

'Does he know she's gone missing?'

Colin paused. Alexander heard the heaviness of it. 'He's not even thinking of her. He's found the real Norah, he says, so the Norah that came to you doesn't exist to him.'

More rain. Alexander let it drown him. He covered the phone with his other hand to protect it, feeling the T-shirt stick to his back. 'What do I do? I can't find her.'

The phone cut out, then came back on Colin's last syllable.

'What? I couldn't hear you.'

'Let it go for now. If she wants you to see her, she has your number.'

'I can't.' The rain stopped. It dripped from his hair over his face. 'I can't give it up.'

A long break this time but Alexander could still hear Colin on the phone, walking now, perhaps away from Donald, his breath regular.

'You know something, don't you? Tell me.'

'Have you tried the airport?'

'The airport?'

'She's only got one place to go, and that's home. I think that's what she's done.'

Alexander killed the call without saying goodbye, already heading to the taxi rank. Would she leave just like that? Would Norah go when she said she wouldn't? He hailed a cab, directing it to the airport, nausea battling in his stomach. Of all the ways in which she could reject him - reject the family - going back to Australia was the worst.

COLIN PUT his phone back in his pocket and turned to find Donald standing cross-armed not far away. Colin indicated the van. 'Lunch, I reckon.'

'Aye.' Donald didn't move. 'You been talking to Alexander.'

'Yeah.'

Donald nodded. 'What's he doing?'

Would it be any use lying? thought Colin. 'He's looking for Norah. She's not answering her phone.'

'Norah?'

Despite himself, Colin had an admiration for the way Donald did not, could not, associate the name with the girl who'd turned up at his doorstep and his missing daughter. It took a rock-solid belief in your own actions. 'Yes. The girl that came to him saying she was Norah.'

Donald's mouth twisted into an amused grin. 'Aye, *that* Norah.' He let his arms drop and glanced at the van. 'You got your piece?'

Colin nodded.

They got their lunches out and sat in the shade of a mangled oak. Donald ate his first sandwich before he said, 'Do you think he's got a thing for this girl?'

'What?'

'Alexander. You know.' Donald jerked his elbows and moved his hips in crude imitation. 'What do you think?'

Colin shook his head. 'No.' He bit into his bread and nearly choked on its dryness.

Donald unwrapped more food. 'You're strange, young lads like yourselves with no girls.' He sat suddenly. 'You're not...?'

What if we were? thought Colin irritably. 'No.'

'Right.' Donald broke his sandwich in two. 'Didn't think so. I mean, Alexander's had some nice girls. That last one, Penny? She was alright. Went back to Glasgow, and he didn't seem to mind.'

Colin nodded. He'd met Penny. She was way too ambitious to be associated with a stonemason when what she really wanted was an architect.

'And Alexander told me about that girl of yours. Alice? Alison?'

Colin felt coldness wash through him. 'Alicia.'

'Aye, sorry. Alicia. She died, didn't she?'

Colin chewed.

'Sorry. I'm only going on what Alexander said to us. She went missing, and they found her dead.'

'We weren't together then.'

'You'd broken up? Just as well, I guess. Would have been

terrible, your girl missing and then...' Donald thought about it, cramming bread into his mouth.

Colin put his sandwich down to take a drink. It was a surprise to him that his hands weren't shaking. He usually felt earthquaked when someone mentioned the raven-haired woman he'd given himself to. Suddenly there was another in his thoughts, a sunset girl with sky eyes.

'You want more?'

Colin had to focus to see the sandwich Donald held out to him. He shook his head.

'Had to make my own this morning.' Donald attacked the last one. 'Julie up already, going on her trek up to the top to help out that woman's group.' He laughed, a snippet of bread flying from his mouth. 'The things women do to keep themselves busy. Waste of time, looking after that old statue.'

Colin found his voice. 'Julie thinks it important.'

'Aye.' Donald laughed again. 'That's what I don't understand. Julie's not even Scottish!' He looked at Colin. 'Well, you'd know about that.'

'You don't have to be Scottish to help out your community.'

'I suppose. Still.' He crumpled his lunch wrap. 'What was she like, that girl of yours?'

'Who?'

'The one that died. What was she like?'

Was he just hugely insensitive or thoroughly mean? Colin studied Donald, the wide-open expression, the frank curiosity. Alexander had first introduced his father as the stone man. Colin had thought it was a mistake on his friend's behalf. Stone mason. Stone man. No mistake, as the next two years showed. Not stone, as in unfeeling. Stone, as in solid and impenetrable. Stone, as in there was no other description for him. It was hard to stay angry with a stone.

'She was a real bitch.'

Donald flung his head back and laughed. Saved by the mirth, Colin stood and packed his lunch things away. Donald followed, still chuckling, content with the answer and on to the next thing, while Colin felt prickly and horrible, *bitch* not being the word that suited the richness of Alicia's dangerousness. *Bitch* was cheap. He didn't want it to be cheap, it made the total experience a one-word issue.

They started on their work without speaking. This job was difficult, an innovative curved wall that formed part of the house while also extending into a secluded courtyard. Alexander was the one who'd agreed with it. He'd sat down with the builder as they went through the plans, making some technical corrections to what the architect had drawn. Alexander had developed specialist skills, thought Colin as he weighed a lump of sandstone in his hands. He had a vision of his friend in ten years' time hosting a stone building restoration television show. Then Donald would see women flock to his son.

Behind him, Donald swore as he scraped his leg on the edge of a rock. Colin turned to help but the big man continued to work, his curse becoming a whistle and then the low hum of the radio's song as the pain faded. The sun came out and just as quickly dived back under a cloud. Colin flicked his sunglasses up to study the stone he'd just placed, shifting it slightly to the left.

The phone vibrated in his pocket. He fumbled for it, letting it fall out and catching it before it hit the ground. 'Alexander. You okay?'

'I'm at the airport. There are nearly thirty flights to get to Melbourne depending on where you stopover. Some are gone already.' In the pause, the PA sounded. 'I asked at the counter and a lot of them have standby seats. She could have gone already.'

'Maybe.'

'You don't think she has?'

Colin changed the phone to his other ear. 'I'm sure she has.'

There was a long break.

'Alexander?'

'I'm here. I don't know what to do.'

'Nothing much you can do.'

'I'll stay here for a while. I'll see if I can find her.'

'And if you can't?'

'I'll see you later.'

The phone finished. Colin thought of Alexander scouring the check-in counters, waiting around security, searching every face as it came towards him. He hoped his friend wasn't arrested. He put the phone back into his pocket.

'You're popular today.' Donald was taking a break, wiping the sweat from his forehead with a purple handkerchief.

Colin shrugged. 'ALIE party tonight. Lots of arrangements to make.'

Donald nodded, drank from his water bottle, and turned back to his work. His old boots, Colin saw, were the same soft brown as the rocks he worked with.

They worked in silence until knock-off time and drove back with the van's windows open. Donald hummed as Colin drove, his fingers thumping a beat on the windowsill. As they pulled up at the house, he tipped his head towards Colin. 'Two days until Sunday.'

Colin saw it then, as clear as Donald. In two days, the real Norah would be here, and Donald would be the hero in his family's eyes. Nothing else mattered.

TWENTY-SIX

Sunday morning. Julie lay in the spare bed listening to Donald fuss around in the kitchen. He'd been up for an hour, not trying to be quiet, rattling through the cupboards as if she'd hidden the crockery and he couldn't find a mug. Sunday morning. There'd been no contact from Norah since Thursday.

One thump of the door and Donald was in, a cup of tea in one hand and a slice of toast in the other. He put them on the bedside table, spilling the tea a little, the toast sliding to the edge of the plate. A hot, dry kiss on her cheek and he was back out the door, turning the radio up in the kitchen, gravelly voice missing the high notes of a song she'd never heard of.

Julie pulled the quilt up under her chin. He'd left the bedroom door open, and she felt exposed. They had not used the spare room before she'd taken to it in recent times. She saw now that they'd made a mistake in positioning the bed like they had. If she sat up a little, she could see Donald's arm as he moved up and down the kitchen bench. If he turned around and peered down the corridor, he'd be able to see her staring at him, night hair tangled and sticking to the pillow, puffy eyes shadowy without concealer. She slid down the bed until his arm disappeared from view, and she could throw the quilt back to slide out without being seen.

Donald hadn't given a time for the visitors to arrive. Obediently, forever the peacemaker, she'd spent the evening making lemon slice and empire biscuits. The baking had made his eyes light up, and it had been tempting to throw the food in the bin. Her cooking had only confirmed that he had done the right thing, that hiring an investigator without telling her about it was an inspired choice. She felt sick thinking about the way he'd been plotting while Alexander had toiled endlessly through Melbourne streets trying to make headway into Norah's disappearance.

And now she'd disappeared again. Or, worse, something had happened to her. Or, best-case scenario, she was coming to terms with her new life and needed time alone to think. She'd be back when she was ready, and it wouldn't be another thirty years. Julie rubbed her sternum as she stepped into the shower. Her chest was aching, not in pre-heart attack, but in a sadly familiar way. It had felt like this for years after baby Norah went missing. It surprised Julie how easily the feeling had returned.

The knock on the shower door made her jump. Donald pulled the door open a crack, letting steam escape and cold air in. He put one eye close to the glass. 'I've rung them and got no answer so they must be on their way.'

The illogicality of his sentence made her frown. 'Well, I'd better hurry up in this shower.'

One of his hands snaked through to touch her belly. 'You are gorgeous, love.'

'Thank you, Donald. Now. You're letting the cold in.'

He snapped back, closing the door gently and leaving the bathroom. She let the water run over her face, sighing. Thirty-eight years of marriage. So much was the same. Donald, ever eager for his wife. She should be flattered. Really. The dullness of it was almost overwhelming.

And if Donald had been Euan?

Julie scrubbed at her hair, rinsed conditioner through it, and got out. She doubted that, given the passing of all those years, Euan would reach for her as she stood in the shower, the evidence of time and childbearing shaping her breasts, stomach and hips. The nimble, young Australian she'd been had matched his restless need for the exotic. That breathless few weeks, clandestine meetings taken as patient-doctor consultations, had fizzed with risk and desire and recklessness. It was not the stuff to build a long-term relationship with. Julie shivered. That it remained so vivid was a sad reflection on the rest of her life.

She took her time getting ready for the day. In the end, she put on a work shirt and tried to play it up with a long, patterned skirt. Donald was sitting at the dining table when she came out, his phone in front of him, an empty mug to the side. 'Any news?' she said.

He shook his head.

She cleaned the already clean kitchen, scraping the toast Donald had given her into the bin. She wasn't hungry, certainly not for cold, hard bread with too much butter. With Donald still at the table, she went from one end of the house to the other, tidying, dusting, rearranging the row of ceramic Australian animals on the window ledge of the bathroom. 'Nothing?'

He didn't bother shaking his head.

She changed out of her skirt and into cropped pants to vacuum, load the washing machine, and clean the bathroom. Saturday morning jobs that had extended into Sunday. Just past one o'clock, she made salad sandwiches and set them on the table in front of Donald. After a moment, she joined him, sliding into the chair opposite and making him shuffle across so he could still see out the window. They ate in silence.

At least, Julie thought as she made a pot of tea and set out the lemon slice and an empire biscuit to share on one of her good plates, Alexander was sensible enough not to be there. Donald had asked him, pointedly, in a conversation in which Donald's voice rose and thickened. Julie was within earshot, trying not to shake her head. Couldn't he see, that enormous husband of hers, that Alexander did not want any part of it? She wondered what he was doing right now as his parents waited in Dryburgh for Donald's discovery.

By four o'clock, Donald had made several more unanswered phone calls, and been on his email several times. The investigator – Con? Callum? Craig? – did not respond. Julie took the electronic tablet from Donald and looked up the agency, frowning at its clumsy refresh and poorly constructed sentences. 'Donald, how did you get on to this fellow?'

He grunted. 'Looked him up one night.'

'Did he ask for money up front?'

'No.' Donald pushed his phone away. 'I gave it to him later.'

'From where?'

'The business account. I put it down as general services.'

Julie handed back the computer and set about chopping up vegetables for dinner. It was easier to keep the smile to herself when her head was down over peeled carrots. Donald roamed the dining room, then the gravelled yard, then the road. When she glanced up, she noticed he had his good shirt on, the one with the faint blue stripes running the wrong way over his torso, and a pang of tenderness hit her. Poor Donald, duped. When he came back in, she handed him a beer, saying nothing. He took it, refused to look in her eyes, and went outside again to sit at the outdoor table, the phone at his ear again.

Hours later, after dinner, she sat with her feet up on the

coffee table. Donald was working in the yard, ratting through the van, back in his old clothes and unlaced boots. There was a crime show on television set somewhere in Oxford. Julie took a ridiculous pleasure in the uncomplicated plot and the views of the Radcliffe Camera. It used to seem so unfamiliar, the greenery and the historic buildings dripping with lichen. She wondered sometimes, if confronted by the dirt and dried grass of a Victorian summer, whether she'd be repulsed.

Evening filtered in. Donald stayed outside. Julie went to find a cardigan, ringing Alexander on the way.

'Mum.'

Julie stopped searching through the wardrobe. 'Alexander, are you alright?'

'I'm alright.'

His tone frightened her, its darkness and flatness. 'I'm ringing to say that they didn't turn up.'

'Who?'

'The investigator. And the girl who said she was Norah.'

'Norah?'

'The other one. The one your father thought he had found.'

'Oh.'

The phone was so quiet, Julie took it off her ear to check that it was still connected. 'Alexander?'

'I heard you, Mum.'

'So what do you think of that?'

'Of what?'

'Alexander! Of the people not turning up.'

'Well, they wouldn't, would they?'

Her cheeks warmed. They wouldn't, would they. There she'd been all day, playing along with Donald, not completely on his side but making biscuits and dressing appropriately only to watch his demise with the sort of delight a competitor in the Olympics might feel if a fellow hurdler fell at the last minute.

She started through the drawer again, yanking out an old red cardigan that really needed to go. 'No. That's right. They wouldn't.'

'Mum, I can't wait for her anymore.'

'Wait? Oh, for Norah?'

'I'm going to look for her.'

'You already have, dear. She's probably having a break from us.' It's what she'd decided. Of course, the poor girl needed time to reflect on what had happened. They needed it, as well. It was for the best; it was a good thing. It was... 'You don't think she has, do you?'

'She's gone, Mum. I feel it. If she was here, she'd contact us. The phone number doesn't even work anymore. She's gone back to Australia. She's gone back to being Claudia.'

Julie felt shivery. 'Why would she do that, Alexander? We've embraced her. We've done our best to make her feel among family.'

'We did. You and I did. Dad didn't.'

'But...' How could she say that it hardly mattered about Donald? 'It couldn't be just that.'

'She was scared that whoever Dad had turned up would fight her for us. I think she didn't want the ugliness.'

'Well, it doesn't matter. There is no other person. Your father's made a costly mistake.'

'The damage is done, Mum. I'm going back to Australia to find her.'

'How? You couldn't find her before.'

'We have her name now. And an area. She must be around Paxton.'

'Melbourne isn't Melrose, remember, Alexander. It's huge. People don't know their neighbours like we do here.'

The phone rustled. Perhaps he was shaking his head. 'I'm not sitting here waiting.'

'Then I'll go with you.'

'No, Mum. What if I'm wrong? If she's still here, she'll come to you. You need to keep Dad from her.'

'He wouldn't do anything, Alexander.'

'No. He just wouldn't believe in her.'

The scorn in his voice twisted in her gut. She walked out of her room and stood at the glass doors to watch Donald. He had tools spread on the ground and sat sprawl-legged on a tarp to sort them. It occurred to her that Alexander had lost his faith in Donald the moment he'd yelled at Norah, but his reluctance to speak anything of Norah over the last few decades had sucked out her own faith in her husband. He'd tried to pack away photos of baby Norah they had when they moved and shook his head when she retrieved them to place them around the new house. But Donald had attempted to find Norah. That should have been enough to revive Julie's religion. If only he'd chosen to be on her side.

'Take Colin with you.'

'I don't think so.'

'Listen, I know he's sceptical about it all but he's a good friend. And he knows Melbourne. Please. Ask him.'

She took the silence as assent.

'Will you wait a few days?'

He hesitated. 'If we've heard nothing in two days, I'm booking the flight.'

'Okay. Alexander, keep... well. Keep looking after yourself.'

'Always do, Mum.'

It was what he continually replied when she said that. She put her phone on the coffee table. A deep uneasiness sat at her core. A mother's grief was enormous, insurmountable. A brother's grief showed itself differently, a blackened mess, something sticky and full of could-have-beens. Until this year, Alexander had kept it to himself. Or, if she'd been more observant, would it have been present in the bouts of unhappiness at school or his dissatisfaction with university? Should she have glimpsed it in the three troubled relationships - that she knew of - he'd had in a row? Should mothers know these things even when their sons are the age they could be parents themselves?

The sound of the glass door sliding open startled her. Donald gave her a rueful smile as he stepped in with his socks hanging from his toes. 'Only me,' he said, sadness drowning his usual vibe.

'Only you,' she echoed, sitting suddenly on the couch.

He paused, kicked his socks off completely, and came to sit next to her. His heavy arm wrapped around her shoulders and held her in its vice. 'I'm so sorry, love. Maybe they've been caught up?'

She nodded, wriggling a little to free herself.

'It must be disappointing to you. Making those biscuits and all.'

She closed her eyes, wishing she could block her ears as well. 'I'm going to bed now, Donald.'

'But it's early!'

'I'm very tired.' She ducked down and managed to escape him altogether. His arm stayed curved on the back of the couch where she'd left it.

'I understand. All that effort-'

'You won't mind if I take the spare bed again? I had such a rough night, and I don't want to disturb you.'

'I don't mind-'

'It's the heat. You know.' She mimed a hot flush. He nodded, averting his eyes at his male mistake. She almost leaned forward to shake him (*I haven't had any menopausal symptoms in two years!*) but let him wallow instead.

The sun wasn't quite down as she shut the door to the spare room. It was clearly too early to go to bed. She put her earplugs in and listened to music as she used her phone to surf every-thing from flights to cat videos. After a while, Donald showered. She heard the water thump off and a quiet as he towelled. She imagined him climbing into bed. He'd be still slightly damp; a trail of water drops on his back where the hollow of his spine sat. He slept naked in summer, his shower-clean skin soft against her cheek when she turned over in the middle of the night. She pulled the earplugs out and turned off the light. After a while, he did the same.

It was dark when Julie rose. The house shivered with Donald's snores. She stole into the main bedroom and took cargo pants and a hoodie from the cupboard. Outside, the moon hid shyly behind clouds and she went back to the kitchen drawer to find a torch. Even then, its short beam was almost useless in the dense darkness of the path. The phone was better, but it was low on battery. She walked slowly, blindly, putting her toes down first like an ancient ballerina.

At the top of the hill, it was lighter. William was hard to see, a looming dark obelisk similar to the trees next to him. Julie shone her little torch on the note box, and opened it carefully, a habit after years of avoiding redbacks in her Australian letter-box. Some notes nestled on the bottom, more than she'd thought. How many days had it been since she'd collected? Time tangled in her mind. What was waiting for her? A cryptic greeting, another line of poetry, the first few bars of a new song? Her anticipation felt unjustified – they were just scribblings, for heaven's sake. Anything, she thought, to stop her thinking of the wasted day.

Something rustled the undergrowth down the path. She swung the torch around, catching the red of rabbit eyes before the creature galloped away. In the distance, across the fields, a fox voiced its lonely bark, perhaps sensing the running rabbit. The eerie noise made the back of Julie's neck prickle. It reminded her of early days in the UK, where sounds were familiar but foreign. The high-pitched wail of an ambulance was the alarmingly wrong tone, the ravens cawed in a different key, and the fox – so loathed where she'd come from – held an almost reverential status for its resonant bark. Here, in the dark, she was reminded that no matter how long she'd lived here it would never be truly home, not while her strongest memories had been set thousands of miles away.

Mission accomplished, she turned to start down the dark path, but a sweep of headlights from the road above halted her. Strange, a car so close to the dead of night. She switched the torch off and stood back against the trees, aware that steeping too far back would send her crashing off the little precipice of the path.

The night fell dark again. Not silent, though. Wind was shaking the trees, rattling leaves against each other and making dry ones scuttle on the ground. Then footsteps, a firm crunching of stones. Julie went down the path a bit, aware that the white hoodie she wore stood out in the slight light. Someone came closer, but she didn't leave. Besides her, who would visit William Wallace at night? A groupie, perhaps, although it wasn't Glastonbury and Wallace was no King Arthur. His modern followers were less hippie-like and more ferocious, daytime-loving fans who sometimes carried fake swords and shields.

The footsteps got louder, slipping occasionally on the steeper parts of the path. Julie shrunk back. It wasn't wise to be hanging around, she knew, but today seemed one of those days when odd things could happen. She waited.

Eventually, a figure rounded the corner and stepped into the clearing. It was long and lean, a man with short hair, and a face shadowed by the night. It went to the note box, lifted the lid, letting something drop inside.

Julie stepped out of hiding. 'It's your story, isn't it?'

Euan stepped back, startled. 'Julie! What are you doing here?'

She shrugged. 'Seeing William. Like I do when I want some peace. Like you do, too.'

He stood very still, silhouetted grey. 'I don't know what you mean.'

'Yes, you do. You know exactly what I mean.' She came closer to him, the moonlight glinting on his glasses and hiding his eyes. 'I know your story, how sorry you are about losing Norah, about how much you miss her.' She took a deep breath in. 'Maybe even how things could have been different-'

'No.'

His loudness of his voice made her blink. The animal in the long grass scuttled away. The skin prickled on her neck. She was alone in the woods with a man who shared the biggest secret of her life. The wind shifted leaves around her. 'Euan...'

'Julie.' His voice was normal again, controlled, even. 'You think you know my story? That's presumptuous.'

'Is it?' Julie lifted her chin. The light had moved a little. She could see the features of his face, a gaze that held hers and a stern mouth. 'Well, why don't you tell me the proper story of Dr Euan Cameron?'

He was quiet for uncomfortably long. Julie shifted her weight to her right leg, half-turning to look down the path, wondering whether to just leave his arrogant self where he was and return home to the house full of snores. She could make a cup of tea, wait until dawn, take a drive to Abbotsford and walk around the gardens.

'You really want to hear?'

She almost lost his voice in a flash of breeze as it rolled through the trees.

'Of course.'

'Well then. Don't say I didn't warn you.'

Julie inched back. 'Warn me about what?'

'The truth.'

'The truth about what?'

'What really happened at the hospital that day.'

Her body hummed in alarm. There was something about the way he was standing over her, his glasses catching glints of light, that reminded her of a horror movie. Just as the protagonists in those movies didn't have to confront the poltergeist, she had a choice. What had happened to Norah as she lay in her hospital cot sleeping the exhausted slumber of a sick baby? Julie swallowed, glanced down the path to safety, and finally turned back to rest her gaze on the sharpness of Euan's face.

'Tell me,' she said.

TWENTY-SEVEN

Alexander woke to the phone ringing. It felt like midnight, although the sun was warm through the window. He leaned over and answered with his face still pressing into the softness of his pillow.

'What are you doing today, son?'

Donald's voice scratched through the phone, low and heavy. Alexander closed his eyes. 'I'm working.'

'So you weren't going to... did you and your mother have any plans?'

'No.'

A grunt.

'What's going on, Dad?'

'Julie's not here. I thought she might be meeting you.'

'Not me.' Alexander held his phone away from his ear, wondering what to say next. So, Dad, they took you for a ride, eh? He didn't want to rub it in then, in the next moment, he wanted to take his father by the shoulders and shake him. See? We had found her already!

'Your Mum will be walking then.'

Alexander put the phone back against his ear. He could

hear his father breathing, waiting. 'Don't worry about her, Dad. She's always going for walks. I'll see you in a few hours.'

'You might as well go straight to the Nicol's in Roxburgh. That's where we are today.'

'Right.'

As soon as Alexander hung up, he checked messages and email. Nothing from Norah. Nothing from his mother, either. He tried Norah's phone number again and wasn't surprised when it failed. He rang his mother. Her cheery voice on the answering message didn't make him feel any better. 'Mum, ring me back.'

'What's up?'

The voices must have been louder than he thought. Colin stood at his doorway, rubbing his face. Alexander heard the rasp of his hand over his whiskers. 'Dad. Wanting to know whether I'm working.'

'And are you?'

'Aye. Are you?'

'Mate, that's not a question you need to ask me.'

Alexander studied his friend. Bleary-eyed and stubbly, typically early morning. Reliable, though. Steady. 'No, suppose not. Hey...'

'What?'

He'd been thinking about it but trying not to. 'Are you leaving soon?'

'Leaving?'

'Will you go back to Australia soon?'

Colin shrugged.

'You are going back, though.'

Colin stared along the corridor. 'Yes.'

There had been a point where Alexander knew that it would not be *Cameron and Astle Stonemasonry*. Thinking about it as Colin stomped wearily into the bathroom, he realised that point had been reached very recently. Back in Australia, Colin had shifted gears down. He was more relaxed, interested in the subtle changes to the city in the years he'd been away. Back in Scotland, something reserved took over his features. Despite being familiar with the work and the environment, Alexander thought Colin looked uncomfortable. It might be how it always was if you shifted countries. Sometimes Alexander had seen his mother give a twitchy sort of shrug out of the blue, as if she was still trying to adjust to something.

He got ready for work, trying Norah's number again and then his mother's. The lack of response made him slam his empty coffee cup down on the table.

'Whoa.' Colin grabbed the cup just as if fell.

'Sorry. No one answering.'

'Let it go for now. You promised your mother.'

'Even she's not answering.'

'Leave it, eh?'

'Nothing's going to change.'

Colin didn't answer. He pulled bread out of the freezer and fed four slices into the toaster.

'Colin?'

'No.' Colin pushed the lever down hard. 'I don't think it is.'

'I'm booking flights.'

'You sure?'

'Aye, I'm sure.'

'Do it then.' Colin caught the toast as it bounced up. 'You want me to come to Australia with you?'

'Would you?'

Colin turned the bread over, stuffed it back in for re-cooking.

'Colin?'

'If I do, I'm not coming back.'

Alexander stared down at where his coffee mug had left a

sluggish ring of brown on the dull surface of the table. Colin's toast sprang up again. The kitchen filled with the sounds of butter scraping on the slightly charred surface. 'It's because of Alicia, isn't it?'

Colin coughed mid-chew. 'What are you talking about?'

'Alicia. It's why you came out here. To get rid of her memory.'

'I came here to learn a trade. I have learned a trade. Time for me to practise back home.' Colin put his plate down roughly.

'I know that's what you said. It was more than that, though, wasn't it.'

Colin sat, put his elbows on the table and clasped his hands in front of his face. The sharp smell of burnt toast came with him. Alexander leaned over and pushed the window up a bit. The street was quiet outside.

'Yes.' Colin let his head drop into his hands. 'That was part of it. It worked, too. At the start.'

'And now?'

Colin sat back, his arms now at his side. 'There are some things you can't un-remember. She's one of them.'

'Norah didn't help, did she?'

Colin didn't answer.

Alexander reached over and took some toast from his friend's plate. It was spread with that black stuff Colin liked, and Alexander's tongue stung with the saltiness of it. 'I'm really sorry.'

'Why are you sorry? It's nothing you did.'

'I feel a bit to blame. Looking for Norah must have had some feeling of looking for Alicia.'

Colin slumped, elbows on the table again. 'No, mate. It didn't. When I helped look for Alicia, I knew she was dead.'

Alexander shook his head. 'But how?'

'Sounds stupid, but I knew. In here.' Colin held his stomach.

'Nothing gave any indication she was alive. She hadn't left anyone with cryptic messages, she hadn't planted any clever little notes, there was no clue to where she was. If she'd planned to go missing, if she'd done a *Gone Girl*, I would've known. But there was nothing. Not one thing that said she was still there.'

'But you knew where she was...'

'I guessed. I was looking in all the spots we'd gone to. Even though she hated every moment of our relationship.'

'Eh?'

Colin broke the last piece of toast in two and gave a bit to Alexander. 'Yep. That's what she said when she left me. Show's what a real charmer she was.'

'She didn't really hate everything.'

'Of course not. But she couldn't have me thinking that what we'd had was in any way special.'

'That's...'

'Yeah.'

They finished eating. Alexander linked his hands behind his head and leaned back. Colin had spoken about Alicia a bit, mainly when he first came over. Then nothing for over a year. Alexander felt a sudden wave of sadness for his friend. Alicia would always haunt him, in the most punishing, unforgiving way. Especially as... 'Perhaps if it hadn't been you who'd found her, things would be different.'

'But I did, didn't I? Washed up on the rocks. I could even see where she'd slipped on the path. There were finger marks where she'd tried to hold on. I saw them and then I looked over and there she was.' Colin stood up, ran a glass under the tap and drank deeply. 'I don't know why she still has such a hold on me. That last time I saw her, she looked like a bundle of rags someone had thrown over the cliff. She wasn't powerful anymore.' He shivered, a violent whole-body shake.

Alexander felt sick, not only at the thought of discovering a girl's body smashed on surf rocks, but at the despair in Colin's voice. 'Maybe what needs to happen is that you find someone else. Someone who can be kind to you.'

Colin turned, his face pale. He put the glass down with a steady hand. 'Well, you find me someone, pal. And I'll get you one the same.'

'Right. Deal.' Alexander pushed his chair back. The sun was on his back, calling him outside. 'First of all, we'd better go fix a wall.'

'Great. The cure to all. Wall-fixing.'

They got going, taking the van through the quiet streets and on the road to the Nicol's. Colin talked of football. Alexander half-listened. Colin wasn't interested in football, not the sort they had here. He was filling the silence and Alexander let him; the words washing over and out the window. Instead, he concentrated on what he was going to do next. Ring Norah at least once an hour. Get home and book a flight if there was no answer. He'd tell Colin once the flight was confirmed and maybe there'd be no more seats. A Colin left behind might be one who stays a bit longer. Alexander wasn't quite sure why that was important when the writing was on the wall. The thought of not having Colin around was unimaginable, part of a crumbling that Alexander thought would not happen. The family was almost complete. Wasn't Colin part of that?

DONALD GRUNTED when he saw them. He was already hard at it, sweat raining from his brow. It was warm, but not hot. 'You alright, Dad?' Alexander said when he saw the redness.

Donald didn't look up.

Alexander turned back to the van. Of course his father wouldn't be talking much. What had he expected? The son turns up again after having a few days' unexpected holiday, saunters back when he feels like it, and then has the cheek to ask if his father – the one who's worked the hardest over the last few weeks – is *alright*? Alexander felt his face warm to match his father's. Still, Donald didn't look right even if he was angry.

Colin took his tools to another work area, leaving Alexander next to Donald. They swung into a rhythm; the pattern of people well-used to working together. There was no need for words. Alexander thought of Norah, wondering whether she too would somehow fit into the family and become part of its machinery, a cog that turned with the rest, dependent on each other? This would mean Donald acknowledging her as a daughter. Alexander glanced at his father, seeing the big man wipe at his head with a shaking hand.

'Dad. What's going on?'

Donald leaned his hands on his knees, letting his head drop. The back of his neck was shining, the collar of his shirt dark.

'Dad?'

'I'm alright, lad. Bit worried about your mother. I didn't see her this morning.'

'But she often goes walking in the morning.'

Donald shrugged. 'Something feels different. She's not answering her phone.'

'Did you try the surgery?'

'Aye. It's not a workday for her. She's not there.'

'She'll be okay.'

Donald nodded, stretching up to stand straight. 'It's unusual, is all.'

'It's been an unusual few weeks.'

Donald put one arm on the wall and turned to look at Alexander. His eyes were bloodshot. 'Aye. Is she off with that girl then?'

'Norah, Dad. Come on. You have to see that.'

Donald shook his head, wiped a hand over his face. 'I don't know what to see.'

'The other, the one that didn't turn up...'

'Haven't heard anymore. Took my money and went.' Donald dropped his head again.

Alexander picked at the mortar line in front of him. Age had made it gritty. Lichen clung to the edges of the stone and spilled haphazardly into the crevice. It's what happened with time. He glanced at his father. So much time had passed since Norah went missing. The fissures must run as deep in his father as they did anyone else. 'I'm sorry, Dad,' he said softly.

Donald shook his head. 'Don't be. My stupid fault for trusting a stranger. I really thought, though, I was helping...'

'I know.'

Donald shook his head again, sharply. Alexander stirred the mortar in his bucket.

'Your mother. Is she with that girl?'

'I don't know. Norah's not answering her phone either.'

Donald straightened, his arm falling to his side. 'They're together?'

'I don't know, Dad. I wouldn't have thought so.'

'But they could be?'

'I guess.'

Donald ran both hands over his stubbly head. 'What if she's taken her?'

'What?'

'The girl! What if she's taken your mother?'

'No, Dad.'

Donald stepped forward. 'Why not?

'Because...' Alexander closed his eyes for a moment. Norah take their mother? Norah, who he knew – he absolutely knew – was his sister?

'Lad.' Donald pulled out his phone. 'I never took you to be a naïve imbecile.'

Alexander flushed. 'I never took you to be one, either.'

At that, his father grinned briefly. He put the phone to his ear and frowned. 'Nothing still.'

'You've left a message?'

'No.'

'Maybe you should.'

'The point of that?' Donald put the phone into his breast pocket.

Alexander shrugged. 'It lets her know that you're worried.'

'She will know that by the missed calls.' Donald rubbed at his eyes. 'The girl. Try her.'

Alexander wiped his forehead. 'I think she's gone back to Australia.'

Donald stilled. 'She's taken your mother to Australia?'

'Dad, Norah wouldn't...' No, Norah wouldn't, but Julie, if she knew that's where Norah was, would. Easily. But telling no one? If she was angry with Donald, that was one thing, but not telling Alexander? No, she wouldn't go without saying something.

'Is everything alright?' Colin had been to the van to get a drink. He stood now with it in his hand, head on one side, eyeing the two Camerons.

'Dad's worried about Mum.'

Colin nodded.

'Colin, tell me,' Donald folded his arms over his chest, 'you are the one least involved in all this. The girl, the one Alexander calls Norah, do you think she could have taken Julie?'

'Taken *Julie*?'

'Julie's not answering her phone. I haven't seen her since last night. Alexander tells me that the girl has gone. What am I expected to think?' Donald turned to the wall, put his steel-capped toe against the stones. 'Do you think she could have taken my Julie?'

Colin stared at Donald. 'Could Norah have taken Julie? No. She's too...'

'Well?'

'I don't know,' said Colin. 'She would not take her, though, it's not her style. Julie may have gone with her, but it would be Julie's idea.'

'Have you checked the house, Dad? Seen what Mum's taken?'

Donald screwed his face up. 'Her phone. That's all.' He got his phone out, dialled again, this time turning away to leave a message. Alexander couldn't hear the words but caught the tone. Pleading, sick to the soul. It made him swallow. His father was always so carefree, his mother was the linchpin for that.

'It'll be something innocent, Dad. Her phone will be on silent. It happens sometimes.'

Donald picked up his trowel. 'It's not. I feel it.'

As his father turned back to his work, Alexander looked at Colin. Colin shook his head slightly, frowning. Donald had decided. His uneasiness was catching. They went back to work as well, but not before Alexander tried both phone numbers again. The same responses. Norah's was definitely disconnected. His mother? Well, she would be doing one of her long walks, maybe the Eildons while the weather was fine.

They knocked off not long after lunch. Donald packed up in an instant, nodding goodbye as he drove out the gate, shrieking the tyres of his van on the asphalt as he approached the gutter too fast. Colin and Alexander took their time, Colin returning to the wall to study an area he thought wasn't aligned. Alexander leaned against the van to wait, idly flicking through flights again.

'Ready?' Colin came back, slammed the back of the van closed.

'Aye.' Alexander put the phone into his leg pocket.

'Looks good.' Colin nodded toward the wall.

'A job well done on this one.'

'Yes.'

Colin came around to the driver's side. They drove in silence back to Edinburgh and just as quietly made their way into the apartment.

There was still no reply on either phone by late afternoon. Alexander roamed the floors, forcing Colin out to get food. Left alone, Alexander felt shut up inside the walls. He went out as well, heading up the hill away from the centre of town. People were making their way home. He passed them walking wearily, bounding along himself until he was deep in suburbia. His mouth was dry, his legs felt tight. When the phone pinged – At last! At last! – he stopped in the middle of the pavement, making a suited man steer hurriedly around him.

She is alright but she's in hospital.

Alexander took thirty seconds to realise that the number wasn't Norah's or Colin's. It was his father. He blinked at it, all sorts of scenarios in his head but mainly to do with the many accidents you could have walking the hills of the Borders. He texted back.

What happened?

There was no hesitation. *I don't know. She won't say.*

Alexander turned and ran down the hill, the journey back to the van as long a trip as he'd ever made.

TWENTY-EIGHT

From her hospital bed, Julie could see through the window to a low green paddock of bald-faced sheep. They were blurry with rain. She blinked a few times, wondering perhaps if fuzzy sheep were part of her brain damage. When she looked away, though, the sparse room was clear and defined as only a ward could be.

Her afternoon peace was broken early. Nurses checked her drip and wounds, took her vital signs with cool hands and calm faces. They'd only just disappeared when Donald came in dressed in one of his best shirts, the top buttons open to reveal sun-bronzed skin and a smattering of greying chest hairs. She smiled at him or thought she did. He was at once concerned and tentatively took up one of her hands. 'Are you in pain, love?'

'No.' Her voice husked. She coughed. 'No, I'm fine.'

He clearly didn't think so. His eyes were welling as he stared, so she patted his hand briskly with her free one. 'Donald, I'm fine.' Her voice was stronger this time. 'Could I please have a drink?'

He sprang away, eager to help, and poured her a glass of water. It was harder than she'd imagined, leaning forward to drink. Everything felt stiff, as if she hadn't moved in years. A sharp pain edged the ribs on her right side. She pressed her hand over it and eased back onto her pillows.

'How's that, love?'

'Better. Thank you.'

Donald pulled the visitor's chair closer to the bed and sat down, immediately searching for her hand again. She resisted the urge to pull away – *I just want to be left alone* – and closed her eyes instead.

'Julie? Can you tell me what happened?'

He'd asked that several times already. The doctor, a chubby bright-eyed woman who surely couldn't have been as old as Alexander, had hushed him before whispering the same question as they steered Donald to the back of the emergency room. Julie had shaken her head. She did it again now, holding her eyes more firmly closed.

Donald cleared his throat. 'You don't have to speak. Maybe you could nod or shake or put one finger up or something? Was it a man? Did he...?'

Julie thought of Norah. She had the perfect image of her, the moment she'd stepped out of the car. It was like a camera's snapshot, only richer. Julie remembered the warmth of the summer air, the heady smell of lavender, the wineglass stem so fragile beneath her fingertips. Norah's dress billowed; her hair lifted gently in the breeze before settling against her cheek. When she'd pushed her sunglasses up, her kohl-lined eyes were soft oceanic blue, her gaze a lighthouse beam across the gravel. Julie knew that part of the memory was fanciful, but it served her well, especially with Donald's breath on her face as he bent over her for an answer. She shook her head.

'Perhaps you don't remember?'

Better that he thinks that, Julie thought, as she feigned sleep. She felt him move away and sit back down in the chair. He would have one ankle balanced on his other knee, a large hand gripping it, jiggling enough to shake the floor. Yes, she could sense the fine trembles through her bed.

What could she tell him that wouldn't break his heart completely? You marry a man whose only fault is that he loves you intensely and you take that love and exploit its forgiveness. She didn't want to be the one to bring him down. She was a coward.

Perhaps she fell asleep for real as the next action in the room was Alexander rushing in, the smell of earth on him. Julie opened her eyes and saw the terror on his face. She smiled, ever the reassurer, feeling the drag across her cheek from the newly dressed scratches.

'Mum, are you alright?'

'Of course.' Her voice was improving. It felt less battered.

'What happened?'

'Don't bother her with questions, lad.' Donald had a warning hand on Alexander's back.

'Sorry. I didn't mean...'

'It's fine, Alexander.' Julie reached for another drink. 'I can't remember what happened.'

There, that was the correct response. The tension eased a little in the room. Donald let out a sigh, Alexander's shoulders relaxed. She didn't remember, so whatever horrible thing had happened wouldn't haunt her. She took up Alexander's offered hand and pressed it lightly.

Not long after the family reunion, the doctor came to let them know Julie would stay overnight. This gave the nurses the nod to usher everyone out the door so Julie could rest. Julie managed a grateful, behind-everyone's-back smile to the nurse who gave her a wink. Donald bent to kiss her goodbye, hovering over her face before deciding there was no clear place to land one, and shifting to the top of head. Julie felt ridiculously child-like and shrunk down slightly so he wouldn't stay long.

Alexander trailed his hand over her arm. She held her hand up in a regal wave as the men left, letting it flop to the bed once they had disappeared.

In the room's quiet, the noise of the night before descended like thunder. Julie kept her eyes on the sheep in the paddock, concentrating on the way they nipped at the grass and jerked their heads sideways to break it. Staring at the benign animals at least kept the vision of his face at bay, but nothing could stop the sound. She wished she'd asked Donald to bring in her head-phones, but then remembered that her phone was lost, left behind somewhere in the estate's woods. She could even picture where it might be: a fallen log that she'd staggered over, the soft mossy patch where her foot had turned, the sharp-edged branches that clawed her arms as they flayed about in a vain attempt to keep her balance. Yes, she had her phone before then – it had been in her hand – but not after. Not when she dragged herself up and fled even further away.

The irony was that, despite her attempts at getting away, she could never un-know what he had told her.

Tears seeped out of her eyes and were absorbed by the wound dressings on her cheeks. She blinked slowly, staring at the sheep again. The rain had stopped outside, but twilight was coming. The sheep moved towards their night resting place. She watched them until they'd gone out of sight and there was no movement to distract her. Sickness came suddenly, and she rang for help, but not before vomiting shamefully over the clean, white sheets. The nurses were nonplussed, guiding her into Donald's vacated chair as they briskly cleaned up. She let herself sob as they worked, and one put a steady arm around her shoulders, squeezing firmly, before they tucked her back in and promised a cup of tea.

By the time she'd had tea with two sugars, a soft cheese sandwich, and an oat biscuit, the tears had gone. A couple of white tablets, and Julie felt herself drifting. It was then that elation set in. A terrible thing had happened. Yes. But her daughter was alive.

ALEXANDER WOKE, his dream world – a weird mixture of dry-stone walling and Melbourne's botanical gardens – fading quickly. The phone tone was generic. He almost didn't answer, but even cold callers rarely rang at three in the morning.

'Alexander, it's your mother.'

He pushed up on one elbow. 'Mum? Are you alright?'

'Goodness me, I wish everyone would stop asking me that.'

'Of course we're going to ask that. You're in hospital and you don't know what happened to you!'

A soft ping of a hospital machine echoed through the line. 'Listen, Alexander. Please don't worry about me. I want you to go after Norah.'

Alexander sat right up, pushing his pillows behind him so he could lie his head back tiredly. 'Now? When we don't know what happened to you?'

'Yes. You need to go now. Alexander, we can't lose her again.'

His mother may be covered in bandages, but if he hadn't seen her for himself, her firm voice was typically Julie. 'You want me to go to Australia?'

'That's where she is.'

'What about you, Mum? Seriously.'

'Alexander, you need to believe me when I say that I will be fine.'

Alexander leaned forward, his palm on his forehead. 'You do know what happened. You remember exactly.'

A long pause with no hospital sounds. She must be on a

landline, he thought. Standing in a corridor perhaps, or alone at the nurse's station as the night workers went about their business. Maybe even in her bed, having asked for the phone. Not sleeping, anyhow. Thinking about what to do next.

'Go,' she finally said. 'Please. Find Norah again. It's the most important thing to do.'

Alexander felt his tiredness leave him, replaced by a heart-pounding exhilaration. 'Okay, I will.'

'Thank you.'

The call ended abruptly. He hoped his mother hadn't collapsed. The sheet caught on his feet as he struggled up, and he pulled at it sharply. He could go on standby at the airport, it was only a matter of packing his things and getting there. In less than an hour, he could be on his way to his sister.

COLIN'S NIGHTMARE was different this time. When he woke, it was a sort of relief to know that the same one wasn't churning over and over in his head. It wasn't about Alicia, nothing to do with her raggy body on its nest of rocks. This one involved pursuit, the endless running and hiding when trying to flee. At one stage, Colin crouched behind the van, the rock hammer in his hand suddenly soft plastic. His pursuer was nearly there – who was it? – and so he ran for the safety of a large oak tree in the distance that shrank the closer he got. Mud sucked at his boots; rain flattened him. He was, he knew, doomed to always remember. The realisation stopped him running. He stood in the mud, arms by his side, a William Wallace statue.

The door slam woke him completely. He grabbed for his phone, but it wasn't time to get up. Something had happened.

The kitchen was empty, so he backtracked to Alexander's

room. The bed was made, his bedside table empty, the wardrobe
door firmly shut. There was an air about it, something reminis-
cent of a motel room. Its occupant wasn't coming back for a
while.

Back to the kitchen. There it was, propped against the
kettle. A brief note written under their shopping list. *Tomatoes.
Bread. Sliced cheese. Going to the airport. Will let you know
what happens.*

Colin put both his hands on the bench, letting his head
drop, before straightening slowly and going back to his room. He
already packed the suitcase under his bed. They could send the
box of extras to him at some stage. He'd got it ready almost a
week ago, not long after the decision to leave took root in his
head. It took Alexander's flight to create one of his own, and
part of him was irrevocably sad. But it was time to go, visa
or not.

It wasn't his plan to go there and then, but by the time he'd
showered, eaten, somehow dressed in shorts and T-shirt rather
than work clothes, there wasn't another choice. He texted
Donald, not wanting to hear his rough voice, and said that he
was going with Alexander. Donald didn't need to know he'd lost
a worker, not this week, not with Julie in hospital. He texted his
parents, too, a warning that he might turn up soon and unexpectedly. In typical coastal behaviour, they said, *no worries,
can't wait to see you, any time is fine, we're here on the beach
with our floppy hats and sunscreen.*

Then there was no reason not to lug his suitcase down to the
bus stop and wait for the airport express.

He paused.

'SIR, we may have one seat on this airline. If you wouldn't mind waiting over there.'

Alexander sat on the edge of the seat, feet clamped widely and firmly on the industrial carpet of Edinburgh Airport. He Googled Claudia Purton again, a sick feeling churning his guts. From her digital footprint, Claudia lived in Melbourne and looked nothing like Norah. Claudia's photos showed a woman with sharp hazel eyes and a fierce black bob. She had strong, tanned arms and an inclination towards singlet tops. There was nothing delicate about her, although he imagined her small. Unless he had the wrong Claudia Purton completely, he now had no idea of Norah's name.

'Sir?'

The airline representative waved him over, smiling. It would be a long flight, two stopovers, forty-one hours in total, but it was his. The nausea dulled. At least, if he was in Australia, he was closer to her.

———

ALL COLIN HAD to do was to grab his suitcase and the back-pack of essentials for the cabin, hail a cab instead of waiting for the bus, and make like a tree. A list of *but, waits* started. But, wait, I haven't let ALIE know I'm going. But, wait, in all this time I've never visited the underground city. But, wait, I have no base to go back to unless I want to live in the theatre room of my parents' kitsch Coolangatta apartment.

He studied his watch. Alexander had probably been gone nearly two hours. Time enough to try for a standby ticket. He was most likely settled in the waiting room, crowd-watching.

Colin pulled his luggage into the hall and went back to stand at the kitchen window. It was still early, so locals were rolling down the hill to their workplaces, most with their heads down. He liked this street and how it was an effort to return. It stamped the end of a working day or a hard night out to heave yourself back to your place of rest. You'd earned it, no matter the reality of the actual day.

It was likely that, when he returned, he'd go back to Melbourne until he could start his own business. Melbourne's hum was the only place for part-time work that didn't interest you but earned you dollars while plotting your proper life. Perhaps he'd ask for work with established stonemasons. They were around, and work in Melbourne was half restoration, half new and commercial. He had a flash of the paddock in Roxburgh, mist hovering over the grass, gnarled oak trees standing guard. No, he couldn't stay in Melbourne, not anymore. Gisborne, maybe. Daylesford. Trentham.

Colin shrugged his shoulders up hard and let them go. Yeah, well, whatever. First, he had to find Alexander. He rang him and the first had no pickup. The second was answered on the last ring.

'Colin.'

'Got anything?'

'Aye. Leaving in five hours.'

'You going to wait there for five hours?'

'I'm already here. I might as well stay.'

'Was the flight easy to get?'

Alexander was quiet for a while. 'No.'

'I'm coming, too.'

'What, you want to sit at the airport for days until you get something?'

Colin looked back through the empty kitchen. He could see the corner of his black bag in the hall. Everything was ready. 'I just think it would be better if I came with you.'

Silence for a long moment. Then, 'Her name is not Claudia Purton.'

'I didn't think it would be.'

'How are we going to find her?'

'We start with the real Claudia Purton. There must be some sort of connection.'

'How do we find her?'

Colin rubbed his forehead with the tips of his fingers. 'How long have you got to do this? I mean, how much money and time do you have?'

'I've got whatever it takes.'

'No, you haven't. Alexander. We just spent a month away. I don't know about you, but my savings are nearly gone. Your father will never forgive me for leaving so suddenly. I'll need work really soon.'

'I'll be okay.'

'You won't, you know.'

'It doesn't matter, Colin.'

For a second, Colin thought Alexander was going to kill the call. Instead, the sounds of rushing people and calm announcements took over. Then his voice came back.

'1245pm is my flight. When I get there, I'm starting where we left off. Paxton. Okay? That's where you'll find me.'

'Okay, okay. I'll get myself sorted and meet you somewhere.'

'Right.'

Colin pushed his phone back into his pocket. A last glance around and there was no point in lingering. He'd send the expats an email. They were used to vagrancy. There wasn't anyone particularly special in that group – Andrea from Sydney tried to convince him otherwise – but he liked them all. Besides them, working had taken up most of his time. He held his hand out to study the callouses on his palm and fingers. Lines of Scottish soil tattooed the skin, criss-crosses of embedded dirt and dust. Maybe he'd have that forever.

He locked the keys inside the flat, thumped his case down

the steps to the front door, and walked into a swift, heavy shower of rain that made him laugh. It was over by the time he'd got to the taxi rank on Frederick Street and back again as he stepped out at the airport. He flicked the water out of his hair before he stepped inside, spotting Alexander almost immediately at Starbucks, no doubt sipping on one of those drinks they described as coffee. He rolled his baggage towards him.

'Hey,' he said.

'Ah,' said Alexander. 'To freedom.'

Colin nodded as he sat beside his friend. Freedom? He breathed out. Freedom. Yes.

TWENTY-NINE

'I can drive.'

Donald glanced at Julie as if the *event* had left her addled. That's how they referred to it, the *event*. It was that young, flush-faced doctor that started it, but Donald had quickly latched on. 'Julie's been involved in an event,' she'd heard him say on the phone to Elizabeth. 'She's coming home from hospital today. Could you tell Euan? Still away? Alright then.'

Julie shivered and reached for her cardigan. Donald tugged it away and spread it clumsily over her shoulders. 'I'll drive, love.'

'You've never driven my car.'

'I drove it here, didn't I? Don't you be worrying.'

She angled herself into the passenger's seat, acutely aware that back pain was now her biggest physical problem and that the last person to occupy the seat was Norah. Donald reached through to do up her seat belt and she held herself back from slapping him away. 'I can do it.'

'Oh. Aye. Alright then.'

He hurried to the driver's seat, thumped into it, and tried to help her again.

'Donald, stop.'

'Sorry, love.'

The truth was that she could have done with some assistance. The latch for the belt was at exactly the wrong angle. Teeth-gritting, sharp flashes of pain happened every time she pushed the clip in. She took a deep breath in, stabbed at the latch until there was a click, and let herself sink into the seat.

'That's a big sigh, love.'

'I'm a bit tired.'

'I'll have you home soon. You can go back to bed.'

But she didn't want to go back to bed. Alexander had texted from the airport, so she assumed by now he was in the air. The hospital had kept her in one further day after the vomiting inci-dent. She lied her way through questions about nausea to get their approval to leave. Nausea? She was full up with sickness, the knowledge she now had so disgusting it was gangrenous. But bed? No. She'd be joining Alexander as soon as she could.

Donald drove like a learner in the little sedan. He kept over-compensating, making the car weave from line to line as he cornered. It was an automatic, and he wasn't used to it. His hand fell uselessly down to the handbrake while his left leg pumped up and down, lost. Julie turned to look out the window so she wouldn't have to see the way his hands worked at the steering wheel as he tried to find things to say.

'You going okay, love?'

'Yes, thank you.'

'If you want me to stop, let me know. I can pull over anywhere.'

The thought of Donald taking the car to the side of the narrow road was worse than him keeping it in the centre of the lane. She closed her eyes, feigning sleep, so he could concentrate on what he was doing.

When they reached home, she would have been out of the

car before he was, but piercing pain held her hostage. She pretended to be looking for a handkerchief in her handbag, waving Donald towards opening the door, while she carefully shuffled around. He looked back as the glass door slid open, but she was out. The pain receded a little now she was standing, but she couldn't help a grunt with the first step forward. Luckily, Donald was emptying the boot of her things and didn't hear.

As she stepped through the door, though, she realised how good the pain had been. Pain kept you distracted. When it eased, other feelings rushed in to fill the gap. The living area, adorned by family photos, looked forlorn. Tears prickled her eyes. Donald bent towards her and she thrust her handbag into his arms to make him, please, go away. She had time to swallow quietly and say, in a quite normal voice, 'I'm going to the bathroom.'

'I'll put the kettle on, love.'

She nodded.

In the closed bathroom, she swallowed some pain killers and checked her phone for messages from Alexander. None. His flight was convoluted, she knew, and some airports had poor communication networks. The last message had been hours before. The next would be hours hence. In the meantime, she had to deal with Donald's solicitousness.

Julie had stiffened herself for a cup of tea with her husband, and was moving slowly back to the kitchen, when the door slid open and Elizabeth came in. There was no use in hiding. The door was exactly opposite the hall, the line-of-sight dead-straight. Elizabeth stopped when she saw Julie, her open-mouthed expression morphing to downright horror the closer Julie came. A hand rose to her mouth, large gems like bottle tops branding her fingers. 'Oh, Julie, whatever happened?'

'We aren't supposed to talk-' started Donald.

'Were you attacked? Was it one man? More?'

'Elizabeth, we aren't-'

'Oh, God, did they...? Did they? Julie?'

Perhaps the tablets were helping. Julie felt a little ethereal, looking down at Elizabeth as if from slightly above. She could see the shocked, melodramatic hand and the whites around her sister-in-law's clear, blue eyes. Donald had a hand reaching out, a silent stop sign that wasn't working. His concern gave him raised eyebrows, and a jutted chin. Julie giggled. It was like a scene out of a bad soap opera, one that you could only watch during the day when most people had better things to do. Next, she supposed, Elizabeth would faint, the back of her hand on her forehead as she sunk slowly to the ground so that her skirt didn't ride up.

'Julie?'

Now Donald was there, leading her with one large hand on her shaking one, the other settled on her back. He lowered her onto the couch, kneeling on the rug to flip her legs up on the couch. The room spun a little. She blinked. His face came into view, a round disc of sweaty skin. She patted his cheek. 'Don't worry, my good man.' She knew they were weird words even before he frowned.

'I'll get tea.' Elizabeth's voice wisped down from the ceiling.

Donald had to move when the tea appeared. He'd been blocking the light. Julie felt better now she could see into her garden and struggled upright. 'Sorry about that,' she said as Elizabeth put the tea on the coffee table. 'I was a bit dizzy.'

'With every right to be so.' Elizabeth sat beside her, putting a bony arm around Julie's shoulders and bumping her head against hers. Julie felt the warmth of her grip, and it was strangely nice. Poor Elizabeth, the poor wife, going about her flippant life without knowing the truth of it all.

'When is Euan back?' Donald almost fell into his chair, knees flopping apart.

'I'm not sure. He said it was a rare opportunity to him to attend. A conference at St Andrew's,' Elizabeth added, her head towards Julie. 'Invitation only. He used to get so many of those after his award. Naturally, he had to take this one.' She slid her arm from Julie's shoulder and took her hand up instead. 'He wanted to be here.'

Julie wet her lips. 'He said that?'

'Yes. Not those words exactly, but that's what he meant.'

It was the right moment, Julie knew, to tell them what happened. She took a sip of tea to ready herself. She would tell them everything, her husband and his wife, and then...And then what? Their worlds would collapse, there'd be trauma and pain. Friends would take sides; the community would falter. Her life would go on hold as she endlessly and uselessly tried to explain why it happened, both to herself and to Donald. He did not have the capacity to understand, not the old information or the new. In the meantime, Alexander was in Australia finding Norah once and for all. That was where she should be, back in her own country, looking for her daughter.

Elizabeth and Donald were both silent, looking at her. They know I'm about to speak, she thought. Tiredness swamped her. 'I can't explain what happened,' she said, feeling them both lean forwards. 'I went for a walk. I know it was late, but I hadn't checked the note box for a while. I went for a walk and I thought I saw someone. I ran. I fell. I can't remember anymore.'

They were weasel words, but they were more than she'd said before. Donald glanced at Elizabeth, who gave him a small nod that translated into *She's talking, that's good*. He nodded back, a smile softening his face.

Julie smiled back at him. Really, she didn't want him to be worried. It didn't matter, not now. 'You found me.'

'I did,' he said happily, grinning now. 'I found you all scratched up and...' He nodded towards the bruises on her arm.

'I fell.'

'You knocked yourself out.'

'Yes.' She felt her head. The lump ached. 'It's all fine now, though. I'll be right as rain in a few days.'

'Right as rain!' Elizabeth laughed, letting Julie's hand go to reach for her own tea.

Even Donald felt safe enough to pull the ring on his beer can. Julie nodded and smiled as they drank their beverages, her concentration only just enough on their exclamations of her improving health as she calculated how long it would take her to get to Australia.

I DO NOT WANT to be me.

For a week, Grace was Katerina Hawley. Katerina's hair was close-cropped and crow-black. She wore heavy eyeliner on her top lid and underscored her lower with blue. Ripped jeans and tight t-shirts with rock band names finished her off. Katerina was hard work. She sneered all the time and became increasingly irritable.

Grace stuffed Katerina's op-shop found clothes back into the collection bin early on Thursday morning. There was nothing she could do at the moment about the black hair, but she'd scrubbed her face clean and applied some chestnut highlights to her hair to bring some joy back. The hardest thing was what to wear now that Katerina was gone. There was not much space in the youth hostel to spread clothes out for a proper look, so Grace put on the items from the top of her case. And, because it was Melbourne in winter, she covered up the free-flowing floral shirt with a thick short coat that had been in the hostel's lost property box. At least her own jeans, devoid of rips, were warmer than Katerina's.

With Katerina gone, Grace walked the CBD with copies of her resume. In a lane as yet undiscovered by the cosmopolitans, the owner was desperate for a barista.

'You done any training?'

'A while ago.' Words fell easily from Grace's mouth, shaped for what needed to be heard. 'I've been away travelling.'

The man grunted, his face red with busy-ness. 'Can you start now? I mean, right now? There's only me here. Think of the day as probation.'

'Sure. Where will I hang my bag?'

The man pointed to a hook behind the outside door. By the time Grace had turned back, he was already telling her what needed to be done.

Grace loved it. She took orders, and there was nothing more technical than a soy decaf latte. She served yo-yos on small white plates with orange serviettes as landing pads. She even made a coffee or two, working with Garry – the owner – and copying his moves exactly.

I love it, she caught herself thinking, *because there is no time to think about Norah.*

At the end of the day, though, when Garry had smiled and given her a token wage as training pay, and asked her back the next day, she was out on the street again with nowhere to go but back to the hostel. It wasn't bad there but crowded with an odour of wet clothes. She walked around the streets instead, weaving in and out of shoppers and workers heading home, not interested in the misty shop windows with their displays of dull clothes. Street lights started flickering on. She sighed, turning for her accommodation.

Claudia stood across the road talking into her phone.

'Claudia!'

It was out before she could stop it. Grace clamped a hand over her mouth. There was no need. The word had been caught in a rattle of trams and hadn't made it further than the person next to her. Claudia had one hand in her coat pocket and a rust-coloured beanie pulled over her ears. She looked so familiar; it was like seeing a photograph of a warm memory. Claudia, who Grace had not spoken with since the night of the decision. Claudia, who was still officially Grace's house mate by virtue of Grace's regularly paid rent. She wondered whether Claudia had sub-let her room, as she had said she could. If so, where was Grace's box of things? Grace blinked back sudden, ridiculous tears and clenched her hands. Claudia had many reasons to get rid of anything Grace had left behind. It was she who'd been abandoned, not Grace.

Grace looked up the street toward the lonely hostel. She turned back to Claudia, who had her phone down and was walking towards the railway station. Thunder rumbled. Grace walked parallel to Claudia until they reached the corner. Claudia disappeared under the clocks. Grace urged the lights to change and ran after her.

There was no need to panic. Claudia hurried to their usual line, where a hundred other people were waiting. At the back of the crowd, Grace kept Claudia's beanie in sight, and boarded the train two carriages back. If Claudia was not going home, she was still heading in home's direction. Grace scrutinised the platform every time the train stopped, but Claudia didn't get off until, there, the home station. It was easy enough to slip into the small disembarking crowd and follow the beanie on to the street.

It was heavy twilight and shadows blackened the footpath as Grace walked about fifty metres behind Claudia. The landscape felt homely. There was the corner electricity pole with its collection of old lost and found notices. The one she remembered about a missing Chihuahua was gone, replaced by a plea to find a ten-year-old tabby cat. Someone had left the picture of a captured floppy-eared rabbit. Did this mean no one had claimed it or had the owner of the notice given up hope?

The two silver birches in the tiny front yard of the corner house were bare. The slim white trunks looked patchy in the low light. Grace put her hand up as she passed, letting their whippy branches run through it. The biggest difference to the street, now that she was in it heading for their house, was that her dad's car was gone. She'd really thought, spending his money on airfares, that she was never coming back.

Grace's step faltered over uneven, cracked pavement. Was that right - she'd never intended to return?

In the distance, Claudia was at the front door, the key scraping loudly into the lock, the door creaking open. Grace walked faster. Claudia had flicked on the hall light. As Grace reached the front gate, walking nonchalantly now, she glimpsed the rough-plastered wall and the coat rack of scarves as the door swung closed. She braced herself for loud greetings within – *hey, you're home! Are you cooking dinner tonight?* – but that was what *they'd* used to say. Claudia and Grace, house mates, task sharers, friends.

Grace walked to the corner and turned back. There was no one else in the street, but she felt shifty. There could be eyes watching through any of the windows facing the road. She pushed the hood off her head, hoping that by exposing her hair she'd look less like a criminal. At the house, she stopped, feigning trouble with her coat zip. It was easy then to turn slightly towards number sixteen, look through the window of the front room, and see, under the gap of the blind, the top of the packing chest she'd taped up weeks ago.

Grace stood there until it was completely dark, the street-light casting her in shadows, her skin prickling. From inside, she heard the television but no people. The door to the front room must have been closed because, now that it was night, she couldn't see any other features. Even the box was just a black thing by the window.

It was getting colder. Light rain fell, the flashing of lightning a long way away but warning of worse to come. Grace had to move. She tried walking past, but her feet turned and went up the one step to the front door. She raised her hand to knock, but instead stretched her fingers out to lay the flat of her palm on the paint-peeling wood. Then she leaned her cheek next to it, a paint curl poking into her skin. With her ear against the door, the low rumble of the television was louder. Something banged from the kitchen – a saucepan of pasta, maybe? Grace could almost smell it, the rich tomato sauce Claudia made from an Italian aunt's recipe, all basil and oregano, with Claudia's special addition of a sprig of parsley.

She stepped back. There was no smell of cooking, only the dankness of rotting leaves. She was shivering now, the cold seeping like oil through her clothes. One step, and she was back to the gate. Two steps, out on the footpath. The empty road space in front of the house shone patchy-rainbow with grease. Three, four, twenty steps and she was running back to the railway station, tears matching the rain on her face, weird thoughts like, *this isn't how Norah would act* racing through her mind and eventually making her slow to a normal person's pace.

It took a sluggish forty minutes for her to be pushing open the door of the youth hostel and inching her way through the dreadlocked corridor dwellers to her bed. Forty minutes in which she decided that she couldn't go on living like this.

THIRTY

Alexander arrived at Tullamarine in the early morning of a day he'd lost. He staggered off the plane. For fifteen hours he'd been jammed against the window with a large, snoring man blocking his way out. He had to wake him to go to the toilet. He woke him several times, not just because Alexander needed the toilet a lot, but because he wondered whether the man, dead asleep from the moment he first did up his seat belt, was going to develop a clot in his leg and die from inactivity at high altitudes. Then Alexander's way out would have truly been blocked.

The airport seemed like any other. People waited glumly at the carousel for baggage that came strewn tiredly on the conveyor belt, the suitcases looking the same with airline tags and use. He didn't even notice his own the first time it did the rounds, but gradually the familiar tawny-coloured backpack triggered reaction. He heaved it on his back and wondered what to do next.

Colin had found a flight leaving six hours after Alexander. It was going via Los Angeles. They'd estimated that he would arrive in Melbourne thirteen hours after Alexander. That was without delays. Which Alexander had. He had no idea of time; his brain was mush. When the flashing neon sign of the motel across the walkway caught his eye, it seemed the only solution. He flung himself into the only room they could offer him and slept face down on top of the bedspread.

Where are you?

The text woke him. Startled, he peeled his face from the bed and rubbed at his eyes until he could type the name of the motel. Half an hour later, Colin knocked at his door. They clasped hands. Colin dumped his bag and locked himself in the bathroom.

An hour later, they sat at the bar staring out at the grey skies.

'I haven't found Claudia Purton's address.' Alexander swirled the last of his beer around the bottom of his glass.

'Doesn't matter. We'll start at the pub in Paxton.'

'Why?'

'That's where she found out about you.'

'Who, Claudia?'

'No.'

'You mean Norah.'

'She said she was talking to the waitress.'

'You can't say it.'

'Say what?'

'Norah. You still don't believe she's Norah.'

Colin put his glass down, missing the coaster so it tipped over. 'She called herself Norah in Scotland, but that's not who she is here. She's had a life as someone else. We can't think of her as Norah here.'

'I can't think of her as anyone else.'

Colin shook his head, looking momentarily anguished. 'Another?'

'No. I'm still recovering from aeroplane food.'

Colin pushed his chair back and went to the bar. Alexander watched him point to something on the food menu and turn back to him. He shook his head. His stomach was churning but not from heated rice and curry. The pub in Paxton was a great starting point, but there was no guarantee Norah would have returned. As for Claudia, who the hell was she?

Colin returned with a Coke. He thrust his phone at Alexander. 'Here.'

'What is it?'

'Somewhere to stay.'

It was an Airbnb in the suburb next to Paxton. 'Okay.'

Colin booked in, swearing at the low battery on his phone. He put the phone down and reached for his drink.

Alexander waited until he'd drained it. 'Let's go.'

Colin rubbed his hand through his hair. 'Ever get a feeling of déjà vu?'

'No. This is different.' Alexander pulled his backpack on. 'We've already found her once. All we have to do is find her again.'

Colin put a hand on his friend's shoulder. 'We didn't find her. She found us. Remember?'

Alexander said nothing as they headed for the airport bus. They sat at the back, their bodies whipping from side to side until the driver got onto the freeway. The city loomed, its lofty buildings lost in mist. It was midnight or dawn somewhere in the world, but in Melbourne it was only just after lunch. The central station was full of shoppers and older people avoiding the rush hour. Alexander felt numb, the light all wrong, the beer sitting nastily in his gut. Colin steered him on to a metro train. The familiar click clack – surely the same all over the globe – settled him. They got off to light rain.

'Straight to the pub?'

Colin eyeballed him. 'Let's get rid of our things. You need

another shower. You're swaying on your feet.'

He followed obediently as Colin walked confidently in the direction of the bnb. Strange, but Colin seemed taller, bigger. Returning home did change him. Or was he reverting to normal? Alexander let his weary thoughts steam. What did *he* look like? A lost traveller? Someone who only had hope and no substance? He was still thinking it when they arrived at the small flat, and Colin put in the code that let them in. It was tinier inside than their place in Edinburgh but who cared? He threw his things down in the nearest bedroom and headed for the shower.

Another hour and they were out the door again. So many hours gone, thought Alexander. Were they too late? He felt better, his body waking up as the day dwindled. He even remembered to text his mother, who replied as if she'd been waiting. Guilt washed over him. His mother, battered and bruised from... what, exactly? Something had happened that had made her more eager to find Norah. He felt the vibes through the satellite connection with their phones.

Let me know the second you find her. The very second.

Her fear electrified him.

'Where's this pub?'

'Not far. Around the corner.'

Alexander glanced around at the terrace houses, the gritty footpath and the multitude of coloured cars parked nose to backside along the street. 'Do you see anything?'

'See what?'

'Anything that could be connected to her.'

'No. Alexander. Come on. We're just starting out.'

Alexander saw the look Colin gave him. It was one of those usually reserved for when you encountered a drunk on the street or someone asked you for money by holding out a grubby hand. Colin wasn't sure of him; thought he was a tiny bit mad. Maybe he was. He tried to smile.

Colin gave a small shake of his head, but then pointed up the road. 'Here it is.'

Alexander remembered it now. The outside was lime-white, while the inside oozed chic. They stepped in from a door set right on the corner and went to the bar. The barman tipped his head to one side. 'Drinks, gentlemen?'

'No. Thanks. We're actually looking for someone.'

'Right.' The barman frowned and scratched his carefully trimmed beard.

'We're trying to track down my sister,' said Alexander, laying on his accent. 'She's gone missing.'

Beside him, Colin twitched. 'Not exactly missing. We think she's come back here.'

The barman raised an eyebrow. 'She your sister, too?'

'No. Just helping him.'

'Right.'

'She was here – we were here – a few months ago.' Alexander nodded towards the table they'd sat at. 'We thought she might have come back.'

'She was here with you?'

'No, she was here afterwards. It's how she found us.'

The barman leaned his elbows on the counter near the cash register. 'Let me get this straight. You're looking for your sister and he's helping. She was here and now she's gone. She found you, but she doesn't want you to find her again. Would that be right?'

Alexander hooked his hair behind his ear. 'When you say it like that, it doesn't sound good.'

'Too right it doesn't. Sounds to me like you're chasing a girl who doesn't want you to find her.' The barman crossed his arms.

'No, it isn't like that-'

Colin put a hand on the counter. 'Do you know Claudia Purton?'

'Is that her name?'

'No. She's... connected with her. With Alexander's... sister.'

'Whose name is...?'

'Norah,' said Alexander firmly. 'My sister's name is Norah.'

'Well, I don't know any Norahs and I don't know Claudia Purton-'

'I know Claudia.'

Alexander swung around. A small blonde woman, her hair tied back in a curly ponytail and an apron over her black jeans, stood just behind them. 'You do?'

'Ruby, I don't think you should say anything.'

Ruby shrugged. 'I worked with Claudia. At *Stillers*. She might not be there anymore. Why do you want to know?'

'They say,' said the barman, 'that they're looking for his sister.'

'I didn't think Claudia had any sisters.'

Alexander felt a wave of jet lag swamp him. 'My sister. We think Claudia knows my sister. She's missing.'

'Are you alright?' Ruby's hand went out as if she was going to hold Alexander up.

'Ruby,' the barman warned.

'He looks like he's going to faint.'

Colin grabbed Alexander by the bicep and started for the door. 'He's fine. He always looks that way. It's his Scottish pallor.'

'Oh.'

'Thanks for the help.' Alexander smiled at the girl as he was steered away. 'And thanks...' but he couldn't think what to say to the barman.

'You can't just say that,' Colin said as they walked towards the city, his grip on Alexander gone. 'You're looking for a missing girl? We'll end up being arrested.'

Alexander shrugged. 'It's the truth.'

'Lie, then. Make something up.'

'Like what?'

'I don't know.' Colin rubbed his hand over his head. 'Anything.'

'That's not helpful. Are we going to Stillers?'

'I think I know where it is.' Colin looked at him sternly.

'What?'

'One week, Alexander. That's all I can do.' Colin's voice cracked. Tiredness?

Alexander shrugged his coat up around his ears. The wind was getting colder. 'Of course,' he said, as if it didn't matter, as if they were looking for a chocolate Easter egg that may have already melted. 'Aye.'

———

'TOMORROW?' Donald stood up from his seat at the kitchen table and paced to the back of the room. 'But you aren't well enough, love.'

Julie didn't bother to say anything. *I am fine. I am fine.* She should get a T-shirt printed. Donald could only see the rainbow colours of her bruising and the deep scratch on her face that was taking its time to heal. They were nothing, dissociated physical elements. Inside, now that was what mattered. Inside, she burned with her mission. It easily swamped any outside difficulties, even that nagging residual back pain. 'The flight leaves at one o'clock in the afternoon. A very civilised time.'

Donald came back to the table and leaned both hands on the back of his chair. His face was tight and scrunched, his head shook from side to side. 'I can't let you, love.'

'Let me?' Julie pushed her chair back and stood as well. The room glowed red for a moment. 'You don't have any say. Let me? How dare you!'

He put his head down further. Now his shoulders hunched, pushing the collar of his Polo shirt further up his neck. 'Julie, love-'

'Don't *Julie, love* me!' Her fury felt good, washing over the emotions of the last few days, the horror of what she'd learned, the betrayal. 'I am going to Australia tomorrow. You know what? I'm not coming back until I find her. You hear that, Donald? If I can't find her, then I won't be back at all.'

He winced, finally lifting his head to stare out at the evening. In front of him, the chicken cacciatore – the first meal Julie had made since the *event* – cooled. Julie's shoulders slumped. A moment ago, she could have flung her plate at her protesting husband, revelled in tomato sauce dripping over the old blue shirt. Instead, she looked at his bent body and shook her head. She sat, picked up her knife and fork, and started eating. He might like it cold, but she did not.

A few minutes passed, and he still stood there. *What is his problem?* she thought. She'd travelled back and forth to Australia before without him raising a sweat. He'd never fussed, never expressed a need to stop her or even come along. He was as unconcerned with her travel as he would be with a trip to the supermarket. She finished her meal and slopped up the juices with a piece of bread before laying her utensils in a neat line across the plate.

Donald turned to her, his hands still clutched on the chair.

'Well?' she said, aware that it was what her mother used to say when her father was at a loss for words.

'What about us?' His voice was so soft she frowned.

'Pardon?'

'Us, love. Us. You and me. What's happening there?'

There should have been a million replies, but the tone of his voice was so desolate she could only shake her head.

'We've been married thirty-five years. That's most of our lives that we've been together. What's happening?'

She swallowed. 'I don't know what you mean, Donald.'

'You must know. Can't you see it?' Donald pulled his chair out, angled it toward her, and sat down heavily. 'What's happened to us?'

Julie gripped her hands together in her lap. 'Relationships change, Donald. You can't expect them to stay the same.'

'But I do, at least part of it.' Donald put his elbows on his knees and spoke to the floor. 'I've always felt the same way about you. From the moment we got together right up to now. Do you still feel the same about me?'

She knew that by not answering straight away that whatever she said was meaningless. Her mouth felt dry. 'Everyone changes.'

'Not me.' He put his hands to his forehead. 'Is that the problem? I haven't changed? I'm still the man you walked to down the aisle, the man you left your country for. I didn't think you wanted me to change.'

Julie closed her eyes. It was such a long time ago. Donald, a fit young man with tenderness in his eyes. A dancer, too, one that could waltz her off her feet in the small kitchen of their old home. He bought her flowers for weeks after they married until she asked him, for the sake of their tight budget, not to. Then he picked wildflowers when he could – Scots bluebells and vibrant heather. It was only last week that the vase on the table had been full of bog myrtle; picked from their garden, yes, but picked for her. 'Donald...'

'This Norah thing, finding that girl after all these years. I know how important it is to you. It is important to me; do you know that? But, Julie, you won't let me in.'

She opened her eyes and found him staring, pleading, at her. 'I don't know what you mean.'

'Our sadness for our daughter. It's not something we've ever shared. We have our own. It's sadness side-by-side, not together. Can't you feel it?'

Julie's chest had tightened so much she felt she couldn't feel anything. Of course, they had grieved together. She'd lost count of the nights she'd spent weeping on Donald's chest after Norah was gone. But did she let him weep? She couldn't remember. She did remember wanting Euan distressed, looking to him – they were so discrete – for comfort, for solace. She knew now that it could never have come. She hiccupped. 'I'm sorry, Donald.'

'For what exactly, love? For not needing me anymore?'

That wasn't what she was thinking. She looked at him, her chest loosening. Did she need him? Had she ever needed him? Without Donald there would be no Alexander and that was the greatest attribute of their union. But had she ever needed him like he so obviously needed her? 'I'm so sorry, Donald.' Tears streamed unexpectedly from her eyes. 'This is all such a mess and you're right in the middle of it.'

'But, can't you see, it isn't a mess. I'm still here, Julie. Still here. Exactly the same. I'm still here for you. I always will be.'

The truth of it was in his watery eyes. His hands reached for hers across the table. She took them, feeling the heat and trembles. It was hard to let her own stay in his when what she wanted to do, what she always did, was to pat and rub to soothe his sorrow in the way a nurse would a patient's or, even worse, a mother would a child's. 'You are a good man, Donald. A better man that I deserve.'

He shook his head. 'No, you still don't get it. Julie, I am *your* good man. I am useless to anyone else.'

She pulled back and shook her head. It was perhaps thirty

years too late, but she couldn't leave without him knowing. She let her breath ease out. 'Donald, Norah is not your child.'

'Norah has gone, love.'

Julie spread her hands out along the table, near his but not touching. 'Listen to what I'm saying, Donald. Norah is not your daughter. She's Euan's.'

'Eh?'

She frowned. He had that look on his face, that one of incomprehension that was so annoying if she was explaining a political concept to him, perhaps, or a theory she had about the reasons for climate change. His dumb look, she'd dubbed it. Not that he couldn't understand, more that he didn't want to. 'Donald,' she said, trying to think of another way of saying it. 'Norah-'

'I heard you the first time.'

Now the look on his face had changed. Red-faced, wide-eyed, stiff-cheeked.

'Donald, it was a rash thing that was done a long time ago.'

'You and Euan. My own brother.'

'You were away in Ireland. That big job you had. A real breakthrough for the business.'

'You and Euan.'

'Yes.' She stopped, pulled her hands in.

He stood, as tall as a giant. 'You and Euan. Norah.'

A trickle of sweat ran down the back of her neck.

'You let me go through the pain of losing my daughter when she wasn't even *my* daughter?'

Her hand flayed helplessly. 'Donald...'

'Don't.' He turned his back to her, his hands on his head and his gaze on the ceiling. She waited for a thundering, primeval bellow that would alert their neighbours two fields away and have the police running into the house with Tasers drawn.

His hands dropped silently to his side. Without looking at

her, he left the room, quietly stepping through the sliding doors, and into the night.

In the deepening darkness, she could only think of one thing. She had killed the love of her husband as surely as she'd driven Wallace's sword into his heart.

THIRTY-ONE

'Claudia finished at Stillers last month. No, I don't know where she is now. Hang on, Tiff might know. Tiff starts in an hour. Hang on, she's not working tonight. Wait, Smithy might know. Smithy, know where Claudia works now? No? Tyson? He's on security. I'll go and ask. Youse wait here.'

Stillers was noise-powered. Music bounced off the wall and mingled with shouts and whoops and the sloshing of drinks onto the already-wet floor.

'What was her name?' Alexander shouted at Colin when the girl left to find Tyson.

'Amy? Amber? I don't know.'

'What?'

'I said, I don't know!'

'Okay, just asking.'

'What?'

Alexander shook his head and gulped at his drink.

Colin's head was pounding in time to the music. They'd been in the club for an hour before they could get close enough to find someone who remembered Claudia. His stomach hurt, and he wasn't sure whether it was from lack of food or something else. The thought of the tiny bnb was heaven, but they had to wait for Amy/Amber if she ever got back from where Tyson hung out.

'Look,' said Alexander in his ear, pulling at Colin's shirt. 'I think that's her.'

The tall, slim girl he was pointing to turned at that moment. 'No. She's not here, Alexander.' *Don't start this again,* Colin thought.

He drank the rest of his beer, trying not to look at his friend. Alexander would be scanning the crowd, lingering on every girl, trying to match Norah to anyone who had vaguely red hair or was taller than average or whose eyes caught his. Déjà vu. He'd gone back to the Alexander of old, desperately seeking Norah. Colin closed his eyes, but Norah came into his head and he had to swallow hard. Sickness rose again. He leaned over to Alexander. 'Listen, once that girl gets back, I've got to go. I need to sleep.'

Alexander stood up. Amy/Amber was back, her ponytail bobbing around her shoulder. 'Tyson says she's working at an office job now,' she shouted at them both. 'Somewhere in the city. A bank.' She took the empty glass from Alexander's hand. 'See youse. I need to get back to it.'

'Thanks!' yelled Alexander to her back as she weaved her way into the crowd.

A roll of nausea gripped Colin. 'I'm going to be sick if we don't leave now.'

They exited the club, the outside cold fresh on their faces. Colin walked slowly, stepping carefully as his stomach eased.

'We could start looking tonight,' Alexander said, but dully.

'Looking for a bank in the CBD at night? I don't think so. Anyway, I feel shithouse.'

'Okay.'

Colin looked up at Alexander. His face was white in the streetlight. 'You not feeling so well, either?'

Alexander shook his head, making his hair fall over his face. 'It's been a big week.'

They said nothing else until they made it to the little flat. There, Colin crashed straight onto the bed, pulling the doona over his still-dressed body and falling straight asleep. He woke during the night to the sound of the toilet flushing but dived back into dreams that were thick with movement he couldn't quite make out.

In the morning, it was clear that they both had some sort of aeroplane stomach bug. Colin stayed in bed, okay unless he moved. Alexander was worse, dashing to the bathroom every hour or so. Colin dozed, waking to drink some water and to the sounds of Alexander. By evening, though, they both had settled enough to sit together in the kitchen for a short while.

'Maybe tomorrow,' Alexander said.

'Maybe.' Colin had been going to make some toast but sitting up required too much effort, let alone putting bread in the toaster.

'Well, I'm going back to bed.'

Colin nodded as Alexander wandered away, idly flicking his lap top on to check for news. He typed in Claudia Purton, and there she was, all sorts of Claudias from all around the world, except that Alexander had shown him the one he thought they were after. She had an intense stare. Not at all, he thought, like Norah's enquiring one, the one where her eyes lit with curiosity.

He shut the computer. Norah's eyes, staring at him across the pillow. The curve of her shoulder, the way her hair fell... One week. That's all he'd given Alexander. Not himself, though. No, not at all.

GARRY HAD work for Grace every day. She came in early morning to help with the breakfast warmth, bringing out plates of eggs to people shuddering with the cold until the gas heater could take effect. Inside the café, muted floorboards and thick brick walls made the place spare but homely. When Garry dismissed her for the day, she stayed on to drink one more cup of coffee. It was grey outside. More than that. It was... *nothing* outside.

On her fifth day, her fifth settling in at the corner table that only fitted one, Garry left his counter-wiping to come and sit with her. It was the post-breakfast, pre-smoko lull. The only other customer was banging away importantly at a computer. A jobless writer, thought Grace, or a would-be executive.

'What's going on, Grace?'

Garry had kind, fatherly eyes although, as far as she could guess, he was not anyone's dad. He was not that old, either, although he had traces of sadness and hard work in the creases around his eyes.

'I'm finishing my coffee and then I'll go.'

'I don't mean that. You can stay as long as you like.' He rubbed at the surface of the table with his cloth. 'Do you have problems?'

She sat up. 'No problems.'

'Sorry,' he said, stuffing the cloth into the pouch of the apron he wore. 'I don't mean to pry. You seem at a loose end.'

She studied him. He'd taken her on, given her a lifeline job. She knew nothing about him except for the two photos he had stuck on the shelf above the coffee machine. A smiling man with a black Labrador, and a 1970s family photo of parents and their awkward teenagers. She tried to remember a photo of her family and came up with one taken at her mother's thirty-fifth birthday. Grace stood at the back of the wheelchair, her father a little distance off. None of them were smiling.

'Grace?'

'A loose end? My life is one big loose end.'

'Can I help in any way?'

'You have.' Grace indicated the little room. 'You gave me a job.'

'That was lucky for me, too. You're a quick learner.'

Grace drained her coffee. 'Thanks. I'll see you tomorrow.'

Garry stood to let her go, adjusting his glasses further up his nose. 'See you then.'

Computer guy was leaving just ahead of Grace. She waited as he flounced out the door, catching it as it swung to close. Garry was back behind the counter with computer guy's plates, his head bent over the sink.

'Garry?'

He turned, expectant.

'What would you do if you had something and then let it go before you realised you were mistaken?'

He smiled. 'Easy. Go get it back.' He brought one hand up. 'Now I'll never see you again.'

'I'll be back tomorrow, don't worry.'

'Take care, Grace.'

She nodded as she left, glimpsing herself in the window's reflection. Her hair had lightened to brown as the semi-permanent black left it and looked patchy. The short cut, which the hairdresser had warned would need more regular cutting, was getting too long to hold its shape. It waved around her ears, sticking out in all directions. Bathroom time at the hostel didn't allow elaborate make-up rituals, so she only put on the thinnest coat of mascara. *I can't have gone further from Norah if I'd tried*, Grace thought. She stopped in the middle of the path, causing the man behind her to do a frowning side-step. It was all wrong, this half-hearted Grace she'd become, but how did she get back?

The bitter day moved her towards the State Library where

the bulk of the helpless went to escape. She took up a position at a computer and started a search for rentals. She'd have to fore-close on Claudia to get a place of her own, and even then it would need to be in an outer suburb. Maybe once she was more settled, she could look for a better job or go back to study or move to the country or something. She sighed and dropped her hand from the mouse. It was hard to know what was worse, breaking her last tie with Claudia or the thought of planning for a future. Idly, she brought up *Cameron Stonemasonry* and flipped through their photos. Nothing had changed. Alexander was still there, his hand on a wall and his hair dangling over his earnest face.

She sat there until hunger drove her outside and to the 7/11 on the way back to the hostel. The fruit and cheese hung heavily from her hand and she was glad to fling it onto her bed once she got there. The food made her feel a little better, enough so she pulled the phone out of the depths of her handbag and finally, after all this time, changed her sim card back to its usual one.

There had been no need to do it before. The card she'd bought for Scotland was in a bin somewhere at Edinburgh Airport, snapped in two with some effort. Katerina would have liked a new card, but she didn't hang around long enough. Who would need to contact Grace here besides prospective employ-ers? Then she'd found Garry without having to worry about contact numbers. She crossed her legs on the bed as she waited for the phone to fire up. Defeat flooded her. There she was, trickling back to her own life after having glimpsed a magical other. No doubt the real Norah was living it up.

The hostel was midday-quiet. Grace lay back, the phone on her chest, and closed her eyes. She woke to the beeps of many texts and blinked her way to sitting, taking a moment to remember why she was in such a gloomy space. The phone felt warm in her hand – she'd been clutching it as she slept. Its screen was full of messages, all from Claudia.

Grace, I'm sorry. Where are you?

You are being stupid and selfish. Answer me!

Do you want me to go to the police? I will, you know.

Please, Grace. I'm keeping your room.

I've been through your things. It doesn't look like you're leaving for good.

Grace! What the?

Okay, I'll give you one month like you wanted.

In the words, Grace saw Claudia. First, the angry face of their last encounter. Second, the way she'd held Grace's hand at her father's funeral. Then, a collage of emotions, the complete range, spread over the years they'd been house mates. The drunk and sober times, the bored and normal times. Claudia had been the one stable thing she'd had. I feel *moor-less without her,* Grace thought.

There would be nothing to lose to go back to their old house and, this time, knock on the door until Claudia answered it. Worst-case scenario: Grace's box gets flung out on the street and the door is slammed in her face. Best-case scenario... Grace didn't dare think. She rubbed at her skull, her fingers catching in unruly hair. She couldn't slink back to Claudia without making some sort of effort to be more herself. Whoever that was. She was definitely not Katerina. But was she still Grace?

JULIE HAD A TRAVELLING HANDBAG, a sensible black one with multiple zipped up areas, perfect for passports and boarding passes. Her cabin bag, she realised now, was not so sensible. Old and heavy, it sat squarely at her feet as she perched on the seat in the waiting area. She studied other people's luggage, picking out a bottle green zipped tote that would be perfect for next time.

If she paused for a moment, she knew she didn't give a hoot about bags or their colours. She was tricking herself, a useful talent. She forced herself to look around. No, that blue case was too big. She liked to tuck something at her feet rather than have it in the overhead luggage and pester people when she needed things out of it.

A loud laugh made her turn. Donald? No, a similarly jovial type, but with brown hair hanging around his ears. She scanned the crowd. She'd left him a note on the table next to a container of ANZAC biscuits, his favourites. Since the revelation, since he knew of her betrayal, he had not spoken to her. Not one word. It was shocking, more than she'd realised it would be. He came into the kitchen the night before and turned his back on the meal she'd made. In the deep, shadowed lines of his face, she saw how utterly wounded he was. As he walked away, she imagined the hall shadows as lines of blood dripping from where she'd hurt him.

The airline counter called her, and she presented her luggage. The whole process of getting a ticket, packing, arriving at the airport and now this handover had been undeservedly smooth. She'd had to spend most of the money her mother had left her on a business class ticket but, even so, it was as if fate wanted her to leave the country to find Norah. Or was it that the country wanted her to leave Donald? She was starting to feel tangled.

The luxuriousness of travelling in her own space wasn't lost to her but, by the halfway mark, Julie felt herself growing distant. Sleep was evasive, as it had been the previous few nights. Through a thickening fog, she watched reruns of old comedy shows, her face stiff and unmoving. They stopped over in Dubai, muggy heat forcing her into the bathroom to change into a shorter-sleeved travelling shirt. Back on the plane, time a stranger, she forced herself to close her eyes and think on Alexander's message about Claudia Purton. It wasn't much, but it was something. Maybe by the time she arrived in Melbourne, some sort of contact would be close.

Norah, she thought, letting a tear slide out from under her eyelid, I'm so sorry.

GARRY HAD SPRAINED his ankle on the way to work, slipping on a rotting plane tree leaf wedged in a crack in the footpath. He hobbled from coffee machine to till, with Grace trying to cover for him by speeding up, darting from customer to counter. Without him saying anything, she stayed on for the day, shutting the door firmly at four o'clock – the official closing time that never was – and turning to her boss. 'Sit down now. I'll do the rest.'

'I'm alright.'

'No, you're not. Now sit. I'll get some ice.'

It was credence to how much his leg hurt that Garry sat immediately, easing his leg up onto a nearby chair and waiting patiently as Grace applied a pack of frozen berries over his ankle, fastening it on with a tea towel.

'Where did you learn that?'

'Scouts. Are you comfortable?' Grace adjusted a cushion under his foot.

'It doesn't hurt as much as it did, if that's what you call comfort.'

'That'll do for now. Stay there and I'll pack up outside.'

'Thanks, Grace. Really.'

She smiled at him, pushing today's paper across the table and making him roll his eyes. As she went outside, she saw him pick it up and scan the headlines. The smile stayed on her face. How ridiculously good did it feel to be useful? Stacking chairs shouldn't be such a source of pride, should it? I'd better think about something to do with my life, Grace thought, rolling the two café tables closer to the door. Unless I stay on here and help Garry grow the place.

She glanced at Garry through the window, wondering how he would feel about that. The street reflection made his image hard to see. People were taking advantage of the sun elbowing its way through the clouds and were strolling from one place to another with their faces tipped slightly towards it. Their images ran across the window, a woman in a business suit, a young man in ripped jeans, an older man wearing blue-framed glasses.

Grace turned. The older man wore a waterproof coat, one faded with use. He was tall with peppery hair and a familiar face. Grace ducked down as he went by, stealing covert glances as she could. Yes, she could see him now, standing on the steps of Julie and Donald's house, a glass in his hand, staring at her as she stepped from the car. Such a stare, she remembered now, hard and direct. Strange, but true. The man was Alexander's uncle, Euan Cameron.

If he was in Melbourne, what about the rest of the family?

THIRTY-TWO

Finally, Colin felt like he could keep down a piece of toast and then, once he started, he couldn't seem to stop eating. Alexander was still asleep as he went outside to track down a supermarket or convenience store or anywhere he could buy a chicken. Chicken? He shook his head at himself as he walked the streets. You get gastro and then you crave chicken. Made absolutely no sense.

It was earlier than he'd thought. Commuters stood around tram and bus stops with their coats buttoned tightly against the icy wind. He'd stepped out with no coat, still in the Scottish summer, and felt the lonely bite of it cut through his thin shirt. There was a 24-hour supermarket on the corner. They didn't have any fresh chicken, but he bought two dehydrated chicken rice meals as a starter.

He got lost on the way back. Although the street names had a familiarity about them, Colin couldn't place the occasional new town house or renovated terrace. This area had once had rows of untidy two-story houses, with short, stumpy verandas guarded by chained bicycles. Rubbish bins had been the decoration of choice, with perhaps a few strands of spiky weeds blossoming out of the cracked pavers. Those houses were still there, but they were fewer than the renos and stood out like black beads strung on a necklace of diamonds.

A girl emerged from a row half-way down the block, pulling a rubbish bin onto the curb. She tugged at it awkwardly while her other hand held a shirt together at the neck. Her legs were bare, as were her feet, and Colin shivered despite himself. She glanced up at him in the distance and moved faster to get back inside before he reached her.

Short, dark hair. The glance came from under a heavy fringe. He couldn't see her eyes, but the jut of her chin was familiar. Claudia Purton?

She might have heard his thoughts. She darted inside, the shirt billowy open from the neck to reveal striped knickers. He looked away, embarrassed for her. He heard the door slam.

As he drew level with the house, he noted its number but kept walking. The front window was covered with a blind and he couldn't hear any noise from inside. He walked on, reading the street name now, recognising it from a map of the area he had in his head. It was easier to navigate once he got to the corner, and he made the three blocks to the bnb in record time.

Alexander emerged as the kettle boiled.

'You feeling better?'

'I think I am. My stomach still hurts, but it's more that I'm starving.'

Colin held up the last of the bread in its bag and one packet of rice. 'This is what's on the menu.'

'Bread first. Got any bacon?'

'Mate, I had to walk miles to get this.'

'Right. Should have walked the other way.'

'But...' Colin stopped and poured water on the rice.

'But what?'

'Nothing. Come and eat something.'

'Aye. One moment.' Alexander disappeared into the bathroom.

It might not have been Claudia Purton. It would be wrong to get Alexander worked up about nothing. Colin rested his hands on the kitchen bench and his forehead on the cupboard above it. If Alexander got even the shred of a thought that Claudia was close by, he'd be stalking the house within two minutes.

A noise made him look up.

'Mum's on her way.'

'*What?*'

Alexander slid on to a kitchen chair and took a slice of bread from its bag. 'Mum. She's on the plane.'

'But is she alright to do that?'

'She says she is.'

'And your dad? Is he coming with her?'

Alexander shook his head. 'Not my dear old Dad. He's at home, no doubt doing the work we ought to be helping him with.'

'Does this seem weird to you?'

'What, flying across the world to find Norah?'

'Yeah, well, weird enough. No, I meant, your mum coming out by herself after she's been in hospital.'

Alexander shoved the rest of the slice into his mouth. 'I don't know what's going on.'

Colin frowned. 'Do we go and pick her up from the airport or something?'

'No, she'll be okay. We go follow our only lead.'

'Claudia. In the city.'

'Aye.'

'With the lead pipe.'

'What?'

Colin shook his head. 'Don't worry. Finish your breakfast and let's go.'

'YOU DON'T HAVE to do this, Grace.'

'No, I don't.'

Garry looked up at her. He was sitting on a stool behind the counter in front of the till and one step away from the coffee machine. Grace was arranging the cakes brought in by Garry's baker brother. Over the last two days, Grace had learned the roles of his family in the business. His sister did the bookwork, along with the accounts for their brother's bakery and their father's garage. Until a few months ago, there'd been a mother helping Garry with the day to day running of the café. She'd died suddenly of a known heart condition, and the café had remained closed for a while. No, Grace didn't have to spend every spare moment helping Garry out, but who else was going to do it? She shrugged at him.

'Well, thank you. I appreciate it.'

'You won't be an invalid forever. And I won't be here forever. Let's work it while we can.'

She'd said it light-heartedly, but her hand trembled as she slid the last apple slice into the display. Garry had his head down, writing a list of supplies they needed. He glanced up, his eyebrows knotted, and then went back to his work. Grace went outside to arrange chairs and gas heaters in the pale winter morning sun.

The truth was, she felt, that there was nothing else she wanted to do at the moment but work at the café. It made her feel... *What's your problem,* Grace? she scolded herself. *Your first new family hadn't worked out, and now you're edging your way into another?* She pushed a chair under a table, catching her finger as she did and cursing out loud.

She went back inside, trying hard not to look at Garry in his centre position. The first customers of the day were trickling in. Regulars. Tom from the travel agent's. Hannie from David Jones. Chiru from the bookshop. Garry took their orders, but Grace was already making coffees in their keep cups, following the exact steps Garry had shown her and pleased with herself for getting better at it every day. Chiru smiled at her as he took his cup, his fudge-brown eyes reminding her – painfully – of someone else.

'So,' said Garry as Hannie was the last out the door, 'new look?'

'What do you mean?'

Garry waved his hand at her. 'Looks nice. And your hair suits you.'

She'd almost forgotten. Yesterday, she had enough cash in her pocket to have her hair done, getting it cut close to her head so they could dye it auburn without too much of a worry. It wasn't her colour yet, and it wasn't Norah's, but it was better than faded black. Then, this morning, her days too full to wash clothes, she pulled out a Norah shirt dotted with flowers and pulled it on over a black singlet.

'Thanks.' She ran her fingers along the edge of the shirt. It was the one she'd been wearing the last time she'd seen Alexander.

'Are you alright?'

She snapped to it, greeting another customer with a nod and not looking at Garry. 'Yes. Sure.'

As she made another latte, she briefly wondered how Alexander was.

THEY GOT off the train at Flinders and walked to the Mall. Alexander had said nothing on the way in. Colin glanced over at his face, pale once more. His hair looked lank and fell over his cheeks in a way that only sharpened the run of his nose. Colin wanted to either pat him smartly on the back or put an arm around his shoulders, he wasn't sure. Coming back to Australia had tumbled Alexander back in time. He'd sat slumped in his seat, tensing for defeat.

The crowds were nothing like the streets of Edinburgh in August, but still they had to either push through or adapt a weaving, awkward walk. They did a bit of both, Alexander adept, Colin noted, at turning his shoulders at the last moment so he could slide through the gap left by two groups of unrelated people. They got to Bourke Street and stopped. A tram dinged its way through, scattering pedestrians.

'There's a tram in the middle of your mall,' said Alexander.

Colin shrugged. 'Welcome to Melbourne.'

'Again.'

Colin rubbed a shoulder against one ear. 'Come on, stop moping. We're looking for this Claudia person.'

'Who works in an office in the CBD.'

'A bank. She's in a bank. You've got the list. We're doing this methodically.'

Alexander pulled out his phone. 'Let's start here.'

It was difficult, of course. You can't walk into a bank and ask about one of their workers – Colin stopped Alexander before he did. They developed a pattern he hoped wasn't putting them on a security interest list. They went in, looked around at who they could see, decided on whether the bank was a formal or informal one, and then guessed whether they would send someone out to get coffee or lunches. No one fitting Claudia's description was in front of the house.

'What do you want to do next?'

Alexander pushed a hand through his hair, making it rain down over his face. 'Keep going. What else is there to do?'

Colin prickled at the uselessness of their quest but kept going, walking four blocks of the CBD with Alexander, and then going back mid-morning as people did go and get coffee.

'Maybe she's changed what she looks like?'

Alexander shook his head. His face was set. Colin felt uneasy. A little bit of craziness was creeping into the way Alexander was scanning the crowds.

'How about we get something to eat? I could use a coffee myself.'

Alexander shook his head and Colin let him go until the streets quietened again in the lull before lunchtime.

'Food. Come on.'

They walked back to the Mall. The wind was up again, cold blasts that made Colin's ears hum. He was looking for a place that was a bit out of the way but would also satisfy Alexander's need for crowds. He pulled his friend towards a laneway where a sandwich board showcased a café. He was almost at the outdoor setting when Alexander stopped, tearing free of Colin.

'There,' he said.

Colin retraced his steps until he could see what had made Alexander freeze.

A woman walked towards them; tidy navy suit stamped with a red banking logo. She was feeling the cold. Her arms were folded tightly across her torso and she was going quickly, a rough-woven handbag bouncing on her hip. Colin studied her face. Winter skin, rosy with blusher and the cold. Clear, cloud-less-sky eyes, the type that were rimmed with darkness so they looked like targets. She lifted her gaze as she drew level to stare back at them, and Colin recognised the woman putting out her bin.

Alexander took one step towards her and instinctively she faltered sideways.

'Claudia Purton?'

The narrowed-eyed reaction was that of a city girl. 'Who wants to know?'

'I'm sorry,' said Alexander, a smile softening his face. 'I'm Alexander Cameron.'

The woman stopped. 'I know you.'

Alexander twitched. 'You do?'

'No, not really. I mean, I saw your picture in the paper.' She looked across at Colin. 'And you.'

'So you are Claudia?' Colin said.

'Yes.' She turned back to Alexander. 'You're that one who was looking for his sister.'

'Aye -'

'Where's Grace?'

'Sorry?' Alexander glanced at Colin. 'Grace?'

'Yes. *Grace*. She went looking for you.' Claudia's face flushed and her eyes shone briefly. She blinked. 'She left. I haven't seen or heard from her since.' She stepped back, pushing her bag to the front. 'What have you done with her?'

Colin held his hands up. 'We haven't done anything. We're looking for someone who came to Scotland to find Alexander. Would that be the Grace you're talking about?'

'What do you mean, looking for her? Where was she? Where did she go?' The strain of Claudia's voice was making heads turn as passers-by caught her distress.

'Claudia.' Alexander's head was down. 'I need to find Norah. Please.'

Claudia hesitated.

'Would you mind if we sat down to talk?' Colin said, in the softest voice he could over the noise of the city. 'Do you have time?'

He saw her assessing Alexander, the slump of his shoulders, the way his hand shook as he hooked hair behind his ears. She moved onto Colin, colder now as she gave him an unswerving glare that made him grimace and give her a half-shrug. 'I've got thirty minutes. It's my early lunch.'

'We were going to have coffee here.' Colin pointed behind him. 'Would that do?'

Claudia glanced into the lane. 'As long as we sit under the heater.'

'Thank you,' said Alexander.

She paused. 'I'll know if you lie.'

'We won't.' Colin put both his hands into his coat pockets. 'There's no need.'

She didn't believe him; he knew from the continued scrutiny, but at least she walked to the little café that had two tables hunched under the umbrella of the gas heater. She sat closest to the main street, positioning the chair away from the table. Colin nodded at her savviness.

'Tell me,' she said, her arms back across her chest. 'What do you know about Grace?'

Alexander put his elbows on the table and leaned towards her. 'We don't know a Grace. We met Norah, who said that her name in Australia was Claudia Purton.'

'Cheeky,' muttered Claudia. 'Clever.'

'She said that she'd seen our picture in the Paxton paper. She knew she was the person I was looking for. My sister.'

Colin saw Claudia close her mouth against what she was going to say. Alexander was looking at her in how he did when he talked of Norah with that evangelistic, little-boy expression that was hard to crush. 'I know the picture. I know the story of the missing baby.'

'So you know it's true.'

Colin cut in before Claudia answered. 'She turned up suddenly, having tracked Alexander down. She knew he was... keen to find his sister.' He tried to keep Claudia's gaze.

'You know what set her off?' Claudia sat up. 'The waiter at the pub said that she had your eyes.' She leaned towards Alexander. 'She was right there.'

Alexander smiled. 'You can see that?'

Colin shook his head. 'How well do you know Grace? She obviously told you she was going to Scotland.'

Claudia sat back. 'I've known Grace since we were at school. We've been flat mates since we were eighteen. There's nothing I don't know about her.' She looked down.

'Except...?'

'Except what has happened to her since she left to find you.'

'Someone must be in contact with her.' Alexander looked up at Colin.

'Does she have any family?'

'No. Her mother died when she was sixteen – she'd been in an accident. Her father died earlier this year.'

'I know that.' Alexander leaned his head into his hands. 'She told me that.'

'Then you know she doesn't have anyone. That's why she was looking for you.'

Colin frowned. 'What do you mean?'

Claudia avoided Alexander, capturing Colin in a hard look. 'She had no family. She was looking for another.'

The door of the café swung open, and a man limped out. 'I'm sorry to be slow. My helper had to go out to get more milk. Can I take your order?'

They ordered coffees. It seemed no one was hungry

anymore because they shook their head at anything else. Colin's stomach churned a little, but whether it was from the days of previous sickness or Alexander's desperate hope – or his own - he couldn't tell.

They sat in silence for a moment. The sounds of distant trams mixed with the murmur of voices and click of heels as people walked by. Alexander stretched back and ran his hands through his hair. 'Norah found her family. So why did she leave again?'

Claudia gave Colin a startled look, and he shrugged at her. 'Alexander,' he said carefully, 'Claudia's known Grace – Norah – for decades. She would know if Grace was really that missing baby. She's just told us that Grace had no family. Grace was searching for someone.' He paused. 'Just like you were searching for someone. It was the perfect storm.'

Alexander stiffened. 'What are you saying, Astle?'

'You know what I'm saying. The girl that found you is not Norah. She's someone called Grace who wanted you as a brother in the same desperate way you wanted her as a sister.'

Alexander stood up, his chair tipping to the ground. 'That's what you've always thought?'

'Claudia thinks that as well.'

Claudia squeezed her arms tighter and nodded.

Alexander shook his head. 'No. You are wrong. I know it sounds mad, but I *feel* it.' He put a fist on his chest. 'I know it. She *is* my sister.'

The door of the café opened again, and the man stepped out with three coffees balanced on his arms. 'Thanks, Grace,' he said, as an aside to someone walking into the lane.

'Garry, you shouldn't-'

Alexander turned at the voice at the same time as Claudia shot to her feet. The woman stopped, milk containers falling from her hands to split open at her feet. There was a 'what the?'

from Garry as he halted suddenly, coffee sploshing down his arm.

Colin stayed sitting, staring at Norah – Grace – standing there in a laneway in Melbourne, her eyes not on Claudia or Alexander, but fixed firmly on him.

THIRTY-THREE

Julie checked her phone again. Nothing. *The very second you find her.* That's what she'd said, and Alexander had agreed. She watched luggage trundle its dismal way around the carousel, hers still out of sight. The flight was a blur, the grey Melbourne landscape looming out of the clouds like a scene out of a post-apocalyptic movie. She was tired to the core, a deep weariness that threatened to make her sit down right where she was, her luggage still on the plane and her phone ominously quiet.

When the only remaining luggage was trapped on its endless cycle and it still wasn't hers, she found an attendant who smiled unsympathetically at her. 'Didn't you hear, madam? We've been calling your name. Unfortunately, your luggage was not transferred in time for your connecting flight. It will be here within twenty-four hours.'

Vaguely, Julie remembered the changeover at Dubai, the hurried journey to the correct terminal, the queues for the toilet in the waiting area long and exasperated. 'Am I the only one whose luggage is lost?'

'No, madam. There are a few passengers with delayed

luggage. May I take your address? We will have it couriered there when it arrives.'

Julie gave them the address of the motel she'd found in Lygon Street and the woman nodded, apologising shallowly once more. She left Julie standing with her sensible black handbag on one arm and the old cabin bag dangling from the other.

On the airport bus to the city, Julie splashed a little cold water on her face from the bottle she'd bought before boarding. The freeway, with its roadworks creating havoc, was familiar despite the years since she'd been there. In fact, she thought, there may be new buildings and shopping centres and DFOs, but its essence was the same. She watched the houses as she passed. Their architecture, red rooves and eaves to the fence, familiarly welcome in a 'don't worry, nothing has changed' way. It made her uncomfortable, like it was a time-shift back to the past. Same same but different.

I am still without my daughter, she thought.

She checked the phone again. There was service, just no message. She rang Alexander, listening until it clicked into its message phase – *Aye, you've rung Alexander from Cameron's Stonemasonry* – and cancelled the call. Almost immediately, the screen lit up. She felt breathless as she answered. 'Hello?'

'Julie, it's Euan.'

His voice made her choke. She grabbed at her throat but kept the phone to her ear. What was he doing, that vile man? She closed her eyes as if to blot out his face but of course it still loomed in her head. Two images: the older, greyer profile and the younger, sharp one, the latter bending towards her to press his lips on hers. 'Leave me alone.'

'I am. I will. Please. I heard you were in hospital.'

She should have ended the call, but what if he was about to explain *why* he'd done it? 'I'm fine.'

'I'm sorry, Julie. I didn't know. I thought you'd made it home.'

'I fell.'

'I heard and I'm sorry.'

She heard his words like they were distant raindrops on a tin roof. How could *sorry* fix what he'd done? She waited.

'Nothing can change the past.' She caught the confidence in his voice. 'I explained-'

'No, you haven't.' She swapped the phone to her other ear so she could shift her handbag to her lap. 'Why?'

He coughed. 'It's difficult to understand, I know. It was a spontaneous decision. I was up for that award. We'd done something very wrong.'

We? She frowned.

He was still talking. 'You were my patient, for God's sake. They could have struck me from the register.' Julie swallowed the bitter taste in her mouth. 'It was a long time ago. Don't think I haven't thought about what we did *every day* since then.'

She wiped her lips. 'I should go to the police.'

The phone line hummed or was it Euan sighing? The noise was lonely, wretched. Julie steeled herself.

When he spoke again, his voice was firm. 'You could go to the police.'

It had been there, that thought, through the police interviews about her accident. She'd watched the junior constables' faces as she told them how she ran from an unknown man and fell, tumbling, out of control, down the steep side of the path. She'd watched them as they gently probed her for more information, delicately stepping around issues of infidelity and abuse. She was honest, to a degree, the one thought clouding her conversations: I should tell them what really happened all those years ago. I should. 'I could,' she said at last. 'If I don't find Norah, I will.'

'If you do find her?'

'I don't know how I'll feel when I get her back.'

'I am sorry it's come to this.'

'Stop it. Stop it!'

Heads turned to her now, fellow travellers trundling into the city. She put her forehead on the cold, white surface of the bus's window edge.

'Julie-'

'Leave me alone, Euan. I don't know what I'm going to do. I need to find Norah first.'

'Is there any sign?'

'I'm waiting for Alexander to ring me.' She pulled the phone away and checked the screen in case a message had come through unnoticed.

'Good luck.'

There was something in his voice, a finality that made her go cold. 'Euan. Where are you?'

He'd gone, the phone dead in her hand.

Numb, weary beyond reason, Julie took a taxi from the station to her motel in Lygon Street, explained to the nodding receptionist about her luggage, got her key and lay carefully on the neat, white bed inside the room, her back aching. A few hours later, she woke, shaking her head and frowning at the strange light outside, to the gentle buzz of the phone still clutched in her hand. 'Alexander?'

'Mum. We've found her. Norah. She's here.'

It should have been a dream come true, but it felt nightmarish. She staggered off the bed and into the bathroom, leaning over the basin and taking great gulps of Carlton air as the tears flash-flooded from her eyes and a thin wail fled her lungs.

'MUM?'

Alexander had turned away from the others, but his voice cut through the city hum. Grace was on her knees mopping up the milk with Garry's apron, Claudia beside her, stone-quiet. Colin sat staring at the table, his fingers drumming a staccato rhythm. Garry had limped back inside to get a bucket and more cloths. Grace itched to go with him, to return to two hours ago when they'd been talking about the business and how a musician or a performance poet might draw crowds on summer evenings. It was a safe conversation, one full of aspiration. Now, here they were, Claudia sullen and Alexander frightened and Colin wary.

She looked up.

'Mum?'

Grace stood. Alexander's back was hunched, cradling the phone. 'What's the matter?'

He swivelled his head around. 'She's making this strange noise.' He had gone as pale as the spilt milk.

'Let me.' Grace held out her hand. Alexander stretched his arm out, and she took the phone, their fingers touching. She wanted to grab them, squeeze his hand in a sisterly grip, but instead she slid the phone out and put it to her ears. 'Julie?'

The sound was like fading wind through pine trees.

'Julie?'

The phone rustled, scraped. Grace imagined it being fumbled across a bed or a bench top. A heavy breath then, 'Norah?'

Grace closed her eyes. 'Grace. My real name is Grace.'

'We called you Norah. That's your real name.'

Grace glanced at Alexander. His arms were folded, and he chewed his lip. 'Where are you?'

'In a motel in Lygon Street. Where are *you*?'

'Not far away. Near the Bourke Street Mall. We're coming to get you.'

'No. I'm not waiting. I'm coming to you.'

'If you think that's best.'

'It is.' Julie paused. 'Listen to me first.' Her voice strengthened. 'You *are* Norah. No. Let me finish. I know what happened. We can prove it later, but know this. You were raised Grace, but you are our Norah.'

Alexander was studying Grace now. His arms fell to his side. She turned so he couldn't see her face. 'What do you mean? What happened?'

'I don't want to say yet.' Julie paused. 'Norah?'

'Please. Can you call me Grace?'

'Grace.' The word stumbled out of Julie's mouth. 'Grace? I might never tell you the whole story. Will it be enough to know that you are definitely Alexander's sister?'

Would it? A few months ago, she didn't have siblings. Grace looked back at Claudia, who was sponging milk into Garry's blue bucket. 'I can't answer that just now.'

'Grace.' Julie sighed. 'I'm on my way.'

Grace held the phone out to Alexander, who snatched it from her and spoke briefly to his mother. The call ended at the same time as Claudia finished.

'Is everything alright?' Garry was through the door again. He stood next to Grace. 'Do we have a problem here?'

Colin stirred, his face flushed as he looked at Grace and nodded his head towards Garry. 'You haven't told him, have you?'

'Stop it, Colin.' Alexander shoved his phone in his pocket and moved towards her. 'Norah...' He wrapped his arms around her.

Grace stood still for a moment, but the pressure of his hug

worked like defrost. 'I had to go, Alexander. There was that other girl.'

'Who?' Alexander's mouth was near her ear. His words rumbled into her.

'Norah. The one your father found.'

'She didn't exist.'

'What do you mean?'

'Just that. There was no other.'

'Poor Donald.'

She felt his arms drop away. 'Aye...'

'Your mum thinks I am definitely your sister.'

'You are.' He stepped back. 'Aren't you?'

'I don't know.'

'She's Grace Worthington.' Claudia spoke firmly. 'She's always been Grace Worthington.'

'Grace Worthington?' Alexander hooked hair behind one ear.

'That's me.' Grace rubbed her arms, suddenly cold.

Some customers walked in to the laneway talking vigorously among themselves. They pushed their way through the café door without looking at the strange crowd standing at odd angles to each other. Grace glanced at Garry. He shrugged, turning carefully, and limped his way inside.

'What happens now?' Claudia had her hands on her hips. 'I mean, you've been away, now you're back. What the hell, Grace? You can't do that and expect life to carry on as usual.'

'I don't. I realise what I've done-'

'Do you?' Claudia tipped her head. 'I've been worried *sick*.'

'Does it matter now?' Alexander's eyes were underscored with blue bags. Grace swallowed. He looked like he hadn't slept for days. Had he lost weight as well? He didn't seem as substantial as he'd been in Scotland. Still, his eyes were bright, fixed on hers, mirrored-blue. 'It's finished. We could start from now.

Leave the rest behind. You, my sister. Me, your brother. Does it really matter if it's not true?'

'You don't think it matters?' Colin took a deep breath in. It shuddered out.

'I know it's the truth.' Alexander shrugged. 'We just take it from here.'

Grace gave him a small smile. She looked at Claudia, whose face was still hard. But it was Colin who struck her the most. He had this twisted, complex look, one that gave her the most hope of all. She felt heat swamp her face. He had said that, if she was Norah, he could like her. What about love her? She ducked her head. 'I can only keep saying how sorry I am.'

'It's not good enough.' Claudia glanced at her phone. 'I have to get back to work.' She stepped across to Grace and gripped her arm. 'Prove you're sorry or I won't ever believe you.' She let Grace's arm drop and turned to go. 'By the way,' she said over her shoulder, 'your room is still there. I'll make your bed up for tonight. And the rent is due. Don't forget.'

An undeserved warmth flooded Grace as she watched Claudia's retreating back. It was gone as soon as she turned. Alexander stood in anticipation, Colin half-facing away with his arms tight. 'What happens now?'

Customers clattered out the door clutching coffees. Garry followed them, stepping carefully, nearly losing his balance on the step. Grace went to him, offering a hand which he took firmly, wrapping his fingers around hers and not letting go even when he was on even ground. Grace saw Colin drop his gaze to her hand, and she slid it out of Garry's.

'I think I'll go,' said Colin roughly.

'What?' said Alexander. 'But Mum's on her way.'

'I can't stay.'

'Colin, wait here a wee while.'

'I'm not waiting.'

'This is crazy.'

'Stop.' Grace put both hands up. Alexander turned to her, the eagerness on his face almost making her cry. Colin, in comparison, was summer-red, his face closed. Beside her, Garry sighed. There are, she thought, wishing Claudia had stayed, too many men. 'Please. I didn't want to hurt anyone. I was just looking for...'

'Claudia told us.' Alexander shrugged. 'You were looking for a family.'

'Yes. I'm sorry.'

'Don't say that anymore.' Alexander smiled. 'I know you're my sister.'

'Come on,' said Colin, 'this doesn't make any sense.' He put a hand on his head and looked at Grace. 'Say that you are his sister. What happened to the real Grace Worthington?'

THE TAXI TOOK TOO LONG. 'Cancel it,' Julie said to the receptionist. 'I'll walk.'

Walking was going to clear her head, settle her thoughts, soothe the tremors wracking her body. It would only take twenty minutes to walk to the city centre, another five to find her children. Within half an hour she would have her complete family back.

Except for the fathers of her children.

Donald, she grieved for. His round, familiar face. The warmth in his hugs. There was time to revive that. If he wanted it. If she wanted it.

Euan. He was a tumour that she would have to cut away.

Julie's walk wobbled. She stopped for a moment, leaning her back against the grimy stones of the Old Melbourne Gaol. People strolled by. Uni students, she thought, noting their bulging backpacks and old shoes. A man lay on the grass, one arm under his head, peace on his bearded face. She took a few deep breaths in and out. Everyone has problems. Everyone has secrets they can't tell.

What was she going to do with Euan's?

Julie walked a little further, but her legs weren't right. Blocking those thoughts was cutting the circulation off to her limbs. She propped against the wall again, closed her eyes. The tigers came out of the shadows and gripped her with their claws.

'You really want to hear?'

She almost lost his voice in a flash of breeze as it rolled through the trees.

'Of course.'

'Well then. Don't say I didn't warn you.'

Julie inched back. 'Warn me about what?'

'The truth.'

'The truth about what?'

'What really happened at the hospital that day.'

She remembered that day. June dull and bitter.

The morning had started with an early walk, her and Euan and Rachel. She'd taken them to the recreational reserve, a known area for dog walkers and Jane Fonda-clothed joggers. Rachel was behind them, photographing the distant city skyline, when Julie had told Euan that her mother suspected something, kept glancing at the baby and then at Euan, squinting at Julie and making her squirm. Her mother was sharp and pious, virulently angry about her daughter's defection to the Northern Hemisphere.

'I remember that we fought.'

'Yes.' Euan's voice was husky. 'You wanted your mother to know the truth. You didn't understand what was at stake.'

'Oh, I understood.'

'No, I don't think you did.' Euan stepped forward and his

*face moved into shadow. 'You didn't consider what the truth
would do to me.'*

Julie bit her lip.

*Euan tilted his head up. 'That morning, after our work, I
went first to the hospital to see a colleague, but he was held up in
consultations. So I went to the ward to see my niece.'*

'Daughter.'

He grunted. 'I went to see Norah.'

'Did you? Did you see her?'

*'Of course. She was asleep, but completely well. I examined
her.'*

'She wasn't your patient!'

*'The hospital was chaotic. There'd been a horrific car acci-
dent. One family had died, another was injured. There was a
baby involved, the father was beating his hands on the desk. I've
never seen a man so desperate, so anguished. The paediatrician
hadn't arrived to see the baby, so I did.'*

'She wasn't your patient, either.'

'She wasn't anyone's patient.'

Julie swallowed. 'What do you mean?'

*'The emergency department had two other accidents come in.
The baby was taken to the ward to wait for the doctor. She was
dead, Julie. It took little to find that out.'*

*Julie put her hand over her mouth. The chaos was easy to
imagine. A community hospital with an undersized emergency
department. A hotchpotch of staff, more used to general medicine
that the effects of trauma. They'd failed the baby, and she had
died in their care. She looked up at Euan. 'What happened when
you told them?'*

Euan stiffened. 'I didn't.'

'What?'

*'I made a decision, Julie. My reputation was on the line. I
took Norah and placed her in the other baby's cot.'*

A fox howled again, joined shortly after by a chorus of frantic dogs. The breeze lifted Julie's hair. She shivered as she brushed it from her eyes. 'Euan, did you swap our daughter for another?'

'I didn't say that I swapped the child. I said that I placed Norah in the other cot.'

'The father. He would have noticed.'

'No. His wife had nearly died. He didn't notice.'

'And the baby, the one that had died... the one from the car accident. What did you do with her?'

'What do you think I did?'

Julie closed her eyes. The ward had four different exits, that was what she'd said to Norah, including a fire door to stairs going up to the fourth floor and down to the basement. The basement had an incinerator that burned all day and night, destroying hospital waste.

She opened her eyes and looked hard at Euan. It was suddenly hard to breathe, and she put a hand to her chest. Euan's silhouette in front of her was frozen, as if he'd turned to rock in front of her very eyes. Cold granite. What he'd been all along.

Her vision blurred as she turned and fled down the pathway into the darkness.

'Are you alright?'

Julie opened her eyes to a stranger, one that spoke in the familiar accent of her country. She stood straight, finding her legs strong again. 'Thank you, but I'm fine. A bit of jet lag.'

The stranger nodded and went on her way.

Julie dabbed at her face, pushed at her hair until it settled around her shoulders, and set her handbag firmly on her shoulders. The truth, however horrifying, was just that. The *truth.* Norah was alive and only a few kilometres away.

Whatever happened next, Julie had her daughter back.

ALSO BY JUNO HARVEY

Being Bronwen

ABOUT THE AUTHOR

Juno Harvey lives in Victoria, Australia, with her family. She has worked as a physiotherapist, creative writing teacher and academic.

https://www.junoharvey.com/

Books of light...and shade.

www.ingramcontent.com/pod-product-compliance
Lightning Source LLC
Chambersburg PA
CBHW030226120726
47903CB00005B/1377